MW00654467

IN BLOOD & DUTY BOUND

In Blood & Duty Bound

The Final Queen of Ombratos, Book One

Erin S. Bales

FALSTAFF
BOOKS
WWW.FALSTAFFBOOKS.COM

For my mom, Karen Bales,
who knew I could do this before I did.
I love you.

"Being a queen of Ombratos requires grace, strength, and a steadfast resolve. First and foremost, the Morovides are stewards of the people, and their queen must be willing to sacrifice everything in order to fulfill that most sacred promise."
-Queen Natali Morovide in a letter to her daughter, Zara

ONE

"Absolute Bindings work best at dawn and dusk, in the shadowy gaps parting night from day, when the world is untethered and afloat in the abyss between light and dark."
-From Galathar Morovide's *Treatise of a Bloody Wanderer*

Princess Renn Belia Violaine Theodora Morovide clutched the wooden rail with sweat-slick hands while, in the chamber some twenty-odd feet below her, alchemists prepared the Absolute Binding that would bring her oldest sister home.

Most of those at the party walked by the rail without so much as glancing down, as if the fate of the heir of Ombratos didn't hinge on the working, a formula comprised of hundreds—perhaps thousands—of letters, numbers, and symbols that covered the circular floor of milky white jade. The colors of the markings changed here and there depending on the materials used for one part or the next. Some substances she recognized, like the watery, brown-black scrawls of henbane or the pasty lines of woad. Others she didn't. But the blending of the pungent aromas reminded her of her twin's secret study, and that helped her maintain her outward appearance of calm.

The chamber below was like a well, open on a single side so the alchemists might enter and leave. Kneeling in the opening, two crimson-robed alchemists painted closer and closer to the formula's edge, and

1

beyond them, more of their colleagues bustled around in the preparation chamber. They had labored since sundown, but as sunrise neared, they toiled with even more purpose, readying themselves for the working to come.

Renn wished she understood more of what they were doing and, at the same time, was very glad she didn't. Not long before Solena left, Renn had, like a fool, asked her twin Parneo what might go wrong with an Absolute Binding, a binding of far more power and risk than an average binding. He had answered in detail and at length. When she'd begun crying, like a child of seven instead of a seventeen-year-old woman, he'd tried to reassure her that all would go as planned for Solena's departure and return, but that had done nothing to erase the gruesome tales of failed workings from her mind.

At another time of year, they'd simply wait for Solena to sail home, but her negotiations had lasted longer than anticipated, and halfway across the world, in the Yent Isles, their storm season was well under way. So, it was either wait six moons until the heir might return home safely, and the additional three moons it took to sail from there to here, or perform the Absolute Binding, which would pull her home immediately.

In truth, Renn wasn't sure why they couldn't just wait, but Queen Theodora, Renn's mother, never asked her to weigh in on such matters.

She plucked a goblet of wine from the tray of a passing maid, then cast an eye around the gallery to see if anyone watched her. No one did. Even Prince Dallan of Tithen remained on the far side of the room, trapped in conversation with a few messeran from her mother's birth cluster. Unobserved, she tilted back the goblet and emptied it in a few gulps.

The instant she swallowed the final drop, a servant in dark-blue livery appeared at her side with a silver tray, and she didn't look as she placed the goblet on it. That was likely the reason the glass's foot hit the edge. The servant, Tomas, old as he was, caught the goblet with a deft hand, but that meant letting the tray fall. The clanging, clattering crash of it hitting the marble floor reverberated off the round walls of the viewing gallery, bounced down from the night-dark glass dome, and echoed up out of the well of the observation chamber. It silenced everyone present, the one hundred and fifteen other highborn, the dozen servants, twice as many palace guards, and handful of varo—the elite force that protected the royal family—as their heads snapped toward the source of the noise.

Renn seldom gained the full attention of the entire court. She struggled for something witty to say, something clever and distracting, but nothing came to mind, and as they continued to stare, her cheeks warmed.

Tomas, who had served the Morovides since before she was born, bowed and said, his voice pitched to carry, "I apologize for my clumsiness, Your Highness." With some effort, he leaned down and picked up the tray. "It shan't happen again."

Before Renn might forgive him, Princess Heshiette, from her spot on a couch not ten feet away, said, "See that it doesn't." Heshi was Renn's next oldest sibling, and even though less than a year separated them, Heshi enjoyed her slightly elevated status.

Tomas dipped his silvery head. "Of course, Your Highness."

Renn touched his arm, mouthing, *Thank you.*

"Would you like another, Your Highness?"

She considered the empty goblet, then the night candle in its sconce on the wall beside the gallery's engraved double doors. The candle burned nearer and nearer to its base, its meager light swallowed up by the clear, steady glow of the globes. Less than three candlemarks remained until the dawn, and the nervousness she had thought to drown with wine broke the surface. She buried her hands in her skirt to hide their shaking. "Not for me."

"As you say, Your Highness." Tomas placed the goblet on the tray and retreated.

The moment of silence broke, and the highborn of Ombratos returned to their talking and laughing and drinking and dancing. They didn't dance in the traditional sense—not this far into the night—but even an excess of wine and weariness couldn't hinder the Ombratian zeal for verbal capering. In pairs, trios, and some larger groups, the men and women of the court had draped themselves around the viewing gallery like a colorful silken quilt. Some sat in chairs; others lounged across couches or even lay on the floor, propped up by down-filled pillows or bolsters. Aside from Messero and Messera Vicchio, who slept leaning against each other on a bench near the main doors, everyone either spoke or waited to speak.

Everyone except for Prince Dallan. Freed from his conversation, he spoke to no one as he cut a path through the room toward Renn, his strong jaw set, his blue eyes fixed and unblinking, wearing the same look as when they raced their horses around the palace grounds, and she was careful not to meet his eye. By unspoken agreement, they had spent the past four moons avoiding one another, but not long after midnight, something had changed, and he had spent the last few candlemarks all but chasing her around the gallery.

She couldn't talk to him. Not yet. Not until the heir returned and everything was settled. As he marched toward her, she searched for an escape. It would be awkward to join the group nearest to her since they gossiped about her clumsiness, and Tomas had ranged too far afield to be of any help. That left her with a single choice.

Renn turned on her heel and strode to Princess Heshiette's corner, where she held court over eleven young men and women sprawled on the floor around her. Renn's silver velvet gown had started to wrinkle the instant her maids slipped it over her head, but even after so many candle-marks, Heshi's violet skirts hung without a crease. Although they shared the same black Morovide curls, not a single hair on Heshi's head strayed out of place, while half of Renn's curls had already fallen from the arrangement atop her head, and whenever she moved, she loosed even more.

The highborn around Heshi either nodded or waved as Renn joined them, but no one stood and bowed or curtsied as they should have, and she didn't press it.

Heshi's followers consisted of siblings who'd never shown much interest or aptitude for taking their family's place in the convocation, the alternate children who stood in the shadows of their older or more ambitious siblings, and they called themselves The Spares. Heshi, the fourth of Queen Theodora's children and third in line for the throne, served as their leader, even though that position might have more rightly gone to Renn. After all, as the youngest of six and a distant fourth in line for the throne, she was the sparingest of spares.

But their differences in age and outlook had proved insurmountable. Since no family outside the royal one was allowed more than two children, the highborn arranged their pregnancies around the queen's, as much as they could with their flowering charms, thereby bettering their chances of marrying into the Morovide's line. Birth clusters, they were called, and Queen Theodora had given birth to her first two children, about ten years before Renn—Prince Dace came first, followed two years later by Princess Solena—leaving a wide gap between her and her so-called peers.

Most days they ignored her, and that suited her fine. Or it had before Solena left for the Yent Isles, before Renn and Dallan had started avoiding one another. She had Parneo, but her twin had his limitations, and truth to tell, she'd grown lonely.

Across the room, Dallan slowed his steps. His position at court—as a ward of the Crown, betrothed to the heir—had cause a mutual animosity to grow between him and The Spares. When Dallan slowed, a drunken Messera Crimmon caught up with him. She pounced, hanging from his arm as she often did in the hopes of stirring jealousy in her husband. Or her lover. Perhaps both. Either way, she would keep Dallan occupied for a while.

Renn sighed and tucked some of her wayward hair behind her ears as she sat on the couch near Heshi's feet. Heshi shifted and poked Renn in the hip with her toe, her means of expressing her irritation Renn had chosen to sit beside her and not on the floor with the others. Having just turned nineteen, Heshi acted as if the eleven moons separating her and Renn were eleven years. Renn stretched, resting her hand on Heshi's ankle, and in response, Heshi huffed and dropped her feet to the floor. Renn bit back a smile, the tremor in her hands abating.

"Enough," Heshi said, the word spoken to her audience but directed at Renn. "Shea, you were saying?"

Shea thought for a moment and then bolted upright and waved everyone in, suggesting a very juicy bit of gossip. Renn had less than no interest in his rumors, but she needed a distraction from her own thoughts, so she leaned in like the others and listened.

THE PALACE GUARDS slated to be on duty for Princess Solena's long-awaited return from the Yent Isles left the barracks for their posts amidst much shouting and false cheer, and soon thereafter, the guards they had replaced arrived back from the party with brittle smiles on their faces, brimming over with stories about the city's highborn.

Palace Guard Getha Barei, not a member of either group, sat on her bunk in the corner nearest the door of Barracks Six and finished sharpening her daggers. She honed the matching pair of six-inch blades, ignoring the others as they talked and laughed and pretended not to taste the same bitterness she did. Nearly every last member of the palace guard had put their name in for the shift of the heir's arrival, and now they all behaved as if they hadn't dreamed for the past few tendays they would be chosen.

According to rumor, those chosen to guard Princess Solena's return stood at the top of the list for entry into the varo. Only the best were selected to try for the varo, and only the best of the best were invited to join their ranks. Getha had spent the last six years in the palace guard training and waiting for an opening but it seemed as if she might be out of the race before it had even begun.

To the pathless hells with this. Getha buckled on her left vambrace. Grabbing one of her freshly honed blades, she slid it in along her forearm until the trigger caught with a near inaudible *click*. She did the same with the right and then stood and faced the merry fools gathered at the far end of the barracks.

"Anyone want to spar?" she asked, her voice pitched to carry above the chatter.

The palace guards turned as a group and stared. At long last, sallow-faced Keska opened her mouth to speak, but Tumolo, who was about fifteen years older than the twenty-four-year-old Getha, sat up on his bunk and beat her to it.

"Why not?" He climbed to his feet, smoothed his tunic over his small gut, and tucked the fabric into his belt. "I'm in." Looking around at the others, he said, "What do you think? How 'bout a little sparrin' to pass the time?"

Coming from Tumolo's mouth, sparring became the best idea the others had ever heard. Those not already on their feet stood, and Rummer patted Tumolo on the back, as if the older man had been the one to suggest the idea in the first place. Keska ran out the door saying she'd tell those in the other seven barracks, and everyone else either paused to pull on more clothing or hurried outside.

Getha waited for the rush to pass, then stepped out into the frigid night. Of all the stars, Blessed Amma shone the brightest, and near to her, the lying moon hung, a sliver of his face shining bright, the rest faintly visible even in its shadow.

Eight barracks stood in a half-circle around the practice yard, empty, but lit by the globes placed in lamps at six-foot intervals about the perimeter, and, true to her word, Keska ran from barracks to barracks, sticking her head inside the doors and shouting about the match. On an ordinary night she would have awakened many, but this was no ordinary night.

Across the palace grounds, a half-mile off, every one of Seedfall Palace's windows blazed with light. Upon the heir's return, the queen was to abdicate her throne, so those asked to join the varo would pledge their fealty to Princess Solena, a queen sure to be one of the finest Ombratos had ever seen. The selection of new varo always galvanized the guards, but the prospect of serving a young, brilliant, vibrant queen such as Solena had added fuel to everyone's desire and excitement.

Getha stepped down off Barrack Six's stoop and walked over to the practice yard. Because no one acknowledged sparring as her idea, she ended up fifth in a line that grew with every passing moment along the practice yard's unbroken fence. After all, if one couldn't climb the waist-high fence, then they deserved to remain within or without.

While she waited, she stretched and, instead of watching, listened to the cadence of the bouts.

Tumolo started out tight, but he loosened up, making short work of Rummer and the two who came after him, and sent every defeated challenger off with little bits of advice on how they might improve their thrust or their stance. Getha had overheard Tumolo at supper saying he hadn't bothered putting his name in for the special duty. "Let the young ones have a chance," he'd said. "I've already proven myself, haven't I?"

Despite his blustering, she knew he wanted varo. Of course, he did. They all did.

Continuing her stretches, she finally looked at the practice yard. Tumolo faced Nerio next, a small-boned man from Barracks Two, towering over him by five full inches. Tumolo had the size and strength, but Nerio had a well-balanced guard and a wicked advance, and might have bested Tumolo if, when he stepped into a lunge, the ankle he'd broken last year hadn't given out on him.

Nerio tumbled to the ground in a heap, and Tumolo signaled his win by tapping Nerio twice on the shoulder with his wooden practice blade. Having established his victory, he offered a hand to help the other man up.

Tumolo expects to become varo. Getha had known the man long enough; he was only gracious when he believed he had the upper hand. Getha scoffed at the falsity of his gesture, but others smiled and nodded, as if it were a genuine show of fellowship.

Nerio slapped Tumolo's hand away—Getha nodded in approval—and climbed to his feet on his own, using his practice blade as a crutch to get him off the field, and at the edge of the practice yard, he tossed the blade into the barrel with the others. Standing on his good foot, he kicked the bad one over and straddled the fence. His breath made white plumes on the air, but sweat drenched his face.

Getha didn't ask the man if he wanted help. Had their situations been reversed, she would have wanted to hobble off on her own to prove she could.

Nerio put his weight on the bad ankle. When it held, he stepped over the fence and limped off toward his barracks, not bothering to wait around for the list. *Poor motherless bastard.* That damned ankle had already cut him from the running.

"Next," Tumolo said.

Getha hopped over the fence. Tumolo lost his height advantage with her, but retained the benefit of his bulk. She went to the barrel for a practice blade.

"Naught but what's already in the ring, Barei," Tumolo said as she chose a wooden sword at random. "No whippin' out those hidden daggers of yours, *pet*."

Getha swung her arms in opposite directions, further loosening the muscles in her shoulders. The nickname and the reproof were meant to get beneath her skin, and though "pet" rankled, she refused to let it bother her. Instead, she focused on the admonition and how she would make Tumolo regret it.

She always wore her vambraces yet had never once used them while sparring in the practice yard. For one, the blades were live steel, which they never used except during designated drills.

Tumolo rushed her, perhaps thinking to catch her off guard, but she deflected his thrust and countered with an empty fade, ghosting past him and angling her practice blade for an upward slice he only just parried. With fast, precise movements, she soon had him huffing as he danced to her tune.

But before she wore him out too much, she relented, so he might have the chance to employ his favored bull offense. Sure enough, he squared his shoulders to her. His eyes narrowed when she dropped into river stance, a form for retreat, but then she held her position for several moments as he battered at her, and his brow smoothed as his suspicions waned. She held until he executed a solid chop-thrust, then started to fall back, letting let him drive her toward the fence and the barrel of practice blades.

When she came up alongside the barrel, she purposely aimed a sloppy cut at his knees. He put a lot of force into his block and, more easily than he'd expected to, knocked the blade from her hand, stumbling through the aggressive maneuver.

Planting her boot in the center of his chest, she kicked out, sending him back several steps. She grabbed another practice blade from the barrel, and in four short moves, had the point at his throat, thereby demonstrating the second reason why she didn't use her daggers in the palace guards' practice yard.

She didn't need them.

Tumolo glared at her, sharp breaths shooting from his flared nostrils. She shifted the blade from his throat and tapped his shoulder twice.

She'd often beat him in practice, but never on a night such as this. He spat at her feet, chucked his practice blade in the general direction of the barrel, and stormed off the field, going to the end of the line of those waiting to spar, a line now about twenty-five people long. He waited until Meritillio had hopped the fence before he called out, "Watch out for Waltham's pet, Meritillio!"

She gritted her teeth at his use of the well-used nickname, not for the insult to herself but for the one to Waltham. Esteemed Varo Hillard Waltham had served the Morovides for over forty years. He was also the first to see Getha's true potential, becoming her mentor, her patron for full Ombratian citizenship, and the closest thing she'd ever had to a parent. However, aside from his general support, he'd never played any favors or pulled any strings on her behalf.

Then Tumolo added, in a mock whisper meant to reach Getha, "Fuckin' forsaken."

Some of the guards gasped, one whooped, and others sniggered. Getha's stomach roiled, but years of practice allowed her to keep her shoulders back and her chin high.

With space so limited in the city-state of Ombratos, on the chance a third child came along, the parents had the choice of leaving together or sending that child out to one of the surplus homes in Shade's Rest, the faubourg just north of the city wall. People insulted those who had been sent out by calling them "forsaken," but no one had thrown that in Getha's face in years. She thought she'd left it behind when she moved up from the city guard to the palace guard, but someone had told Tumolo, and because she'd made him look like an ass, everyone knew.

She swallowed the lump in her throat and showed Tumolo her back. *"Use your anger,"* Waltham said in her mind. *"Channel it."* So she did. Meritillio was one of her strongest opponents, but when she knocked him to the dirt in a single series of moves, the laughter ceased.

"AND WHAT WOULD Queen Theodora have to say about that?"

Though Renn had ceased listening when the Spares had begun gossiping about poor Messera Leas, a woman who remained in love with a messero despite his recent marriage, the queen's name caught her ear.

"I don't know," Heshi said. "But I think you should ask her when she comes back."

Heshi's cronies cackled at this response.

"Wait!" Renn said, shouting to be heard above the laughter. "The queen is returning for the Binding?" When Theodora had retired to her rooms after second dinner, Renn had thought herself free for the rest of the night.

"Of course she's returning," Heshi said. "*Mother* should be here soon."

Renn searched the gallery and found their elder sister, Linore, in the same secluded alcove she'd occupied for the last few candlemarks. She sat with her forearms resting on the table, and her hands entwined with those of the woman seated across from her.

Heshi leaned in. "Let them be," she whispered. "Let Perfect Linore grab Mother's attention for once."

Ignoring her, Renn rose and charted a course around the opposite edge of the gallery from Dallan, who remained in Messera Crimmin's sloppy company.

As Renn passed through the gentle darkness cast by the pillars holding the high roof aloft, she neared a group of grey-haired highborn, a handful of the few men and women still alive from her grandmother's cluster. She slowed as Messero Casteau climbed from his chair to his feet and began addressing the women on the couch next to him in hushed tones sharpened by a striking urgency.

"It's not enough, I tell you," Casteau said. "The market must be taken in hand, or it will continue to thrash about like an intractable child."

"I agree," said a woman, "but this is not our most pressing issue." Messera Nissot's slight lisp made her easy to pick out. "She won't care that we are paying more than twice in taxes than the lowborn. She'll overturn the grazing law, and then where will we be?"

"We need her, Milasa." That quiet voice belonged to her sister, the younger Messera Nissot. "Too strong a hand is better than no hand at all."

A sigh and a rustle of fabric. "You're right," the elder Messera Nissot said. "Theodora should have stepped aside years ago, but we mustn't let the girl or her Tithen prince-consort run roughshod over us."

They spoke about Solena, then. Solena would have called the group out, then distracted them all from their discontent with a profound thought or a clever turn of phrase before steering the conversation toward productive talk. But it was one thing to know that and another to know how to do it, and so Renn said nothing. Instead, her eye was caught by a triptych of maps all but hidden in the alcove behind her.

The first depicted the major walls of Ombratos, and like most maps of the city-state, was oriented with the east to the top. The most prominent object was the city wall, more commonly known as The Gift. In the painting, which took a bird's-eye view, the Gift looked like a barrel cut in half lengthwise. To the west, along the coast, it ran in a straight line. Then, to the north and south, it bowed outwards in two gentle curves, creating the barrel's staves. Far to the east, the wall collided with the Cassedent Mountains. It was assumed that the structure continued through the mountains themselves, but without digging into them, and possibly compromising the Gift itself, nothing was proven, making it a favored subject for debate among alchemists or the extremely bored. On the map, the cartographer had diplomatically represented the proposed connection with a straight, dashed line that mirrored the sea wall.

Two other walls were marked on the map, and they looked like a barrel's hoops, both stretching from one side of the Gift to the other. One was the curtain wall for Seedfall Palace, an unremarkable construction. The other was the Hedgerow, a wall of green marble that separated the highborn of the city from the lowborn. No one knew where the marble came from. Either it had been brought in or mined into nonexistence. At any rate, there were three gates in the Hedgerow, one for each of the Pillars of Alchemy: Binding, Transformation, and Balance, and the cartographer had marked their locations in a fine hand.

There were, of course, many other walls in Ombratos, but none large or important enough to make it onto the map.

The second map depicted the Sap River. Its wellspring came from an underground source in the Cassedents. It ran in a fairly straight line west, passing through the palace grounds, under the curtain wall, running down the middle of the Bole—the highborn's neighborhood—before passing under the Hedgerow and then splitting off into dozens, perhaps a hundred or more, streams in the lowborn part of the city, also known as the Branches. Three of the widest streams, ones that were almost as wide as the Sap at its most expansive stretches, fed all the way out into Crown Bay, the immense cove that served as a small inlet of the Farouche Sea.

The third map was clearly newer than the others, with its starker lines and sharper handwriting. Its orientation was different from the others, with north at the top, and it vaguely delineated the neighborhoods among the Branches—the Chestnut, the Tangles, the Fallen Leaf, and so on. To the north of the city, Shade's Rest appeared like a barnacle clinging to the Gift. Miners and the unmarked made up most of its population, and though Renn had never been there, she'd heard its occupants were rather rough and ready.

The map went so far as to depict the Road's major fork—to the northwest, the Sea Road ran along the coast, and the Wood Road ran to the northeast, into the heart of the Karskil Forest. The Karskil, with its blood-red leaves year round and the many stories of people disappearing into it, provided much fodder for tales of monsters and specters hiding among the bone-white branches. Along the bottom of the map were a few of Ombratos's farms, but it stopped well before it reached Xanti, their only neighbor to the south. The rest of Althea reached far to the north, also well beyond the map's reaches.

Renn didn't know how long she'd been staring at the maps when a woman's high-pitched laughter startled her from her reverie. *Where was I going?* She looked about and caught sight of another one of her other sisters, Linore. Leaving the alcove with the maps, and forgetting them almost as soon as she walked away from them, she continued on, tucking the gossip about the grazing law away to share with Solena later.

In both coloring and temperament, Princess Linore was the sibling who took most after their sandy-haired, gentle-hearted father. She and Ductora Gesso, a priestess who'd been spending more and more time at the palace as of late, said little as they stared across the table at one another, but Linore glanced up as Renn approached the table.

"Heyla, Renn," she said in her high, breathy voice.

Like a surprised bird taking flight, Ductora Gesso disentangled her hands from Linore's, scraped her chair back, and almost tore her ash-grey robes in an effort to find her feet and bow. "Fair evening, Your Highness. Or"—she peered around Renn toward the night candle—"should I say, fair morning?"

"Fair morning, Blessed Ductora," Renn said. She patted the air. "Please, do sit. I just came to let Linore know the queen will be returning soon."

Ductora Gesso's face paled, and before Linore could say anything, she bowed again and scurried off. Linore stared after her but didn't give chase.

"I'm sorry." Renn sat in the vacated chair. "I just wanted to warn you. I didn't mean to run her off."

Linore shook her head. "It's fine. This silliness will be over soon enough."

If anything happened to Solena, Linore was next in the line of succession, and becoming a queen of Ombratos meant being Bound to the throne with a prince-consort so as to ensure the continuation of the bloodline. Once Solena returned, married Dallan, and was Bound to the throne, Linore would be free to enter the ductoran and devote the rest of her life to Amma.

And Ductora Gesso. After all, joining the church required vows of poverty, obedience, and devotion, but not chastity.

Linore faced Renn, her light eyes gentle with sympathy. "How are *you* doing?"

Her kindness brought all of Renn's nervousness, all of her fears for Solena back to the fore, and her throat tightened. Without thinking, she put her hands on the table and laced her fingers together, sparking the bloodmark on her palm. "What...what if something goes wrong?" she asked, the mark tingling.

"Shh." Linore held out her own hands, revealing fingertips studded with puncture wounds. "I've barely ceased praying since I awoke yesterday."

Renn unlaced her fingers, and as she broke contact between her hands, the thumb-sized bloodmark on her palm faded away. She touched the prayer locket she wore around her neck on the same chain as her flowering charm. Though she wore the locket every day, it had never occurred to her to ask for Amma's mercy or protection on Solena's behalf.

As if reading her thoughts, Linore said, "It's not too late. Pray now." She rose. "I have to go find Lolly." Renn's confusion must have shown on her face because Linore clarified. "Ductora Gesso. She could be halfway to Rhyllex." She touched the top of Renn's head, then went off to find her lover.

"*Pray now.*"

Renn, meaning to do just that, stood and returned to the balcony overlooking the working. The circle had widened even farther, and a single alchemist worked at the edge. She—the slender, scarred hands jutting from the sleeves of the crimson robe were too fine-boned to be that of a man—finished a bright, yellow-green line, sat up, corked the bottle she had been using, and tucked it into a fold in her robe. From a different fold she pulled out a ceramic jar filled with brown paste. She opened it, and a loamy, grassy scent rose up from below, bringing with it a sudden urge to go riding.

"Smells like the stables."

Though Prince Dallan had lived in Ombratos as a ward of the throne for the past fifteen years—since he was seven and Renn three—his words still retained a bit of Tithen lilt, and the familiar, spicy smell of the tonic he used in his hair eclipsed that of the loamy paste. He leaned against the rail next to Renn, so close their shoulders touched, and her nuisance pulse quickened. They had grown up together, been raised as siblings, but she had never had much success in thinking of him as a brother.

It will be easier once he and Solena are married. Doubt tugged at her. *It has to be.* She refused to become Messera Leas, pining over a relationship that could never be.

She slid away from him. "That it does."

He followed. "Speaking of the stables, we haven't been riding together in ages." He bumped her shoulder with his. "We haven't even spoken in ages."

"Four moons," she said, moving away only half as far, but she kept her eyes trained on the alchemist. *Don't look at him. If you don't look at him, you'll be safe.* "Not ages."

He sidled over until the fabric from his shirt brushed against her arm and faced her. "Four moons, two tendays, five days, and twelve and three-quarters of a candlemark," he said, his breath warm on her cheek and neck. "To be precise."

That he knew, down to the candlemark, how long it had been since they'd last spent time together... She couldn't help it. She looked at him, really looked at him, for the first time all night. The dark green tunic he wore set off his golden hair and bronzed skin in a way that brought heat rushing to every inch of her flesh.

Then he grinned, that damned dimple creasing his left cheek, and she was lost. All of her thoughts and good intentions scattered like dandelion fluff in the wind as she shifted and their arms once again touched.

His smile deepened before falling away to reveal an expression far more intimate. "There you are." He reached out, and the tips of his fingers grazed her hand, leaving burning trails in their wake. "I've missed you."

Having mislaid any desire to move away, she closed her eyes. His and Solena's would be a political marriage, not a love match. Even so, a marriage it would be. She opened her eyes and spoke, the words tumbling out in a rush. "I don't think we should talk again until after the wedding."

She waited for sadness or irritation, perhaps even outright anger. Instead, "That's the thing." The grin returned to his face. "After tonight—"

Shouts rose up from the alchemical chambers below.

Oh, thank Amma! Renn stumbled back, putting a couple of precious feet between her and Dallan. The preparation chamber, the place where the alchemists planned the working being carried out on the floor of the observation chamber, was on the floor below her. She peered over the rail as far as she dared, but she couldn't see more than a foot into the room.

The yelling grew louder, and one of the voices sounded like her twin. *Parneo?* The queen hadn't wanted him at the working, so he should have been in his suite. Renn listened for him, but too many voices shouting too many different words made it impossible to pick out the individual speakers or the reason for the argument.

Renn straightened, and the main doors to the observation chamber opened. Not waiting to be announced, Lady Helenia rushed in alone.

That the lady rushed in by herself would have been startling enough— she was often trailed about by a phalanx of highborn, all entranced by her long-lashed eyes, which seemed blue or green or grey depending on the light, and her fall of waist-length hair that shone like burnished copper— but she also appeared perturbed. Usually the woman was as still as a frozen lake and, as Solena had once quipped, only half as warm.

She stopped to search the room and, seeing Renn and Dallan, approached them. Dallan bowed as she came near. "What is it, Aunt Helenia?"

Unlike Dallan, Lady Helenia wore the traditional Tithen tattoos inscribed across her forehead and down around her eyes, and at the moment, agitation creased the fine blue tracery. She pulled out her white skirts, sketched a brief curtsy for Renn's sake, and spoke to her. "I don't know enough to say. I was touring the preparation chamber when the prince came in. Everything seemed well enough at first, but then he began cursing and shouting."

Renn didn't need to hear more. She grabbed her skirts, crossed the gallery, and ran through the doors, out into the hall. Through the high windows, ponderous clouds blotted out the coming dawn, promising a morning of cold rain. Down the hall, from an open door designed to be hidden in the wall's carved paneling when closed, voices echoed up a staircase. She slipped through the door and hurried down to the preparation chamber.

A crimson bulwark of alchemists stood along the workbenches lining the walls, their arms spread out as they either protected their materials or attempted to block them from view. In the middle of the floor, Renn's twin, Parneo, lay on the floor clothed in his dressing gown, shouting nonsense as his keepers struggled to hold his thrashing arms and legs.

The keepers, ductoran acolytes dressed in pale blue robes, spoke quietly among themselves as they strove to coordinate their efforts, and nearby, the high alchemist paced back and forth, throwing his arms around and bellowing about "thoughtless people upsetting the precise and urgent delicacy of my process!"

A mad scene, but familiar enough where her brother was concerned.

She shoved past a few alchemists, who stepped back and bowed as soon as they saw her, and entered the tumult.

"What in the pathless hells is going on down here?" she demanded. At the sound of her voice, Parneo ceased his shouting, though he continued to fight the men and women clutching his limbs.

High Alchemist Marcal Daniau stomped toward her. "They're stopping him from destroying my working, that's what."

One of the keepers winced, and many of the alchemists gasped. Solena had said of Marcal that he was a brilliant man, but sometimes his tongue and his temper got the better of him, and he needed to be reminded to whom he spoke.

Renn channeled her sister as best she could and said, "Perhaps you would like to reconsider your last statement." She wanted the words, and their implied threat, back as soon as they left her mouth—she'd spoken too bluntly, using a hammer where Solena would have used a blade—but she couldn't retrieve them, so she'd have to see things through.

Turning his wild eyes in her direction, Marcal opened his mouth to speak, and Renn readied herself to order for him be taken away. She'd never had anyone arrested before, and she didn't relish the thought of doing so, but she'd backed herself into a corner. Amma must have been watching over her because his first assistant, Kitra Rande, interceded by putting a hand on his arm. She whispered in his ear, and whatever she said calmed him.

Marcal rubbed his sleeve across his brow, leaving a dark, wet smear on the fabric. "I beg your pardon, Your Highness."

Renn stifled a sigh of relief. "It is given." Then she knelt by Parneo's head, forcing everyone else in the room to kneel as well. The untamable curls she and her twin shared haloed his face in an inky aureole. She stroked his fringe back from his red, sweaty face, and soon he had settled enough for the keepers to let him go. When they did, he pulled his arms and legs inward, and put his head in her lap.

She looked up at Marcal. "What happened?"

He frowned. "Absolute Bindings are very complex, you see?"

Though she liked the materials and the rituals of alchemy, she had no passion for the details, so she didn't quite understand the complexities of Absolute Bindings, but she nodded as if she did, both to urge him to continue and to avoid a lecture.

Marcal sniffed. "Your brother—" Kitra nudged him. "Ah, that is to say, *the prince* came down here and insisted upon observing. He was rational enough then, so I agreed to it. But he watched Ithan for only a short while before he started shouting and carrying on."

Renn didn't recognize the name. "Who is Ithan?"

An alchemist of middling age near the front of the crowd raised his hand, his cheeks and the scalp beneath his thinning auburn hair the same color as his robes. "I'm Ithan. Ithan Virey."

"What were you doing that might upset the prince?"

Though it seemed impossible, the color in face Ithan's deepened. "I wasn't... I didn't... "

Kitra jumped in. "He was showing Lady Helenia one of the materials, Your Highness."

Parneo sat up, his skin grown pale and waxy. He pointed at a startled Ithan. "Truth can't be measured, only weighed." He spoke with a single voice, but somehow it sounded like many. "If the truth is too heavy, then the scales will break, and lives will be lost."

Even the imperturbable Kitra seemed thrown by that pronouncement. Parneo fell back, repeating the words over and over, and Renn wrapped her arms around him, pulling him to her.

Most likely, neither Ithan nor Helenia had done anything to set Parneo off. Though alchemy often calmed him and brought him back to himself—he'd been stable for almost two full moons after inventing the globes—this morning the fog in his head obscured too much. Rubbing his shoulders, Renn rocked him until the mutterings ceased.

When he quieted, she held him at arm's length. He continued to rock on his own and wouldn't meet her eyes. She climbed to her feet, reached down to help him up, then pressed a hand to his cheek, the skin-to-skin contact again sparking her bloodmark. Like a child, he closed his eyes and leaned into her touch, a night's worth of stubble rough against her palm.

"I think it would be best if the prince returned to his bed," she said.

His keepers surrounded him. She handed his care over to them, and they ushered him toward the stairs, leaving an embarrassed silence in their wake. She hated the kind looks and the piteous stares.

"Resume your work," she said, her tone sharp.

One of the alchemists jumped, and they all rushed to comply. Leaving them to it, she followed Parneo and his keepers back up into the hall, where the queen, her handmaids, and her prince-consort waited.

Two

"Due to the mighty wall the Ombratians call 'the Gift,' the Great Purge failed; therefore, we shall never know what might have been lost—or, dare I say, gained —with the annihilation of the Fallen and their alchemical practices."
-From Danlan's *Histories of the Known World, Vol. 3*

After Meritillio came Keska. Then Paveseau. Then Cremonesco, Lussin, Irconi. Then Getha stopped noticing names or faces and simply fought. She battled each newcomer as sweat soaked her tunic, and the fabric clung to her skin. She pushed her muscles hard, and when they grew lax and weary with effort, she pushed them even harder. She fought and fought, proving herself over and over again, until a voice cut through the fog.

"It's up," someone shouted. "The list is up!"

As if waking from a dream, Getha returned to herself to find an exhausted Nott standing several feet away from her. In what appeared to be a relieved concession, he tapped the ground twice with the tip of his blade and shuffled off the field, where the line had dissolved into a crowd. Tumolo didn't so much as glance back as he left his spot two from the front.

Two from the front? Had she really taken down that many opponents? The realization thrilled her, but her joy was short-lived in the face of the list of those invited to try out for the varo. She feared her name wouldn't be on it, but her heart, beating a rapid tattoo against her breast in a way that had

18

nothing to do with her recent exertions, didn't seem to share the same concern.

Wait. Wait until everyone else has had their peek, then, when it's all clear...

Even as she thought that, she crossed the yard, dropped her practice blade into the barrel, and hopped the fence. She jostled past those waiting to examine the list, uncaring of the curses and complaints that rose in her wake.

Tumolo stood nearest the board, a bright globe dwarfed in his meaty paw, his girth blocking her view. She tried to peer around him, and he shoved her back, his expression lost in shadow. "Amma's blood, Barei. Stop breathing down my damned neck. You'll get your chance." He returned to the list, and like a boat in the bay, she let herself be shoved to and fro by the crowd, willing herself to be patient, be calm, be still—

"Is this a fuckin' jape?" Tumolo turned around and faced her. "Here," he said, handing her the globe.

She reached for it, but he let it drop and it thunked against the frozen ground, rolling under the notice board as he walked away. Everyone hesitated before grabbing for the globe—a part of them, like a part of her, probably still expected the burning glass ball to be hot—but then she snatched it up and raised it so its bright glow could illuminate the list.

Starting at the top, she worked her way down, each name spelled out in an even script, each guard someone she had overmatched in practice more than once, and with every name, her misbegotten hopes sank a little further.

You should have waited, she told herself. *Why didn't you wait?*

Then she reached the bottom of the list, and there, scrawled in a different but familiar script, *Getha Barei.*

A tide of emotions swelled within her. Before she could separate any of them, a large hand gripped her arm, and while she remained in shock, yanked her from the throng. Someone plucked the globe from her as she passed. At the ragged edge of the group, the grip swung her around.

"How'd you do it?" Tumolo demanded, his beady eyes wide, a vein on his forehead bulging. Edrich Tumolo hadn't been one of the names she'd skimmed past. "How'd you do it, *pet?*" He spat the nickname at her.

She pointed toward the practice enclosure. "You saw how I did it." Around her, everyone stared. "You all saw how I did it!" She jerked her arm from Tumolo's grip. "Now, piss off."

She shouldered past him and stalked away, keeping her head high as she made for the barracks, eager for a quiet place and a bit of solitude in which to sort her thoughts.

But Tumolo dogged her. She bounded up the steps in a single leap, and he stomped on every one, shaking the stoop. *So be it.* If he wouldn't leave her alone in the barracks, then she'd find someplace else to go. She undid the leather thong holding back her sweaty hair, and left the straight, shoulder-length brown strands down to dry. Then she peeled off her sopping tunic and breastband, tossed them into the laundering basket against the wall, and grabbed clean ones from the box under her bed.

Tumolo didn't come any closer than the foot of her bunk. As a rule, the guards respected one another's bunks as if they were private rooms. "Tell me."

"Back off." She wrapped the fresh breastband around her chest and adjusted it before slipping the tunic on.

"Are you tumblin' Waltham?" He took a step into her space and gripped her arm again. "Is it true you're ridin' the pole of some frail old man?" His words came low and even, but the girl who'd grown up on the streets of Shade's Rest recognized the danger in his tone. "'Cause I don't see any other way some danky, *forsaken* chit who's been here half as long as me gets her name on that Amma-lost list. I mean, we all know he prefers men, but you're mannish enough then mayhaps..."

She flexed her free wrist, and with a quiet *snick*, a dagger fell into her hand. In a smooth motion, she brought the blade up.

He pulled her closer. "I'm going to—"

She pressed the blade to his throat. His body stilled, but the fire in his eyes continued to rage.

"You done?" she asked.

His mouth worked as he seemed to consider several responses. Finally, from between clenched teeth, he ground out, "Done."

Bullies. They were the same on both sides of the wall. She removed the blade and reset it in the vambrace. "Then let me pass."

Tumolo took a couple steps back. Behind him, guards had gathered around the door, inside and out, to watch their little show. She shoved past Tumolo and out through the knot of people, then she forced herself to walk over the frozen ground, past the list, ignoring the stares on her back. Unless she wanted this trouble with Tumolo to grow, she needed to fix it sooner than later. Or did she? By next tenday, she might be a varo.

Her whole body tingled like her bloodmark when it sparked, and the moment she passed the bathing house, she broke into a run. Running always cleared her mind. She ran away from the barracks, away from the practice yards and the stables and Menders' Row. Her feet pounded the earth, then crackled and squeaked over the crushed-shell paths closer to Seedfall.

In the hall, Renn watched Parneo avoid the queen, all but pressing himself against the far wall from her.

Every Morovide queen gave birth to a set of twins. She had to, it being a requirement of the position, a rule etched into their bloodline. A boy and girl had to be born to every generation, and as the portraits around the palace could attest, the siblings all came into the world bearing the same coloring, the same willowy height, the same fine features. Queen Theodora was herself a twin. But her dark hair was streaked with white, and Renn and Parneo's narrow features had been softened on her sallow face, their height reduced by the bow of her shoulders, their slender figures buried under years of indulgence and indifference.

The queen's brother had taken his own life before Renn and Parneo were born—accidents of alchemy or acts of madness always claimed the lives of the male Morovide twins—and if she and Renn agreed on anything, it was their desire to keep Parneo from either, or both. But their thoughts on how to do so differed drastically.

The moment Parneo and his retinue were out of earshot, the queen hobbled over to Renn, relying on the cane she used more and more often these days, though only in the presence of her family and the servants.

Prince-Consort Corlin stayed back, stroking at the salt-and-sand-colored whiskers on his upper lip and staring at the floor. Father never interceded when Theodora came after her, and she tried not to resent him for it. Everyone in their family knew only Solena could shield Renn from Theodora's ire, and she had done her best to avoid the queen during Solena's absence, succeeding fairly well up until this moment.

Renn curtsied to the queen. "Fair morning, Your Majesty." She nodded to her father. "Fair morning, Father."

"Why was he down there?" Theodora asked. She thought keeping Parn away from alchemy might keep him safe.

Renn shook her head. "I don't know, Your Majesty."

"Was it your idea?"

"No." *But I would have brought him down there if I had thought of it.*

"Then whose idea was it?"

So much had happened this night, and so much had yet to happen, that Renn's nerves, already as tight as lute strings, snapped. "Well, his keepers were there, so I suppose it was his. Parneo does have a mind of his own, which you might know if you ever spent any time with him."

Behind the queen, Father's mouth fell open. Horrified, Renn snapped hers shut, lowered her eyes, and gripped her skirts in anticipation of whatever punishment might befall her.

Theodora sighed. "You are an exhausting creature, aren't you?" She turned to Father. "Shall we go in?"

Renn swallowed around the lump in her throat. The sting of a slap would have hurt less.

The queen lifted her arm, and Father stepped forward, the faint smell of whiskey on his breath, squeezing Renn's shoulder as he passed. He took the queen's hand, and thus steadied, she gave her cane to one of the maids. When she waved, the doors to the observation chamber opened, and a page announced her. The highborn within cheered and fell, or rose, to their knees as she entered.

The list of places Renn would have rather been than in a room with the queen could have filled volumes, but... *You're not going in there for her. You're going in for Solena.* So, while everyone's attention was on the queen, she slipped back inside. Linore and Heshi already waited at the balcony, and the queen and prince-consort joined them. Then the queen gestured for everyone to stand and come forward, and the highborn rushed in, with everyone jostling for a position near the rail.

Only two people remained out of the crush. Dallan and Lady Helenia sat near the door, on the bench formerly occupied by the Vicchios. Eyes shut, she appeared to doze, but the tightness in her shoulders gave her away. Dallan didn't bother feigning indifference. He squinted his eyes shut and gripped the edge of the bench with such force his knuckles were white. The first Absolute working he'd ever attended was when Solena was sent away. His aunt, having arrived in the city after Solena's departure, had yet to witness one, but it made sense that she wouldn't want to watch. Though the Tithen had a long-standing alliance with the Ombratos, their people still disapproved of alchemy and the sacrifices it required.

"Come along, Renn," Linore called, patting the only open space left along the rail.

THE SOLES of Getha's boots slapped against the marble steps leading up to the varos' wing of the palace before she remembered that this night even Varo Waltham would be on duty.

She stopped a third of the way up the stairs. At the top, in a pool of globe light, Varo Nostros guarded the door, her dark hair braided around the crown of her head, her black uniform coat sleek, the silver hilt of a gently curved varo blade hanging from her belt. Getha pictured herself in the woman's place, wearing one of those coats, the weight of an identical blade on her hip.

"Need something, Palace Guard Barei?"

Getha shook off her reverie, and Varo Nostros looked down at her from the top of the stairs. All of the varo knew Getha's name because of her relationship with Waltham. "No."

"Then clear my perimeter." Getha nodded and turned to go, but Varo Nostros stopped her halfway round by speaking again. "Making that list is one thing. Passing the tryouts is a whole other. No one wears one of these"—she touched the hilt of her blade—"who hasn't earned it."

Did the varo think of Getha as Waltham's "pet" too? "I know."

"Good." Varo Nostros straightened, returning her attention to the wider area. "Best of luck to you, Barei."

Distrusting her sincerity, Getha made no response. Instead, she ran down the steps and headed off toward the Gift. The light from the globes along the path seemed dimmer as the night lifted. Brightness limned the jagged peaks of the Cassedent Mountains, lightening the palace grounds and casting the world in shades of gray.

Her name was on the list, plain as plain. Then again, her name on the list had been Waltham's doing, written in his hand. Same as with the city guard, then the palace guard. She didn't know how to cozy people, didn't know how to make them like her, and few wanted to give a woman raised outside the city a chance. So Waltham always had to step in and exert his influence.

She wanted to speak to him, even if she already knew what he would say. *"I just prop open the doors. Your skill gets you inside."*

But she resented that she needed him to prop open doors for her, *especially* since he claimed her skill got her through them. Even though he said it, some niggling doubts always lingered, and for once, she wanted to pull open a door and step through it all by herself. Only then could she be certain her achievements were of her own making.

Of course, she would never, ever tell Waltham that. Guilt tugged at her for even thinking such thoughts after everything he'd done for her.

She slowed to a walk, lifted her hands, and rubbed her thumb against her left palm, sparking her bloodmark. Waltham had found her out in Shade's Rest nine years earlier and given her a second chance at life, and after that, he'd offered to be her patron, fulfilling her lifelong dream of receiving a bloodmark and allowing her to become a legal citizen of Ombratos.

When her bloodmark faded, she sparked it again and again. No matter what anyone called her, she had been touched by Amma, and when she died, she would walk the Starry Path at Amma's side along with Tumolo and the rest of the Fallen.

She jumped the low, wooden fence of the apple orchard and jogged between the rows of winter-naked trees. A wind kicked up from the north, setting the branches to clattering, and clouds scudded in, blanketing the sky, promising rain, maybe even a bit of snow. Heedless of the weather, she continued on, the Gift growing closer with every step.

The Gift was a wall, a magnificent structure that surrounded the whole city-state of Ombratos, every inch of it seventy-two feet tall and twenty-one feet thick, and marked every nine feet by long, squared-off merlons that looked like teeth, as if the wall was a massive mouth opened to the sky in eternal praise of their Blessed Amma.

Though the city guard patrolled the areas of the wall around the rest of the city, palace guards walked its length around Seedfall Palace. The smooth surface of the wall looked the muddy yellow of marrow in the predawn light.

Alchemists claimed the Gift, so named for its part in saving their people from the Great Purge, was made from actual stone, manufactured by alchemical processes buried within the Lost Pillars. But they couldn't explain the total lack of cut marks or seams along every inch of its length, and Getha preferred the ductoran's teachings that named the wall a gift from Amma, formed some four hundred years earlier, in the Fallen's greatest candlemark of need, from prayer and light.

She touched the wall, enjoying the tingle in her palm as it sparked her bloodmark. For so much of Getha's life she had stood on the other side of the Gift, wishing she had a bloodmark, wishing she belonged inside. Now she had her mark, but she hardly belonged. Not that she would give up trying. Ever since she'd learned of the varo, the chosen few who dedicated their lives to protecting the Morovides, she'd wanted to be one of them.

So no matter how her chance had come, in the next tenday she would take it, prove herself worthy, and join their ranks.

The palace bell rang, announcing the sunrise. How they knew the sun had risen when clouds blocked it out was beyond her, but the bell rang, which meant Princess Solena was at last on her way home. Getha closed her eyes and whispered a prayer to Amma that the princess might have a safe journey. While she prayed, she reached under her tunic and tugged on the chain that bore her flowering charm and prayer locket. She slipped her thumbnail into the catch on her locket, opening it, and pressed the pad of her thumb against the needle therein.

The needle's familiar bite drew no more than the usual drop of blood. For a simple prayer, Amma required no more than that.

Taking a deep breath, Renn strode to the balcony and stood beside Linore, and the highborn pressed in around her, their excited presence close at her back. The alchemists had left the ritual chamber below. Writing covered the floor, all but a circle the size of a splayed hand at the center, and a wooden plank, a bridge of sorts, spanned the working from the preparation chamber out to it.

Sweat again slicked Renn's hands as she gripped the balustrade. Light gave depth to the glass dome above, and the palace bell rang in the distance, announcing the arrival of dawn. Up on the wall, the night candle guttered and went out.

Theodora clapped twice. "You may begin."

High Alchemist Marcal walked out onto the board and knelt at the end. He chanted some words of incantation—Renn wished Parn stood next to her to translate them—and then took a bottle from one of his many pockets. He repeated the words of the incantation, uncorked the bottle, and poured its contents, Solena's blood, into the circle's focus. They had collected her blood before she left and kept it for this exact purpose, to use as the key, the bridge that would carry her home.

He repeated the incantation, the repetition growing faster and faster until it sounded as if he spoke one long word over and over. When it seemed like the chanting might continue forever, Marcal's voice choked off, and he jerked forward. He put away the bottle, then he took out a short dagger and pressed the tip to his thumb.

In alchemy, any bodily fluid could be used as a catalyst for a working, but blood was considered the most sacred because it demanded both pain and sacrifice. A ruby of blood welled out, and he let it drop into the pool. With this, he claimed the working, tying off the flow of energy from the Unknowable Beyond. That much Renn remembered from Parneo's terrifying explanation. Marcal climbed to his feet on unsteady legs and stumbled out of sight. Another alchemist lifted the board and pulled it out behind him.

Renn held her breath, but for the longest time, nothing happened. Then, from the center of the perfect circle of blood, darkness spilled up into the room like red wine poured into a goblet of water, and it rose and flowed into the air, probing about with gossamer tendrils. One of the tendrils reached the edge of the working, and the murky cloud spread, filling almost the entire ritual chamber before coming back together to form a shape, a figure fashioned from shadow and starlight and the black spaces between the worlds of the living and the dead.

A head appeared and then shoulders, arms, hands, all of it forming a familiar silhouette, and colors swam out of the black, filling the figure and pushing back the darkness. Bright colors, a swirling array of life, fractured and gamboled, then tumbled together into recognizable patterns, and Solena's face flickered into relief. She had her eyes closed, her mouth pressed into a hard line, as if she might give Renn the scolding she had expected from the queen. Emotions, too many to be contained, welled up inside Renn and tears ran down her cheeks.

Solena—her tall, beautiful, imperious sister—was coming home.

Bit by bit, every part of her reformed, and in the span of a hundred heartbeats, she stood before them, no longer a figment of color and light, but a person with weight and substance. She wore a strange dress that covered one shoulder and left the other bare, and the smell of some exotic spice wafted up from her. When she was fully formed, she stumbled out of the circle of blood and opened her eyes.

Her gaze swept the gallery, stopping on Renn. Solena lifted her hands and laced her fingers together in their private signal. A burden Renn hadn't even known she carried slipped from her shoulders, and she let go of the balustrade to do the same. Solena nodded to her, then turned to look at the queen.

Theodora's jaw tightened beneath her quivering cheeks. She blew out a short breath and said, in a loud, clear voice, "Yes."

Solena reached into her bodice and pulled something from it. She raised her clenched fist, showing the item to be a glass bottle, and tossed it to the ground, shattering it in the center of the circle, covering the portal in yet more blood.

In that instant, the world turned on its side and righted itself, and darkness splashed into the air like ink spilled across a page. Solena gasped, backing toward the wall. Her chest and throat worked hard, veins standing out like taut cords in her neck. From the panic blossoming on her face and the way she clutched at her throat...

She couldn't breathe. Fear clenched around Renn's mind and every shaky breath felt like treason. "Help her!" she cried at the alchemists standing in the opening of the preparation chamber. *Why aren't they helping her?*

The shadow forming next to Solena flickered and solidified, and colors pushed back the darkness to reveal a man with warm brown skin several shades deeper than hers, and short, waved hair the bright red of saffron. A circlet rested across his brow. He, too, was clad in strange clothing, his face and body contorted in a rictus of pain. But, even in his agony, he turned in the direction of Solena's desperate wheezes.

"It's too much, Solena." Theodora's shrill tone grated in Renn's ear. "Let him go!"

Solena reached out to the coalescing man. Her hand passed through his shape, diffusing it and returning him to smoke and shadow. She screamed silently as he disappeared, and her red face crumpled, but she staggered over to the circle and dragged her bare foot through the blood, smearing it across the floor of the chamber and destroying the portal. Tears streamed down her purple cheeks. She let out a hitching gasp and fell to her knees, clawing at her chest where the bodice of her gown pulsed outward.

"Help her!" Renn shouted again. Unsure what she might do, she tried to move from the rail, but the crush of highborn behind her trapped her in place. "Will no one help her?" When nobody answered, she closed her eyes. *Blessed and merciful Amma, please help her! Help—*

A sound like the breaking of branches and the rending of silk, a sound akin to so many others and yet unlike anything she had ever heard before, split the night and echoed through the gallery. Her eyes flew open. A torrent of blood gushed from a ragged, gaping hole in Solena's chest, poured out between the jutting white claws of her broken ribs, trickled over the torn fabric, skin, and muscle, leeching the color from her face and the light from her eyes.

Soon the working on the circular floor was obscured beneath a hellish crimson sea with Solena's empty body kneeling at its center.

GETHA STILL PRAYED when something deep in the earth rumbled, and the whole world shifted. Opening her eyes, she caught herself against the wall. Though the shaking lasted but a handful of heartbeats, it seemed to go on forever before it ceased with the same abruptness as it had begun.

The muscles in her right leg cramped and twitched from alchemy shock, and she struggled to keep her feet. A heaving sound came from above, and she staggered back, just missing being vomited on by a palace guard retching over the wall's edge. Her stomach turned as the sick splashed against the Gift, marring its perfect surface.

"Sorry," the guard called down. It sounded like Jaseaux.

Getha waved the apology off. Alchemy shock bothered some worse than others, and the bigger the working, the stronger the reaction. That was it, then. Princess Solena had returned home. In praise, Getha returned to the Gift well away from Jaseaux's sick, pressing her calloused palms to the silky, unbroken face. *Thank you, Blessed Amma, for returning the princess—*

The Gift shuddered, rippling beneath her hands, like the skin of an animal shaking water from its coat.

She jumped back. Had the wall just...moved? An absurd notion, one she might have rejected outright if not for the ghost of its shiver lingering on her skin and the throbbing of her left hand. She lifted it and, in the center of her palm, her visible bloodmark pulsed, not in time with the beating of her heart but in rhythm with something else entirely.

She reached out again, her hands trembling as she pressed both palms to the wall. The instant her skin touched it, her bloodmark stilled. Afraid it would and afraid it wouldn't, she waited to see if the Gift might move once more. She stood there waiting for something—anything—to happen.

But the Gift stood as quiet and still as the grave.

Above, the clouds opened, releasing a deluge of icy rain, and the down-pour soaked Getha to the skin in moments. She didn't mind rain, but the cold was too much to bear, so she gave up her vigil and ran back toward the barracks, dreading the almost two-mile trip. To take her mind off her discomfort, she imagined herself pledging fealty to Queen Solena, and because of this, as she neared the northern wing of the palace, she mistook the first scream for a cheer. But she didn't mistake the second. Or the third.

She halted in the driving rain, trying to determine the source of the screams. A door in the palace, the one closest to the observation gallery, flew open, and dozens of people—highborn, servants, and even a handful of palace guards—spilled from Seedfall, their mouths agape in horror, their faces streaked with tears. Once outside, some staggered away in a daze or slumped into the mud, sobbing. Others ran off into the storm, their shrieks trailing behind them like nightmarish standards.

Getha didn't know what had happened or if she could help, but the Morovides were in the observation gallery, and even as a mere palace guard, part of her duty was protecting the queen and her daughters.

She dodged through the trickle of bodies still pouring forth from the palace, but just as it ended and she was about to slip inside, a hard hand on her shoulder stopped her.

"Thanks, Barei," Varo Nostros said from the doorway. Her face was pale, yet set and determined. "But the royal family"—she glanced behind her—"is secure. You're not needed here."

Then the varo stepped back and shut the door.

Getha turned to see if any of the wailing, shaking people sprawled in the sodden grass required a physicker or an alchemist and vowed to herself she would never, not where the Morovides were concerned, ever be told again that she was not needed.

SOUND AND SENSATION came back to Renn in a rush, and all around her, people screamed and shoved and retched and cried. She clung fast to the balustrade, the wood beneath her fingers the only solid, certain thing left in the world. Someone bumped into her, but her grip on the balustrade saved her from going over the edge.

"What happened?" she asked, as she righted herself. But the person who had knocked into her had already gone.

The blank-faced husk that remained of Solena slumped and toppled over, falling to the floor with a wet *smack*, the weight of her sending undulating ripples in the blood, rolling outward. Renn followed one of the waves as it traveled along and broke against...

It broke against something the size of her fist, a thing that shone dully in the unforgiving light of the globes. She pressed her hand to her chest; her racing pulse throbbed wildly against her palm.

The thing wasn't a thing. It was a heart. It was Solena's heart.

Renn's knees gave out, and she slid to the floor, no longer able to feel the beating in her chest. No longer able to feel anything at all.

29

THREE

"To win a Rhyllexie bride, a suitor must kill a snow bear, carve out the beast's still-warm heart, eat it, then lay the bloody pelt at her feet. It is an appropriately barbaric custom for this obdurately barbaric people."
-From Danlan's *Histories of the Known World, Vol. 6*

Dace Morovide, bow and arrow at the ready, lined up his shot. Through the trees, in a clearing not thirty feet from where he stood, a snow hare sat on its haunches with its ears up, listening. Seven hares already hung from his belt, but there were plenty of mouths to feed back at the keep and no one would complain about more meat in the stew.

With no wind, clouds hung heavy in the sky. If not for the hare's black eyes and the black tufts of fur at the tips of its ears, it would have been impossible to see amidst the drifts of snow.

Dace let out a slow, steady breath, brought the bow up, and—

Crack!

The snapping of a branch sent Dace's arrow wide, where it disappeared into the snow. The hare dashed off into the woods.

"Eh, eh." The sound, like the panting of a dog, identified the disrupter as Swey the Cloud Face. All Rhyllexie had two names, the one given to them at birth and an honorific from the tribe. "I apologize, the Prince. I was

30

coming to tell you we're heading back, and you are quite easy to find with that hat."

Dace touched the red woolen hat his *kärlief*—the Rhyllexie had no separate words for "husband" and "wife"—had knitted for him his first winter in Rhyllex. "No trouble," he said, swallowing his irritation. He slung his bow over his shoulder and turned to the other man. "But you owe me an arrow."

Swey nodded and made his strange sound again. Like Dace, he was wrapped head to toe in hunting furs and leathers. Though shorter than Dace's six feet and two inches by at least half a foot, Swey was broader across the shoulders and chest, and his hair and beard, white for the winter season, met on the sides of his face, making it appear as if his flat, wide face rested in a bird's nest. Just looking at him made Dace's beard itch, and he gave the short, black hairs a good scratch. Because of the way his beard curled when it grew too long, he preferred to keep it trimmed close. In truth, he preferred no beard at all, but there was a saying in Rhyllex—*A man without a beard is a man without balls.*

Swey tipped his head to the side, back in the direction where Dace had parted from the others, then turned and started walking. Though Dace would one day be Swey's chieftain, the small man didn't bow or scrape before him, and after ten years in the north, Dace didn't expect him to. Leaving his arrow for lost, he broke into a jog.

"How did you fare?" Swey asked, when Dace caught up to him. The path they walked through the Denkiefer was wide, the trunks of the trees far apart to accommodate the far-reaching branches of the broad, winter-bare canopy overhead.

Dace touched the bodies hanging from his belt. "Not bad. You?"

"Not good." Swey held out his empty hands. "Unless—eh, eh—you ask the hares!"

Dace joined the Cloud Face in laughing and was still chuckling when they climbed down the steep verge and stepped onto the North Road. A quarter of a mile down, amidst a small herd of horses, a group of ten Rhyllexie men and women worked, stringing the massive, palmate antlers of a felled ness to a few of the saddles. Nesses were large by nature. The males grew to seven feet at the shoulder, but this one must have been at least nine.

As Dace and Swey neared the group, one of the women looked up from her work and saw them. Filise the Loose Tongue grinned, revealing her sharpened incisors, and planted her boot on the beast's flank. "How do you like that?" she called. "Tonight, we feast."

Dace's hares were nothing compared to the ness, and an old self-loathing, a sense of being less-than, reared up within in, bringing with it the urge to cast away his paltry offerings. But then he thought of how much Agahara loved the downy pelts, the way she looked wearing them, and the feeling passed.

The wind kicked up, the clouds broke, and sunlight hit the snow in a dazzling array. The Rhyllexie cheered, some of them wordlessly, others that the sun was a sign of their ancestors' praise. Even though it did nothing to lessen the cold, the sun was a rare treat during the snows, and Dace closed his eyes, turned his face up into the light, and silently thanked Amma for it.

"We should try to return before it disappears again," a man—it sounded like Knai the Bear—said.

Filise and the others finished working while Swey and Dace went to their horses and prepared to ride. The Rhyllexie favored stocky-legged, barrel-chested horses with shaggy coats the color of cloudy ice. They were practical beasts for this part of the world, but they looked dull standing next to Dace's Windspear.

His lithe Ombratian filly—a gift sent to him on his last birthing day—was the color of chestnuts, with white socks and a star between her eyes. While the other horses waited patiently for their riders to mount, Windspear danced and shook her mane, and when Dace came close, she snuffled his furs in search of treats. He grabbed the bridle, tugged her nose out of one of his pockets, and checked the saddle's girth.

"Climb up on that silly thing," Knai said from ahorseback, "and let us be away."

He, Swey, Filise, and the others rode off, the dragging ness creating a deep furrow in the middle of the snowy road. Dace led Windspear over to the verge and, using the incline as a mounting block, leapt into the saddle.

The instant he landed, Windspear took off, forcing him to find his stirrups on the fly. He reached the others within moments, shouting that he would meet them back at the keep before leaving them behind. Windspear wore studded horseshoes, but he kept her to the clear path at the center of the road and took pleasure in the sun on his back, the frigid wind in his face.

As he raced along, the road eased into a slight incline, and the stone walls of Vomek Keep rose above the hill. Bit by bit, the keep came into view, and soon Dace reached the edge of the barren plateau surrounding the hill on which the keep sat.

Back when he first saw it, he remembered thinking it a cluttered mess of barren stone walls and steeply pitched roofs. Aside from a decade's worth of aging and the new roof on the armory, it appeared no different now than it had then, but the sight filled him with a pride he'd never experienced gazing upon his mother's palace.

He stopped and waited for the others so as not to make those stationed at the portcullis raise it twice. Shouts and shrieks of laughter came from within, sounds of people out in the courtyard enjoying the sun, and Dace, eager to join them, urged the others to hurry.

Before too long, the hunters came along, and chains rattled as the portcullis rose. Dace charged Windspear up the hill and ducked beneath the still-rising iron teeth. As expected, he found most of the tribe in the courtyard. Children, and more than a few of the adults, laughed and shouted and played, tossing snowballs at one another or building snow sentinels, while elders stood off to the edges and watched. To one side of the main doors of the keep, a group of young women with newly sharpened teeth and young men only just in short sleeves sang a call-and-response song, the singing a prelude to more serious flirtations, like gift giving or wrestling.

In the way of parental instinct, Dace knew at a glance neither of his sons were among the dozens of children and wondered where he might find them.

Then the rest of the hunting party entered. Juna the Red Leaf caught sight of them and cried out, and everyone circled around the felled ness. Leaving those that had taken the beast down to their glory, Dace guided Windspear toward the stables, where he left her in the able hands of Essön the Belt and the Ostler, who'd learned to care for his skittish Ombratian filly.

Dace was at the edge of the courtyard when the Young came darting up to him dressed in short pants and a long-sleeve tunic—his inside clothing. Gunnur the Young, named for his greatmother, was a striking boy. He bore his mother's deeply bronzed skin and dark, hooded eyes, and Dace's height and curls. Because the boy was tall for his age, he stood out among the other children, even more so in the winter moons, when his black hair, rather than shifting to all white as most Rhyllexie's did, grew in streaks of black and white.

Most days a line of children trailed him everywhere, but at the moment he was alone.

"Come, Papa," he said, his eyes shining with excitement. "There's... It's... " He ran around in a tight circle. "Come!"

"Easy, now," Dace said. "Where's your shadow?" There was a tug on his coat, and he turned to find his six-year-old son staring up at him.

"Fair day, Papa," Isaak said, a somber expression on his serious little face. He, too, shared his mother's coloring and heavy lidded eyes, though unlike the Young, his hair changed to a proper Rhyllexie white during the winter seasons. But his other features were pure Morovide, fine and narrow, and reminded Dace of Parneo.

A trickle of fear ran down Dace's spine as it always did whenever he was reminded of Isaak's resemblance to Parneo. "There you are!" Dace said, shouting his anxiety away. Isaak wasn't a twin and hadn't been born to a Morovide queen, so there was no reason to think he might develop Parn's skills or his madness.

Dace swept his younger son up—the boy was light as a wisp—and tossed him into the air, eliciting an excited shriek. He propped Isaak on his hip and, with his other hand, ruffled the Young's hair. "How are my boys?"

"Don't." The Young ducked out from under Dace's hand, then looked to see if anyone had noticed. He was just ten, and such casual contact wouldn't be frowned upon until he wore short sleeves, yet he already shied from Dace's touch more often than not, especially in the presence of others. It was a shallow cut, but the pain went deep. Though Dace remembered what it was like to be the Young's age, he wasn't ready for his son to become a man.

Did Father feel the same way? It wasn't the sort of question one put in a letter, so unless Corlin made the trek hundreds of miles north to Rhyllex, Dace doubted he would ever have the chance to ask.

"Will you come, Papa?" The Young leaned in and whispered, "It's Pyry and Pekka."

The brothers, both Dace's friends, fought every winter, but this year was worse than most, the acrimony stemming from a foolish disagreement over who in the autumn had cut and hauled more grain. It had been the talk of the winter, and if the snows didn't melt soon, many thought them headed for a blood match.

"Yes," Dace said, waving his hand. "Lead the way."

The Young made a line straight for the main building's antechamber, which was large enough for two dozen grown men to change in, with common hooks along one wall and shelves as long as the room and as high as the ceiling on the other. Dace set Isaak down and stripped off his *vervärmen klädij*, leaving the coat and overboots on the empty hooks for anyone who might need them. In his personal space on the shelves opposite, he deposited his scarf, gloves, belt, and his red woolen hat.

When he was in his short sleeves, his scarred forearms bared, the Young danced around him, hopping from foot to foot. "Hurry, Papa."

Dace patted the air for patience and knelt down in front of Isaak. If there was to be a blood match, he didn't want his younger son there for it. "Here," he said, handing the hares over. "Take these along to the Cook."

The hares were skinny ones, but Isaak struggled to hold them aloft, so Dace showed him how to carry them over his shoulder. With the load settled, Isaak headed off for the kitchens, looking like a tiny peddler hunched over by the burdensome weight of his sack.

"Come!" The Young tugged on Dace's arm, his excitement overriding his need to play the man. "We'll miss it."

"Yes, yes. Lead the way."

The Young darted into the great hall, and Dace followed. At three-hundred-and-fifty feet long and two-hundred feet wide, the great hall at Vomek Keep was the single largest room Dace had ever seen. The grand ballroom at Seedfall could have fit inside it twice with space to spare. During Rhyllex's all-too-brief warm season, the great hall stood vacant, an empty cavern bereft of purpose. But this was the snow season, and it was anything but empty.

The Young cut a circuitous path through the forest of tents that reached from one end of the hall to the other. The tents were almost identical in their construction, leather walls stretched over wooden frames, but each family decorated their own tent by their own means. Some sewed into the leather and others painted it. Some carved the wooden frames or stained them. Hair, fur, feathers, bones—both animal and human—they were all used to distinguish one home from the next. The one mark every tent bore was the profile of a rearing snow bear above the door, the symbol of the Vomek tribe.

In the afternoons, the keep usually bustled with activity, but with so many people outside, the hall was quiet. Dace and the Young passed through the east end, where the people of Yost lived, just as during the warm moons they lived in the village to the keep's east.

They skirted the hall's center firepit, one of the five common pits large enough to roast an ox, and crossed over into the western end, where those of Wessow camped. Dace looked for Agahara along the way but saw no one other than a handful of dozing elders and a couple of mothers with babes too young to be taken out in the cold.

A quirk of the architecture meant sound didn't carry far in the hall, so Dace heard nothing of the fight until they were almost on top of it, not until he stepped from the tent forest into the High Lane, the open passage along the north wall.

"I'll cut your ears off and feed them to the dogs, you shit-stain!"

"Not if I cut off your hands first and feed them to the ness!"

Pyry the Plain and Pekka the Corner Eyed were toe to toe, both shouting at the tops of their lungs. Beyond them, about twenty or so of their tribe-mates contributed to the noise, urging on one or the other, and at their fore, of course, was Sturr the North Wind, his color high and his eyes gleaming.

Dace and Sturr the North Wind were of a height, but the other man was broader by half, and of Dace's detractors within the tribe, the North Wind was their leader. Dace had been told more than once that the North Wind had set his aim at Agahara when they were children, and perhaps that jealousy was the seed, but after so many years in the same tribe, the hatred between the men had grown thick on both sides.

The Young bounded forward, but Dace caught his arm and held him back. "Stay here." The Young balked and opened his mouth to speak. "I mean it," Dace said, cutting off the protest before it came. "If this goes to a circle you can come, but until then, you will do as I say."

The Young lowered his eyes. "Yes, Papa."

As Dace approached the brothers, Pekka shouted something he missed, but he caught Pyry's response. "How do you know? You can't tell your mouth from your ass."

Pekka spat, and the phlegm and spittle landed in Pyry's beard. Sturr and the others cheered. Trifling with Pyry's beard, which he always kept in three neat braids, was asking for a challenge, with Pyry the Plain ready to give it. His mouth twisted into a snarl and his upper teeth pressed hard into his lower lip, but before he might speak, Dace stepped between the brothers and cried, "*Vasgievollen!*"

The shouting ceased, and everyone stilled. Sturr's flushed cheeks beneath his white beard turned florid. "You dare—"

"*Vasgievollen,*" Dace repeated. "*Vasgievollen, ystänur.*" *Vasgievollen* simply translated to "challenge," but the way in which it was spoken, and to whom, determined the seriousness of it. That was why he'd added *ystänur,* the Rhyllexie word for "tribemate" or their closest approximation to "friend."

Those with their heart set on a blood match crowed their displeasure. Both brothers seemed relieved, yet Dace knew neither would thank him for his intercession—it made all of them appear soft—but he didn't care, not with his son watching.

"No," Sturr slapped the smooth skin of his forearms for emphasis. "That is not right. That is not how things are done, the Weak Lander."

The title, dropped by most years earlier, rankled, and Dace bit down hard to stop another challenge from flying off his tongue.

"Enough!" An older woman, her long, white hair in a braid that no longer changed colors with the seasons and hard eyes set in a hard face, stepped out into the lane.

Pyry was the first to bow. "Chieftain," he said, the greeting echoed by the other tribemates, with Sturr's deep voice coming last.

Dace bowed. "Mother."

Gunna the Peacekeeper dipped her chin to acknowledge those of the tribe, but her eyes never left him. "I must speak with the Prince."

"A challenge has been offered," Sturr said. "It must—"

"It will be met later," she said, her attention unwavering. "I need to speak with Dace." His first name was near unrecognizable as she struggled with the Norrish sound. That she attempted it all—in front of others, even —signaled that something was off, and his heartbeat quickened when she gestured for him to follow her away from the crowd.

Dace caught up with Gunna in a shadowy alcove along the wall. "What is it?" He checked to make sure the Young was out of hearing range. His son's brow was creased, but he remained where he was. "Where is Agahara? Did something happen to her?"

Gunna made a slashing motion with her hand. "Your *kärlief* is well."

Letting out a breath, he leaned over and placed his hands on his knees. "Thank, Amma."

"But," she said, the gravity in her tone drawing him back upright, "a message came from your family." He looked at her empty hands. "In my study."

His stomach jumped into his throat. There was a single means by which a message might arrive directly in the chieftain's study.

"Go," Gunna said. "I'll tell Isaak and the Young what's happening."

"The Seedling is in the kitchens."

"I'll find him. Go."

Without another word, he headed for her study at a run, leaving the expansive great hall and charging through the keep's winding side passages.

Chieftain Gunna's study was narrow, long but not very deep, with a low ceiling braced by thick wooden supports. At one end, a fire burned in an open pit, the smoke rising and escaping through a hole in the roof. At the other stood Gunna's desk, and in the corner behind that, a blood-soaked slip of paper sat where it had for the past eleven years, beneath a bell jar on a knee-high wooden plinth, waiting for an important enough message to come along.

Carved into the rich honeywood were dozens of alchemical formulas, their shapes familiar but their meaning obscured by his lack of knowledge. He had once considered entering the academy, just as he'd considered entering the ductoran or the varo, anything to avoid the uselessness that was his birthright. But then Parneo was born, and by age four, showed more aptitude for the artful science than Dace ever would, so his search for purpose had continued.

He crossed the room in a few long strides, then stood over the bell jar, anxious to pull it away yet afraid to do so. Visible through the warped glass, words were etched into the blood, a message of such import there hadn't been time to send it by normal methods. Like a man standing at the edge of a cliff, he clasped the cold glass knob at the top of the jar, took a deep breath, and lifted the cover away.

The slip of paper was small, no longer than his pinky finger, so the message was short. *Solena dead. Accident. Return home. Funeral.*

Bell jar still in hand, he took several steps backward, and when his legs hit the edge of Gunna's chair, he dropped into it. The ancient wooden frame squeaked its protest, but he barely noticed.

Solena was dead. He'd been two when she was born and couldn't remember a world without her in it. She had always been there, ready to take that which had never been his to start with. For a brief time as a child, he'd believed that, as the oldest, he would inherit his mother's throne, until his father had taken him aside and explained to him why he wouldn't. That talk had given rise to a one-sided rivalry with Solena that had driven him and shaped his entire life.

"The Prince?" Agahara the Bold—Dace's *kärlief*—walked into the room. Her long white hair hung around her shoulders, blending with the snowy rabbit fur of her gown and contrasting with the rich warmth of her skin.

"Mother said you received news from your family. Has there been an attack?"

Solena is dead. Unable to speak the words aloud, he picked up the note and handed it to her. She took it from him, no more than the heat from her hand brushing his skin, and read it.

"What is this last word?" she asked.

"Funeral." One of a hundred words for which there was no Rhyllexie equivalent. "It's a death ceremony."

She narrowed her dark eyes. "But your sister is gone. She is no more." Her statements hit him like physical blows, but she seemed unaware. "What is the purpose of such a ceremony?"

A good question. What was the purpose? "A funeral is a way for people to..." The Norrish word "mourn" required another explanation. "To share in a loss."

"I see," she said, though it was clear from the crease between her white brows she didn't. Even after more than a decade of marriage, she was as beautiful and as inscrutable to him as the day they'd first met.

Solena is dead. Grief wrapped its hands around his heart and squeezed, and he longed for the comfort of Agahara's touch. He wanted her to wrap her arms around him, hold him close, and whisper meaningless consolations in his ear. But he'd learned when he was a child the futility of wishing for something that might never be, and so, instead of hoping for Agahara to reach out to him, he grabbed her, pulled her close, and pressed his lips to hers.

Coupling was one of the furthest things from his mind, but it gave their physical contact the meaning it required.

He lifted her onto the edge of the desk, rucked up her skirts, and pressed himself against the warmth between her legs. His movements were frantic, driven by his desperation, and she matched his urgency, writhing against him until his body responded, then tearing at the laces of his breeches and guiding him inside her.

While he thrust, she licked and kissed her way up his left forearm, stopping and closing her teeth around a bare spot of skin near his elbow.

"No!" He pulled his arm from her mouth before her sharpened incisors broke the skin. He didn't want any scars from this encounter, didn't want any marks to remind him of this day.

Agahara straightened and wiped her lips. When Dace took a step back, she stood and arranged her skirts so they once again fell down over her hips. Looking up at him, she tipped her head to one side, then she placed a hand on his hip and ran her fingers along his thigh, bringing them around to cup his now limp cock.

The confusion in her expression deepened as she released him. "Death is natural, *kärlief*, the one constant of life."

He laced up his breeches and said nothing because there was nothing to say. She was right.

"Do you want to go to this"—her upper lip curled as it always did when she spoke in his native language—"funeral?"

Dace had promised himself long ago he'd never return to Ombratos, not for any reason. But this was Solena, and his family would expect him to come, as would their people.

Setting the paper back on the plinth, he turned it over to the side colored with his blood. Then he took his eating knife from his belt and used it to pierce a fingertip. When a fat ruby of blood welled from the cut, he asked Agahara to hand him a quill. She gave him one from her mother's desk, and he dipped it into the blood.

"I have to," he said. They neared the end of the snow season, making it safe enough for travel, and in his mind he already composed the response telling his mother he was coming. "I have a responsibility."

"What responsibility?" Agahara asked. "To whom?"

Her questions brought him up short because he didn't know how to answer them. "In blood and duty bound"—that was the Morovide family motto. He thought of the countless times he'd heard his Grandmother Violaine and then, after she passed, Solena say, *"A Morovide's first duty is to her people."* But they had referred to the Fallen, the citizens of Ombratos, and who were they to him now? Some were his parents, his sisters, his broken brother. Inheriting the throne was Linore's nightmare, and his mother would be slower to abdicate to her, slower to turn over her responsibilities to a daughter less ready to lead. Or would she? And what of Heshi and Renn, little Renn, who still wrote often and had always worshipped Solena as if she were Amma herself. *They are my people, aren't they?*

Seeming to sense his struggle, Agahara pointed to him, then touched her face, tracing the spots on her chin and cheeks where his beard covered his face. She bared her incisors and ran her hand along her forearms. Closing his hands into fists, he flexed his muscles and his scars, the scars she'd given him, the pattern of their lives together, pulled.

He was a Morovide, so his first duty was to *his* people.

"To whom?" she asked again, and this time, he knew the answer.

Dipping the quill again and putting pen to paper, he wrote, *Apologies. Snows too deep. Will pray.*

Though the words were written in blood on blood, the letters stood out, stark and legible. He spoke the incantation etched around the face of the plinth and touched his bloody finger to it four times, leaving a mark at each point on the compass. He placed the bell jar over the message and stepped back, gesturing for Agahara to do the same.

For the span of several heartbeats, nothing happened. Then it felt as if the room tilted on its side, and his message disappeared, signaling its delivery. With a sound like a sharp crack of thunder, the plinth split in two, and the bell jar slid toward the floor, but Agahara reached out and caught it before it fell.

"Here," he said, taking it from her and setting it on the desk. His head pounded from the alchemy shock. "We have to burn them now."

Agahara hefted up one half of the plinth, and he took the other. They set them on the fire before he returned to the spot where the slip of paper had fallen. On one side, his mother's message to him remained. Part of him wanted to keep it so he might read it over and over until it made sense. But Agahara watched him, and so he tossed the paper into the fire too, his bloodmark tingling as the working to which he was Bound burned.

FOUR

"Be you rich with coin or friends or family,
Death makes beggars of us all."
-Final lines from "Tarry and Torn," a song sung at Tithen funerals, author
unknown

Renn spent the four days after Solena's death riding. With whichever varo was assigned to her each day, she rode over every inch of the palace grounds—across the sprawling lawns leading down to the guarded wall separating them from the rest of the city, up into the wooded hills that marked the land between the edges of Ombratos and the Cassedent Mountains, back and forth across the rushing currents of the River Sap.

She, and the varo trailing behind her, rode hard from dawn to dusk. At night, she fell into her bed and was claimed by exhaustion, only to be chased back into shaky, sweaty wakefulness by blood-drenched nightmares a few candlemarks later. That was when she would rise and leave the stifling confines of her bedchamber to walk the halls of the palace, keeping to the smaller, lesser-used corridors, always careful to avoid the observation chamber. Eventually, the first hints of dawn colored the sky, releasing her to start the cycle over again.

The morning of the fifth day broke cold and gray, with a wet chill that settled deep into her bones. When Renn returned to her rooms to have her maids dress her for riding, one of them, Editi, told her the funeral would be that evening.

"What about Dace?" Renn asked. "Is he here already? That's impossible."

"No, Your Highness," Nessa said, braiding Renn's hair. "The snows are too deep for him to return."

A flash of anger seared through her. How dare he miss this as he had missed so much else? She took a deep breath and told herself not to blame him. *He would have come if it were possible.* She repeated it to herself, hoping it was true even as she suspected it wasn't.

She rode hard all morning, until she and her horse—that day an ash-colored gelding called Salt—were covered in mud. She rode through the woods to the foot of the Radix Waterfall, the head of the Sap, and spent the afternoon sitting on a rock at the edge of the deep pool into which it fell, staring down into the churning water, letting the deafening roar drown out every sound, every thought, every feeling.

Too soon, the gray skies began to darken. Renn climbed to her feet and wiped the wetness from her cheeks. Her body was so stiff it took several tries to clamber back into the saddle. Varo Deniel, who waited beside his own horse less than twenty feet away, moved in her direction, but when she waved him off, he didn't offer to help her again, for which she was grateful.

Once mounted, she and the varo followed a trail along the Sap back to the stables. The clouded waters crept by beneath the crusty fringes of ice lining the banks. In the warm, torchlit stable, she handed Salt's reins over to Khea, a young groom whose dark hair hung down her back in dozens of thin braids. She wore a black strip of fabric tied around her arm above the elbow.

Renn scraped a hunk of mud off Salt's flank and scratched his rump. "I hope I didn't ride him too hard."

"Never do, Your Highness."

"At last," said a male voice behind Renn.

She turned to find Tomas standing behind her. "Yes?"

He bowed to her. "The queen requires your presence."

Does she think I've forgotten? "I'm on my way to the pavilion now."

"She's in the palace, Your Highness."

She tried to ignore the relief that came with the thought of avoiding the pavilion for even a moment longer.

He examined her from bottom to top, taking in every inch of her wretched, mud-soaked state. "Perhaps the princess would like to change. I believe the maids have set out your mourning attire."

She smoothed her curls back from her face, and her fingers touched something. She pulled it out. A twig. She no doubt looked a fright, but the idea of putting on a black shroud brought bile to the back of her throat. It was too much. "Khea, where might I find one of those strips?"

Khea paused, then untied her own and handed it to Renn.

"Thank you." She gestured to Tomas, and with lips pressed into a hard line, he took the band and secured it around her arm.

Then he led her from the stables, across the grounds, and into the palace. The queen's chosen meeting room seemed to be on the far side of Seedfall, and now that Renn's routine had been broken, she began to realize how poorly she'd treated her body over the past few days. Her muscles, especially those in her thighs, arms, and abdomen, cramped and ached. She pulled off her gloves and tucked them into her belt, exposing chafed and blistered hands. Her lips were cracked, her cheeks raw and wind-chapped. The pain was intense, but it was clean. Unsullied. Pure. It was the sort of pain a salve or rest could ease, and she welcomed it.

After several minutes, they arrived at a little-used study on the second floor of the Snow Wing and stopped just beyond the open door. She knew the room, though she couldn't remember when she'd last been inside. A long table of golden honeywood ran the length of it, and a portrait of Ombratos's fifth queen, Renn's great-several-times-over-grandmother Caren hung on the east wall, hidden away because of her strange choice to be painted with a bright green tree frog in each hand. Outside, the full darkness of night had fallen, turning the room's windows into mirrors. Renn stepped to the side to avoid catching a glimpse of her reflection, and Tomas sidestepped with her, sighing as he removed her filthy cloak.

She walked through the door to find four people already seated at the table. Her twin, Parneo, and Prince Dallan both stood as she entered. Dallan wore a jacket of black velvet over a charcoal silk tunic. The somber colors and the shadow of whiskers across his jaw suited him, and when their eyes met, a deep and visceral longing jolted her. Shame arrived hard on its heels, and before the heat in her chest might rise to her cheeks, she cast her attention elsewhere.

Heshi did not stand, but that was her right as one of Renn's elder sisters. More telling was her appearance. Heavy circles darkened the skin beneath her eyes, her hair hung loose from its pins, and her mourning gown was so wrinkled she might have slept in it. Next to her, Dallan's aunt also remained seated, though she did so contrary to protocol. A jeweled snood held back Lady Helenia's long, coppery hair and she remained in white, the proper color for mourning in Tithen, but that too seemed an act of defiance, as did her cold stare.

Renn wanted to channel Solena and put the woman in her place, but the very thought of Solena sapped her of her strength. So she ignored the breach, and though Dallan pulled out the chair beside him, Renn took the open seat nearest her twin.

Five days' worth of stubble covered Parneo's cheeks, and the stench of chemicals coming from his black clothes burned the inside of her nose. His keepers stood close by, but his eyes were clear. Closing the space between their chairs, she reached out and took his hand. He squeezed her fingers, his grip tight, and the sharp pressure brought tears to her eyes. She squeezed back. Pure.

Footsteps approached in the hall, and with no fanfare, Prince-Consort Corlin entered, followed closely by four of the queen's advisors. Father's face was pinched with grief. He was not a small man—it was as if, in recent years, he thought his girth should match the queen's—but he suddenly seemed very small. And old. His salt-and-sand hair was uncombed, and he hadn't used any wax on his whiskers, so they hung ragged over his top lip and down the sides of his mouth. He sat at the table on Renn's other side, and the advisors took chairs set along the wall.

"Father? Are you...?" She wasn't sure how to finish the question.

He looked over at her, his blue eyes watery and shot through with red. "I'm a'right, poppet. I'm a'right." The words wafted out on a cloud of spirits. While she had been riding, he had crawled down to the bottom of a bottle, both of them hiding in their own ways. She touched his arm, and he patted her hand.

The *knock-shuffle* of the queen using her cane preceded her arrival. Then she and Linore came around the corner, followed by their varos and the queen's maids, and everyone, including Lady Helenia, stood while Father helped Theodora into her seat. The chair groaned with the effort of supporting her, but it held nevertheless. Once settled, the queen nodded, giving everyone leave to sit, and her attendants left the room, but before the last handmaid could close the door behind her, Lead Varo Orli entered and took a spot along the wall next to the scarlet-haired Varo Maurius.

A lead varo trained and coordinated the varos, though on occasion he or she might also guard the queen or a guest of particular import. Orli had held the position for the last nine years, but as he'd hadn't watched over

Renn since he was a simple varo and she a child, she knew nothing about him aside from what she'd learned during the queen's tourneys. The man was a strong and ruthless fighter, and she was glad she'd never have to face the end of his blade. His gaze roamed the room, never alighting anywhere for too long. When it stopped on her, she was quick to look away.

Linore sat with her narrow shoulders hunched. Pinkness rimmed her eyes and patches of hectic color mottled her cheeks. Next to her, the queen appeared much as she always did, overburdened and miserable, but she stared at the band around Renn's arm.

Her mouth twisted in disgust. "Do you really think it appropriate to honor your sister in such a common manner?"

Her question found its mark. What had seemed so right in the stables now seemed childish and silly. Renn swallowed around the lump in her throat and stared at the table.

One of the advisors cleared her throat. "I beg your leave, Your Majesty. There are urgent matters of state requiring your—"

Queen Theodora held up a hand. "I am aware. But I'm certain our guests"—she gestured toward Helenia and Dallan—"don't wish to hear of such things. Those matters will keep until tomorrow, will they not?"

Lady Helenia leaned forward; her reflected shape wavered across the polished wood like a shadow moving under water. "Your Majesty, I think we have been rather patient here."

"Indeed." The chair creaked as the queen shifted in her seat. "My alchemists are looking into the matter of the...incident." She cleared her throat. "There are questions still, but we are proceeding with the assumption the prince survived."

Renn was going to ask "What prince?" but Heshi beat her to it. It was the first she had spoken, and her voice was hoarse.

"The man Solena tried to bring through with her," Theodora said. "The crowned prince of Baumo."

Why—

Linore slapped her hands on the table, making Renn jump. "You're forgetting the most important part, Mother." Her expression hard, each word snapped like the breaking of a branch.

Theodora gripped the head of her cane so hard her knuckles turned white. "In accordance with the conditions set forth in their marriage contract—"

"No," Parneo whispered. Renn put her hand over his.

"—should anything happen to her—"

Parneo jerked his hand away. "No," he said louder. "No, no."

"—then the established Binding carries—"

"No!" Parneo clutched the sides of his head. "More time," he shouted at the ceiling as he scrabbled at his ears. "I was supposed to have more time! They said more time, more time, more—" His speech devolved into meaningless whimpers and shrieks.

Renn grabbed for his hands, but his well-trained keepers reached him first. One of them took his left wrist, another held his right, and they pressed his hands together at the center of his chest. A third, this acolyte a shorter young woman with yellow hair, steadied his head against her belly. He jerked and shouted for a few moments more, but then he began to settle. The shouts trailed off, and the twitching lessened, and soon he'd calmed enough for his keepers to release him. The last to let him go was the young woman, who patted Parneo's hair before stepping away from him and slipping something into her pocket.

A flowering charm. That was the item the acolyte had returned to her pocket. Even Parn's keepers understood how alchemy calmed him. Why couldn't the queen see it too?

"Please," Theodora said quietly, "take him to his rooms."

Renn spun around to face her. "But he's fine n—"

"To his rooms," Theodora repeated. Her eyes shone as she stared at the globe sconces hanging over the table. "This day is hard enough already."

Renn mouthed *"I'm sorry"* to Parneo. His gaze once again clear, he mouthed back *"No need."* His keepers eased him from his chair and ushered him out.

"In accordance with the conditions set forth in Solena's marriage contract," the queen said, going on as if nothing had happened, "the Binding established during their wedding ceremony carries over to the next heir."

Renn scrambled to return to the subject at hand. Marriage contract? Wedding ceremony?

"Apologies, Your Majesty," Messero Noa, one of the queen's oldest advisors, said, "but are you saying the heir was married before she... the accident? To the prince from Baumo?"

"Yes."

A shocked silence gripped the room, and Renn's eyes flew to Dallan, who sat with his hands in his lap, his head bowed. He looked up at Renn, found her already staring back, and smiled. Hope, thready as a lark's song, trilled within her.

47

"What does this mean?" Lady Helenia said.

The strange, angry creature inhabiting Linore's body snorted. "The marriage contract and Binding were fashioned to extend beyond Solena's death. Which means"—her voice grew thick and her eyes glittered—"I am now married and Bound to some strange man I have never met."

That explained the bitterness. Linore's future in the church, her future with Ductora Gesso were both gone, consumed by her duty to the throne.

Lady Helenia said, "I'm still not sure I follow."

Messero Noa half rose from his seat. "If I may, Your Highness?"

Linore covered her eyes with her hand and nodded.

"A queen of Ombratos must be Bound to the throne with her prince-consort to ensure the direct continuity of the bloodline."

Lady Helenia raised an eyebrow, creasing the tattoos on her brow. "What if the woman is barren or the man impotent?"

Father beat the messero to his answer. "Then the Binding doesn't take, an' she picks another one. Or another."

Though he slurred, he spoke with authority. Had he been the queen's second choice? Or her third or fourth? He had always seemed so devoted to her that Renn had just assumed theirs a love match, though she wasn't sure why. When Renn was eight, not long after Dace married the Rhyllexie, she'd asked Solena if she thought their parents loved one another. Solena had smiled sadly and said, "Amma has already given us so much, Renn. We can't expect to marry for love too."

Yet, there had been such passion on Solena's face when the prince appeared, such despair when she severed the connection.

"Did she love him?" The question sprang unbidden from Renn's lips, and everyone turned toward her. "Solena," she explained, unnerved by the attention. "Did she love the prince?"

Linore glared. "Does it matter?"

"I suppose not," Renn said, lying to deflect Linore's ire. It did matter to her, though; it mattered that Solena might have found that happiness before she died.

"That is all well and good, but what of us?" Lady Helenia's Tithen accent was sharper than Dallan's, and she clipped off each word like an irritated gardener attacking a wayward hedge. "What of the intended marriage between Prince Dallan and your heir? Did you consider that?"

Tension filled the room as everyone waited to see how the queen might react to the lady's impertinence. Theodora drew her shoulders back and grew very still. "I considered everything."

"Everything?" Lady Helenia breathed out a humorless laugh, and strong emotion stirred beneath her icy surface. "I know there was never a formal contract drawn up between Dallan and the heir, but does an Ombratian's word mean so little?"

As if her honor and the honor of her people had not just been impugned, the queen gestured in Heshi's direction. "I believe there are alliances that might still be made."

With that, she silenced Renn's tremulous hope. Renn didn't look in Dallan's direction this time. She couldn't.

Lady Helenia remained quiet, perhaps waiting for more. When it became obvious a marriage between her nephew and the queen's third daughter was all that would be offered, she stood, her chair scraping against the floor. "Then I think we have nothing more to speak of." She crossed the room, threw open the door, and stalked through it.

Dallan rose and bowed. "My apologies, Your Majesty." Glancing at Renn, he raced after his aunt.

"Tomorrow," the queen said almost under her breath. "I will fix it tomorrow."

She held out her hand to Father, and he found his feet to assist her in doing the same. Love match or not, they walked out together arm in arm, her cane thumping against the floor. Varo Maurius followed them as they entered the hall and veered to the left, but Lead Varo Orli exited and turned to the right, the direction Lady Helenia and Dallan had gone. Did he think her so angry she might try something? Linore sniffled, Heshi went to console her, and they, too, left together, trailed by the advisors, who chattered among themselves in hushed tones.

Soon, save for Varo Deniel, Renn was alone, and the time for Solena's funeral had arrived.

FIVE

"The Ever-Watchful Eye rewards the ever ready."
-First Tenet of Burk

Lady Helenia Briain tipped her head back against the door and continued to grin at the ceiling as a sense of relief settled over her.

Her meeting with the queen could not have gone better, and for the first time in a long while, her life had returned to her control. She moved from the door and sat on the cloth-of-gold counterpane, sinking into the feather-stuffed mattress. The windows' brocade curtains had been pulled to keep out the night's chill, a fire danced in the grate, and the room smelled of the lavender soap with which the servants washed the linens and the beeswax they used to polish the honeywood furniture, all of it a vast improvement over the dank, rat-infested prison cell where she'd been convinced she would take her last breaths.

Without a new message from Mayve, Helenia reached into the pocket of her skirt for the last one she'd received. Helenia and Mayve were sisters, though not by blood. For a while they were sisters-by-law, married to brothers, and yet, since Mayve's divorce and Helenia's widowing, they weren't even that. No, they were sisters by choice, tied together by a bond forged over twenty-seven years of friendship.

Mayve's letter, written in a code the women had spent years developing, started by explaining how her plans to assassinate Princess Solena in the Yent Isles had failed. Helenia pushed back the anger that rose once again in reading about Mayve's second failed assassination attempt in the Isles. After all, her first failure had led to Helenia's imprisonment and disgrace. But, as always, the next part of the letter, the part in which Mayve spoke to the necessity of their actions, soothed her. Helenia was not as devoted to the cause of Tithen expansion as Mayve, few were, but she did believe in it, and Mayve's insistence that Helenia's humiliation had played some part in the larger mission took some of the sting from her memories.

Besides, Mayve wasn't the only one who had failed.

The letter closed with Mayve asking Helenia to sabotage the alchemical working bringing Solena home. *One gift is acceptable. But as we both know, two would be insuperable.* Mayve had, long before anyone else, seen Ombratos for what it was: a nut overripe for the cracking.

The wall around Ombratos had proved surmountable the moment the Morovides had welcomed her son Dallan, and then Helenia, to Seedfall, but the threat of Princess Solena had ranged beyond their reach the day she had left for the Yent Isles. The working had been their last chance, and Helenia had tried to do as Mayve had asked. She'd spent close to a candlemark in the preparation chamber, returning twice under the pretense of an insatiable curiosity about the process, but with the number of alchemists around and the sheer volume of components, she'd never known where or how to start.

But one of Mayve's agents had succeeded where Helenia had not, and the heir was dead. Helenia wished she knew by whose hand. It couldn't have been the flop-haired footman who brought her messages or the traitorous messera who'd spent the whole of the night gaping at that indifferent messero.

Mayve had almost a dozen agents in and around Ombratos, and in Helenia's mind, none of them fit the role of assassin. That, in its way, explained his or her success. It was a little unsettling not knowing who Mayve's other agents were, but Helenia took solace in the fact that if she couldn't identify them, then they couldn't identify her.

Helenia owed Mayve so much. Carhal had married Helenia, and in doing so, lifted her far above her station, but Mayve was the one who had taught Helenia how to survive, and Helenia hated disappointing her. But soon Helenia might prove herself in other arenas. She ran her finger over Mayve's standard farewell—*For Tithen.*

Their land, Tithen, was, for many, many years, an island of strife. An island of occupiers and slaves, of natives so weak they allowed themselves to be subjugated again and again. For centuries, men and women went to the island of Tithen intent on claiming ownership over the fertile fields, the forests of iaradann trees, and the tireless workers who couldn't rise up and who would rather live with chains around their necks than leave.

Some of those who came were driven back; others succeeded. But none ever eradicated the Tithens because it was understood that as long as they worked their land, the fields never laid fallow, never went barren, and only the Tithens knew when an iaradann tree was ripe for harvest.

Harvested in season, iaradann wood was as hard as iron and coveted at every market in Althea. Out of season, and it was useless, as soft as cheese, and wanted by no one. With Tithens around, rain came when the land thirsted and held off when it didn't. Tithens kept the worst of the sea storms at bay, and some even believed they had tamed fire.

And so, whether through genuine belief or fearful superstition, ruler after ruler allowed a certain number of Tithens to live, while scores of young women—elemental wives—gave their lives to maintain those fictions. Due to their sacrifices, their people survived long enough for Burk to free them.

During Burk's Age, Tithen went from a nation of slaves to a nation of fighters, and these days, with both elemental wives and iaradann trees now rare, their most profitable export was mercenaries. But Mayve believed her people deserving of more. Capable of more.

"We've kept to this island long enough, Helly. We need to grow. It's time for us to conquer."

Before Helenia left for Ombratos, she and Mayve had agreed putting Dallan on the throne was their best option, the goal in taking Ombratos to force the issue of Tithen expansion. If, somehow, Adameth and his shrinking band of conservative supporters won out, then Ombratos would serve as little more than Mayve's refuge in a war between the small nations. But if Mayve and her rising tide of progressives had their way, Ombratos would become the mainland hub for a new Tithen empire.

Helenia wanted the throne, of course she did, but even she could understand that taking it for herself was too risky to chance. People had respected Carhal, but they'd merely tolerated her, and in the wake of her trial, she was too hated, too likely to bait the conservatives and swell their numbers. So Dallan would be their figurehead while she ran the city as chancellor. She understood this, and yet the necessity for her nephew's presence galled her all the same. She and Carhal had led Morleon as partners, and the city had flourished with their combined leadership. If not for one kind deed—taking the blame for Mayve's failed assassination attempt —followed by the most horrid event in her life—Carhal's sudden death— Helenia might have been queen.

A scratch at the door startled her from her thoughts. Dallan had caught up to her, then. "One moment," she called.

She stood, smoothed her hair and gown, and schooled her expression into a scowl. Her nephew would expect anger, and after he'd "calmed" her, sympathy. His look when that engorged tick of a queen promised him Princess Heshiette had spoken volumes. He lusted after the youngest, Renn, even a fool could see that. But his desire remained a piece of a larger puzzle she'd yet to solve. Mayve had her plans, but with her back in Tithen, Helenia needed to do what she thought best, and at the moment, she rode along on her instincts, trusting them to lead her in the right direction.

She took a deep breath. "Enter."

Her maid, Pia, opened the door and cowered in the hall as if fearing a blow. "I-I'm sorry for disturbin' you, my lady."

Helenia's appearance of anger in the wake of her meeting with the queen had been a necessary pretense, but now she dropped it for actual contrition. Servants were allies no highborn, especially those planning to overthrow the crown, could afford to lose.

"My apologies," Helenia said as she strode over to the doorway. "Please express my deepest apologies to the man at the door as well. My behavior was unforgivable. I was... My meeting with the queen didn't go as I'd hoped."

Pia relaxed her shoulders, but the tension around her eyes stayed. "I'm sorry to hear that, my lady. Would you like I should draw you a bath and ask your guest to return later?"

"Who is this guest?"

"Lead Varo Orli, my lady." Pia glanced in the direction of the suite's entryway. "Said you would know why he'd come."

Well, aren't we eager? Helenia suppressed another smile. "Prepare the study and see him to it. Where is the prince?"

"I don't know, my lady," Pia said, but she rubbed a hand over the black band tied around her upper arm, her way of voicing the obvious without speaking it aloud.

It bordered on insolence, and yet Helenia liked the girl even more for it.

"Shall I find the prince?"

Helenia weighed her options. Dallan and Orli both required attention, but if Orli demanded his first, so be it. Let Dallan attend the heir's horrifying funeral. "That won't be necessary. Please see the lead varo to the study, and let him know I will be along shortly."

Pia curtsied, and Helenia, nodding her thanks to the girl, closed the door. Her disagreement with the queen served as good justification for staying away from the funeral, not that she had ever planned to go. For such a forward country, the Ombratian ritual of burning their dead was almost as barbaric as their means of tapping into the Unknowable Beyond by bloodletting, or their mad worship of some mythical being.

She crossed to her dressing table and sat in front of the mirror. With her fingertips, she touched the puffiness beneath her eyes and the wrinkles around her mouth and wished the room lit with candles rather than the less forgiving globes.

As the days passed, she slept less and less, and her forty-eight years were starting to show. *"Sleep defies the wicked and the sly of heart."* It was her father's voice she heard, a line from an old poem he'd always quoted at her whenever she complained of being tired. Despite the way he had raised her, she hadn't set out to be wicked or sly, and yet life had found a way of making her both.

But the tattoos around her eyes—the fine blue lines denoting her family and her completion of a compulsory year of martial training—helped to hide the wrinkles across her brow, and no grey strands marred her hair, her best feature. She combed through her copper-colored locks, then reached into the bodice of her white gown and adjusted her breasts so they sat higher. She also shortened the gold chain that held her flowering charm, placing the silk-wrapped green stone at the hollow of her throat.

Even though the Fallen tried to make their magic seem so civilized, it repulsed Helenia, as it would any good Tithen. Sure, they dressed it up and called it alchemy, veiling it enough for the Tithens to turn a blind eye when they needed to, but all one had to do was watch one of their complicated ceremonies—ceremonies that always ended with the slicing of flesh and the spilling of crimson—to know the truth in their practices. For Burk's sake, they even called themselves the Fallen.

Yet, as much as their magic sickened her, she could acknowledge some of its benefits. Take the flowering charms. She'd refused to believe in their effectiveness until she'd been in the city long enough to understand how the charms had shaped the women's lives.

She rose, left her bedchamber, and walked to the study at the end of the hall. The room was dark, heavy with carpets across every inch of the floor, emerald velvets, and leather furnishings. Two servants waited by the door for her instruction, and Lead Varo Lucador Orli stood at the window, holding back the curtains and staring outside. She waved the servants away, and they left without a backward glance or a shared look between them.

In Ombratos, women and men often met in private, the scandal being if either or both of them were married or otherwise promised to someone else. The flowering charms meant that a woman's virginity wasn't treated as some precious jewel that required guarding at any cost.

So Helenia wore a charm for appearance's sake, for the freedom it brought her, though she couldn't bring herself to complete the vile ritual. Not that she needed to. Putting the price of blood magic aside, it would be profane to allow a man to enter her while she still wore white, both in her eyes and under Burk's Ever-Watchful Eye, and she had no intention of removing her mourning in the foreseeable future.

The servants' footsteps receded down the hall. Orli had attended the meeting as she'd asked, but she hadn't dared look at him in the course of it. His mask wasn't as well formed as hers. Take this moment. From the way Orli dropped the curtain and turned, she knew his intent and steeled herself against it.

Forgive me, Carhal.

Orli crossed the room in a couple of long strides, grabbed her waist, and pulled her to him. He kissed with all the grace of a starving man set loose upon a feast, and she bore it for as long as she could before tipping her head back so he might slaver on her neck for a while.

Part of the design in coming to Ombratos was making solid connections and important allies, and she maintained a bevy of suitors all for the purpose of hiding this one. Orli was in no way the cleverest, the richest, or the handsomest of her swains. True, he was better looking than her beloved Carhal had been, but that was not saying much. Word did have it that Orli was the best fighter in the city, but even if he wasn't, he did have two very important qualities she found nigh on irresistible. His position as lead varo...

"You were right, my darling," he said, his breaths hot and moist against her ear. "That sow queen will ruin us all."

...and his traitorous contempt for Queen Theodora.

He stepped back and ran a hand over his bald head. "I did not want to believe Princess Solena"—he drew a line up the center of his chest and kissed his fingers—"may she walk at Amma's side, had wed that *foreigner*." He spat out the word. "But Amma knows I'm not surprised."

How odd that he hadn't ever made mention of considering Dallan, another foreigner, equally unworthy. It spoke to Mayve's forethought in sending her son to Ombratos so many years earlier. Helenia guided Orli over to the couch in front of the fire and sat while he removed his varo blade from his belt so he might join her.

"Perhaps I'm wrong in this," she said, "but it didn't seem to matter to her that she might be destroying a century's-old alliance with Tithen."

Propping his blade on the edge of the couch, he sat so close less than an inch separated them. "No." He sighed, lifted a lock of her hair, and wove it through his fingers. "You're not wrong, my love."

When she was young, her father had trained her to spot what he'd called pebbles, people small enough for men like him to pick them up and move about however he liked. It took a practiced eye to see pebbles, especially ones like Orli who pretended to be boulders, but her pa had taught her the markers—a bit of overeagerness here, a touch of bitterness there—and so she'd followed her instincts, prodding Orli little by little, seeing if he was light enough to slip into her pocket.

This was long before she'd learned Orli had been Theodora's first choice for her prince-consort. Before she'd learned of the failed Binding between the two, the eventual gesture of naming him her lead varo, putting him in a position that forced him to protect her and the man who'd taken his place. Helenia's instincts, honed at her pa's knee, had allowed her to sense Orli's well-earned resentment long before she'd tracked it back to its source.

She mimicked his sigh. "That's too bad. You know how much I wished we might come to an agreement. But she offers so little."

"A marriage to Princess Heshiette is all she has while that prince lives and his Binding to Princess Linore holds. She's too shortsighted." He released Helenia's hair and touched the flowering charm at her throat. "We mustn't allow her to drive our great nation into the ground."

We. Our. He didn't know all of what had happened to her in Tithen, but she'd told him the truth in that she never wanted to go back, and he'd come to believe she considered Ombratos her home. She did, or she would very soon, just not quite in the way he thought. "Ombratos *is* a great nation," she said, "but did you not pledge your fealty to Queen Theodora?"

Traitors often ventured down one of two paths—they abandoned their morals, becoming little more than uncontracted mercenaries, or they cobbled together their own set of virtues and then followed those with the righteous fervor of the converted.

"I did." He stared into the fire for half a minute, then slapped the seat of the couch. "But when I made my oath to this queen, I also took an oath to the crown. The moment she became unworthy of that crown, half of my oath was severed."

She traced his jawline to draw his attention back to her. "I knew when I met you that you were a man of convictions."

He kissed her again, and she let him as her thoughts wandered. How could she use his power, his realigned loyalties to suit her goals? She feigned less knowledge of Bindings than she actually possessed, and she suspected they were the key since everyone in Ombratos seemed tied to some person or another.

From what she'd gleaned, Bindings tied one object to another, be it a person to a place, as with Princess Solena and Seedfall, or a person to an object, as with the queen to her throne, or a person to another person, like Princess Linore and the Yentish prince, and the detailed formulas dictated every form of the Binding, from how long one held to the amount of power behind it. She knew all this, and yet the solution remained beyond her grasp.

When Orli left off kissing her, she placed her hand on his knee and asked, "What of these Bindings?"

"What do you mean?"

She began dragging her nails up and down his wool-clad thigh. "Are you not Bound to serve her?"

"I am," he said, squirming in his seat.

She ranged a bit higher with every pass. "Is that not an obstacle?"

"It, uh... " He closed his eyes and dropped his head against the back of the couch. "As long as I'm not given a direct order, no."

The flesh on her scalp tightened. She neared something important. "Well, what would you do if one of your varo disobeyed a direct order?"

He startled her when his head snapped up. She thought he might be angry, then he gripped her hand, not in anger, but like a blind man grasping for aid.

"What is it?" she asked, careful to keep her body still and her voice gentle.

He settled himself as if for a confession. He drew in air and opened his mouth, but he didn't speak. She waited while he repeated the process. Nothing.

She laid a hand on his cheek. "Please."

"I want to tell you," he said, "but I can't."

"You can," she said, holding back her frustration. "You can tell me anything."

He nodded with resolve and said, "They aren't ab—" He choked on the word. "Aren't—"

What is he playing at? "Don't you trust me?"

"I'm sorry, but I can't tell you." He glanced down at his lap, and his cheeks flushed. "Not unless... "

Disappointed that his seeming confession was nothing more than an attempt to tumble her, she slid away from him, stood, and smoothed her hands down her skirt. "I think you should go."

He reached for her. "Wait." His florid cheeks and neck grew even darker. "I can do it myself, but—"

"You can do what yourself?" She no longer cared to hide her frustration. Why had she wasted so much effort on this man?

"My Binding... " His expression closed as he draped an arm over his lap and stared into the fire. "Forget it. If you wish me to go, I will do so in a moment."

He winced when she cast her arm out to point toward the door, but she stopped short of ordering him to leave. If his efforts were a ruse, then they were quite elaborate. He was a pebble, of that she was certain. She had already staked her life on it. Trusting her instincts a little further, she lowered her arm and sat back down beside him. She touched his leg, and the relief on his face drove her to resume her earlier movements.

They sat in silence, the only sound the whisper of her hand on his lower thigh, then his upper thigh. He gasped when she cupped the laces of his breeches. "Thank you," he said with an almost pitiable amount of gratitude.

"Nothing more." She didn't want to disappoint Mayve, and she didn't wish to fail, but her vow to Carhal's memory meant more. She tugged at the laces, and with another silent apology to her departed husband, slipped her hand inside, pleasuring Orli as a Tithen maiden might.

He groaned, closed his eyes, and the words came tumbling out. "My lead varo was very strict. A bully. She, uh, used to do things."

"What sorts of things?"

"As punishment—to make us stronger, she claimed—she ordered us to keep out hands at our sides while she forced others to hit us. Or she might make us to hold our breath until—ah!" Helenia slowed her strokes. He licked his lips. "Until we... until some of the varo fell into faints. It was rumored that she even used her power to coerce some of the varo into her bed."

"*Until* we..." Orli's lead varo had done this to him, and it haunted him still. He began growing soft in her hand, and on his face, fear and shame overtook his arousal.

"Were you one of them?" she asked quietly.

"No!" He opened his glassy eyes. "But I bear my own scars."

She imagined these scars he spoke of were both literal and figurative. "I'm sorry."

He turned his head away from her. "You don't think less of me?"

She wasn't sure if she did or not, not without further consideration, but she knew the answer he needed to hear. "Of course not." Laying a hand on his cheek, she moved his face until their gazes met. "Never."

He sighed, relief clear as dawn on his face. His eyes slid closed again. She didn't want to press too hard too fast, so she worked in silence, waiting for the tension to fall from his face. When his breaths grew ragged, and he seemed distracted enough, she asked, "Are your varo Bound to you in the same way?"

Taut veins stood out like cords in Orli's neck, but he managed a single, shaky nod, and a charge like lightning traveled up her spine. *There!* That was it.

Helenia had already gleaned that every varo who entered the role committed to a Binding in order to serve. So, if Orli's predecessor could make him go against his own body's natural impulses—if that sadist was able to dictate whether her varo breathed or not with her words alone—well, that meant her, and therefore Orli's, control over their varo was absolute, did it not? In other words, not only were the varo Bound to serve the Morovides, they were Bound to serve their leader, too. Meaning that, since Helenia controlled Orli, the varo were not an obstacle to overcome, but a tool to wield as she and Mayve saw fit. Any disappointment Mayve held about Helenia's inability to sabotage the working would wither away the moment she heard this news. The bit about Helenia stumbling across this information by happenstance... That she'd keep to herself.

However, one very large question remained: Why was Orli suddenly able to speak of these abuses? Surely, his former leader bound her underlings to silence. Was it because the woman was dead, a fact of which Helenia was not entirely sure?

"Please," he gasped, and Helenia realized she'd stopped moving. "Please, my love. More."

She redoubled her efforts and carried Orli quickly to his pinnacle, taking more satisfaction than she expected to in the proof of her undiminished skill, demonstrated by way of his shuddering appreciation. She used her kerchief to clean them both, then he took it from her and tossed it into the fire.

The Fallen burned their bandages, rags, and blood moss, destroying their blood so it couldn't be used against them, but was there some ritual of alchemy where they used a man's seed? She sat upright. Perhaps the power of bindings waned when the bound individual was sufficiently distracted. Or, if they spilled their bodily fluids. Mayhaps both were required. The subject certainly demanded further study.

She remained lost in thought while he relaced his breeches, and when he offered her a spot in the crook of his arm, she hesitated.

The narrowing of his eyes told her a corner of her mask had slipped. "I risk everything with you, Helenia," he said, his voice as rigid as the sword beside him. "How much do you care for me?"

They had met when he was assigned as her guard on her first full day in the palace, and in the course of that day, she had discovered a man waiting for the right chance, the right reason, to abandon a life he no longer wanted. So she became his excuse, his reason, but she'd always kept him at arm's length, at a distance she could manage while she still mourned her husband and the life they had shared.

Now Orli wanted more, and rightly so. They both risked everything by even talking as they did, and whether she liked it or not, whether she cared for him or not, no longer mattered.

She slid into the space he offered and pressed her cheek to the rough wool of his jacket. "I care for you every bit as much as you care for me."

Silence followed, and though she knew he mustn't, for half of half-a-heartbeat a small part of her wished for him to call her out on her lie. But, of course, he didn't. Since Carhal's death, there was no longer a single living soul capable of telling her lies from her truths—none that she had ever met, anyway.

"All that matters," he said, rubbing her arm, "is that a Morovide remains on the throne."

Her shoulders tensed, and she disguised it as a stretch. "Why is that?"

"Because this is Ombratos, and that is how it has to be." He said this in the manner of a lead varo speaking to his subordinate. To him, this was not a suggestion but a mandate.

We'll see. That pushed the schedule back again. She could work Orli around on this—she could work him around on anything, of that she was certain—but it might take a couple of tendays. Perhaps a little more.

Or perhaps less, if you abandon your whites. That was Mayve's voice in her head, the voice of ruthless practicality. But Helenia had worn white for less than a year, so a couple of tendays or more it would be.

That settled, she turned her mind to the wider picture. In addition to her efforts with Orli, Dallan needed to be dealt with. At Mayve's insistence, he remained in the dark, ignorant of the designs that hinged on him, but perhaps the time had come to change that. Like Orli, he, too, would balk at the notion of claiming the throne from the family he'd grown up with, but for all his charms, Dallan was another pebble, another person to be picked up and moved around as she wished.

She sensed that the plan, her new plan, neared completion. In Fallen parlance, she'd finished the working and simply required a catalyst.

SIX

"Transformation and Balance vanished with the forming of the Gift, and though some might argue we are now limited in our abilities, experience suggests Binding is the only pillar of alchemy we have ever truly needed."
-From Starla Siderine's *Binding: The Remaining Pillar*

Unlike the palace guards and her varo, Renn hadn't anticipated or dressed for the cold on Seedfall's roof, where the winter winds blew at full-strength over the Gift. On the grounds below, dark shapes huddled around the domed funeral pavilion, with the highborn closest, surrounded by the alchemists, ductoran, and any lowborn considered wealthy or important enough to attend, while the palace's off-duty servants, guards, and other workers stood at the fringes. The dome hid the body from sight.

While Renn watched, the queen walked around the side of the palace with a servant on either side of her, each carrying a globe to light her way across the lawns. The procession behind her included Father, Heshi, and Linore. Poor Linore, who moved along with the bowed-back gait of a much older woman.

I should be with them. Protocol demanded Renn's attendance in the pavilion, but the one person in her family who would have gone to the trouble of seeking her out and demanding her presence could no longer do so. Solena would be so disappointed, and that knowledge weighed heavily on Renn, but she couldn't bear the thought of once again laying eyes on her sister's lifeless body.

Up in the sky, Amma hid her twinkling face behind thick clouds. "Coward," Renn whispered, not sure if she spoke of Amma or herself. An icy wind blew between the merlons, and she shivered, her teeth chattering.

"Shall we retire within, Your Highness?" Varo Deniel stood about ten feet from her, half-lit in the glow of the nearest globe. "I fear a chill," he said over the high collar of his riding coat.

She cupped her hands around her mouth and blew on them. "The lie is appreciated, Deniel. But I won't go. Not until it's done." She meant it. She wouldn't leave the roof until the ceremony's conclusion. She might be weak, but that much she could do.

"Very good, Your Highness."

She strove to keep her mind blank as she waited, refusing to think of the meeting, or poor Linore, or Solena's body, wrapped in sheer white silk and laid atop a plinth of stacked wood. Or Dallan, promised now to Heshi. Another frigid gust combed through gaps between the merlons, and she ducked into the lee of one of the stone pillars. A flash came from the pavilion as the ductoran set the pyre alight.

Under the dome, the oil-fed fire climbed high, and she imagined herself close enough for the heat of the flames to tighten the skin on her face and for the smoke to bring tears to her eyes.

A ductoro stood at the pavilion's edge, silhouetted against the flames, his hands pressed together in prayer as he invoked Solena's funeral rites. Though too far away to hear him, Renn remembered the words the ductora had spoken at her grandmother's burning several years earlier. *"We return this body to the sky, lifting this Fallen to Amma's side so she might lift others who have passed and lead them to the Starry Path."* A pillar of oily smoke rose from the chimney, Solena rising to Amma's side.

How am I supposed to live without her?

The wind shifted, and a gust caught the pillar of smoke, shredding it into delicate ribbons that disappeared off over the mountains.

I can't.

The full, final truth of Solena's death hit Renn square in the chest. She gritted her teeth, but a ragged cry tore loose from her throat. To hold off the grief, she kicked the wall, first with one foot, then the other. Her riding boots protected her feet, so she fell on a merlon instead and dashed her bare fists against it, again and again until sharp pains shot through her hands and up her arms. But the hurt of losing Solena was stronger; it went

63

far deeper and refused to be denied any longer. Cries wracked her body, weakening and then ceasing her blows. Dropping her head onto her hands, she gave up and let them take her.

Around her, the relentless wind blew on, carrying her sobs and Solena's ashes away into the night.

IN THE DISTANCE, a door slammed shut, and someone, it sounded like Dallan, said something Helenia couldn't make out. Then, louder, "No, it cannot wait until morning. Where is my aunt?"

She disentangled herself from Orli's arms, and they both moved to opposite sides of the room. He limped as he sometimes did when he was tired—she suspected an old wound—and strapped on his sword, and she smoothed her hair and gown. Private meetings weren't frowned upon in Ombratos, but it was considered vulgar to be discovered in the course of a tryst in a common area. Had they been in Tithen, she would have cared not a whit. How could anyone care for a reputation that had already been so thoroughly tarnished? But the same could not be said for her name in Ombratos, where the withdrawn, inward-looking nature of the Fallen had enabled her to start anew.

There were still things she might lose in Ombratos, and she drew comfort from that.

Footsteps approached down the hall and brought with them a memory of sitting at the desk in her husband's study, troubled by the recent fights with her husband but unaware of his sudden death, unaware the footsteps belonged to her brother-by-law and his guards as they came to the office to arrest her—

The door, the actual one in front of her, swung open, and she returned to the present as Dallan, who, Burk bless him, did not bear any physical resemblance to his father, entered.

But her relief was fleeting. Dallan's hair was mussed, his shoulders hunched around his ears, his hands clenched into fists, and he paced back and forth. She'd never seen him so perturbed.

"Dallan," she said. He kept pacing. "Dallan?"

"Here now," Orli said, hand on his sword. "Is something wrong?"

Dallan seemed to notice the man's presence for the first time. "Why are you here, Lead Varo, and not at the pavilion?"

Orli tucked his hands behind his back and stared off to one side of Dallan. "I failed her, my lord."

Does he mean Princess Solena?

Dallan didn't ask. Instead, "May my aunt and I have the room?" He formed the order as a question, allowing Orli the courtesy of acceptance. Her nephew had few skills, but his courtly manners were impeccable.

Orli bowed his acquiescence and, with a last glance at Helenia, left, closing the door behind him. Dallan sat on the couch Helenia and Orli had just vacated and stared into the fire.

She wanted to demand an explanation, but she'd learned over the last four moons that when pressed, Dallan tended to dig his heels in. Though he looked nothing like his father, King Adameth Briain—the current leader of Tithen, Helenia's former brother-by-law, and her greatest enemy, Dallan had received a generous portion of his father's stubbornness, so she waited while he worked around to it on his own.

At last, he leaned back and said, "I wasn't going to marry Solena, and I won't marry Heshi."

Helenia's chin dropped, and she raised a hand to cover her gaping mouth. He hadn't planned to go through with the marriage to Solena? Very little shocked her these days, but that did. "What were you going to do, then?"

"Not marry her." He sat forward again. "You have to renegotiate the contract."

She fought to keep pace. They didn't require a marriage, but they did require a contract; they needed a reason to remain in Ombratos. Her uproar in the meeting had served to show Orli how lax the queen had become in her rulership, but it had also been meant to unsettle the woman and force her into a protracted negotiation, buying Helenia more time to solve the puzzle before her. "That was my intention—"

"I'll only marry Renn."

A night filled with surprises. The way Dallan said her name... He didn't just lust after the princess; he loved her. Or thought he did. After all, what did a twenty-two-year-old know of love? Yet, if he believed it, that made it true enough for him.

She didn't want to give him ideas, but a morbid curiosity forced her to inquire, "Then why don't you ask her to run away with you? Surely your mother would take you in."

He looked at her as if she'd grown a second head. "I can't ask her to leave."

"Why not?"

"She's a Morovide."

It wasn't the first time she'd heard the royal name brandished like a talisman. "What does that mean?"

He thought for a few moments, then shrugged. "It means what it means."

She stifled her frustration. In Ombratos, "Morovide" was more than a name. It served as shorthand for something she'd yet to comprehend, and the way her nephew used it against her now proved he understood Ombratos and the Fallen in a way neither she nor Mayve ever could.

He was also right, even if it was for the wrong reason. He couldn't ask Renn to run away with him, not in a practical sense. Besides forcing Helenia back to Tithen, the last place she wanted to go, it would cause a rift between the countries, and another between her and Orli.

But if she didn't do as Dallan asked, then a different rift would form, and he might return to Tithen anyway, dragging her with him. He had a vague notion of her reasons for leaving their homeland, but, as with most things, the subtleties were lost on him. The threat of Tithen hovered over her like a specter, and in her desperation, she shifted the pieces around and around, scrambling for the pattern.

Dallan, perhaps sensing her distress, reached out to put his hand over hers, and his earlier words, his stubborn defiance echoed in her mind, *"I wasn't going to marry Solena, and I won't marry Heshi."*

The answer came to her in a rush so powerful it made her head swim. When the lightheadedness passed, she placed her other hand over Dallan's. "Let me talk to her."

His face lit up like a globe. "You'll do it?"

"I'll do it." Then she couldn't help but return his infectious grin, especially since it might be one of the last she saw for a while. "I'll renegotiate with the queen tomorrow."

RENN WEPT until only a mountain of glowing embers remained of the pyre. Exhausted and raw, she dragged herself to her rooms and fell into bed, where she slept through the night untroubled by nightmares. She woke close to midday and, instead of ringing for her maid and asking to be dressed for riding, she lay in bed and stared out the window at the palace guards patrolling the garden beneath an overcast sky, wandering between the burlap-shrouded rose bushes wrapped up tight for winter.

She wasn't better, far from it, but the sharpest edge of her grief had been filed down. It remained keen enough to cut, and to cut her deeply enough to bleed her dry, but Solena wouldn't have wanted that. No, Solena had expected the most and demanded the best, both from herself and from Renn. Though Renn hadn't always succeeded in living up to Solena's exacting standards, and sometimes she'd even railed against them in her mind, she'd never wanted to disappoint Solena, so she'd always tried.

Why should that change just because Solena was gone? If anything, Renn owed it to her sister to live her life as Solena might have lived hers. Not exactly, of course, since Renn would never be heir to the throne, but she could find other ways.

She wanted nothing more than another day alone, a day to wander through her rooms, napping or weeping as she wished, but she'd already neglected her duties for far too long. Taking a deep breath, she rang for her maids and, when they arrived, asked to be dressed for afternoon tea. The older of the two, Nessa, simply nodded, but the younger, Editi, smiled at her and sighed with clear relief. A few tears slipped loose as they laced Renn into the black silk mourning gown, but Nessa wiped them away with a gentle hand.

"You want we should take it off?" she asked. "No trouble to neither of us to fetch your leathers."

A *yes* sat on the tip of Renn's tongue, but she closed her eyes, took a deep breath, and thought of Solena. "No," she said. "Please continue."

Varo Arias awaited Renn at the door to her suite, the guard dressed warm for a day of riding.

"I'm sorry, Varo," Renn said. "I should have sent word about the change in plan. However, I'm not leaving the palace, so if you'd like to go and dress more appropriately for an inside watch, I'll meet you at tea."

The corners of Varo Arias's mouth dipped downward naturally, but she pulled them down even farther in response to Renn's suggestion. "That won't be necessary, Your Highness. Your safety comes above my comfort."

Renn left it at that and started down the hall. She'd win Arias over some day. Just not this one.

She headed toward the Sun Wing. Her maids had informed her that with visiting dignitaries still at court, all of the highborn were expected to attend, so afternoon tea would be in Seedfall's largest reception room, the one adjacent to the palace ballroom.

The footman announced Renn at the door. Everyone rose, and more than a few surprised faces greeted her, but she held her chin up and pretended not to notice them. Groupings of tables and chairs had been placed around the room, creating areas to sit and sip and speak while leaving enough space for people to walk around and intermingle as they liked. On a sunny afternoon, the five sets of windowed doors let in more than enough light, but on this gray day, globes had been set in colored glass bowls on all the tables. They helped offset the darkness outside and in; almost everyone wore black in accordance with Ombratian mourning custom.

Almost. Near the center of the room, Lady Helenia stood out, a pillar of white in a sea of black. Renn's hands clenched into fists, and she didn't realize until that moment how angry she was with the Tithen woman for forcing the queen into the position of betrothing Heshi and Dallan. If the lady hadn't pushed so hard, perhaps Renn might have had a chance to do something, to have...

Dallan shifted beside Lady Helenia, distracting Renn from her anger. He looked absurdly handsome in his dark clothes—the belt around his tunic showing off his trim waist, his golden hair pulled back into a tail, revealing the strong line of his jaw. She met his gaze, and for a span of several heartbeats, it was as if they were alone. Then a man at a table near the door side-stepped into her eye line, cutting her loose. She and Dallan needed to talk, but she had no idea what to say. What was there to say with him promised to Heshi?

Renn dipped her head, giving everyone leave to sit or return to their previous activities. Noise rose as people resumed speaking and bustling about, and she prepared to find a table in the center of the room, when something else caught her eye.

As usual, fancier tables and more comfortable chairs had been set in every corner. With five Morovide women, Renn had, as the youngest, been expected to do as the other attendees and intermingle. But, with Theodora, Linore, and Heshi already seated in their respective corners, there was an extra space.

Unsure of what to do, Renn looked first to Heshi, sitting where Linore once had, in the corner nearest the door. Her Spares crowded around her like puppies anxious to suckle from their mother, and she preened before them. In the next corner, Solena's corner, sat Linore. Four grey-robed ductoran perched on the chairs at her table, but none appeared to be her beloved Ductora Gesso. Aware of Renn's plight, Linore met Renn's gaze, yet she offered no more than a shrug.

Renn gritted her teeth and turned to the queen. Beside her, Father smiled his encouragement, but for once, she didn't need it. Theodora, her expression blank, glanced toward the empty corner and lowered her chin in a tiny nod. Looking away to hide her surprise, Renn nodded back and went to take Heshi's old place. It seemed a foolish thing to hope for after so many years, but perhaps Solena's loss had changed something between Renn and the queen.

Renn had little time to adjust to her new position. The instant she sat, a servant placed a cup of steaming tea before her, and a man arrived right behind it. The hammered medallion hanging around his neck identified him as a member of the Sea Road Council. As for his name... He was a short man, with dark hair and ears like plates. Or jug handles. Handles.

She gestured to the chair beside her. "Please join me, Counselor Handlan."

The servant set a second teacup on the table, and Handlan slid into the chair beside it.

"I'm so glad you're here, Your Highness." She liked the soft twang of his Sea Road accent, the way it cradled all the vowels. "We haven't had a chance to speak since I arrived, and I'm leaving in the morn."

"Yes," Renn said. "I apologize for my absence."

Handlan shook his head as he took a sip. "There's no need." He placed his cup back on its saucer. "I lost a sister when I was a boy."

"I'm so sorry."

"Thank you, but it was long ago." He touched his fingers, counting the years under his breath. "Seventeen—no, eighteen—eighteen years past this summer."

"Please forgive me for asking, but do you still miss her?"

He laid his warm hand on her forearm. "Every single day."

His kindness brought tears to her eyes, and she blinked to hold them back.

"Now," he said, politely ignoring her sniffling, "if you'll allow me, I shall take my leave." A line had formed behind him, snaking along the wall and out into the center of the room. She nodded, and he stood. "I hope we have the chance to speak again soon under happier circumstances."

She had to compose herself before the next person joined her. With a strength developed from years of recovering as quickly as she could from Theodora's barbs, she found her equilibrium, and from that moment on, she noted everyone who sat, but accepted their condolences without actually listening to them. Her line shortened bit by bit as the afternoon passed.

Eventually the Messeran Vicchio joined her, and while they spoke, she glanced up to see how many more people waited. Her heart sank. The Vicchios were the last. She'd hoped Dallan might come by to talk, maybe wait at the end of her line until—

She stopped herself there. She had to let go of her childish fantasies of being with Dallan.

Across from her, Messero Vicchio climbed to his feet and helped his wife to hers. Then everyone stood, including Heshi and Linore, which meant the queen was making her departure. Father supported Theodora on one side and Lady Helenia walked on the other. No doubt they sought to further solidify the plans between Dallan and Heshi.

Renn's stomach clenched into a hard knot. She'd resigned herself to Solena marrying Dallan, but Heshi? The thought of watching the two of them wed and then build a life together made it difficult to breathe. The walls of the reception room pressed in on her, and the collar of her gown choked her. Why was it so damned tight? The Vicchios made their farewells, but instead of giving them leave, Renn left herself, hurrying out into the hall. She needed to be outdoors, on horseback. Away.

The halls flew by in a blur. At her rooms, a servant opened the doors for her, and there, on a bench in the entryway, sat Dallan. He looked up as she walked in and climbed to his feet. His presence shocked her, yet didn't surprise her at all, as if she'd conjured him with her very thoughts. Then again, perhaps she had. Perhaps this Dallan was a figment of her imagination, born from her frustration and misery. That certainly seemed likely, given the hopefulness on his face.

Varo Arias went ahead to search her suite, and her maid Editi came hurrying around a corner. She dipped into a low curtsy and said, "I hope this is acceptable, Your Highness. I told the prince you were out and to return later, but he insisted on waiting here, and—"

"That's fine." So he was real. "Leave us."

Editi curtsied again and scurried off.

"You should go." Renn had to throw Dallan out before he said something foolish to further break her heart. "You can't be here."

"Renn, I—"

Varo Arias returned. "All is well, Your Highness."

If only that were true. "Would you see Prince Dallan out?"

Varo Arias held her arms open as if to corral him out, but he stepped away from her. "Renn, please. Let me say one thing, and then I'll go if you still want me to."

Don't do it! Renn closed her eyes. "Varo, please wait in the hall."

"As you wish."

The instant the door closed, Dallan grabbed Renn's shoulders. She opened her eyes but kept them downcast. He dipped his head and tried to meet her gaze, but she stared at her feet, refusing to look up.

"Renn, listen to me. Are you listening?"

Let him speak, then send him away. She nodded.

"I spoke to Aunt Helenia last night. She's fixing it. I told her, and she's fixing it."

Must he make everything worse by speaking in code? "Told her what?"

"That I want to marry you. That I love you."

Those last three words struck her like lightning. She snapped her head up and looked into his eyes. "You love me?"

He chuckled, the sound gentle and sweet. "Of course I do." Raising his hands, he touched her cheeks. "For as long as I can remember."

"What about the marriage contract?"

"That's what Helenia's fixing. She's renegotiating it so we can be together. We talked, and with Solena breaking the agreement in the first place, my aunt believes we have the leverage to get what I want." He tucked a wayward curl behind her ear. "What we want."

She didn't have any words. Or she had too many. Either way, nothing came out, and all she could think to do was the one thing she'd been wanting to for ages. She wrapped her arms around his neck and kissed him.

HELENIA WAITED for Queen Theodora in a private salon tucked down a side hall not far from the reception room, and she might have found the location and the size of the room insulting had it not such a well-used feel to it.

The one window looked out on Seedfall's forest and the Cassedents, and below the window sat a desk, the top of it cluttered with correspondence. A few different tapestries covered the south wall, all pastoral scenes featuring horses, and on the north wall, above the fireplace, hung a rather stern-faced portrait of Queen Violaine, Theodora's mother. A severe woman, but a fair queen according to the stories. An embroidery loom sat next to a chair before the fire, an expanse of white fabric stretched across the loom, the project on it only just begun. Or so Helenia assumed. For now, a stitched depiction of Seedfall Palace floated adrift in the center of the fabric, as if nothing else existed beyond it.

No globes lit the room, only candles and the fire in the grate. That gave the room a warm and cozy feel, minus the old queen glaring down from the mantel. With a bit of redecorating, it was the sort of place Helenia could imagine visiting often once the palace was hers. But at the moment the room spoke for the woman who most often used it, and while Helenia waited, she tried to reconcile the information around her with Queen Theodora's current temperament, as well as the woman she'd been before taking the throne.

According to Mayve's file, which she'd had copied and delivered to Helenia for her trip to Ombratos, young Princess Theodora had caused her mother no end of trouble. Sole heir to her mother's throne after her sister succumbed to the child's cough at age twelve, Theodora spent most of her days with those in her birth cluster, shirking her duties to the crown for as long as possible. She adored riding and held races on the grounds as often as possible, betting exorbitant amounts on herself and winning more often than not.

She ran wild until her father fell ill and asked to see her married and settled before he died. At that point, her life capsized. She chose Orli for her husband, but the Binding to him failed in some way, forcing her to marry Corlin instead. Her father died days before her wedding, and not long after, her twin brother killed himself.

It then took Theodora and Corlin several years to conceive their first daughter, not that they were able to stop there. After two more painful births and several miscarriages—no one was quite sure how many, and on that point, Helenia hadn't cared to pry—Theodora at last gave birth to twins, which finally allowed her to stop. Helenia remained unsure why the queen had been forced to reproduce like a broodmare until she had a set of twins, but that highlighted the odd nature of Ombratos—so progressive in some ways and so backward in others.

In the end, Theodora's blithe nature had curdled into callousness, her wildness tamed by years of hardship, and some part of Helenia did pity her for it. But a person's history could only account for so much of their actions and decisions, and Helenia's sympathy meant nothing in the wider world, where the strong rose and the weak fell. At a certain point, a woman needed to take claim of her life. Otherwise she risked having it torn from her hands.

The door to the salon opened, and Helenia stood to curtsy as Queen Theodora entered. A servant followed the queen to the chair beside the embroidery loom, then helped her down into it. When the queen was seated, the servant quietly asked if she required anything else.

The queen said no and sent him out, then, "You may go too, Varo Nostros."

Helenia had intended to ask for a private meeting, but it seemed neither she nor the queen sought an audience. Interesting.

Near the door, Varo Nostros saluted. "As you say, Your Majesty. I will be right outside." The latch clicked shut behind her.

Queen Theodora took a few moments to situate herself in her chair, long enough that Helenia's legs, still in mid-curtsy, began to quiver, no doubt a punishment for her behavior in their meeting the night before. Unsurprising coming from a woman with only the bluntest of weapons in her arsenal.

"Please sit," Queen Theodora said at last.

Helenia, determined not to flop back on to the couch like a caught fish tossed into the bottom of a boat, straightened her legs and lowered herself slowly. "Thank you." She had spent several candlemarks considering how she might play things at this meeting, deciding to present the same face she'd shown since her arrival. However, first, her fit of bad temper required an apology.

"If I may, Your Majesty?"

Theodora, not taking her eyes from the fire in the hearth, flicked her fingers for Helenia to proceed.

"My conduct at the meeting last night was unforgivable, especially given the circumstances of the evening. I'm afraid the announcement caught me off guard, and I've never been at my best when knocked a-kilter."

"Few people are."

Not exactly an acceptance, but Helenia pressed on. "As inappropriate as my actions might have been, my nephew was not the one who broke his marriage contract."

Theodora looked Helenia in the eye. "There was no formal contract."

"But there was an agreement made when the queen of Tithen sent her son to you."

"Yes. And how is *Duchess* Mayve?" Theodora asked, emphasizing ever so slightly Mayve's new title—an elegant, unexpected parry—and Helenia noticed how kind the room's candlelight was to the wearied queen, giving glimpses of the vibrant young woman she'd once been.

"She is disappointed, I'm sure."

"I'm sure." Theodora ran a finger down the edge of her embroidery frame. "The truth of the matter is, Solena arranged much without my fore-knowledge or consent."

Although Helenia had been raised among gamblers and thieves, she couldn't tell if the queen lied or not.

"I understand," Helenia said. "A mother can only lead her children so far before they choose to venture off on their own."

"Indeed."

Such an apathetic response. And that was it, wasn't it? Theodora considered her victory in the war guaranteed, so she fought this battle without care for whether she won or lost, and that made her impossible to read. So, because Helenia couldn't figure out her opponent, she simply played the dice in her hand.

"You mentioned last night that we might come to another under-standing."

Theodora sighed. "I am tired, Lady Helenia, so let us speak plainly. What would you like?"

Helenia had been so focused on moving forward that it wasn't until her talk with Dallan that she'd realized the only way forward was back. "We would like a formal contract drawn up between Dallan and Princess Heshiette."

"I see," Theodora said.

Helenia, having nudged Dallan in Renn's direction when they parted ways in the reception room, assumed he was in the act of professing his love at this very moment. "We would also like the announcement made as soon as possible."

The queen ran her finger around one of the windows on the embroidered palace. "Then I shall have the contract drawn up tonight, and tomorrow, at the start of convocation, I will announce the betrothal of Prince Dallan and Princess Renn."

Helenia's skin prickled. "You mean Princess Heshiette, don't you?"

"Excuse me?" the queen said, moving from the window to the whorls carved into Seedfall's main doors.

Had she really not noticed the slip? "You said Princess Renn, Your Majesty."

"How careless of me." Theodora looked up and met Helenia's gaze. "I meant to say Princess Heshiette."

Helenia stared at the indecipherable queen. Was it possible that they, at least in this, wanted and expected the same outcome? That required Theodora's awareness of the attraction between Prince Dallan and Princess Renn. True, Helenia was in the process of orchestrating her own nephew's heartbreak, but that served a greater purpose. Could the queen be so cruel to her youngest daughter just to extricate herself from an undesirable alliance? Based on how she treated the girl, she'd proved herself more than capable.

Theodora shifted in her chair. "Is that all?"

"It is." With the groundwork laid, the only thing left to do was wait. "Thank you, Your Majesty. Tithen looks forward to a long and fruitful partnership."

"As does Ombratos." Theodora reached into a basket beside her chair and pulled out a bell. She rang it, and the servant returned, assisting the queen from her chair and the room.

Helenia took one last glance around—the salon was going to make a fine office—and left, prepared to avoid her nephew until the announcement. One of her suitors, Messero Aude, had invited her and several others on to his pleasure ship for a dawn sail. They would sleep early in the evening, then awaken after midnight to drink and eat and watch the sun rise over the Cassedents. If she timed everything right, she'd arrive just before convocation.

Messero Aude, handsome and as bland as a bowl of tepid milk, waited for her in the main hall. He kissed her hand. "The others should be here in two flaps of a robin's wing."

While he droned on about the new sails on his ship, Helenia sent a quick prayer to Burk. Princess Renn was the only part of this over which she had not an ounce of control.

What began as Renn and Dallan's first kiss had stopped just short of coupling. They finally had time, and Renn meant to take advantage of it.

With kiss-swollen lips and a love bite on her left breast, she had spent the whole of the following day feeling drunk as she finally allowed herself to fully imagine what her and Dallan's life might be like together.

Then Theodora had announced Dallan and Heshi's betrothal, and

Renn's mind, her body, everything had gone numb. Hoping to stay that way, she'd returned to her rooms, lay down on her bed, and fallen asleep, only to be awoken a candlemark later by someone pounding down the door. That someone turned out to be Dallan. All he did was touch her hand, and the numbness shattered, releasing her anguish. She'd lost the two people she cared most for in the world within a tenday.

She shattered, and Dallan had wrapped his arms around her, holding her close while she cried. Eventually, her sobs grew less violent, and his nearness overwhelmed her. Even though he was no longer hers, even though it was wrong and selfish, she kissed him.

She loved him with her whole heart and nothing seemed bigger or more important than that. They'd started kissing and the years of unfulfilled desire caught up with her, carrying her to the edge with a thrilling speed. In the final moments before, Dallan had been the voice of reason, asking if she was certain, and she—reveling in his love, in their shared ardor, in that which was neither pain nor grief—had consented, spurring him onward.

Though she'd imagined what coupling might be like, both in the abstract and with Dallan, the reality of the act, of being so intimately joined with him, had been a revelation. She'd felt vulnerable and exposed and powerful and cherished, all at once. And though there had been some fumbling, they'd found their way through together, as partners did.

Now, tucked into the crook of Dallan's shoulder, Renn ran her hand back and forth over the golden hairs on his bare chest. Moonlight shone through her bedchamber windows, illuminating their clothes, strewn about the floor.

He snuggled her close and kissed the top of her head. "We'll find a way to be together, whatever it takes."

That seemed impossible, and yet she believed him. She had to. Sitting up, she removed the chain holding her flowering charm. The act of giving one's partner a flowering charm was a symbolic gesture, a suggestion that the giver considered the receiver someone worthy of having children with. She took Dallan's hand, pressed the charm against his palm, and closed his fingers around it. "I love you."

He grinned and slipped the chain over his head. "I wondered if you were ever going to get around to saying it."

"Yes, well"—she lifted the blanket covering them and peered beneath —"I wanted to see what I was getting before I committed to anything."

"Is that right?" He poked her in the side, in her most ticklish spot.

She shrieked, wriggling away from him, and for a minute, they acted as if they were much younger, tussling as they had before maturity had complicated things between them. They wrestled around until he straddled her on the bed, and the silliness fell away. With him leaning over her, the flowering charm hung from his neck. She tapped it and set it swinging.

"Now that you've seen me, Your Highness, do I meet your standards?"

She pulled him down and kissed the tip of his nose. "I think you'll do."

His expression grew serious. "I will never marry anyone but you."

"Nor will I," she said, and she meant it.

THE WIND RAKED its salty fingers through Helenia's loose hair, and bright sunlight made knife-edges along the waves. She clutched the starboard rail of a Tithen ship, the *Forweary*, as the shape of Ombratos grew smaller and smaller in the distance.

So close. Everything had played out so very close to perfection, and yet, at the last instant, fallen so very short.

Helenia tried to help Dallan and Renn sneak about, the goal being an elopement that would tie Tithen to Ombratos even before Helenia and Mayve's plans began to play out. But the prince and princess's illicit affair had only lasted for three days before the queen discovered it. Helenia was furious with the woman's sudden astuteness. Queen Theodora, known for her apathy and ineffectiveness, turned into the model of competence and efficiency with an alacrity that, for once, outstripped Helenia's. The queen had called for a meeting with Helenia and Dallan, a late-night meeting held in a more austere, more official meeting room than her private salon, and used the affair as a reason for annulling the marriage contract. The queen's haughtiness, Dallan's anger—all things Helenia might mitigate. But Helenia hadn't anticipated Theodora's parting lines.

"I would have been happy to see you married to any of my daughters, Prince Dallan, but Lady Helenia insisted on a betrothal to Heshiette. What a pity."

A spiteful blow, cast for whatever reason, that sent both Helenia and Dallan reeling, and she'd kept him from heading off to find Renn with a desperate warning. "If you take Renn away from here tonight, you and I both know her mother will never allow her to return." Burk be praised, it had worked. Dallan had returned to their rooms to pack and refused to speak to her further. Once aboard the ship, she'd begged him to listen to reason, but he'd barred himself in the captain's quarters below decks, the best accommodations the sailors could offer a prince on such short notice, and kept his own counsel.

Orli she'd left with a kiss and a promise to return—a promise she intended to keep. For how little he knew of her true heart, he was right about one thing. Ombratos was her home. But she had to return to Tithen before she could claim it because the only way forward was back.

Or so she hoped. Dallan's anger was not a part of her plan, and she wasn't yet sure how to assuage it. She'd betrayed him, and there were fewer obstacles harder to overcome.

Down in the water, a length of wood—a board, one end splintered and broken—floated by. It seemed like it might get dragged into their wake, but then a swell caught it and sent it in the other direction. Helenia closed her eyes and remembered what it had been like to walk from the prison a free woman. She was going to fix this. She had to. Dallan's father, King Adameth, had already destroyed her once; she wouldn't allow a Briain man to ruin her life again. Nor would she miss out on putting Theodora's head on a pike.

WHEN RENN TURNED down the hall to Dallan's rooms and saw the doors to his suite standing open, she slowed, and as she reached the doorway, her heart skipped a beat.

In the sunlight streaming through the open windows, servants bustled about the rooms, polishing and dusting. Cloths draped the furniture, and Dallan's trinkets and books were missing from the shelves near the entry-way. A footman, Eateau, walked by with a bucket of soapy water in one hand and a brush in the other and noticed her standing in the doorway. He stopped and bowed.

"Where is the prince?" she asked.

"Prince Dallan and Lady Helenia left not long before daybreak on a ship bound for Tithen, Your Highness." He reached into a pocket for a folded piece of paper, which he held out to her. "He left this for you."

With shaking hands, she unfolded the page. On it, a short message written in Dallan's flowing hand explained that Theodora had found them out and, as a result, had sent him and his aunt away.

However, she cut the bonds of my betrothal to Heshi as well, freeing me to marry whomever I should please. Your mother is angry now, furious with us both, I'm sure, but time heals all hurts, and I swear to Burk and Amma and every god that has ever existed or will exist, I will return to you.

As she finished the letter, the footman stepped toward her, worry creasing his brow. "Are you well, Your Highness?"

She wasn't. Her sister was dead, and Dallan was gone. She had never been less well in her life. *Go. Follow him to Tithen.* The idea popped into her mind, and she would do it. She would follow him as far away as the Yent Isles if she had to. She spun on her heel, intending to do just that, only to find the queen waiting for her in the doorway.

Behind Renn, fabric rustled and the bucket hit the floor as Eateau knelt. "Your Majesty."

"Leave us," Theodora said, limping inside with the help of her cane.

More rustling as the servant clambered up, hurried from the suite, and closed the door. Theodora limped closer, and Renn fought the urge to back away from her. Amma knew when they had last been alone together.

Theodora stopped a few feet away. "How could you do this? *Why* would you do this?"

Renn decided to tell the truth. What else did she have left to lose? "I love him."

Theodora barked a humorless laugh. "What does that matter?" Renn didn't have an answer for that. "And where are you going now? To chase after him? How do you think that will make me look? How do you think it will make Ombratos look? We have already been weakened by our loss—" Her voiced cracked. She cleared her throat and continued. "By our losses. Would you make us appear even weaker? What about Parneo?"

"Stop!" She had to bring up Parneo, didn't she? Renn had never despised her mother more than she did at that moment. "Why are you acting as if you care? I mean nothing to you."

"I care because you are a Morovide," Theodora said, not denying it.

"I didn't choose to be a Morovide!" Tears pricked Renn's eyes, but she refused to let them fall. "I didn't choose any of this."

"No." Theodora looked down and gripped the head of her cane even tighter. "None of us did." She tapped her cane against the floor. "You will stay and find a use, or I shall find one for you."

Without another word, she turned, limped to the door, and knocked on it with her cane. Someone opened it from the outside. Then she walked off, leaving Renn to think about what she'd said.

Dozens of choices swirled around in Renn's mind, but none came to the fore and presented itself as the right one. What about Parneo? If she left him and then he... and then if something happened to him, would she ever forgive herself?

I will return to you.

She read Dallan's letter again, refolded it, and tucked it into her bodice, next to her heart. Outside of Dallan's suite, Varo Nostros rejoined her, following her to Parn's rooms. When he wasn't there, Renn knew where to find him.

His workrooms were in one of the abandoned shops down on Menders' Row, and she arrived at the height of the midmorning bustle. Servants, merchants, and various smiths toiled away in the shops while others walked up and down the row carrying baskets as they fetched items or brought them to be repaired.

A farrier with bulging arms and a leather apron noticed her and called out, "Morovide on the row!" After that, she bowed, and like a gust of wind blowing across a wheat field, the news traveled along, dropping heads as it went.

Renn passed the bowed forms, wishing she'd hidden herself under a cloak. The last thing she needed was more people reminding her of her position and her duty, but there they were, every single one of them wearing a black armband, bringing to mind her plan to live her life as Solena might have lived hers.

About halfway down the row, four keepers, different ones from the night of Solena's funeral, huddled together in front of the door to Parn's workrooms. They seemed to be engaged in a whispered argument, and didn't notice as she and Varo Nostros neared.

One of the acolytes stomped his foot and said in a whisper-shout, "It was less than a candlemark!"

Another acolyte whispered something too low to hear. When the first acolyte saw her and Varo Nostros coming, he shushed the others and fell to his knees. The other keepers looked, then moved to bow, but Renn darted forward. "Please don't."

The tense acolytes remained upright, though they did step aside so she might reach the door. Varo Nostros fell into a resting stance, with feet shoulder-width apart and hands clasped in front of her waist. As with all of the varo, Nostros knew she was to remain outside here. Renn, ignoring the meaningful looks passing among the keepers, scratched at the hard, unpainted wood. She waited and raised her hand to scratch again when the latch squealed, and the door flew open.

"Come in!" Parn grabbed her wrist, yanked her inside, and slammed the door shut behind her. His workrooms, two small, low-ceilinged chambers connected by a door, were usually ablaze with globe light, but the globes were covered, and the sole source of light came from the back room, where the shutters of the single window stood open.

Shelves of alchemical materials and reagents loomed against the walls, but she couldn't make out any of the labels in the shadows. "Your keepers out there are in quite a state."

Parn moved to the far side of his worktable in the back room. Two items sat in the middle of the otherwise empty table. They looked a little like healing charms, but larger, and she couldn't begin to imagine what they might do.

"They lost track of me for a bit last night," he said, as if it were nothing.

"Lost track?" That wasn't good.

"Yes, yes, just for a bit. But don't worry. A bit is less than a bite." He waved her into the back room with him. "Come." He picked up one of the two identical charms—pink stones the length of her palm wrapped in silver wire—and held it out to her. "Here."

She went, though she had no intention of letting his disappearance slide. If Theodora found out... Where had he gone, anyway? Had he come looking for her?

"This one's yours," he said, tossing the charm at her.

She caught it and waited for him to explain its purpose. After all, Binding charms didn't work without a chant and the application of blood. But then Parneo slipped the other around his neck, and every thought fled her mind when his face changed shape.

For a repulsive moment, his flesh appeared to be made of wax. His features took on new dimensions while they slid around, finding their homes on his narrowing, elongating head. Meanwhile, his hair faded to an unremarkable shade of brown, as did his eyes, and he grew taller, skinnier, with lankier limbs and a slight hunch to his shoulders.

Renn held her breath until her brother's body settled into that of a stranger's. Then she let it out all at once. "Parn?"

The stranger smiled and nodded.

This caused Renn's head to ache, for it both was and was not her brother's expression on his face. "How?"

Her question earned her a larger, equally head-splitting grin. "It was very simple." The timbre of his voice had also changed, though the cadence of his speech hadn't. "I rediscovered Transformation."

He said that like it was nothing, as if reclaiming one of the Lost Pillars was something he did as often as he changed his clothing. As if Transformation and Balance had been eradicated from alchemy just this tenday past, as opposed to hundreds of years before either of them were born.

Remembering the charm he'd thrown to her when she'd entered the room, she lifted it up by its chain. The miracle dangled in front of her, real as anything. Her cheeks ached, and she realized she was smiling, too.

Renn thrust the charm out toward Parneo/not-Parneo. "Show me how."

SEVEN

"Your sins have forever stained your people. As Amma as my witness, the schism between the Wandering Fallen and the Fallen shall never be mended."
-Leader Thethen Morovide to his younger sister, Queen Orane Morovide

Jos sat on the back steps of his Aunt Bosk's wagon, a small length of charcoal in one hand and a clean piece of bark in the other. Aunt Bosk always camped at the edge of the caravan, so her wagon had the best view of the southern road into Derlest some forty or fifty feet away. Her wagon also didn't have a furious caravan leader stomping back and forth inside it.

Just thinking of his father, or, as he preferred to be called, Leader Oveno, Jos's hand tightened, and the charcoal stick snapped into pieces that fell into the trampled grass. He closed his eyes and lay back, trying to ignore the edges of the steps digging into his spine. This far north, a chill clung to the air with icy fingers, but the spring sunlight did all it could to break winter's loosening grip.

Things between Jos and his father had been tense *before* he left for his Tempting. Since his return, they neared unbearable.

"Your grandparents forced me to endure the Tempting for twice as long as you did, and after I came back, I never once considered returning to that Amma-forsaken place! If your mother hadn't..."

Jos rubbed a hand over his eyes. To avoid rehashing every moment of

83

that morning's argument, he reminded himself the Tempting wasn't something his father had dreamt up to punish or trap him. Even though Jos had never heard of it until coming to live with his father's caravan, it was an old tradition, almost as old as Ombratos itself.

As Aunt Bosk had explained it to him, in the darkest candlemark of the Purge, the Gift was either created or discovered, and the followers of Amma, the Checormetans, took refuge inside the impenetrable structure. Once the danger had passed, a disagreement arose.

One group, led by Orane Morovide, thought they should remain within the Gift, where they were safe. Those led by Orane's older brother, Thethen, believed the nomadic tenets of their religion demanded they return to their wagons and the road. Rancor built between the two groups, pitting sisters against brothers, fathers against daughters. On the verge of civil war, the Checormetans split into two factions—the Fallen, who would stay within the wall as the seeds of Ombratos, and the Wandering Fallen, who left, as they believed Amma wished them to, for the uncertainty of the road.

Jos couldn't fathom the courage it must have taken to leave the harbor of the Gift back then, with the Purge less than a decade past. Despite his father's belief that he been raised a "godless cretin," Jos had, in fact, been raised to respect Leader Thethen's bravery and to admire the sacrifices his ancestors had made in Amma's name. Those sacrifices were why he and his mother had lived as they did.

But his father held on to too much of his ancestor's anger. After Orane Morovide became Ombratos's first queen, Thethen Morovide hated her with a fervor that never waned during his long life, passing that hatred on to his children. His grandchildren, however, found it harder to despise people so far removed from themselves. Afraid they lusted for the ease of living amongst the Fallen, Thethen sent his grandchildren away to Ombratos, to see how they lived. One stayed, but the other five returned to his caravan filled with their own righteous hatred, and at that year's Grand Convocation, Thethen held those five up as ideals, saying, "They will burn even brighter in Amma's eyes for having walked through the fire and come out the other side."

Jos valued tradition. He believed in Amma and blood magic and the continued search for the Lost Pillars. He, too, even believed the Fallen had misinterpreted Amma's Word with the intent of justifying their choice to remain within the Gift. However, he also believed the Tempting nothing more than a meaningless test imagined up by an angry, bitter old man hoping to poison the well for future generations.

These days, most Wandering Fallen were sent to live near Ombratos when they were seventeen or eighteen to "experience the temptation of its embrace." Jos hadn't been sent on the trip his father referred to as "a journey into the foul pit of pathless hells" until he turned twenty-five. He'd overheard others in the caravan say Oveno wasn't the first caravan leader to favor his child, to try to ease the weight of the Tempting from his shoulders.

But they all knew that wasn't the real reason Oveno had waited.

Light footsteps approached on the grass. *Anell.* The wagon jostled as Jos's half-sister climbed up beside him. "Papu's so angry he's about to start pissing vinegar."

Jos almost teetered off the steps. Anell was nine, and if their father heard her talking like that, he really would piss vinegar—right after he blamed Jos for teaching her such a phrase, of course. "Where did you learn that charming phrase?"

Anell giggled. "Gent said it to Nora over by the wash wagon."

Gent and Nora's wagon was on the far side of camp from theirs. "They heard us, then?"

The smile left Anell's face. She grabbed one of the feathers in her hair and ran a finger along the quill. So Gent and Nora hadn't been the only ones listening in on the argument.

"Why do you want to leave the caravan?" Anell peered up at him with her long-lashed brown eyes. "It's not because I hid your paints, is it?"

"Oh, no, Mouse. That has nothing to do with it."

He set down his piece of bark, scooped Anell up, and sat her on his lap, facing the road. A skinny bundle of elbows and knees, she seemed destined to grow into a tall, slender woman like her mother. He wrapped his arms around her and rested his chin on her head.

He wasn't sure how to explain to her how confining the caravan was, how their father strove to crush him under the weight of his disappointment, how he longed to return to life as he and his mother had lived it.

His mother, Rahel, and father had never been of the same caravan. Jos's conception occurred, as so many did, at the Great Convocation. Rahel had explained to her son that beyond his creation and birth, her and Oveno's relationship was never meant to be. Both full of passion, they coupled and fought with equal fervor, driving everyone around them mad, and when the Convocation ended, at the behest of their families and friends, they went their separate ways.

Jos had asked his mother several times over the years if she'd loved his father, or if his father had loved her, but a wistful smile and a shrug was her only reply. It wasn't until Jos met Oveno, until Jos saw how deeply Rahel's death hurt him, that Jos understood his mother's reply for the confession it had been.

Regardless, a few moons after the Convocation, Rahel discovered her pregnancy and sent word to Oveno, as was right, but before he might reply or arrange a meeting between their caravans, everything else went very, very wrong.

Centuries before Jos's time, the Mad King of Baltwull—who also claimed to be a god—declared the Fallen evil. He whipped his devoted supporters into a frenzy of hatred, giving birth to bloodhunters, roving bands of indoctrinated vigilantes who took it upon themselves to gain their own bloodmarks so that they might correctly identify and eradicate the Fallen from their world. The king and his bloodhunters caused the Purge, spreading lies and hatred throughout every corner of Althea.

Eventually, the Fallen created their impenetrable city; the mad king, who was, as it turned out, not a god, died; the Wandering Fallen learned how to hide in plain sight; and the bloodhunters fell by the wayside. Mostly. As with all cults that are never truly eradicated, small numbers of bloodhunters still roved the countryside, looking for the Impure so they might be wiped from this world.

Rahel was in her sixth moon, when bloodhunters found her caravan and sussed out their true nature as Wandering Fallen. The hunters came in the night, in the dark, like the cowards they were, and laid siege to the caravan. Men, women, and children were torn from their beds and slaughtered, their wagons burned while the bloodhunters howled and celebrated.

In the madness, a man had knocked Rahel to the ground with a passing blow to the head, and she writhed on the ground, cradling her round belly, praying to Amma and waiting for the end to come. Only, it hadn't. Rahel was at the edge of the caravan, cast into shadows by the growing flames, and it was there that she met another bloodhunter. According to Rahel, the bloodhunter, a woman, stood and stared down at her, rubbing her own gravid belly with an unreadable expression on her face.

Quickly, decisively, the bloodhunter reached down and grabbed his mother, helping her to her feet, setting her bloodmark tingling with a false sense of connection and goodwill. After a wild look around, the bloodhunter guided Rahel away from the madness, accompanying her at least half a mile down the road. Nothing but a single word passed between them, and the bloodhunter spoke it to Rahel.

"Run."

Rahel, heartbroken at the loss of her family and friends but spurred on by the growing life inside her, did as she was told. Too afraid of life on the road, she never joined another caravan, never attended another Grand Convocation. Instead, every few years, she and Jos moved to a new town or city, finding a tenement or cottage to live in. In that way, they followed Amma's peripatetic teachings in spiritual, if not literal, practice.

Truth told, even if Jos could figure out how to explain his upbringing to his father, he wasn't sure he would. It was the height of hypocrisy for Jos to accuse Thethen of well-poisoning from one side of his mouth and do the same to his family and the caravan from the other. Oveno and Anell had their own paths to walk. Jos just wished his father might respect Jos's feelings as Jos sought to respect his father's.

Out on the road, a merchant dressed in a colorful patchwork coat shuffled out of Derlest, pushing his jingling cart full of bits and bobs. Had it not been for the scowl on his face, Jos might have waved him down to see if he had anything to trade.

The merchant saw him looking and raised a hand in a rude gesture, stopping for a moment to spit and shout "Filthy road rats!" before continuing on.

Jos hugged Anell closer. He hated to think what the merchant might have done if he'd guessed who they truly were.

Most Wandering Fallen thought themselves safe because they traveled under different guises. Some groups performed as mummers or storytellers; others moved from place to place as workers for hire or tinkers, and those in Leader Oveno's caravan posed as artisans and merchants. But no matter the face they put on it, all the caravans wore the marks of their belief like targets.

The lone, angry merchant continued down the road, and when he passed behind a copse of elms, leaving the road empty, Anell wriggled around on Jos's lap until she faced him. Tugging down the edge of his collar, she laid her hand against his chest, over his heart. His bloodmark—the one forced on him the day he joined his father's caravan—tingled and flared, visible on his palm, sparked by her touch.

But she didn't care about the mark on his palm. She had one of those too, given to her at birth. Instead, she pulled her hand away and watched the bare spot on his chest, as if something might have changed since yesterday or the day before that. Or any day since he'd returned from his Tempting and refused his Second Mark.

Anell let go of his tunic and resettled herself so she once again faced the road. "Is Papu angry 'cause you failed your Tempting?"

"Failed" was one of Oveno's words, and it angered Jos to think Anell believed he'd done so. "No," he said, careful to keep his voice even. "The Tempting isn't something you can fail."

"Oh."

Based on the frown in her voice, he pictured the lines that creased the corners of her mouth when she was confused. He wished he could catch that expression in his drawings, but since he'd returned from Ombratos she'd been questioning too much, and her changing truth made it impossible to sketch a clear image of her. It was frustrating—she was at a charming age, and his fingers itched to capture it—but her questioning also gave him hope that she wouldn't grow up to be as dogmatic as their father.

"I thought the Tempting was a test," she said.

Jos wanted to explain, but he held his tongue. His problems with Oveno were his own. "Don't worry, Mouse. Yours is a long way off." He tickled her sides. She shrieked and wriggled off his lap. "Want to watch me draw?"

While he leaned off the edge of the steps, picked up his bark, and then hunted through the grass for his broken pieces of charcoal, she clambered up to rest beside him. He found two lengths still long enough to use. Handing one to Anell, he used the other to start a drawing of the rude tinker.

He gave the man a larger head and a more bulbous nose, understanding as he pulled and smudged lines across the bark that the merchant had lost much in his life, so he drank and lashed out in the hopes that others might share in a small measure of his constant pain.

Jos was less than halfway finished when Anell put her hand over it. "He makes me sad. Draw someone else."

So he did. A fat farmer was the next to ride by, driving a wagon pulled by a mismatched pair of oxen. Guessing from the health of his beasts and the girth of his belly, he was a happy man. The likeness of him on the bark seemed to catch the sunlight and hold it, and some of the tension eased from Jos's shoulders.

When the merry farmer passed around the curve leading to the gates into Derlest, Jos switched to a pretty young woman headed out of it. Short, fair of face, and gifted in the breasts and hips, every line he pulled was neat, tidy, and proper. She was attractive enough, but he missed the taller women of Ombratos. Despite the warnings from the men in the caravan, he'd lain with a few in his time there, and if he were honest with himself, his desire was a small measure of the force calling him back. But that was a single drop of water in a bucket filled to the brim with reasons.

The pretty girl walked to the edge of the road, lifted her pale green skirts, and stepped onto the verge to approach the caravan. She picked her way over the patches of yellow grass and around the verdant thatches of new.

Anell shifted against Jos. "What do you think she wants?"

"Let's find out." Raising his voice, he said, "You didn't need to risk your skirt for my sake."

The woman came to a halt. "Excuse me?" Her guttural Baltwullian cadence made the question sound like an accusation.

Jos gave her his most charming smile. "If you wanted to speak to me this bad, you could have waved me over from the road."

Dropping her skirts, she frowned at him. "Does your caravan bear Josiah Porthain?"

Anell started, and Jos's heartbeat sped up, but he was growing used to the sound of his name coming from the mouths of strangers. "It might," he said. "Why are you looking for him?"

"My lady sent me to find the man who painted the portrait of Pator Michel Engel."

Jos had finished the piece not two days ago, and asking to keep a bit of the coin he earned for doing so had been what set his father off that morning. *"You would take food from your sister's mouth? Bosk's wagon is falling apart. Would you deny her a new one? You will return to that Amma-lost place a beggar or you won't return at all!"*

The woman continued, "Is Porthain here or not? Mutta Jannike Kirsch demands his presence."

His breath caught. Everyone who passed through East Baltwull knew of Mutta Kirsch. Outside of the royal family, her status and influence in the country were unmatched. The idea that the mutta had seen his work excited him. To think that she had viewed it and now wished to speak to him...

He stood, and she offered her right hand to shake—no one outside of Ombratos greeted one another with their left—but he showed her his charcoal-smudged palm as an excuse to avoid contact, and instead gave her a little bow. "Heyla, then. I'm—"

"He's my son"—Oveno came charging around the side of Bosk's wagon, cheeks flushed—"and he does not jump for any noble."

The woman stumbled back a few steps, almost losing her balance when she stepped on an overgrown tuft of bright blue periweed.

Jos's father stopped just short of the wagon's shadow. "Your mutta may *request* Josiah Porthain's presence, but demanding it will get her nowhere." He jabbed a finger in the direction of Derlest. "Go and tell her that."

The woman sniffed, snatched up her skirts, and marched away, toward the road. Anell leapt down from the steps and scurried off.

Jos turned to face his father. He was a tall man, large in every way, with tanned skin and light, sandy hair that hid the gray. People often remarked on how Jos favored his father, unaware their similarities began and ended with their appearance.

In this moment, Oveno's broad, lined face was creased in triumph.

Fury, raw and ugly, seized Jos by the throat. "You had no right to send her away like that. She asked for me."

"I am your leader." Oveno pounded the side of the wagon with his fist. "I have *every* right."

"You don't!" Jos had drawn his father before. The man was solid black against solid white, hard lines, heavy and stark. "Why can't my choices be my own?"

Oveno lowered his head and rubbed a hand over his beard. "I should have expected this."

He always did this. When Jos spoke in a calm, rational manner, Oveno raved at him, and when Jos shouted, his father affected weariness, as if Jos's anger was all too much for him. So Jos fought to rein in his fury.

Until he was twelve, Jos had lived a handful of places, always in houses or tenements. He and his mother had owned a wagon, but they'd used it for travel, not to live on the road. With his father's caravan, Jos had visited every major city and port in Althea, but he had never been anywhere alone until he went to Ombratos. He hadn't realized how much he missed putting down roots. He'd never had such a chance to explore his skill as an artist, and he'd never felt safer than he had in a city surrounded by thousands of people with bloodmarks.

He had tried explaining that to his father—all but the last part—but the man didn't listen, didn't understand, or didn't care.

"What?" Jos asked when his father didn't continue. "You should have expected what?"

"I know you think she protected you." Oveno tugged down the corner of Jos's collar and jabbed a finger in the same spot where Anell had touched him, the spot where every Wandering Fallen who came back from their

Tempting bore their Second Mark, and then pulled his finger away to point at Jos's bare flesh. "But she ruined you."

Jos smacked his father's hand away. "Is that why you took me in, to fix me? Just because I don't want what you want doesn't make me broken."

"That's enough." Aunt Bosk came up behind Jos and laid a hand on his arm. She, too, looked much like Oveno, and the brother and sister shared many of the same heavy lines on the page. But where Oveno's image refused even the slightest contours, Bosk's gave way to the occasional smudge or curve.

"Jos," she said, "why don't you go back to your wagon?"

Oveno opened his mouth, but Jos walked away before he might speak. Bosk had a way with her brother. Let her deal with him.

Sunlight dappled the ground where Jos walked, and he sought to lose his anger in the beauty of their camp. A wood surrounded the south of Derlest. With the continuation of the red-leaved trees, many thought it part of the Karskil Forest and so avoided it, but as all the seasoned travelers knew the Karskil didn't start until a good mile and a half outside the city. At the moment, Oveno's caravan stood alone in the shaded clearing, and Jos trudged through the almost empty camp. Only a few adults had remained behind for the day, to watch the children and craft more of their wares.

In sight of the communal fire and the children playing Pare the Wind near it, Samis sat in the back of his wagon and worked at his handloom. Though it took Jos through the children's path, he crossed on the far side of the fire from Samis, who would chatter Jos's ear off if he let him. The children, including Anell, came at Jos in a mob, then broke around him like water breaking around a stone in a stream.

Gent and Nora waited on the steps to the wagon Jos shared with his father and sister, and they climbed to their feet as he neared. The two of them had met on their Temptings, which they had both taken at the more usual age of seventeen. Slender Nora had a couple of inches on the rounder Gent, and where he was dark, she was fair, but they fit together in way that was difficult not to envy. Their lines were gentle, the shading light, and Jos couldn't sketch one without including the other.

"Heyla, friend," Gent said. "Rough morning?"

Jos sighed.

"Here." Nora gestured to the step. "Sit. Talk."

As much as he wanted to unburden himself, he held his tongue still. Unlike Anell, Gent and Nora had already found their path, but Jos didn't see the point in speaking ill of the leader they'd sworn to follow. Better to retreat into his art. "How about you let me draw you again?"

Gent looked like he wanted to insist they all speak, but Nora embraced Jos around his middle and laughed. "Whenever you'd like. We love your sketches, don't we, Gent?"

Gent's gaze shifted to his wife, and she drove away his concern. "We do."

"Good," Jos said. "Let me get my supplies."

He went into the wagon, sat on his bed, and took out the portrait he kept under his mattress. The small painting, his first, was faded and poorly rendered, but even in his shaky hand, he'd caught his mother's unbroken lines, her shadowed luster. She wouldn't have understood his desire to return to Ombratos either. The difference was, she would have listened. She would have tried.

He collected his supplies, including the portrait. He'd kept the painting on the wall next to his bunk for a year before his father—not angry, but sad—had asked him to please take it down. Their mutual love for Rahel should have been a bridge, and yet somehow it had become a wall, one neither of them knew how to scale.

Chalk and paper in hand, Jos went back outside.

TWO CANDLEMARKS LATER, everyone in camp came together around the central fire to share the midday meal. Jos stared down into his bowl. Never subtle, Bosk had made collection pot stew, a symbolic dish often saved for convocations.

Jos scooped up a hunk of potato and let it fall back into the gravy. Gent and Nora had eased a measure of Jos's anger, but his unhappiness ran deep, made worse by the way Oveno now acted as if all was settled and well, dandling Anell on his knee, making her giggle by pretending to steal her nose.

A bright, jingling sound came down the road, and soon two sets of matching silver dun mares rode into view pulling a closed-top carriage enameled in the exact same pale green of the Kirsch woman's skirt. Jos and several others stood, and the children even ran to the road to watch it pass. When the carriage slowed and stopped in front of the caravan, they cried out and returned to the group.

A servant in a deep green livery that complemented the coach climbed down from a perch in the back, opened the door, and offered assistance to whomever sat inside. A delicate, gloved hand appeared, and its owner turned out to be a small gentlewoman clad head-to-toe in dove gray. Once her feet were planted firmly on the ground, she let go of the servant and walked over to their fire as if she crossed through a fine sitting room.

No one spoke or moved. It seemed even Oveno was stunned into silence.

The highborn woman approached the wide-eyed Gent and asked, "Are you Josiah Porthain?"

Jos cleared his throat and found his voice. "I'm Josiah."

The woman turned her head toward him and looked him up and down, taking his measure. "You are Porthain? The one who painted Pator Engel?"

"I am."

"I see," she said. "Then I am Mutta Jannike Kirsch, and I have come to *request* your presence."

Before Oveno could object, Jos handed his bowl to Dwyer, who stood beside him openmouthed, and said, "I will gladly give it."

At this, Oveno found his voice. "How dare you? I—"

Mutta Kirsch's glare staunched the flow of Oveno's ire. They stared at one another, reminding Jos of two large dogs growling over a scrap of meat, and Oveno looked away first. Jos knew his father backed down for the sake of the caravan, but it was startling to witness all the same. Not wanting to miss his chance, Jos bowed, stepped around the fire, and offered Mutta Kirsch his arm. This prompted a wry smile from her. She laid her gloved hand atop his, and together they returned to her impressive carriage.

The inside proved to be even more opulent than the outside. His feet sank into the thick carpet, and he could almost stand straight without his head touching the roof. White velvet cut through with strands of black covered the walls, giving the illusion of depth, and buttery leather benches faced forward and back. Mutta Kirsch, who stood at her full height inside with room to spare, took one bench and offered him the other. He lowered himself onto the well-stuffed seat, the leather beneath his hands the finest kid.

Mutta Kirsch allowed him to settle before stating her business. "I would like a portrait of my husband."

Jos tore his attention away from the richness surrounding him. "I am honored that you might seek me out, mutta."

"But...?" Her stare went right through him, and his fingers itched to draw her, to balance the scales.

"But," he said, "this seems like a lot of trouble to go to for a simple portrait."

Another wry smile. Either the mutta thought very little of him or he amused her greatly. "I saw the painting you did of Pator Engel. I have known that man for many years, more years than I care to admit to." Unless Jos missed his mark, the woman was at least sixty, close to the same age as Engel. "He is a dear friend, but he has never been what one might call a handsome man. However, in that portrait..."

She looked away from Jos as if imagining the painting in her mind. "In creating that portrait, you saw past his face. You saw past his watery eyes and weak chin, and you painted the truth of him."

The hairs on Jos's arms rose. Many responded to his work the way Anell had to his drawing of the merchant—they sensed what lay beneath the charcoal or oil paints—but not since his mother had anyone spoken of his skill in such a plain manner.

"You have a gift," she said, again staring at him in her unsettling way. "I saw it in another many years ago. Though, in her, it took a different form."

Jos sat back on the bench. It had never occurred to him that others might share his ability. He had worked at honing his eye and his hand, but drawing out a person's truth, taking a little bit from them and trapping it with his charcoal or brush, had come as natural to him as breathing. And this woman knew something of that.

"Will you do it?" The way the mutta asked the question suggested she already knew the answer. Even so, she added, "I will pay whatever you ask."

Not even Amma herself could have stopped him. "Let me get my supplies."

Jos skirted the caravan, relieved when only Aunt Bosk and Anell met him at the wagon.

They waited outside while he went in to collect his toolboxes from under his bed and his portrait. He stood and rested him arms on the bunk where Anell slept above him. The acrid stink of his supplies clashed with other homey, familiar scents worn into the wood and fabric. Unsure why he did so, he grabbed the edge of the quilt Anell's mother had sewn for her, covered his mouth and nose with it, and inhaled. The blanket smelled of fresh straw from her mattress, the musty rot of the flowers she hid beneath it, and the rosemary soap Nora made and sold and that they used for the caravan's washing.

"I think it will be good for you and Oveno to spend a few days apart," Aunt Bosk said, when he came out.

Jos didn't disagree. He hugged her, let her go, and turned to Anell. She ran at him and leapt into his open arms, and he squeezed her tight. "See you soon, Mouse."

She pressed her face into his neck, snuggling for a moment, then she bit him.

"Ow!" He dropped her to the ground and put a hand to the spot. It was wet with spit, but she hadn't broken the skin. "What was that for?"

She grinned up at him with childish madness. "See you soon!"

Gent, Nora, and most of the others waved to Jos as he returned to the carriage. Oveno was nowhere to be seen.

Jos's toolboxes rattled with brushes and tinkled with bottles as he handed them up to the servant, and on the ride into Derlest, neither he nor Mutta Kirsch broke the silence between them. Older people, like children, were sometimes harder to draw. The older a person grew, the more they tended to cling to certain parts of their lives, their successes or their failures or the point in their life when they felt the most alive or alluring. But that was what Jos had given Pator Engel, and the mutta seemed happy enough with it.

Passing through the city in her carriage was a far cry from traveling through it in the caravan. Instead of the hard looks and accusations of "road rat," people bowed when they rode by. Even so, the Kirsch home wasn't as immense or magnificent as Jos expected it to be. A high wall ringed the grounds, and they had to pass through a heavily guarded gate in order to enter, but the plain, if well-made, stone building didn't seem worthy of someone of the mutta's supposed wealth and status.

Perhaps that was because everything missing from the exterior was on full display in the home's interior. All of the coin saved on the size of the building looked to have been spent on decorating the lesser number of rooms and halls, which were covered from wall to wall in excess and splendor. The mutta's feet made barely a sound across the carpeted floors as she led him past room after room crammed full of antiquities. Tapestries and paintings covered the paneled walls and flew by in a whirl of colors and vague impressions. He hoped he might have a chance to study them later.

The moment they turned down a dark hall near the back of the house, a smell—heavy and strangely sweet—coated the inside of his nose and mouth. A servant in the dark green livery, all but hidden in the thick shadows surrounding a set of doors at the end of the hall, opened the doors and followed them into the darkness inside, where the scent pressed over his face like a hand.

Mutta Kirsch asked the servant to pull back the curtains. The light the servant let in revealed a bed, and in the middle of the bed lay a creature that might have once been a man but now resembled a monster, a horrible thing with blackened limbs, sunken cheeks, and cracked, bleeding lips.

She's brought me here to paint a dead man.

Mutta Kirsch bowed over the monster and, with a gentle hand, smoothed down the yellow-white strands of hair clinging to the ashen skull. With that, the corpse sucked in a ragged breath. Jos's stomach heaved, and he swallowed the bile that rose in his throat.

Somehow the mutta stared down at the monster with love in her eyes, more love than Jos had thought existed in the world. "This is my Alric, Josiah, and I want to remember him how he was, not as he is." She kissed Alric's brow. "I need you to paint his truth."

Jos spent the next tenday at the manor, and every day, Mutta Kirsch told Jos stories about Alric, about the stern, stubborn man she had married and fallen in love with. Though her Alric had been generous in many ways, he'd refused to ever sit for a portrait, so she showed Jos his study and his clothing, she had her cook prepare the dishes her Alric had requested most often, and one afternoon, her niece came over to sing Alric's favorite song, a mournful ballad about duty and honor in the face of insurmountable odds.

Every night, Jos spent candlemarks studying Alric himself, trying to make out the shape of the bones beneath the rotting skin, trying to find the hearty soul she described in the man who lay dying before him. Never before had it taken him such work to commit someone's likeness to the page, but he was grateful for the way the effort occupied his mind. He pushed so hard a barrier within himself gave way. It was like the first time he had caught the exact look in his mother's eyes or the precise details of her hand. He tapped into a deeper level of his skill.

Whenever the mutta wasn't telling him about her Alric, he peppered her with questions about his ability, and she didn't discourage him from asking, yet she answered almost none of them. This frustrated him, though it surprised him little.

He took a single candlemark on his second afternoon in the house to sketch an image of her, and the drawing revealed the clear, bright face of a handsome, twenty-year-old version of the mutta surrounded on all sides by a shadow of words and shapes. They covered the whole rest of the page, hundreds of words and shapes that were indecipherable even to him. In truth, the picture, at odds with the woman he was coming to know, disturbed him, and not wanting to keep it, he slipped it under the wardrobe in Alric's room, where it might or might not ever be found.

Despite the mutta's reticence to answer his questions, he continued to ask them, and on the fifth evening, she shrugged and admitted that she knew as much about his skill as he did. "I know enough to recognize it when I see it. I made you think I knew more to entice you to come with me."

He pressed her that night about the woman she had known, the one she had claimed shared a different manifestation of his same gift, but she refused to say more. Or she did until the seventh night, when, after a few bottles of wine over a long meal, she took a rather unladylike gulp, swallowed, and said, "A kiss."

Jos, in an effort to match pace with his hostess, polished off the last few drops in his goblet. The world swam before him and his well-oiled jaw seemed to move without his bidding. "Are you asking for one or offering?"

Mutta Kirsch laughed. "Neither. That was how my friend discovered my truth." She touched her lips and her cheeks turned the delicate pink of a much younger woman. "With a kiss."

He looked away to give the mutta the privacy of her memory. A woman who read others with her kisses. How many others out there shared his gift, and in what form? The possibilities seemed endless.

Eleven days after arriving at the Kirsch estate, on a rainy morning, Jos finished the painting, but he held off on sharing it with the mutta for almost a candlemark. Though he was certain he'd captured the man's very essence, the strong, proud pator on the canvas bore not even the slightest resemblance to the suffering man in the bed.

It was either his greatest triumph or his worst failure.

Using the needle he kept amongst his supplies, he pricked his finger and offered a silent plea to Amma before calling a servant to tell the mutta he was done. Mutta Kirsch, when she came, entered the room with deliberate steps, and Jos stood between her and the painting until, with a deep breath, he stepped aside.

She stared at the image a long time. Then she approached the painting and reached out. "Alric."

Jos clasped her shaking hand to him to stop her from touching the canvas. "It's still wet, mutta."

"Oh, Alric," she cried. She said his name over and over as tears spilled down her face. "Oh, my dearest Alric."

Jos took his leave from the house a short while later. Mutta Kirsch walked him to the door, handed him a purse heavy with coin, and pulling him down, pressed a dry, powdery kiss to his cheek. "You may find yourself in great need one day. I hope that you do not, but if you do, you must not hesitate to seek me out."

He couldn't fathom begging this great mutta for a favor, no matter how dire the circumstances, but he smiled and humored her. "Of course."

She pinned him down with one of her stares. "I mean it, Josiah. My pockets are deep and my reach is wide. You have given me a gift without price, and nothing I do will ever be enough to repay you."

Jos declined the offer of a ride back to the caravan. The purse Mutta Kirsch had given him held thrice the amount of coin they had agreed to, more than enough to buy his own wagon and a couple of animals to pull it. He walked toward the east side of Derlest, where the traders dealt in live-stock. The sun hung low in the sky, shining sidelong onto the city beneath clouds still spitting rain. He slowed by the first pen, where a herd of donkeys caught his attention.

A man, his clothing muddy from a day's work but well cared for, wandered over. "Fine day, chap. Can I help you with sommat?"

Jos squeezed the fat purse in his pocket. "I'm looking for a few beasts strong enough to drag a small wagon all the way to Ombratos."

EIGHT

"Don't ever let down your guard until you're certain of your victory."
-Waltham

Getha sat on the roof of the stables. She couldn't stand horses—
with their giant teeth and their stamping, kicking hooves—but
aside from the palace battlements, where she wasn't allowed
unless she was on duty, the view from the stable roof could not be matched.
So she sat there, breaking her fast with a steaming mug of sop, waiting in
the cool shadows of the Cassedents for the sun to rise above the peaks and
warm her back.

A light mist shrouded the valley, but beneath it, the city-state of
Ombratos sprawled out before her. The vast lawns of Seedfall reached
down to the curtain wall, patrolled day and night by the palace guard, and
beyond that lay the Bole, where the hearths of the highborn huddled and
preened. Another higher curtain wall separated the Bole from the rest of the
city, built from a vein of green quartz discovered in the mines. Ombratians
called it the Hedgerow.

The bulk of Ombratians lived on the far side of the Hedgerow, where
the steady flow of the River Sap broke into channels, creating dozens of
canals throughout the lower parts of the city. The highborn referred to the
whole area as the Branches, but Getha had spent two years in the city
guard, and she well knew the individual neighborhoods therein—the

99

Chestnut, the Blossom, the Acorn, the Tangles, the Mire—each with their own rhythms and rules. The river flowed through these neighborhoods down to the sea, where everything from two- and three-masted carnos to ocean-rigged round ships to dinghies floated at the docks in Crown Bay.

And circling the whole of the city, the Gift. With the wall, and nestled as the city was between the mountains and the sea, Ombratos was the most fortified nation on the Althian Coast. Waltham liked to call their city The Nut—*A nut that several armies and rulers have broken their teeth trying to crack.*

This morning, as the sun had yet to rise, the golden color of the unmarked stone appeared paler, almost a bone-white. She thought about the wall rippling beneath her hand, but the memory was as fleeting and difficult to grasp as the tattered remnants of a dream. Perhaps that's what it had been, a mad dream. Or perhaps alchemy shock. Not that it mattered. She touched the black band around her arm. The stories of the princess's death, every horrid, stomach-turning detail, were impossible to avoid, but Getha had climbed up onto the roof to clear her mind, so she returned to her beloved city.

Outside of the Gift, the city's farmlands reached to the south, and Shade's Rest blighted the north. Given the steady stream of miners and traders settling there, the faubourg grew a little larger every year, but soon it would reach its limits. The Sea Road Council's official declaration of their borders meant Shade's Rest couldn't expand much farther up the coast without an incursion into the Sea Road, the Wood Road, or the Karskil Forest.

As always, the sight of the forest sent spider-like chills down her spine because it looked like a lake of blood. The crimson leaves of the trees in the Karskil never changed color and never fell, and that hellish expanse—home to fell creatures, untamed links to the Unknowable Beyond, and other unimaginable horrors—reached to the horizon, spanning all the way up to the southern border of East Baltwull. Not that she had ever been that far north, but she could read a map.

Though the Wood Road hadn't a council to declare their borders, they did have quite a few homesteads on the outskirts, and no one took violating the edges of those properties lightly. There was a saying that a person had to be stubborn or stupid to settle on the Wood Road, and from what she'd heard, most who did were both.

But Shade's Rest's expansion, or lack thereof, no longer concerned her. She'd spent the first sixteen years of her life out there, living in a surplus home, then walking the streets as a city guard, yet Ombratos was where she'd always belonged.

The first rays of sunlight shot over the broken teeth of the Cassedents, casting an orange glow over the sky and burning off the mist from the waking city beneath. Getha swallowed the last of her sop and stood. Six years in the palace guard, and as long as she passed the final test to join the varo, this day would be her last. History, protocol, stratagem—she had done well in every task put to her, and today was fighting. The very thought of having a blade filled her with a powerful calm. As the city bells tolled to signal the opening of the city gates, she hooked the mug onto her belt, and ignoring the short ladder, jumped down into the hayloft.

"Shit!" a stable hand cried out, brandishing her pitchfork like a weapon. Broken stalks of hay covered her clothes and stuck out of her short, greying thatch of hair. "Didn't know you were up there. Scared the piss outta me, girl."

At almost twenty-five, Getha was hardly still a girl. "Guard," she said as she trudged through the hay to make her way to the ladder leading down from the loft.

"What's that, girl?"

"Guard." Getha grabbed the ladder and swung around onto it, the rails polished smooth from years of countless stable hands doing the same. "I'm called 'Guard,' not 'girl.'"

The woman frowned. "As long as you keep sneaking onto my roof, I'll call you what I please." She returned to her work, shoveling hay over the open side.

Getha climbed down, and the six grooms at the base of the ladder glared at her. They didn't like her on their roof, but they'd yet to stop her from going up there, and until they did, their scorn was a small price to pay for a few scraps of solitude and that view.

She headed outside. As she passed one of the stalls, the horse in it snorted and kicked, pounding its hooves into the door. Childhood instincts that she couldn't have been rid of even if she had wanted to took hold. She twitched away from the sounds, her feet carrying her to the far side of the aisle and her wrists flexing to release the daggers from her spring-loaded vambraces. Blades slid into her hands, and she rounded on the beast, falling into the steady, wide-legged wall guard stance.

The horse—a huge black creature that might have ridden straight up from the pathless hells—snorted again and tossed its head around, but it was secured behind the locked door of its stall.

Getha's pounding heartbeat slowed and laughter reached her ears. Back by the ladder, the grooms were doubled over, leaning on each other's shoulders as they pointed and howled in her direction. An urge to stick the motherless bastards came and went as Waltham's voice echoed in her mind, *"You don't earn respect by the tips of your blades, not anymore."* Claiming what little dignity she had left, she straightened, tucked the knives back into her vambraces—resetting the internal triggers—and strode from the building, showing the fools her back.

She couldn't care less what those grooms thought of her, but perhaps she would wait a while before returning.

Outside, mindful to watch for piles of horse shit, she made haste across the enclosed yard, leaving by way of the gate that led to Menders' Row. Low white buildings, housing every sort of smithery from farriers to tinkers, lined either side of the narrow road, and a wave of heat rolled over her as she jogged by a smith's open door. All of the doors she passed were painted black for the fallen heir.

Amma guide you and keep you, princess.

Getha had prayed on it, but couldn't fathom why Amma had taken the heir from them. Princess Solena had been different. Special. Unlike most highborn, she'd cared about everyone in the city, from the richest noble down to the poorest streetling. But Amma, in her great wisdom, must have had a reason, and it was up to the Fallen to now walk the path before them.

A tall, lithe figure turned on to the row at the far end. Princess Renn. From what Getha had heard, the youngest princess was kind and never intentionally abused her position. Yet people also called her silly and vain, and the obsessive riding had disturbed them all. Not to mention the business with the Tithen prince.

Vicious gossip, that, and regardless, the princess was a Morovide, and therefore to be treated with respect. Getha stopped and prepared to bow as the princess neared. But halfway down the row, the princess ducked through one of the doors, leaving her varo to wait outside with a cluster of acolytes. That seemed odd, but Getha shrugged and continued on. The highborn did a lot of things that confused her.

The row let out at the practice yards, and at least fifty palace guards and varo already gathered around the fences, most talking in their own groups since varos didn't usually mix with guards after rising in the ranks. But everyone, no matter their rank, watched yard servants roll empty barrels through the dirt at Varo Tems Maurius's behest.

"Set that one there," Orli's second-in-command said, pointing to a spot near the northern fence. He wore his scuffed leather sparring armor, his ginger, shoulder-length hair in a tail at the nape of his neck. He had been in charge of their tests, and this morning she'd expected him to do little more than observe, but his dress suggested otherwise. "Put a long sword in that one."

A servant carrying an armful of practice blades stepped forward and slid a wooden long sword into the barrel.

Maurius spoke to Getha over his shoulder. "Are you planning to be late, Guard Barei?"

She shook her head. "No, Varo."

"Then you'd best keep moving."

She hurried around the enclosure toward the palace guard barracks. Lead Varo Lucador Orli stood alone at the fence, in the shadow cast by Barracks Eight. A person passing him out in the city wouldn't look twice at him, a balding man of middling height and middling build, but a trained eye would note the way he carried himself, the stillness wound inside him, waiting for release, and not only look twice, but move to the other side of the street.

Like the others, he watched Maurius set up, and he too wore sparring armor. Would the candidates be expected to fight both men? Having seen Orli's remarkable skill on the field, she both welcomed and feared the prospect. She ran past him and up the steps into Barracks Six. Despite the candlemark, everyone was awake and buzzing about the last trial, and by some miracle, Tumolo was out on duty. She crossed to her bunk to strap on her armor, and without paying attention to what was being said, let the excitement in the room flow into her.

Back outside, a gentle warmth in the morning air promised a nice day ahead, winter at last giving way to spring. Every guard and varo not on duty milled around the practice yard now, guards on one side and varo on the other. Along the fence between the groups, an audience of highborn had formed with a cluster of servants behind them.

Even in Ombratos, Getha was considered tall for a woman, but she was of a standard height for the guard. Balancing on the balls of her feet, she looked above the heads of those around her, through the growing audience, for Waltham's familiar head of disheveled white hair. She swallowed down her disappointment when she couldn't find him. For a man of seventy, most days he was still as sharp as ever, but his thoughts were starting to slip in places and there was a real chance he had forgotten.

Maurius walked into the center of the yard, clapped his hands for quiet, and addressed the group of guards. "As you well know, we have two openings in the varo, and while you are all still in the running, Guards Frena Catala, Nils Roher, and Getha Barei are currently in the lead for these positions."

No surprise there. Those two had been hard on her tail all tenday. She took a deep breath. *One last test.* Catala and Roher smiled their wry lovers' smiles at one another and shook hands.

"Yeah," a voice called from the back of the group, "but who's on top?"

Everyone laughed, including Catala and Roher. Japes about their relationship were standard fare, and somehow they shared in the amusement, even though it came at their expense.

When the noise tapered off, Orli stepped forward, looked right at Getha, and said, "Barei's on top."

The remaining murmurs and giggles cut off.

"Ah." Maurius rolled back on his heels, hands clasped behind his back. "Planning to take this seriously now, are you?"

Orli continued to stare at Getha. She didn't know him, so she wasn't sure why he had painted a very large target on her. Was it to push her or to push the others?

Behind her, someone—it sounded like Leeson—took the first shot, whispering, "Don't know why she's even up for this. Amma-lost forsaken."

Under the guise of stretching out her fingers, she rubbed her right thumb over her left palm, sparking her bloodmark. Let them call her what they liked. Waltham would tell her to put some iron in her spine and to hold her head up high, so she did just that, and Orli shifted his hard stare away from her.

Maurius stopped at the other end of the yard. "This last trial is simple. The varo"—six varo jumped the fence and spread out between the barrels—"will be the assailants. I am the queen. You"—he waved at hand at the assembled palace guards in contention—"will enter in groups of eight and do your best to defend me. The trial ends when either all the assailants are disabled or I have been captured or killed."

Getha's heart sank. She had hoped this would be a one-to-one challenge or her alone against multiple varo. Guards were taught to fight together, but she didn't trust any of them at her back for a battle as important as this.

"Questions?" Maurius asked.

Roher raised a hand. "Which weapons may we use?"

"Neither you nor the varo will be allowed to enter with anything." He walked over to a barrel and knocked on its hollow side. "Everyone will have to use whatever they find in these."

Getha ran her hands over the tooled leather of her vambraces, wondering if she should remove the blades or take them off altogether.

"More questions?" Maurius asked. "Last chance. No? Fine. Wait here, and in a moment we'll call the first group."

Whispers flurried around Getha as she undid the buckles to her left vambrace. Once it was off, she tucked it under her arm and started on the right.

"I'll hold those for you."

She spun around, and Waltham stood before her, holding out a gnarled hand. His weather-beaten skin, grooved all over with deep lines, and his posture, stooped with age, always made her think of an ancient tree.

"You came," she said, almost dropping her vambrace.

"So I did." He pointed toward the varo waiting on the far side of the yard. "I even offered to fight with them." Varo was a lifetime appointment and Waltham still held the title, even if he had been "tucked away into a corner," as he called it, for years.

"What did they say?" She finished taking off her right vambrace and handed both over to him. Her arms felt bare, but she was less troubled by their loss with Waltham nearby.

"They thanked me for my offer but declined. Imagine that." He reached out and tapped her helm. "Remember. Be fast, be bold... "

"Be brave and wise," she finished. "I will. Wish me luck?"

He shook his head. "I only do that for those who need it." He peered around her, putting on a kindly old grandfather face. "Catala, Roher!" Their group stopped talking, and the two of them turned to look. When they did, Waltham smiled and said, "Best of luck to you both!"

Catala narrowed her eyes, and Roher waved uncertainly. Dropping the act, Waltham winked at her and walked away.

GETHA'S GROUP was last up, and it included Catala and Roher. They waited on the far side of Barracks One, out of sight of the practice yard, but well within hearing distance of the cheers and gasps from those watching.

The group agreed they needed a leader, and Catala stepped up, assigning positions in an odd manner. Instead of distributing their strongest fighters throughout, she placed herself, Roher, and Getha at anchor. Getha held her tongue. The fight would be harder than necessary, but that didn't bother her.

Before long, their group was up. As they approached the training grounds, the noise from the audience grew. It seemed that the news of Catala, Roher, and Getha's positions in the competition had spread, as most cheered for either Catala or Roher. Getha found Waltham in the crowd and gave him a solemn nod, which he returned. Then, not meaning to, she caught the eye of Lead Varo Orli. Clad in armor, one hand resting on the hilt of his varo blade, his gaze drilled into her with an unnerving intensity.

Getha shook her head, casting all thoughts aside from the impending battle aside, and entered the training ring.

Although Getha's group began with eight and the varos six, the varo had a fighting force less than a quarter the size of the palace guard, and they trained to face overwhelming numbers. Which meant five palace guards—their spearhead—fell in the initial assault, taking out a single varo along the way. That left Getha, Catala, and Roher to deal with the remaining five varo on their own, and with three to five, they couldn't defend their "Queen" on all sides.

Catala had had her chance. "To the fence!" Getha called, and to her surprise, Catala and Roher retreated with her.

They herded Maurius back, and Getha glanced into the barrels she passed. *Empty. Empty. Shit! Empty.* So far, all she'd found was a hand-and-a-half sword and a flail. Though she had no use for the flail, Waltham had taught her better than to pass up any weapon, and she'd tucked it into her belt. She held the blade.

Moving fast, they reached the fence before the varos's second advance. Roher defended the "Queen" on the left, Getha on the right, and Catala at center.

Damned Catala. Somewhere, that lucky chit had found a pair of matched blades. But she held them in front of her, blades down, in the snake guard, a stance better suited to attack than defense.

"Wall guard," Getha said, shifting into mountain peak.

Catala shook her head, and then the five varos were on them, charging as a pack, now relying on the strength of their numbers.

Two varo came at Getha together, the one on the right bearing a long sword, the other a short, curved falchion. They attacked in a pincer formation, each driving forward from an opposite side. But she rushed the one on her right, dodging inside the varo's wide swing and jamming her blade into the woman's exposed armpit before shoving her away with an elbow.

One down, four left.

The varo on Getha's left lashed out and overextended his thrust by the tiniest bit, but the extra half inch, the extra half second, was all she needed. She grabbed his wrist, jerked him forward, and cracked her blade across his knuckles, causing him to drop his falchion and pulling him off-balance. Twisting his arm around her middle as if he were a ribbon and she a maypole, he ended up pressed to her back. She pushed against the dirt, driving them together into the fence. The rail hit him in the small of his back, and he bent backward over it, trying to carry her with him. She raised her foot and stomped down on the inside of his. When he cried out and loosened his grip, she ducked beneath his arm and spun, dragging her blade across his belly with a hard swipe.

Three left.

Behind her, Roher had fallen. A varo held out a hand to help him up from the dirt, something he wouldn't do unless they were both out.

Two.

Catala struggled to hold off both her opponents. She tended to add flourishes to the ends of her moves that looked good, but each one cost her precious time. Getha shifted to the right for a better vantage and ran into one of the barrels. She looked inside. Empty. In her head, she heard Waltham's voice saying, *"Why couldn't the barrel be a weapon itself?"*

She knocked the barrel on its side and kicked it forward. The varo closest to her tried to half-step, half-jump over it, but she caught her foot and tripped. She hit the dirt hard, and Getha was on her. Turning the varo over with one hand, Getha drew her wooden blade across the woman's throat with the other.

One.

The varo fighting Catala swept his leg out, but she stepped into his sweep instead of avoiding it. He recovered, but it was now two-to-one. As Catala closed with him, trapping his sword between her blades, Getha jabbed her blade up into the dent at the base of his skull, careful to stop before making actual contact.

Because she pulled her movement, the varo was unaware he was out until Maurius stepped forward, a smile on his face. "That's enough, Fino. It's over."

Fino glanced back and, seeing Getha, growled a curse, tossing his sword into the dirt.

"Shit, Getha!" Catala said, dropping her guard. "I had him. If you'd just given me two more—"

The alarmed look on Maurius's face was Getha's only warning. She ducked into a crouch, and the swing meant for her caught Catala in the chest, hurtling her to the ground. Orli followed through with the wooden shortsword and came full circle, leaving Getha no chance to wonder what in the pathless hells was happening. She could only react as Orli came for her like a man possessed. Over and over, she blocked his hammering blows and searched for any sign of an opening, but none came. He charged at her, battling her with a savagery that was all the more frightening for the lack of emotion in his face. He forced her back and back until she hit the fence, and then, in two lightning fast moves, he cracked open her guard and sent her blade flying.

Both physically and mentally unarmed, she grabbed the flail from her belt and whipped it at his head. He held his blade up and the flail's chain wrapped around it. Let go, she told herself, but before she could, he yanked both it and her forward, driving his fist into her chest. Pain blossomed outward from the contact point, and her air rushed out in an endless breath. When she tried to suck in another, she couldn't.

He jerked the flail from her, and she fell to her hands and knees, gasping and choking. Knocking off her helm, he grabbed her hair and pulled her up into a kneeling position. Tossing aside the practice blade, he pushed her head to one side, drew his varo sword, and slid his blade into the resulting gap between her gorget and cuirass. She thought he would stop there, but a burning sting and the hot runnel of blood down her back made her heart pound even harder, and she closed her eyes, certain she was about to be executed.

Why? Tears threatened to spill from beneath her closed eyelids. *Whywhywhywhy?*

With same abruptness of his initial attack, Orli removed his blade and released her hair. She opened her eyes as she flopped down, still struggling for breath, into the dirt.

She fought for air until, with a gasp, she drew in one small breath, and then another.

A woman in the audience said, "I wonder what in Amma's name that was about."

Getha sucked in a larger breath. *You and me both.*

Maurius came over, and together, he and Orli moved away from her, speaking in hushed tones too quiet for her to overhear. Getha sat up, rested her arms on her knees, and found Waltham in the crowd. He stared at Maurius and Orli, his mouth pressed into a hard line. The whispered discussion continued for a while before it turned heated on Maurius's part. He jabbed a finger in Getha's direction and then hooked his thumb over his shoulder, pointing to where she, Catala, and Roher had made their stand. Orli listened and displayed about as much emotion as a blank wall.

Maurius paused, and in that pause, Orli said a single word, one that was clear even from where she sat. "No." After that he said something else, sliced his hand through the air, and walked away, vaulting the fence to leave the yard and heading toward the palace.

Maurius stood there until Orli was out of sight, then he moved, his limbs and back stiff, into the center of the ring and clapped for attention. "Our new varo"—the words sounded like they were being ground out of him—"will be Frena Catala and Nils Roher."

A gasp came from the crowd, and Orli might as well have returned to hit her in the chest again. Then she caught sight of Waltham crossing the practice yard toward her, and everything about the moment struck her as humorous. Hysterical laughter built in her chest, and she tried to hold it back, but the harder she tried the more it built and the more it built, until it bubbled forth, spilling from her in high-pitched bursts.

"Getha?" Waltham bent over her, touching her shoulder. "What's wrong? Getha? Getha!"

His concerned tickled her further, and the laughter poured forth, stealing her breath, creating an ache in her side.

She'd wanted the chance to fail, and now she had. All on her own.

NINE

"After their hard-won liberation, the Tithens began training every man, woman, and child to fight in the hopes of placing their freedom out of reach of the next conquerors that, at some point, will come to call."
-From Danlan's *Histories of the Known World, Vol. 1*

Despite Helenia's repeated attempts, Dallan refused to speak to her aboard the *Forweary*. In fact, he refused to so much as leave his cabin. Meals were left by his door, then collected, untouched, a few candlemarks later. Had it not been for Nye, the scrawny lad who went into Dallan's room to empty his chamber pot, she would have feared her nephew had thrown himself into the sea.

So she spent much of the voyage sitting at the base of the ship's rear mast, staring out at their wake. With every moment that passed and every mile they crossed, they drew nearer and nearer to Tithen and the tightness in her chest grew.

The only way forward is back. So much for that. Some small part of Helenia wondered if the queen had known what she was doing when she told Dallan she had asked for the betrothal to Heshiette instead of Renn, if somehow Theodora had suspected Helenia and Mayve's treachery all along. But that implicated them in Solena's death, and the queen would have seen them hang for that. More likely, Theodora was a miserable woman who enjoyed spreading her misery around.

If only returning to Ombratos didn't require Dallan. But it did because in order to claim the city for herself, she needed ships, weapons, and warriors to wield them, all of which his mother, Mayve, had, and even though Helenia and Mayve called each other sister, her involvement depended on Dallan's. Mayve was the lock and Dallan the key.

"Land!" The call came from atop the ship's forward mast.

Lightheadedness descended on Helenia. Gripping her skirts, she took some deep breaths to steady herself. When she left, she hadn't expected to ever step foot on her homeland again. *Too late to turn back now. Better to meet it face-to-face.*

She started to stand when a few strands of straw fell down onto her white skirt. She jumped to her feet, brushing them away, and took several steps before turning back. More straw floated down to the deck as the wind wife rustled in her stinking, filthy nest on the platform above. A stiff breeze snapped the sails, and the wind wife stilled, raising her arms to the sky. They stood out against the low clouds like sticks laid out on a bed of ashes, the holes through her palms looked like open mouths crying out for mercy, and in a hoarse voice that cracked and wavered, she sang her praises to the Unknowable Beyond.

There was no mention of Burk in her song since the rituals and rites she performed were from long before the Final Liberation. Even so, a sailor went to the base of the mast and said, "May the Ever-Watchful Eye see you and keep you, *brídgaoh*." A new blessing addressed in an old tongue. The thick tattoos around the sailor's eyes indicated that she, unlike most of the crew, was of the Terrefosk clan. It was strange being back among so many painted faces. Carved Eyes of Burk ran down the length of the mast, and the sailor kissed her dirty fingers and pressed them to one at shoulder height that appeared faded from hundreds of similar blessings.

The sailor hastened off, and in quick succession, six more hurried over to offer their own words and kisses. The last, a man with a jaw like a block of wood, stared at Helenia as he waited, the narrowing of his eyes questioning why she didn't do the same. Really, she respected the elemental wives for their sacrifices as much as the next Tithen. The women who chose to enter one of the four orders gave their lives in service to the rest of their people. But the toll their sacrifices wrought upon them...

When Helenia was nine, a fire wife, a *brídtin*, had lived in the rooms below her and her father, and even after so many years, it turned her stomach to think of the woman's slack cheeks, her haunted eyes, and the burned and blackened skin that stretched over her bony hands. A girl entered the order at fourteen, the same age at which every other Tithen started their required year of military training. But while those who trained in the martial skills could leave once their year was up, an elemental wife promised her whole short life away. Most were lucky if they reached thirty.

How or why the alchemists of Ombratos weren't also consumed by their connection to the Unknowable Beyond ranged outside of Helenia's understanding. Chances were, the secret hid in the blood they spilled. Or perhaps the secret lived in their mysterious god, Amma.

The Burk that Helenia prayed to had been an actual man, the man who had liberated the Tithens. In doing so, he had claimed his people's worship from Necoriana, the also once-living woman who had founded their island, the woman to whom the elemental wives still prayed. The Rhyllexie worshipped their ancestors, the odd Xantish their unborn descendants, and the cynical Baltwullians eschewed religion altogether, but only the Fallen and the Wandering Fallen were mad enough to deify some unseen, unknown entity that never had and never would walk the land.

"I'm sorry, *brídgaoh*. May the Ever-Watchful Eye guard you and guide me." Helenia kissed her fingers and pressed them to the smooth, touch-worn spot on the mast. The elemental wives unsettled her, but she needed every blessing she could get if she was to turn the tide back in her favor.

Careful to avoid the sailors swarming over the decks, she walked to the bow. The tall stone watchtowers along the coast seemed to rise out of the sea as the ship neared Tithen. Her beloved Carhal, a duke in name, but a historian at heart, had loved the watchtowers, and the sight of them brought the pain of his death rushing back.

By some divine providence, Dallan joined her at the rail, startling the sorrow from her before it took hold. Like most things, heartbreak suited her nephew. He still wore the black mourning clothes of Ombratos, and that, along with the four days' worth of whiskers covering his cheeks and neck, made him appear both older and more serious. A peacock turned raven.

Taking his presence as encouragement, she laid a hand on his arm. "How are—"

He winced and pulled away from her. "No."

"I can explain."

"I don't care."

The tightness in her chest increased, and she scrambled for a different tack. "What about Galleford?" She kept her gaze trained on the sea, waiting with a morbid hunger for the capital to come into view. "Are you planning to visit Curmholt?"

He gave her a derisive, sidelong glance. "Of course. Can you imagine the reaction from my father if I traveled through Galleford and didn't visit the palace?" He snorted. "Some of us know better than to test the almighty King Adameth."

Careful. If Dallan guessed how much she wished to avoid his father, he might demand she accompany him out of spite. "I thought I might ride ahead and meet you on the far side of the city. Then we can head off to the duchy of Morleon—"

"No." Immediate. Firm. Decisive. "I'll be traveling to Morleon alone."

After days spent stewing in his own anger, Dallan seemed harder, more king-like, and the irony that he was becoming the man she needed him to be even as he pulled away wasn't lost on her. "I'm sure Mayve would like to see both of us."

"And I'm sure you can make other arrangements."

She fought the urge to push for what she wanted—after all, she had pushed in Ombratos and look how that had turned out—but she couldn't allow him to travel on without her. It took a full tenday to reach Morleon, and she needed every one of them to try and win him back.

The ship rose on a swell, Galleford came into sight. The capital, immense and imposing, sat crouched in an opening along the eastern coast, and sheer cliffs stretched out to the north and south, promising a briny end to any ship that ventured too close. Though the other coasts were fortified, to approach the island from any direction other than the east was considered an act of war.

The wind wife cried out, and the air shifted, sending the *Forweary* into the channel that carried them toward Galleford far too fast.

A man stood at the end of one of the docks. The black-and-white-striped plume in his helm marked him as a commander of a mercenary company. He removed his helm as the ship approached, and he turned out to be one of Dallan's older brothers, Seifan. Helenia's hopes for a swift and shadowy passage through Galleford died a quick death.

But out of that darkness, another idea began to form.

Beside her, Dallan slapped his hand against the ship's rail. "I brought nothing for him."

Since he wasn't expected to bring a gift for Seifan, "him" meant their father, King Adameth, her former brother-by-law. The last time she had seen him was the day she had been stripped of her land, her title, and a large swathe of her dignity.

The only way forward is back. Fighting off a rising tide of emotion, she said, "Gift him one of the crates of globes."

Dallan nodded, his shoulders relaxing slightly. This faint show of gratitude presented to Helenia the start of a reconnection with Dallan. Too bad that merely speaking of facing Adameth seized her in its icy grip, preventing her from taking the opening she'd just created. A lump formed in her throat, and she didn't trust herself to speak without crying or to move without shaking.

In what seemed like the blink of an eye, the *Forweary* docked, the bridge between ship and port erected. Dallan crossed first and left young Nye to help her.

When they were both ashore, Seifan approached Dallan and, ignoring Helenia, saluted. "Your safe return is welcome, brother."

Dallan bowed. "I am glad to once again be under Burk's Ever-Watchful Eye."

Though the brothers were as close in age as two siblings might be without sharing the same womb at the same time, one had to look very close to find any resemblance between them. If Dallan showed off the best his bloodlines had to offer, then Seifan showed off not quite the worst, but also not far from it.

Seifan was a stocky man, wider in the chest, but several inches shorter than Dallan. His hair, a dirty blond compared to Dallan's golden locks, hung down his back in lank braids, and his black eyes were like gimlet holes bored into the center of his broad, ruddy face. But in Tithen, Seifan had an advantage over his brother in the complicated tattoos that covered his heavy brow, which spoke of a lifetime's worth of distinction and service in Burk's name.

"Tell me," Seifan said. "How do you like returning to Tithen with your tail between your legs?"

Theodora had sent word about their return on one of the sleek knife boats that had passed the *Forweary* on their voyage. No surprise there.

But the news of Dallan's disgrace had little to do with the enmity radiating from Seifan. At eight, he had been quite old enough to be aware of what it meant when his attractive younger brother was sent to Ombratos instead of him. Having not seen the boys together since then, Helenia had always thought Seifan blamed Mayve, but it seemed his enmity reached beyond her.

The clouds chose that moment to release their burden. Fat raindrops fell on the wooden dock, giving them brief warning before the sky opened up. The servants overseeing the movement of Dallan and Helenia's baggage from the ship rushed them to their waiting carriage, but not before they were both soaked through. Having no desire to see Galleford again, Helenia shut the curtains over all the windows. Dallan reopened the one closest to him and stared out it while he played with some charm on a chain around his neck. A flowering charm.

They rode in silence, and upon their arrival at Curmhalt Palace, they weren't given the chance to bathe or change, but Helenia's shivering as she stood in the antechamber to Adameth's throne room had little to do with the drafty stone halls or her dripping skirts. Her new plan might succeed, but it wouldn't be easy.

The Master of Ceremony drove his copper-capped staff down against a steel circle set into the wooden floor. Though there was a time when she had been afforded three raps, the staff landed but once. "Lady Helenia Briain."

The Ombratians had used her title out of respect. Beyond their royalty, the Fallen bore no further distinctions within their ranks, so they cared not a whit for the various titles given to Tithen nobles. But coming from the Master of Ceremony's mouth, "Lady" sounded little better than a curse. Yet, in the face of death, it was a petty slight, and she clung to her minor irritation as one might cling to a raft in a troubled sea.

Like the rest of the palace, Curmhalt's throne room had been built to intimidate any who stepped inside it. The short hall was empty of furnishings but filled with people. Blocky wooden pillars broke up the space and held the high-vaulted ceiling aloft. A rose window, the stained glass depicting the Ten Stations of Burk, took up much of the far wall. When the sun shone through it, the different sections lit up the room with a rainbow of colors, but in the rainy gloom, lit from the inside by torches and candles, the pictures in the glass were flat, lifeless.

Harsh whispers chased Helenia down the hall. These people, the nobles of Tithen, their favor had mattered to her once. She had needed them, if not as friends then as allies. But she had been tried twice, for treason and in the court of public opinion, and though she had avoided the chopping block, her reputation was tarnished beyond repair. She squared her shoulders and forced herself to look at her detractors as she passed.

The men and women who lined the hall appeared much as they always had. The nobles of Tithen liked to show off in their dress. Yards of fabric laid over wide panniers made the women walking barges, and the men wore golden chains wrapped around the curled wigs fashioned long enough to brush the floor. Jewels the sizes of various birds' eggs were set in gold, and they perched on fingers or dripped from ears or around necks. This marked show of opulence, once commonplace to Helenia, now stood out as the basest demonstrations of newly earned wealth and status.

Let them play their silly noble games while I vie for the fate of nations. Rather than worry her more, that thought settled her, and she let it carry her.

Behind her, the Master of Ceremony rapped on the floor four times and called out, "Dallan Kellifer Briain, fourth son of Adameth and Prince of Tithen."

They had stricken Mayve's name from the title in the divorce. What did Mayve make of that? Helenia's concern distracted her, and she made the mistake of looking straight ahead.

King Adameth's angles were so stark he might have been chiseled from granite. He had kept his head shaved for as long as she had known him, and elaborate tattoos circled his black eyes. There had never been any love lost between her and her brother-by-law, but his scorn, like so many other things, had been easier to bear before Carhal's death. Before the trial.

He wore leather armor that was creased and dull around the joints, and that it didn't creak when he moved proved it well-worn and meant for more than show. A naked blade, Ever-Watchful Eyes inscribed down the length of it, rested against the side of his throne.

A shiver racked Helenia's body at the remembered sensation of its cold edge pressed against her throat. She swallowed and returned her gaze to the floor. When she reached the farthest spot from the throne at which it was respectful to stop, she fell to one knee and stared at Adameth's feet. Silent submission. That was how she had survived before and how she would do so again. With any luck, it was also how she'd bring Dallan back to her side.

Another four raps. "Seifan Alger Briain, third son of Adameth, Decorated Commander of Wolf Company, Master of the Sword, and Prince of Tithen."

Dallan reached Helenia's side and stopped, bowing but not kneeling. With quick steps, Seifan overtook them both, climbed the steps to the dais, and took a place behind his father's throne. Helenia kept her head bowed, but, now that Adameth's attention was on his sons, she raised her gaze to see how this little reunion played out.

Adameth nodded at Dallan, and Dallan cleared his throat. "I bring gifts from Ombratos, Father." A pair of servants brought forth a small wooden crate.

"Do you?" Adameth said. He gestured toward the plain box. "And are these meant to make up for your shameful return?"

The nobles laughed outright, not even bothering to hide their titters behind their hands. The tips of Dallan's ears turned a bright shade of crimson, but he kept his head held high.

Next to the king, a young woman with hair the color of carrots shifted in her more delicate throne. How could Helenia have missed his new wife, her hair and tattoos naming her as one of the Praely girls? Young, perhaps even a couple of years younger than Dallan, she rubbed at the small bump of her belly under the shelf of her enormous breasts. Had Adameth even waited until the ink was dry on his divorce papers before taking this girl to his bed?

The girl—Helenia couldn't remember her first name—pointed at the crate. "Is this all?" she asked in the high, nasal whine of a child.

Dallan asked one of the servants to open the box. "Begging your pardon, Queen Bethana."

Bethana. That's right

"I think you'll find the trinkets to be small, but impressive. There is nothing else like them in the whole of Tithen. In the whole of Althea, even."

She sniffed and sat back in her chair. The top of the crate came off, revealing a nest of wood shavings. The servant pawed through the shavings and pulled out a couple of unlit globes, but without the fire burning within, they looked like nothing more than balls of cloudy glass. Adameth motioned the servant forward, and he carried the globes up to the dais, placing them gently in the hands of the king.

"I want to hold one," Bethana cried, and Adameth, with an indulgent smile, handed one to her. She closed an eye and pressed the ball to the other, peering into its murky, unlit depths.

"They're called globes," Dallan said. "They're a light source, like a candle or a torch, but they don't give off any heat or smoke."

"Doesn't look like it gives off much of anything," Adameth said, giving the other to Seifan, who held it like he might a hunk of dried horse shit.

Dallan hesitated. "It requires a sort of, uh, catalyst to spark the flame inside."

"What's a catalyst?" Adameth asked.

Helenia misliked his tone, and she expected Dallan to dance around the meaning, but he took a deep breath and ran straight at it. "Blood. It needs a drop of your blood and then you need to say a couple of words. It's as minor a working as they come."

Adameth grabbed the globe from Bethana's hand. She opened her mouth to whine, but a look at her husband's face warned her off it.

"Do it," Adameth said.

Dallan's brow creased. "I beg your pardon."

The king sat forward in his throne and held out the globe. "Bleed on it and say your little words," he said, unaware of the forbidden nature in the Ombratian culture of what he asked for.

Proof Dallan had been among the Fallen for far too long, proof he was more Ombratian than Tithen, he blurted out, "No. Never."

A tense hush gripped the room, and Helenia bit down hard on her upper lip to hold back her smile.

"What?" Adameth's soft-spoken word should have been lost in the great room, but it cut through the silence like blade through silk.

Dallan held his ground. "I'm sorry, Father," he said, not sounding very sorry at all. "It's just that the globes are yours, a gift to you, and it's considered inappropriate to ask someone for their blood."

Adameth, already as motionless as a statue, somehow stilled even further. "It is, is it?"

He stared at Dallan for a long time, and Helenia's lungs burned from the breath she held. The men were so alike as to be total opposites, their animosity blooming from that which they saw of themselves in the other.

With sudden movement, Adameth unfroze, sat back, and tossed the globe over Dallan's head, into a knot of nobles. Most of them cried out, stepping back, but one brave man reached for it. It slipped through his fingers, and a couple of ladies shrieked, no doubt expecting it to land and shatter. But it did nothing more than hit the wooden floor with a loud *thock* before rolling beneath a woman's skirt.

The same man who had reached for the globe as it flew through the air, knelt and stuck his hand under the voluminous layers, eliciting another shriek, and pulled out the glass ball. He turned it over in his hand and then held it above his head. "Not so much as a crack, Your Majesty!"

Amazed whispers floated up into the rafters, and even Adameth showed some interest at that. He beckoned the man forward, took the globe back from him, and examined it himself.

Dallan shrugged, his relief evident in the loose set of his shoulders. "Though the glass appears delicate, they can withstand quite a lot of abuse. I've even dropped one myself a time or two."

Seifan, not to be outdone, stepped to the center of the dais, tucked the globe he held under an arm, pulled a dagger from his belt, and dragged it across his palm, leaving a line of blood. *Idiot.* That wound would take an age to heal unless he allowed a fire wife to burn it closed. Sheathing his dagger, he wiped his bloodied hand over the glass. "If you are too much of a coward to share your blood, little brother, then tell me the words to say."

Dallan smiled at Seifan's ridiculous presentation. "A single drop was all you required."

Adameth slammed his fist down on the arm of his throne, the sound echoing through the room. "Seifan gives more than is necessary and without being asked. I see no humor in that. Tell him the words."

Dallan told Seifan the words, repeating them several times before Seifan's pronunciation was correct, but the moment Seifan spoke with the right inflection and in the proper tone, the globe flared to life, the light bright and clear, if tinged red from his blood.

Many in the room gasped. Seifan's hand twitched around the glass ball, and Bethana jerked away from the one in her husband's hand, as if it might burst into flames of its own accord. Adameth alone seemed unmoved by the wonder, his face unreadable as he stared at the globe.

Dallan bowed. "It has been good to see you, Father, but the road to Morleon is long and night approaches. If you have no objection, I shall take my leave."

"No." The word came out before Helenia might stop it. But Dallan couldn't go and leave her in the wolf's den. Not before she had her chance to win him back.

"Helenia," Adameth said, not bothering with her title, and she closed her eyes.

The only way forward is back. The only way forward is back.

When she opened her eyes, she found Adameth walking toward her, naked blade in hand, and her tremors returned in force. He came closer and closer, until he towered over her. He stood there for a moment, then, in a swift move, held out the blade. She flinched away from it, but he only used it to tease out a fold of her skirt.

"You're still in white. I'm sure my brother would be touched."

His words teetered on the edge of sarcasm, but didn't quite cross the line. Adameth had always hated Helenia as much as he loved Carhal, and at this very moment, he wanted to deny her love for his brother. But despite others' doubts, he'd known and believed in Carhal's ability to hear truths. This meant when Carhal told his brother Helenia said she loved him, and her words resonated in his mind with their truthfulness, Adameth had been forced to concede her sincerity. So, questioning her love, even now, meant impugning Carhal's legacy, which Adameth would never do. It was an internal war for Adameth, one waged in the small ticks across his face. She wanted to poke him, to call him out for it. A year ago, safe behind the bulwark that had been her marriage to Carhal, she would have. Much had changed in the past year, however, and her survival, her victory lay in her silent submission.

Adameth dug the point of his sword into the wood in front of her knees. "Kiss the blade and pledge your fealty to me," he said, his voice ringing out in the hall.

He had demanded the same of her when last they spoke, and the hate she bore for him then was as it was now, as deep and endless as the sea. Her nails bit into the skin of her palms. "Again?"

He moved in and said, "Again and again. As many times as I wish."

His threat that she might be forced to relive this humiliation at his hands whenever he pleased might have cowed a lesser woman, the sort of woman who didn't understand how someone might sacrifice so much of her pride and still be able to live with herself. Yet Helenia had learned at her father's knee that pride was a false idol worshiped by the foolish and the dead.

"Do you need to be reminded of the words?" Adameth asked, sounding like a man offering a woman his hand to dance.

She shook her head, requiring no assistance to remember the words that had saved her life. "I pledge my fealty to you, King Adameth, and to Tithen, today, tomorrow, and for the rest of my life. May Burk watch over you, keeping you above all others in his sight, so that you may rule over us in your infinite wisdom and grace."

"Very pretty," he said. Then he tilted the blade toward her face. "Only you forgot something."

The Ever-Watchful Eyes along the blade stared at her with their empty, baleful glares, and bile rose in her throat as she pressed her lips to the icy, unforgiving steel.

When she moved back, he handed the blade off to an attendant, placed a finger under her chin, and forced her chin up so she might face him. As he did this, a litany sprang into her mind. *One day, one day, one day...* One day this man would die by her hand. But this was not yet that day. She met his eyes for a fleeting moment, then looked away as if incapable of more.

Expecting a dismissal, she started when he leaned in close. "Will you run off to Mayve now?" he whispered, his question for her alone.

She held back a ruinous laugh. He feared her and Mayve together; he always had. "I'll send your regards."

He chuckled, surprising her again. "Don't bother." Forgetting her efforts at submission, she raised her eyes and met his gaze. "Oh, Helenia, I wish you could have seen how quick Mayve was to give me my divorce once Morleon was on the table."

Not satisfied with her humiliation, he'd conjured up a lie to rattle her even more. The pain of losing Morleon still stung, but Helenia had agreed with Mayve that she'd rather see the duchy in Mayve's hands than in those of a stranger. She knew better than to take his bait, and yet, "What else was she meant to do when you offered it to her?"

Adameth's face lit up, and Helenia braced herself for his next cruelty. "You misunderstand." He shook his head. "The plan for our divorce, for Mayve to take Morleon, she offered it to me." He pressed his cheek to hers. "She offered it to me the very night my guards arrested you."

His words struck her like a hand to the face. "You lie."

"I don't. But without my brother's skill, you can't be certain, can you?"

"I can," she said, with far more conviction than she felt.

He smiled at her and stood. "Now you may take your leave," he said over his shoulder as he walked back to his throne.

Shaken to her core, she stumbled to her feet with the lack of grace of a woman twice her age and shuffled from the room.

Adameth lied because he wanted nothing more than to drive a wedge between her and Mayve, but tears clouded her vision. She didn't even realize she'd returned to the antechamber until Dallan stopped and offered her his arm. She took it, allowing him to lead her down the hall. They passed an open door, and he turned back.

Those who held positions of the crown were given offices near the throne room in which to conduct their businesses. This study, with its heavy mahogany furniture and yards upon yards of golden brocade, was as overdressed as the nobles they had left behind, but a crackling fire burned in the grate. Dallan led her inside and sat with her on the couch in front of the fire. The warmth of it did little to comfort her.

She offered it to me.

"I'm sorry," Dallan said, his voice drowning out the echo of his father's. He stared at his hands, and his hard shell broke away to crumble at their feet.

The plan, she reminded herself. *Your plan to win Dallan back.*

He shrugged. "That whole mess with Father was my fault. I suppose you can see why I return to Tithen so seldom."

She nodded, his forgiveness bringing the tears back to her eyes. He opened his arms, and she embraced him, clinging to his solidity, the surety of his kindness. Her gambit had worked. Adameth, in humiliating her in front of his softhearted son, had given her one of the greatest gifts she had ever received.

That witless, prideful jackass had just handed her the key.

Holding Dallan tighter, she reveled in her triumph and did her best to ignore the sliver of doubt lodged in her heart.

TEN

"Experience often teaches us the lessons that words cannot."
-Waltham

Getha lay on the roof of the stables, her hands pressed to the spot on her chest where Orli had hit her. Though the worst of the pain had eased, a growing bruise throbbed under her fingers. Stars like salt spilled across a field of black filled the sky above her, but Amma's face shone brightest of all. In Getha's mind, she relived the fight over and over. She remembered every thought, every choice, every movement, and Maurius's announcement of the new varos echoed in her ears. Had the secrets of Transformation never been lost, she would have paid an alchemist every last coin she'd ever saved for a charm to turn her into a worm or a snake, some sort of creature that might wriggle underground and live in the darkness without worry or care.

The roof shook as someone climbed the ladder to the hayloft. With her scheduled to be on duty this evening, perhaps it was another guard sent to find her. She didn't bother sitting up. Who cared about the warnings they gave for first infractions? Her otherwise unblemished record might suggest that she did, but it was already too late to unbreak that bowl.

The door swung open and hit the roof with a *thunk*. She couldn't stop herself from jumping to her feet, knives in hand. The shadow outlined by the light coming up from the stables snorted. "You do have some life left in you. Good to know."

"Piss off, Waltham." She relaxed her stance and shoved the blades back into place with more force than needed. One of the springs gave way, releasing the knife back into her hand, and with that, the dam she had built over the past two days broke and a searing river of anger burst forth. "Goat-fucking-shit-breathed-son-of-a-motherless-bastard!"

"Well," Waltham said, sounding taken aback. "I'd say I've been called worse, but... "

She hadn't meant to point all her fury in his direction, which made her even angrier. Falling to her knees, she slammed her blade down into the roof. "Shit!"

Waltham reared back, but punching that hole in the roof was like punching a hole in a bucket; all of her rage drained away, leaving her feeling empty and useless.

"You finished, then?"

Releasing the knife handle, she slumped back on her heels.

He reached out. "Give me a hand, will you?" She grabbed him, her bloodmark tingling as it met his, and helped him climb the last few rungs. Then he let go, brushed off his gnarled hands, and grunted as he sat beside her, facing out at the city, blowing out a low whistle from between his teeth. "Would you look at that?"

She turned. Ombratos showed a fine face in the day, but it shone even prettier at night. The windows of the palace glowed, globes marked off the straight, even streets of the Bole, wavering torches spilled golden puddles across the Branches, and bobbing lights danced in the harbor. Even Shade's Rest gleamed out beyond the Gift. She had come so far. So far, but no farther.

Our new varo will be Frena Catala and Nils Roher.

She put her head in her hands. "What did I do wrong?"

He sighed. "Let's not head down that road."

Part of her hadn't wanted him to answer. Or at least it hadn't until he didn't. "No," she said. "Let's. What did I do wrong?"

"Listen to me, squirrel." *Squirrel?* He hadn't called her that in years. "I think it's best if you—"

"Stop." She calmly pulled her knife out of the roof. The whole first inch had snapped right off. Ignoring that, she set the blade down between them. "I know I've been behaving like some fluttery highborn, but I'm better now. You can tell me true."

He paused, then said, "You did nothing wrong."

"Nothing?" The pain in her chest returned. "Then why wasn't I made varo?"

He sighed again, the sound carrying with it the weariness of a man twice his age. "There are obligations that come with the title... When they say you're a varo for life, they aren't lying. Those Bindings last forever, and they're tied very tight."

She picked up the blade and pressed the broken tip to her left palm. "Not to mention how unworthy I proved to be."

"No," he said. "You proved too worthy."

What in the pathless hells is that supposed to mean? "Too worthy?" Waltham gentled her on occasion, but he had never lied to her, not even to give comfort.

He patted her arm. "If you still want varo—the title, the Binding, the weight of it all—then eventually your day will come."

His faith did more to bolster her than anything else. "You think?"

"I do," he said. "Keep up with your studies and your training, and you will distinguish yourself in such a way that no one will be able to ignore."

He made it sound so simple. So possible. She thought of Orli, of the viciousness of his attack in the ring. "What good will that do me if the lead varo hates me?"

"Don't you worry about that," Waltham said, his voice going flat. "The varo is a lifetime appointment, but no lead varo can hold that position forever." The stark line of his profile was black against the star-draped sky. "Not even Orli, no matter what he believes."

A chill brushed the back of her neck, her hairs standing on end. Waltham had been set off to the side within the varo before she ever met him, so it was easy to forget the history behind his title, easy to forget that within his wrinkled, bowed body beat the heart of a warrior.

Then Waltham grabbed at his side, at the once-broken ribs that sometimes still ached, and moaned, the warrior retreating. "Now swallow down the last of that pity, get on your feet, and help me down before I fall. Rolling off a roof is no way for an old soldier to die."

She tucked the broken knife into her belt and stood. Seedfall boasted one of the finest bladesmiths in the city; she'd have to make a trip to Menders' Row in the morning. "What is the way for an old soldier to die?"

"With a blade in his hand and a curse on his lips."

She laughed, reaching out for him. "So shall it be."

Getha rose before the dawn and strapped on her vambrace with the unbroken blade, leaving the other behind. She finished running her second lap around the outside of the palace as the first rays of sunlight speared through the morning haze and the city bells began to toll three. The day promised to be a warm one. Running back to the practice yard, she joined the early training session, pushing herself hard to make up for her missed day.

Once complete, the training captain called her over and served her official notice of her warning. She finished by saying, "I'm surprised at you, Barei. Never thought you would be the sort to fall apart like that. Try not to let it happen again."

Behind Getha, the whispers of the other guards buzzed in her ears, her name and "forsaken" jumping out among the otherwise insensible murmurs and hisses. Instead of standing at the bathing trough with them, she chose to rinse off in the Sap. Menders' Row would be on her way back, so before she went to the river, she returned to her barracks to retrieve her broken blade and vambrace.

There was a spot not far from the palace where the river narrowed and the current slowed enough that someone careful might wade in and not have to worry about being swept off her feet. A crescent of muddy sand jutted out from the west bank. Setting her vambrace and knife on the grassy ridge surrounding the tiny beach, she knelt in the sand, took a deep breath, and dunked her whole head beneath the flowing waters.

Her face ached with the cold, and the frigid ice melt stole the breath from her chest. When she couldn't stand another moment, she rose with a gasp, her wet hair hanging around her face like a curtain, and across the narrow stretch of river, a horse pawed at the dirt of the riding trail, sending up small clouds of dust.

Getha swept her hair over her shoulders, bowing her chest out as runnels of freezing water ran down her sweaty back and sides. And found Princess Renn, wearing a rough pair of riding leathers with a hole in the left knee, staring down at her from the saddle.

The princess gave a little laugh. "You're a braver woman than I."

How did someone reply to that? Getha had spent many a candlemark standing guard in the princess's general presence, and she'd learned the proper form of address, but none of the Morovides had ever spoken directly to her before.

A bit of advice from her training returned to her. *It's not a palace guard's place to have an opinion. Always agree with a member of the royal family, even if asked to speak your mind.* But mindless agreement ran against Getha's very nature.

"How so, Your Highness?" she asked, trying to sound respectful as she did.

The princess raised an eyebrow, giving Getha doubts as to her success. Waltham had told her to distinguish herself, but he probably hadn't meant for her to do so with impertinence. She was about to apologize when the princess smiled and pointed at the river. "That water must be terribly cold. I don't think I could even stand to dip my hand in there."

Relieved, Getha decided to at last follow her old lesson. "Yes, Your Highness."

The princess's smile faded. She untucked a long black curl from behind her ear and pulled it in front of her face. Tossing it aside, she said, "Of course." Then she clucked to her horse and rode off toward the stables.

Waltham often called the highborn inscrutable, and this encounter had done nothing to discourage Getha from that notion.

She continued rinsing off and was chilled through when she finished, but the sun and a brisk pace soon warmed her. She arrived at the row to find it filled with people from the palace going about the day's business. The metalsmiths worked in several open shelters near the end of the row, and heat poured from their forges, adding to the warmth of the day. The surplus home where Getha grew up had been next to a farrier's, and the ring of metal against metal brought comfort and loneliness in equal measures.

At the bladesmith's enclosure, Getha spoke to one of Darazo's apprentices, a young man about eight years her junior named Sabrian.

"Darazo was called up to the palace this morning." Sabrian set down his polishing and hurried around the table to take a stack of burlap off an old barrel near the door. "If you want to wait, he should be back soon."

The heat of the forge and the hopeful expression on Sabrian's face convinced her she'd rather wait outside. She hooked a thumb over her shoulder. "It's a bit warm in here for me. I'll be on the row."

His face fell, but she turned away from his disappointment and stepped outside. Though it had been at least four moons since her last tumble, she had neither the time nor the inclination to roll around with some untried youth. Even if that youth did have a nice smile and well-muscled forearms. A cool breeze cut down the row, and she faced into it, allowing the wind to brush her still-drying hair from her shoulders and any lingering frustration from her mind.

"Excuse me," a servant said, cutting around her.

Moving out of the thoroughfare, she stood near the rungs of the short fence marking the bladesmith's shop. She needed to think of a positive way to make herself stand out, and if she did so sooner than later, it would cast Orli in a poor light for refusing her the position.

Orli. What had Waltham meant when he said that he wouldn't be lead varo forever? *No matter what he believes.*

From the direction of the practice yards and the stables, a quiet fell over the row. People stepped to the walls and bowed one after another, like a wave nearing the shore, and Princess Renn strode through the center of it, the hole over her left knee that gaping and closing with every step. Some called out blessings as she passed, and she waved when they did, but the movements were curt, her smile tight. Perhaps even princesses grew tired of all that bowing and scraping everywhere they went.

The only person not bent in respect was the varo who walked half a step behind her, his head swinging from side to side as he looked at every person and into every doorway or window they passed. Roher. The sight of him in his varo uniform hit Getha like an elbow to the gut. Torn between concern that the princess might talk to her again and not wanting to seem cowed by Roher in his new position, she bowed before protocol demanded and looked up the instant Princess Renn passed. She met Roher's eyes, and the swiftness with which his gaze slid from hers told her exactly what it needed to—that they both knew that his varo blade, his title, his role rightfully belonged to her.

Cold comfort, but Getha embraced it all the same.

The princess slowed and stopped about twenty feet down, at the same door she had entered several days earlier. She spoke to Roher, her voice low, but Getha caught the last few words. "...and no one other than my maid is allowed to enter. Is that clear?"

Roher nodded and put his back to the building. The princess opened the door partway and, with a furtive glance up and down the row, slipped through the crack before the door snapped shut behind her.

The princess's actions struck Getha as odd even for a highborn, so she did her best to watch the door without seeming to watch it. With the princess out of sight, noise on the row returned to its former din as servants hastened to and fro on their errands, gathering up whatever bits of news or gossip they could along the way. The door, behind which the princess did Amma knew what, remained closed.

Just then, Darazo, the man Getha waited for, appeared in the crowd, a bulging leather satchel slung over one narrow shoulder. He reminded Getha of a dagger, silent and sharp on all sides. Coming to an abrupt halt before his shop, he bowed a little and waved for her to enter before him. She had never seen him in such a fine mood. Not wanting to spoil it before she had to, she hurried inside.

Sabrian straightened in his seat as she walked in, but slumped back down over his polishing when he noticed Darazo following her. Darazo set down his satchel on the end of Sabrian's table and held his stub-fingered hands out to her. She hesitated, then laid the blade in one and the vambrace in the other. He lifted the blade—one of six he had made especially for her—and the missing tip earned her a reproachful glare, his good mood waning. Of course, that glare did nothing to rival the storm that crossed his face when he tried to slip the knife into its broken catch.

"I'm sorry," she said.

He stared at her.

"I'm so very sorry, Master Darazo. Can you fix it?"

If he refused her, it wouldn't be the first time. Unlike many at the palace, he seemed to like her, but he was fickle in a way that only a genius of his craft could be. After a long, hard look, he set the blade and the vambrace on the table next to his satchel. He covered his eyes with his right hand and then held up two fingers. Two days.

"Thank you." She rushed out before he changed his mind.

While she'd spoken with Darazo, clouds had stolen across the sky, but the quality of the light, the persistent, dazzling glare, told her they approached midday, which brought the start of her shift. Part of her expected Roher to be gone, the princess having moved on, but the varo remained at his post, and Getha's curiosity grew.

She had little time to waste and no intention of being late, but something told her to wait a few moments more. Walking to the far end of the row, she tucked in behind the tree that provided a bit of shade for the fletchers.

As people hurried off to eat or serve the midday meal, the crowd thinned, and Getha was about to leave when an unfamiliar woman with yellow hair, a basket on her arm, and a bounce in her step caught her eye. The yellow-haired woman, dressed in riding leathers similar to those the princess had worn, skipped less than ten feet down the lane before a servant, a scullery worker judging by the livery, ran into her, knocking the basket she carried to the ground.

The scullery worker rushed on without apologizing or missing a step, and the yellow-haired woman, on the short side for an Ombratian, responded to the rudeness with a broad smile. As she bent to pick up the fallen basket, she even laughed. Without a care, she brushed dust from the wicker with a sleeve that hung down to her fingertips, and when she continued on, her cuffs dragged in the dirt. She walked for a few feet, then lifted her left leg in a little hop-step, and a hole gaped just below the knee.

Getha's confusion deepened when the woman approached the door where Roher stood guard, and he stepped aside to let the stranger through the door.

A thousand thoughts, few of them sensible, flew through Getha's mind. While she thought, she left her position near the tree. The obvious answer would be to confront Roher, but instead of doing that, she circled around the end of the row in the hopes of finding a window in the back.

Amma be praised, she found one. Crouching down, she crept along the wall until she came to it, then she rose inch by inch and met the weathered slats of closed shutters. But a knot in one of the wooden boards had worn away to create a narrow hole where the shutters met in the middle. She pressed her eye to the gap, and a fall of undyed muslin further blocked her view.

Behind the muslin, wood scraped against hard-packed dirt and a basket rustled. Putting her lips to the narrow slit between the shutters, Getha blew. The curtain billowed inward and flipped off the side, giving her a brief glimpse of the back of a yellow head before the muslin fell back into her way. Getha waited a moment, then blew again. The curtain opened, and the edge caught on something, clearing her view. So as not to cast a moving shadow around the room, she remained as still as possible.

The room was empty but for a worn table and a single chair, on which the yellow-haired woman sat with her back to the window. On the battered table, a globe lit every corner and surface from its expensive copper sconce. A pile of papers rested at one end of the table, a covered bowl at the other, and set between the two, an even line of unrecognizable tools. No sign of the princess, but a closed door suggested at least one other room. What if the princess was trussed up, laying on the floor right below the window? Roher seemed unconcerned for his charge, but as he had proved by looking away from Getha, they both knew she would have made the better varo.

She released the catch on her working vambrace, and the knife fell into her hand. Inside, the woman stood, went to the door to check the latch, then turned and placed her back to it. Getha raised her arm back to hammer in the old slats—*one good hit, maybe two*—when the woman reached inside her tunic and pulled out...

If pressed to name it, Getha might have called it a charm but for its size. The full length neared the size of her palm, and instead of being wrapped in ribbon or thread, a cage of thin silver wire bound the cloudy pink stone. It hung around the woman's neck on a length of fine silver chain, and she turned the charm, or whatever it was, over and over in her hand.

Then she slipped the necklace off over her head, and right before Getha's eyes, the woman...changed. Her body stretched, narrowing in the breasts and hips but growing in height. The yellow hair curled and lengthened, and as if a shadow fell over the room, darkened slowly, the flaxen glow soon eclipsed by locks the sheen and color of a raven's wing. She raised long-fingered hands to touch her nose and lips. While the changing hair had held Getha attention, the woman's face had shifted from the rounded prettiness of a lowborn to the delicate, fine-boned features of Princess Renn Morovide.

Getha managed to hold herself up until the princess turned from the window, at which point her knees gave out and she fell to the dirt like a sack of turnips. Though she had never seen it before, she knew she had just watched the forgotten art of Transformation. She, one of the forsaken, one of the children unworthy of being brought up within the protective shadow of the Gift, had been chosen by Amma to witness the reclamation of a Lost Pillar.

She reset her blade, and with her hands in her lap, she sparked her bloodmark over and over, trying to remember how to breathe.

ELEVEN

"Transformation requires the head of a scholar, the heart of an artist, and the soul of a trickster. Even the most practiced working may yield unexpected results."
-From Galathar Morovide's private journal

Several days later, in the front room of Parneo's secret study on Menders' Row, Renn closed her eyes and hung the Transformation amulet around her neck. She'd been experimenting with it for a little over a tenday, and she'd started living for the moment she donned her second skin. Turning into someone else let her forget how much she missed Dallan and how much she still wanted to chase after him. It allowed her to leave the ineffectual princess behind as she became a lowborn, as she became someone with purpose.

As the change took hold, she wondered about the other face and body, where they had come from or how Parneo had formed them. She thought to ask him when the shift finished, but then the thought slipped from her mind and left a blissful dullness in its wake. Beyond her more high-minded reasons for liking the change, she also loved that dullness. Transforming hung a sheer veil between her and the rest of the world, and that distance made the absences in her life easier to bear.

Everyone else in her family had something to occupy their days. Parn had his alchemy and Father his drinking. She didn't know what Dace was up to since his last letter to her sat unopened on her desk, but Heshi spent every waking candlemark, and most of her non-waking ones, with The Spares. Theodora had receded even further into her hole, and Linore ruled the city in all but name. She also slept more and more, whenever her presence wasn't required, and ate less and less, making her appear like a specter, one that had died of starvation.

A royal family in another country might fear for their throne, but Ombratos would never leave the Morovides' hands because it couldn't. The throne was Bound to their bloodline and theirs alone. So they muddled their way through, traveling along the path on which they'd been set, together, yet apart.

Parneo knocked on the closed door between the front and back rooms of his study. "Are you finished?" he asked, and she could practically hear his irritated glare.

She smiled to herself. At least she had Parn. "Almost." She adjusted her breastband, and once it was loosened, she tucked the heavy Transformation amulet inside, next to Dallan's letter.

"I just need the jar of crushed deathtick beetle." The latch clicked, the door opened a crack, and a hand poked through. "You could find it and hand it to me." He wiggled his fingers.

Renn looked around. Every surface, from the shelves lining the walls to the worktable taking up much of the center of the room, sagged under the weight of books, papers, and hundreds of jars and vials, which bore every sort of chemical, powder, or liquid an alchemist might need, and all of them were labeled in Parneo's cramped scrawl. Even by the bright light of the four globes perched around the room, it would take her an age to find a tiny bottle of beetle dust.

She slapped his hand. When he pulled it back, she shut the door. "One more moment and I'll be done."

Though new to dressing herself, Renn had found the trick of it: determine the correct positioning of the clothing *before* putting it on. She located the front of the tunic and slipped it over her head, and then slipped into a pair of breeches with a single tie around the middle, a lowborn fashion for which she was grateful. It hadn't been too difficult undoing the laces on Dallan's highborn breeches, but fixing them up again had looked a bit tricky.

Stop. Since she'd yet to think of a way to bring him back, she had to trust what he'd said in his letter, that he would return to her.

Breeches on, she strapped a purse onto her belt. She'd never worn one, and the heaviness of the coins on her hip surprised her. Decent at last, or decent enough for her brother, she unlatched the door and sat on a stool to slip on her boots. Another trick she had learned—sitting while putting on one's shoes. That lesson had come at a cost, to which the yellowing bruise on her elbow could attest. Parneo, ever sympathetic, had been fascinated to discover that the wound carried over from one form to the other.

He propped open the door with a worn stone bust of Queen Elissianne —smiling as he did so, as if the irreverence of using it for such a purpose gave him some sort of pleasure—and went straight to one of the shelves. Wrapping his hands around a huge ceramic jar, he hefted it up and carried it into the other room.

"Is that the crushed beetle?" She stood and followed him through. The back room was much neater, but out of necessity, it being where he conducted his trials. "That seems like a lot."

Ignoring her, he opened the jar and scooped two heaping spoonsful of the finely ground powder into the bowl in the center of the table. She loved this Parneo. Everyone else saw the confusion and the fits, but this keen, intense young man was the brother she knew best. He picked up a knife and sliced open the narrow stem of a gillyflower with a steady hand. Only alchemy could center him like this. Only alchemy quieted the voices in his mind, the voices that he alone heard.

She ran her fingers along the edge of his worktable. "Come with me."

After all of her masquerading around Seedfall as a lowborn, she was leaving the palace grounds, and butterflies danced in her belly at the thought of entering the city without guards. Not to mention the task of finding the man in the night market and asking him questions she didn't understanding about a process she barely comprehended.

But she didn't have to go alone. Parneo had his own amulet. Identical to hers, it hung on a peg next to the door.

"Are you sure you won't come with me?" she asked.

He used the flat of his blade to collect the slime inside the gillyflower stem.

Taking a different tack, she said, "I don't know why you made yours if you aren't going to use it." Goading him had worked often enough when they were children.

But less so now. "I did use it." He wiped the slime off the knife and into the bowl, where it almost seemed to writhe around in the beetle dust.

"Once," she said. "You used it once." Parneo's other form was a tall, weedy boy with black eyes and a mess of dirt-brown hair. "Don't you want to see what it's like to be a lowborn, what it's like to walk around without a swarm of keepers dogging your every move?"

He shook his head. "That wasn't the purpose of this experiment."

"Then what was the purpose?"

"To see if I could do it. To see how it felt." Pride crept into his voice. "Both were successful."

She reminded herself it was a lot harder for him outside these walls, away from his alchemy, surrounded by people, and decided to stop pushing him. "What are you working on?"

He set down the knife and handed her an empty vial. "I need more."

A pang shot through the middle finger of her left hand. "So soon?" Though she always used a healing charm and the slices healed well enough, she thought a scar might be forming on the digit from how often it was cut.

"I'm on the brink of something." He leaned over a page to make a note on what looked like a very complicated formula. "And you don't bleed much, so my supply goes quickly."

"Terribly sorry. What if I sliced down the length of my arm? Would that be enough blood for you?"

"Yes," he said. "Quite." He peered at her over his lenses, which had slipped to the end of his nose. "But that amount of blood loss might kill you."

She shivered. She adored this Parneo, but sometimes he could be practical to a fault. He kept the penknife he used to "extract samples" in the other room, so she went to fetch it. Strong fumes stung her eyes and the inside of her nose as she dipped the knife into a jar of pure alcohol.

Returning to Parneo, she handed him the blade. "Not too deep."

He took her finger, always the same one, and grabbed it with his scarred alchemist's hands. She turned her head away and clenched her teeth. Blood had never bothered her, not before, but now the sight of it made her stomach churn. The blade bit into her flesh, and she started. He held her tight. With Solena gone, Parneo was the only person she felt close enough to let spill her blood.

"I just wish you had another source," she said.

"Linore or Heshi's blood would be as useful as yours, I'm sure."

"And I'm sure either one of them would tell Theodora about this study so she could have it pulled apart."

"True." He squeezed her finger, coaxing every last drop from the burning cut. "Done," he said, dropping her hand.

He'd filled less than half of the vial, yet her finger ached as if he'd wrung it dry.

He stoppered the glass tube, set it aside, and pulled a familiar charm from his pocket. Threads of clean linen wrapped around a bloodstained hunk of soapstone no larger than a quail's egg—a healing charm. He wiped her finger clean with the linen and put the charm in her palm, then he mouthed the incantation as she spoke it—*"inte ac vitgarar"*—and when the charm began to give off a faint glow, he eased her fingers closed around it.

The tenderness caught her by surprise, and a fierce wave of love and protectiveness for her twin swept over her. Before he could return to his work, she pulled him into a hug. He stiffened and kept his arms at his side —in truth, it was a little like embracing a wooden bedpost—but for once, he didn't try to squirm away.

"Maybe," he said, his voice tentative. "Maybe now that I'm older..."

"Oh, Parn." She squeezed tighter. "No matter what you discover, Theodora won't let you attend the academy." She let go and stepped back. "You know that, right?"

The muscles in his jaw tightened, and he bent over his formula. She hated admonishing him, but his desire to enter the Academy of Alchemical Studies never waned, and in this, he forced her to be the voice of reason. Which had developed its own irony, given how she pined for a man who might never return. Without thought, her hand rose to the spot where her flowering charm had hung. She missed the actual moments they'd spent together, but she also longed for the parts of their life they had yet to share, so who was she to crush her twin's dreams?

"I'm sorry," she said.

Parn, already lost again in his work, looked up at her. "For what?"

She didn't know how to explain without telling him she'd stayed in Ombratos not because of him, but because that was what Dallan had asked of her. "Never mind."

The glow of the healing charm faded, meaning the wound on her finger was gone. She opened her hand, and if not for the slight lingering pain, she could have believed it had never been cut. She set the spent charm on a corner of the table, then went to the window.

"Are you sure *I* shouldn't go to the academy?" she asked. "Linore did say High Alchemist Rande was looking into this too."

His head flew up. "Rande? But I thought Tusson—"

"Everyone thought Tusson," Renn said, naming the alchemist most had expected to succeed High Alchemist Marcal. "Turns out Kitra Rande took the office this afternoon."

"Oh."

She unlatched the shutters and drew them back. Most of the color had drained from the sky, and the warmth from the day was fast retreating. Amma winked at Renn from the sea of black overhead, and she aimed a blasphemous gesture at her in response. Childish, she knew, but she didn't care. Her prayer locket sat in a drawer of her desk that she hadn't reopened since the day of Solena's death.

Renn poked her head out into the alley behind the row. A few crickets—their song rising as the sun finished setting—lurked in the otherwise empty shadows. She tried to throw a leg over the sill, but her reduced height and shorter legs made that impossible. Grabbing a stool from the front room, she placed it under the window, climbed up, and straddled the sill.

Parneo fiddled with something on his worktable.

"I won't be gone for too long," she said. "Any last bits of advice?" She pulled a folded page from her purse and waved it at him. "Any last questions I should ask?"

"No." He stopped and turned. "Yes. One." Snatching the page from her hand, he laid it on the table and added a line to the list of questions he'd already given her. Then he handed the page back to her and returned to his work.

She held the list up to the light. *Do you source any compositional reagents?* "I have no idea what half the words in these questions even mean."

"You don't have to," he said. "You just have to remember the answers."

"Easy enough for you to say." She refolded the page and tucked it into her purse. "Stay out of trouble while I'm gone, dear brother."

He grunted, and a shuffling noise came from the alley. She stared into the heavy shadows. Just the night before she'd heard some servant telling another a story about a huge rat that had come up on him in an alleyway while he pissed. She'd assumed he'd been out in the city, but what if it was at Seedfall?

Now leery of rats, she dismounted the sill and lowered herself into the alley. Once both feet hit the ground, she made haste to the end of the row and circled the stalls where the metalsmiths and the fletchers worked. Heat from the banked fires in the forges and the sharp scent of glue hung in the air.

Keeping to the shadows, she peered around a splintery old support beam. Parneo's keepers sat around a barrel outside his door, tossing bones together and laughing. They knew what her brother did behind the door, but he'd never had a fit inside those walls, and so long as he didn't, they had no reason to violate his sole refuge of privacy.

Varo Roher, on the other hand, stood apart from the keepers, scanning the row and every person who strode by. Guilt plucked at her. He would be punished if anyone found out what she was doing, what he was unwittingly allowing her to do, but he couldn't be stripped of his title or position. The Binding ceremony guaranteed that. Plus, the chances of her being discovered were slim since no one other than her and her brother knew Transformation was even possible.

She straightened and walked past the end of the row with all the sureness of a servant going about her business. With the tight, abbreviated strides forced on her by her lowborn form, she made her way across the palace grounds and headed for Seedfall's main gate.

With any luck, tonight might be the night she garnered her first real clue as to what had happened to Solena.

TWELVE

"There are secrets in my words, whole workings trapped within them. It is my greatest hope they are buried forever; it is my greatest burden to know one of my descendants will unearth them."
-From Galathar Morovide's private journal, burned the day before his death

Getha spent that afternoon patrolling the Child's Garden. Circular rows of pansies—or peonies?—surrounded a fountain in which the water arced from the center plinth rose and fell onto tinkling bells. The door she guarded led to a polishing room always busy with servants, making it an absurd point of ingress for anyone hoping to enter the palace unnoticed, but she had been assigned to guard it, and so she did, walking back and forth along the cobbled paths while the dark-eyed flowers bobbed their heads in the passing breezes.

Protocol dictated she spend at least a third of her shift standing beside the windowed, high-framed door, but today she couldn't stop moving. After a full tenday of following Princess Renn on her evening excursions around the palace, the time had come for Getha to act.

The princess—or, more likely, Prince Parneo—had discovered the secret of Transformation! Lost for hundreds of years, yet they seemed no closer to sharing their revelation with the church, the academy, or the queen now than they had when Getha had first witnessed the princess's miraculous transfiguration. Instead, Princess Renn traipsed around the palace grounds talking to servants. Getha didn't know what sort of amusement the princess derived from such a game, but the frivolousness of it, the selfishness, sickened her.

Telling someone was the logical solution, but a tiny bit of doubt remained because there was a chance, albeit a small one, she was mistaken. For all her recent obsession with watching the princess, Getha had seen her shift forms only the once. What if her eyes had deceived her? Waltham would listen to her. He might even believe her, but then what? What if she really was wrong?

The evening bell rang, and her stomach lurched. Before she did anything, before she told anyone, she needed to be sure.

Within minutes, Bosier, a slight, bug-eyed woman with a hard-to-shake mountain stance, arrived. She marched up to Getha, stood at attention, and said in a loud, firm voice, "Palace Guard Bosier declares on duty."

Getha matched her stance and tone. "Palace Guard Barei declares off duty."

"Have a good night," Bosier said, relaxing and rolling her shoulders.

Relieved from her post, Getha ran off to grab some food. In the guards' eating lodge, she passed by the roasted capon for a knobby old apple that had probably been in a root cellar since autumn and a thick slice of dark-nut bread slathered in butter. She stuffed them down, the salty richness of the bread making up for the tartness of the apple, while she walked to her barracks.

Tumolo sat on her trunk, chatting up her bunk neighbor, Hoefen. Tumolo's anger over their confrontation had waned in the wake of her refusal into the varo, but Getha's soreness remained.

"Move."

Tumolo glanced at her. "Toss off, Barei." On the next bed, Hoefen smiled as if he'd said something clever.

Getha gritted her teeth. Every moment spent dealing with Tumolo was one where she could be missing the princess's transfiguration. "Get off my trunk."

Tumolo shrugged. "What's the rush? Have a date?" Hoefen laughed. Getha's refusal to couple with anyone in the guard was well known. Tumolo shook his head. "Poor fellow. Doesn't know what he got himself in for."

That's it. She turned to Hoefen. "Are you interested in tumbling him or not?"

Hoefen's idiotic smiled dropped from her face. She blinked, looked at Tumolo, then at the floor. "I... I suppose... "

"Yes or no?" Getha demanded.

Hoefen glared up at her. "Yes."

"Wonderful." Getha shoved an open-mouthed Tumolo off her trunk in Hoefen's direction. "Then go find some dark corner, and let the rest of us be."

Lorri, who had looked to be sleeping in the bunk on the other side of Hoefen's, sat up, her short hair sticking out in all directions. "Shit's sake, Barei. Leave 'em alone."

This elicited a chorus of grunts and agreements from around the room. Getha turned her back on them. Fighting and fucking, that was all that ever happened in the palace guard. Since her talk with Waltham on the roof, her hunger to join the varo had returned, stronger than ever. She belonged with them, and dealing with the likes of Tumolo and the rest just made her even more determined.

She changed out of her uniform, checked her vambraces—both in working order thanks to Darazo's repairs—and charged out into the gloaming. Running later than usual, she sprinted across the grounds to the alleyway behind the row. Several windows along the way were open to the sunset and the evening air, but one had a yellow-haired girl straddled the sill, talking to someone within. Getha often watched the girl she thought to be the Transformed princess from a distance, but a stack of barrels and the deepness of the shadows at this later candlemark allowed her to get closer than she ever had before.

As she neared the window, her heartbeat pounded in her ears. Tucking into the lee of the barrels, she struggled to listen.

"...remember the answers." Having heard Prince Parneo's ranting around the palace, she recognized his voice.

"Easy enough for you to say," the yellow-haired girl replied. She sounded a little like Princess Renn, but not enough to eliminate the last of Getha's niggling doubts. Next came the shuffling of papers before, "Stay out of trouble while I'm gone, dear brother."

There! Getha twitched, the scuffing of her boot against the dirt loud in the narrowness of the alley. She stilled and held her breath. No one but Princess Renn would call Prince Parneo "dear brother." It was the proof Getha needed, assuming she hadn't given herself away.

A long moment passed before there came the rustling of clothes and the scratch of feet landing in the alley. Getha crowded as far as she could into the shadows of the barrels, but as it turned out, she needn't have worried. The princess scampered past Getha's hiding spot without so much as a glance. Had she turned right at the end of the alley, Getha would have let her run off to play her game with the servants. Had the princess turned in the direction of the palace, as she had every night before, Getha would have gone straight to Waltham to tell him what she knew.

But instead of turning right, the princess slowed at the end of the alley, looked around, and rushed off to the left.

Don't lose her. Not sure why it mattered and yet certain it did, Getha heeded her instincts and hurried along after the princess.

ONCE SHE NEARED THE PALACE, Renn stepped from the grass onto the globelit, crushed-shell paths, enjoying the way the shells creaked and crackled beneath her feet. At every split in the path she told herself she could turn back, she could find another way. Then she would picture Solena gasping for air and continued forward with renewed vigor. Parneo refused to say that anyone had been responsible for Solena's death, but Renn had to find out, one way or another.

Movement on the path ahead stirred her from her thoughts. Two highborn strolled toward her arm and arm, and she stumbled when she recognized the foppish Messero Ralward and the apple-cheeked Messera Skalina. Both heirs of their respective houses, a marriage between the two might mean—

Renn shook her head. *You're a lowborn tonight. Start acting like it.* Slipping up on the palace grounds was one thing. Out in the city, it could be disastrous.

So, when the couple neared, she stepped off the side of the path to let them pass, bowing and wishing them both a fine evening. She hadn't expected them to return the sentiment, but neither so much as looked at her. She never sought out attention, but she didn't exactly like being treated as if she didn't exist at all.

She straightened and returned to the path, concentrating on the main gate and wondering if she would have any trouble getting through them.

TURN. Turn. Turn!

Getha, hanging back in the shadows beyond the circles of globe light, sucked in a hissing breath as the princess walked up to and right past the final break in the path, and she slowed in her tracks as the princess continued on to the privet-lined drive leading to Seedfall's main gate.

If there was ever a time to go tell Waltham what was happening, this was it. But first she would have to find him, then it would take ages for her to explain and even longer for him to wrap his mind around the situation.

Besides, how much trouble could a princess get up to in the Bole? She couldn't possibly hope to range beyond the highborn neighborhood. Getha would follow the princess through the streets for a while, let her have her little adventure, then snatch her up and bring her home. Waltham might not approve, but he had told Getha to distinguish herself, and she imagined herself bringing the errant princess before a teary-eyed queen grateful to see her youngest daughter home safe. Though everyone knew Princess Renn was not her mother's favorite, she was still the woman's child, and mothers—*most* mothers, anyway—cared for their children.

Getha further imagined revealing that Prince Parneo had rediscovered one of the Lost Pillars, and she could almost hear the gasps, could almost see the chagrin on Orli's face when the queen demanded to know why Getha hadn't made varo.

The princess hesitated as she approached the gate, and a sensation equal parts disappointment and relief rushed through Getha's limbs. But the sensation abandoned her the moment the princess squared her shoulders, strode up to the gate, and asked to be let through. Palace Guard Getts and Palace Guard Lexorianan opened the gate without any fuss, and the princess turned to flash Getts a smile as she ducked out. From the triumphant spring in her step, she wasn't aware of how much more difficult it was to get back in.

Getha's left arm tingled up to her elbow. She'd been sparking her bloodmark over and over while she watched. She released her hand and let the mark fade away. The princess wouldn't have any trouble returning because Getha would be with her.

Thinking ahead to the moment she escorted the princess through the gate, she fished in her purse to ensure she carried her chit. All the workers, palace guards, varos, and even the highborn outside the royal family were Bound to lacquered wooden tickets that allowed them quick passage in and out of the gate. Her fingers brushed against the chit's smooth surface, and she lost her final reason to stall.

Taking a deep breath, she counted to twenty, then pursued the princess into the Bole.

Being outside the walls of Seedfall alone was terrifying and freeing and wonderful.

On the seldom occasions when Renn called on her peers, she rode out into the Bole on horseback or in a carriage with four varos and twice as many palace guards surrounding her. Walking past the homes on foot, every gate barred to her, the hearths seemed larger, more imposing, and without a phalanx of guards surrounding her, she felt naked.

She kept her sight trained on the Hedgerow, the wall between the Bole and the rest of the city. Three gates stood in the Hedgerow, each one representing a pillar of alchemy, and she couldn't resist heading straight for Transformation Gate. Her path took her by Lamplighter's, the Bole's lone drinking house. She'd passed a few evenings sitting on the rooftop terrace, drinking, talking, and gazing out at the rest of the city. As she neared the establishment, a memory came to mind of Solena laughing at something so hard she spilled wine down her skirt, which had only made her laugh harder.

Renn's sight blurred, and she dashed away the tears that fell when she blinked.

Set into the green stone of the Hedgerow, the Transformation arch reached about forty feet at its peak, and the wrought-iron gates set into it were closed and locked for the night. The Blossom neighborhood rested on the other side of the pickets, and along its shop-lined streets, the globes gave way to torches. Lowborn crossed in and out of the wavering pools of light as they went about their lives, and a few glanced up at the gate, or past it to the Bole or the palace, as they went by, but none lingered.

Two city guards stood watch on the Bole side of the postern, a man and a woman, and the woman moved to open the door as Renn neared.

"Long day?" she asked with a smile. "Did the messeran not want to let you go before you served 'em their beddy teas?"

Chuckling, the male guard scratched his round belly.

The amount of contempt in the female guard's voice startled Renn. Talking with the servants, she'd heard a lot of gossip about the highborn, but never such outright disdain. Unsure of how to reply, she bade a fine evening to the pair of guards and stepped through the door. She came around to the iron gate and noticed someone striding into Lamplighter's. All the way up the hill, the palace appeared very far away.

Tucking away the guard's scorn for the highborn away to examine later, Renn turned and faced the street. She'd done it. She was out in the Branches alone. Not only that, but she had a man to find and a page full of questions to ask him. According to the servants she'd spoken to, Brailen Natts, called by everyone simply "Natts," could always be found at the night market. She'd never been to the night market, but she assumed it was where they held the day market, on the Meet.

Orienting herself in that direction, she started off again.

SHIT. Getha pressed her back against the door to Lamplighter's, her heart racing.

As expected, the princess had wandered the streets of the Bole, but then she'd turned toward the Hedgerow, and Getha had panicked until she remembered they were on the road to Lamplighter's. It took Getha a moment to work out why the princess might head there disguised as a lowborn, but she came to the conclusion the princess hoped to play a trick on her friends, an even better jape than fooling the lowborn at the palace.

Anger had nearly driven her to snatch the princess up before she could further profane the miracle she paraded around in. Yet Getha hung back long enough for the princess to approach the door to Lamplighter's. And for her to walk on by.

No. The anger had curdled in Getha's belly as the princess neared the gate. *That's not... She can't be...*

Princess Renn had waved to the city guards at the gate, closed for the night. The female guard said something to her, then opened the postern door to let her out, and as the princess had stepped around to peer back through the gate, Getha had ducked into Lamplighter's doorway to avoid being seen.

The doorway of Lamplighter's, where she now stood. *Shit, shit, shit.*

Out into the city? Was the princess mad? This wasn't good. Not good at all. A small voice at the back of her mind piped up—*Then again, saving the princess from the safety of the Bole is easy compared to saving her from the wilds of the Branches.*

That, she reasoned back, *is because there are real dangers out there at night for someone walking alone. Amma forbid she wander as far as the Meet. Or the Tangles.*

Then a scene came into Getha's mind of Princess Renn telling her mother how Getha had rescued her from getting lost or being roughed up by streetlings. The grateful queen would offer a boon in the face of such bravery, and Getha would say, *"I ask only for the chance to serve you more faithfully, Your Majesty. I ask only for another chance to earn a position among your varo."*

She could almost taste the varo's oath on her tongue, could almost feel the queen's blade touching her shoulders as she was sworn into their ranks.

She abandoned her fancying and peeked out just in time to see the princess walk away from the gate. Getha's heart jumped up into her throat. Every bit of her grand planning would be for naught if she lost the girl in the city.

Leaving her hiding place, she rushed toward the postern door.

THE SHOPS in the Blossom clustered near the Hedgerow and gave way to block after block of small but well-kept homes with bright doors and shutters, and boxes of flowers hanging from the windowsills. Renn had heard the neighborhood was where many of the city's skilled workers lived, but she'd never explored it for herself.

Many of the houses were dark and shut up tight, but light and a rhythmic, unfamiliar sound—*whoosh, thump, whoosh, thump*—spilled from an open door. Inside, a white-haired man sat at a ten-foot-tall wooden framework with even rows of threads running every which way. He moved his feet, and the wooden frame shifted, taking half of the rows of thread with it. *Thump.* Then he passed something through the opening, *whoosh,* and moved his feet again, shifting the frame back to its original position. *Thump.* Over and over again. He worked at a remarkable speed, his attention never wandering, and bit by bit, a lovely piece of patterned fabric stretched out before him.

The endless repetition calmed her. She might have watched him all night long, but then a salt-laden breeze swept down the road, carrying on it the strains of an upbeat melody. *The night market. I must be closer than I thought.* Though she wanted to stay longer, she left the man's doorway and continued on.

The streets grew busier as Getha and the princess neared the Meet, and Getha tightened the distance between them. Of course the princess headed toward the night market. Of course.

Twenty feet ahead of Getha, Princess Renn strolled along, her head turning this way and that as she looked at all the people, most in their finest dress. Obviously no one knew who she was, but soon she would be mistaken for a road rat or a farmer's daughter, a stranger to the city and therefore an easy mark. The heavy purse on her hip didn't help matters either. The gawping and the coin made her a thief's dream come to life.

Getha closed the gap to fifteen feet.

Pinchers waited all moon for the market. Getha had patrolled it when she served in the city guard, and in those crowds, a pincher would have the princess's purse in less than half a candlemark. When they counted their pull, they'd hunt her down, find a way to trap her in a back alley, and try shaking her down for more.

Ten feet.

Princess Renn turned a sharp corner, and Getha shoved past a pair of slow-moving girls giggling and meandering along arm in arm to follow. Around the corner, the number of people and the noise from the market increased, and it took Getha a heart-stopping moment to find the princess's yellow head.

Seven feet.

A mix of children and adults bunched and crowded near the end of the road, held there by the city guards regulating the bridge traffic. The night market happened only three nights a moon, those nights when the moon was fullest, and everyone who waited to cross the bridge over to the Meet did so in good cheer. Princess Renn didn't speak to anyone, but she waited in line like everyone else and did so with a pleasant smile on her face.

In small groups—Getha elbowed a man out of the way to be in the princess's—the city guards let people cross the bridge from one side, then the other. Getha, Princess Renn, and a boisterous extended family of seven clomped over the wooden structure. Beneath the bridge, the River Sap rushed along. Their group reached the other side, and Getha and the princess were on the Meet, at the fringes of the night market.

Some claimed the Meet to be part of the Commons; others argued it wasn't. In this case, the truth meant little and less. The Meet was where the Branches of the Sap came together—or as the lowborn tended to think of it, broke apart—an open area at the easternmost end of the Commons. Built on a natural plateau, the large, flat space was paved with cobblestones, and narrow bridges, like the one they'd just crossed, spanned and connected the wedge-shaped pieces of land.

They stood on the largest piece, and at its center towered an immense twelve-foot-high platform called the Queen's Table. The Table functioned either as a dais from which the queen might address her subjects, or as a gallows. Since the start of Theodora's reign, it hadn't been used much for either.

Uncaring or unaware of the superstitions, Princess Renn ignored the groups parting to either side of the Table and walked beneath it.

"Heyla, girl," a man called into the deep shadow through which she passed, slurring his words and wagging a dirty finger at her. "That's bad luck for you."

"No, it hain't," a woman countered. Two small children clung to her hips like panniers. "It's bad luck for the queen."

"Don' matter none," the man said, waving at her and throwing off his balance. "It's bad luck fore and aft either way, even for us just bein' here." He righted himself and set his attention toward the princess, who exited the other side unaware of the commotion she left in her wake.

"Gonna tell her what's what, I am," he said, dropping a fist into his other palm. "Knock her one for bringin' down—"

He took a single step before Getha snatched his tunic and yanked him back. She had two inches on him, and he peered up at her with bleary eyes.

"How's about you go home and sleep it off?"

Opening his mouth, he let out a rancid belch, and Getha's years of serving in the city guard returned to her in a nauseating rush. She pointed the man in the direction from which she'd come and gave him a little push. He stumbled off toward the bridge, where an actual member of the city guard could deal with him.

Let them, Getha thought. She'd paid her dues.

Turning, she caught sight of a yellow head standing in the crowd around a street performer and sprinted beneath the Table, ignoring the shouts that dogged her.

ACROSS THE BRIDGE and beyond the Table, Renn discovered the bare expanse of the Meet lost under rows and rows of tents, some of them silken, others patchwork, and tables covered with wares. The day market wasn't anywhere near as large, and the light of the full moon and the shifting glow of fire from the street torches gave the night market a mystical air the day market could never hope to match.

Not to mention the excitement. Every twenty or thirty feet, bards and buskers competed for attention and coin, and the smell of so many bodies in one place was challenged by the scents of fancy oils and cooking food. Renn let the crowd carry her along like a twig floating on a stream. She'd been told Natts hung around the ale tent at the market's center, and the stream of people was certain to end up there at some point.

Off to her right, a woman lifted her voice in song, the sound cutting through the din like a sailing boat dashing through the waves. It drew Renn in, and she wove through the crowd to find her, which she did at the next intersection. The singer was of middling height, somewhere between Renn's lowborn form and her actual one, but she stood on a plinth, and it raised her above the masses—as if her lovely voice didn't already do so. Each note she sang fell to the earth like snow, and the haunting melody tugged at Renn's heart, making her yearn for something she couldn't name.

Coppers filled the bowl at the woman's feet, but she deserved more than that. When the song ended, Renn reached into her purse, pulled out a silver, and tossed it, the gleaming coin shining amidst the sea of tarnished red.

The woman's face lit up. "Thank you!" She climbed down off her plinth, snatched up the silver, and tucked it into the bodice of her dress, then grabbed Renn's hands. "Thank you, messera! Amma's blessings on you."

Messera? Renn's cheeks warmed. The silver had marked her as high-born. A foolish slip. Beside her, a boy of thirteen or fourteen took off his cap and bowed. She tugged her hands away from the singer and hurried off, ducking down the nearest row of tents. As much as she wanted to spend the whole evening exploring the night market, as much as it tied her stomach in knots to think about approaching this man she didn't know, the time for flowing along with the stream had passed.

Halfway down the row of makeshift shops, she stopped at a booth of combs, carved wooden combs next to filigreed silver ones and carved golden pieces with jewels sparkling in them. She wrenched her attention away from beautiful wares and set it on the large man perched behind them. "Which way to the ale tent?"

The man picked up one of the golden combs and laid it on his chubby

149

palm. The comb was shaped like a bushy-tailed squirrel with two emeralds in place of the eyes, and he held it out for her inspection.

"Yes," she said, falling in love with it instantly. "It's very nice, but if you could just point me toward the ale tent."

The comb seller stared at her. "Hain't running a charity, girl. Information costs." He tipped the comb so the jewels caught the light.

"How much?"

The man looked her up and down. "Ha' gulden."

Half a gold? That seemed far too much, but she had already wasted enough time and she did want the comb. While the man wrapped it in a square of silk, she counted out twelve silvers and dropped them into his waiting hand.

He handed over the comb, which she tucked into her lightening purse, then pointed toward the end of the row. "Down here till the end. Turn south and cross over the next few bridges. Tent's big, white, and has sots stumblin' round it. Can't miss it."

She considered asking the seller if he knew Natts, but worried what another answer might cost her, so she nodded her thanks and followed the seller's directions.

THE BOY BOWED to the princess, and Getha sighed at the princess's ignorance. *A silver to a night market singer? Why not just wear your tiara?*

From the way the boy eyed the princess when he came up, he aimed for her purse. When the princess cut down a row, he dashed off in the opposite direction to find a couple of his friends. Getha let him go. She and the princess would be halfway back to the palace before they returned.

Down the seller's row, Princess Renn stopped at one of the tents to buy something. *Let her buy her one little trinket.* Once she finished, Getha would sidle up alongside her, grab her arm in a gentle hand, reveal who she was, and...

Instead of wandering from the seller's tent to another, the princess walked away with all the haste and purpose of someone who recalled an important assignation, and Getha's curiosity rose, causing her to once again abandon her plan.

She kept pace after the princess, tracking her yellow head as it cut through the meandering shoals of market-goers, meaning to catch up with her past this tent or over the next bridge, but never quite doing so. *Now, you idiot! It doesn't matter where she's going or who she's meeting. Do it now!* Over and over, she excoriated herself for being seventeen different colors of stupid, yet she waited, desperate to know what sort of meeting a crown princess of Ombratos might have at the night market.

RENN WIPED her sweating hands on her breeches and reviewed what she knew about Natts. He worked for—or with, depending on whom one asked —Phineas Talp, a merchant and the city's largest importer of fine alchemical goods. From what she had pieced together, Talp specialized in procuring hard-to-find items, the sorts of things needed for a major working like the Absolute Binding that had ended with Solena's death. None of the servants she'd questioned had been able tell her exactly where to find Talp, but it appeared to be common knowledge that Natts never missed a night market and that he spent those evenings drinking and gambling in the ale tent.

She joined the end of a line waiting to cross the next bridge. The white ale tent was indeed impossible to miss, and as her stomach roiled, she laced her fingers together, making her and Solena's special signal and sparking her bloodmark.

GETHA FOLLOWED Princess Renn over the bridge and onto the island bearing the tattered old ale tent. There, the princess stopped, tilting her head as she took in the sight.

During Getha's stint in the city guard, she hadn't minded patrolling the night market, but she'd loathed ale tent duty. Or, as she'd called it, retch duty since she'd always ended those nights with someone else's vomit on her boots, down her sleeve, or on one Amma-forsaken shift, in her hair. Even now, a round-shouldered boy of twelve or thirteen heaved into one of several buckets outside the main entrance while his friends stood nearby, pointing and sniggering.

It hadn't helped that most of her fellow guards partook in the ale tent's offerings. Two guards wandered by, and based on their rolling gaits, that tradition hadn't changed either.

The princess, as if spotting her quarry, took off toward a group of five young women about Getha's age. Were those the people she had come to meet? Was it possible they were all highborn disguised by Transformation? What had the prince called them a few days ago? Amulets.

True, the women had the bearing of miners; they all wore single-piece buttonfronts and had pipes either in their hands or hanging from their mouths, but if one of the Lost Pillars had been found, then anything was possible, wasn't it?

The princess said something, and the women laughed, the sound grating against Getha's nerves. They *were* all highborn, a bunch of stupid highborn women flitting—

Princess Renn spoke again, and one of the women, the one whose short, brown curls clung tightly to her head said, "Why're you... " Getha lost the rest of the question under the musical sound of another of the boy's heaves.

Getha lost the princess's reply, but another woman, her sharp features wreathed in a bluish cloud of pipe smoke, said, "In there," and gestured toward the tent's entrance.

"Thank you," Princess Renn said, and she strode off in that direction.

Getha shook her head. If the princess hadn't come to meet these women, then who was she looking for?

"Careful," the curly haired woman called after the princess. "He knows what he's doing, but he'll leave ya with a gift whether yer wantin' it or no." To illustrate her meaning, she reached down and scratched her crotch, sending the rest of the women into gales of laughter.

Princess Renn entered the tent, and Getha's burning curiosity left her. *Time to end this evening once and for all.*

Even with the flaps at both ends wide open, the inside of the tent was loud and hot from the lamps hanging overhead and the press of bodies. Adding to the charm, the whole place reeked of sweat and ale. Twelve huge casks guarded by the soberest of the city guards lined the left side, and at a mismatched grouping of tables and chairs, sat a motley collection of Fallen.

Only in the ale tent did a woman from Chestnut rub elbows with a man from the Mire. The Fallen were one people under the flag of Ombratos, only like tended to like, with the cozy merchants looking down on the dirty dock workers, or the strong-armed miners sneering at the soft-hearted, soft-headed artisans. But not in the ale tent during night market. In the ale tent, drink made equals of them all.

It took Getha a long moment to find the princess, and that was because Princess Renn had already made it halfway across the tent, where she spoke to a man seated with his back to Getha. He wore his long, dark hair in a tail at the nape of his neck, and something about the way he moved or the cant of his shoulders tugged at her.

She struggled to place the man until he stood, revealing his profile, and then she felt as if she'd plunged full-on into the freezing waters of the Sap. Her hunger to become varo had pushed her into making a series of bad choices this night, but those poor choices were swallowed up by the nightmare unfolding before her.

Most thought Phineas Talp a merchant, an importer of rare alchemical goods, but that was because he cut a profit tidy enough to explain away his other activities. Slavery was illegal in Ombratos, but trading with Xantish slavers wasn't, and few cared when passed-out travelers disappeared from alleyways. Talp paid well for dock workers not to notice when his transport vessels, crewed by poor souls from the Tangles, returned with fewer sailors on deck, and if an orphan or two went missing from Shade's Rest, no one missed them, not when their purses were lined with gold.

Phineas Talp was a hawk draped in a sparrow's feathers, and Brailen Natts, the man now offering the princess his arm, was his number one enforcer.

When Princess Renn took Natts's arm and together they headed toward the tent's far opening, Getha broke into a panicked run, darting through the crush of tables and benches, knocking into people and shoving them over in her rush to reach the princess.

She careened into a thick cluster of drinkers, and seeing no other way through, jumped onto a bench to climb over a table littered with dice and coppers. The men and women sitting around the table cried out as she stepped into the middle of their game, and fast as a snake, one of the women snagged Getha's ankle. Getha tore from the woman's grip, but she'd already lost her balance, and she pitched headlong into the broad backs of a couple of men sitting at the next table.

Suddenly she was down on the cobbles with people on their feet all around her, shouting and stomping around. Ale soaked the front of her tunic, and her sleeve was caught beneath someone's heel. She shoved that foot away and rolled, and someone else's boot landed on her thigh. She kicked, freeing her leg, and scrambled beneath the nearest table, scraping her back along the edge as she clambered out the other side.

The way to the tent's opening cleared in the ruckus, and Getha sprinted for it, bursting out into the night. There, her chest heaving, she spun in circles, looking in every direction, but Natts and the princess were gone.

THIRTEEN

"It's always better to fight with partners at your back than it is to fight alone."
-Waltham

F ear flapped around in Getha's skull like a bird that had flown in a window and couldn't find its way out again. She stood there, plagued by images of the princess hurt or, Amma help her, dead. Dead. If the princess died—

Right behind Getha, a man shouted something, startling her from her daze.

Think, Barei!

Natts didn't know the yellow-haired girl was Princess Renn. How could he? But the princess knew who he was; she'd asked the women outside the tent about him in particular. The one woman's warning returned to Getha. *He knows what he's doing, but he'll leave ya with a gift whether yer wantin' it or no.* Was that what the princess was after? Her Prince Dallan had left her, so now she hunted a good tumble in the wilds of the Branches?

Anger surfaced, and Getha clung to it in the manner of a drowning woman clinging to an oar.

Natts and the princess might head anywhere in the city, but the most likely spot was Talp's Court, his alehouse in the Tangles. If she didn't find them there, then she'd go to the docks. And if she couldn't find the princess at the docks, her next stop would be the jails, followed by a long walk up onto the Queen's Table and a short, sharp step off the side.

A swell of fear crashed over her, so she reached again for her ire. *Princess Renn is nothing more than a fool girl looking for a tumble.* She clenched her hands into fists, and the dread receded. There were a dozen different ways to Talp's Court from the Meet. She checked her vambraces, then chose a direction and took off.

Perhaps her luck had turned, and she'd run into the princess on the way there.

It hadn't, and she didn't.

For most of Getha's two years in the city guard, she'd patrolled Crown Bay and the surrounding Mire, but she ran through the warren of the Tangles, where tenements rose, crumbled, then were rebuilt amidst the ruins, to the best of her memory. She rushed along the pitted roads, past houses with walls shored up by logs and alleys piled high with refuse. Not the finest homes, but every Fallen with a bloodmark who wanted a roof over her or his head was promised one within the Gift, which was more than could be said for those who lived out in Shade's Rest.

After her third wrong turn, she arrived at a busy intersection rich with the smells of roasting chestnuts and night soil. Sweat pooled beneath her breasts and trickled down her sides. Talp's Court was nearby, but where? *Where?*

A clanking line of manacled gongfermors came down the road, pushing their rattling wagons. Getha's eyes watered with the unspeakable stench, and she and those at the other corners covered their noses and mouths as they waited for the wretched parade to pass. Six city guards escorted them, the lower halves of their faces hidden behind rags soaked in perfumes or oils. Having served that duty more than once, she knew their assignment was as much a punishment for them as it was for the criminals who pushed the wagons.

Both the criminals and the guards were trapped, just like her. Or was she? A stiff breeze carried on it the salty kiss of the ocean. No one knew where she was or what she was up to. What if she walked down to the docks and sought passage on a ship headed for Tithen? Better that than to hang for losing...

No. She'd never run from anything, and she wasn't about to start now.

With the reeking prisoners rattling away, she crossed the road, and on the far of the intersection, a pair of lads crossed in the opposite direction. The skinny boy dragged his feet and glanced into every corner, but the short one walked with a bow-legged swagger and spoke with his cracking voice pitched to carry.

"Gonna have a full pitcher tonight, see if I don't."

The skinny boy muttered something, and the boaster laughed, grabbing between his legs. "Fa can suck me dry, he can. We earned it!"

Getha changed direction to trail after the lads. Sure enough, two blocks later, they fetched up at the end of a long, narrow alleyway. The buildings to either side of the alley leaned in, creating a valley between them, and at the far end a woman guarded the main doors to Talp's Court. When the lads entered the alley, Getha passed it, then circled around to stand on the far side of the street.

While she waited for the lads to enter, she slid her thumbnail into the catch on her prayer locket, found the needle with her forefinger, and pressed. *Dearest Amma, please let her be inside.*

As she walked through the wavering circles of torchlight, the hairs on the back of her neck rose. No doubt, in the shadows above, archers hid, waiting for someone to twitch the wrong way.

A lump of a woman guarded the door. One of her eyes stared straight at Getha; the other pointed off toward Amma. A flash of copper gained Getha entry, and inside, noise from the main room echoed down another kill hall, this one barely wide enough for two people to walk side by side, with murder holes dotting the ceiling.

Talp's Court, another of the man's legitimate ventures, was where the city's worst liked to gather, and if half of Ombratos had crammed into the ale tent, then the other half was here, crowding the low-ceilinged hall with smoke, noise, and the ripeness of unwashed bodies.

Robbery, fleecing, assault, and murder tended to be night work, but scores of men and women sat at the bar or at the rectangular tables running along the length of the room. At the far end of the hall, some even danced, whirling around to a tune spun by a trio of fiddlers. Though it seemed like midnight, it was early in the evening yet, and the joy of the night market had spilled over.

The main hall hadn't changed much since Getha's single visit years before. Patrons drank at scar-topped tables, sitting on new chairs or chairs sturdy enough to have survived the last brawl. A bar ran along the full length of the west wall and faced a cracked, wavy mirror that served well enough to let someone sitting at the stools know if anyone crept up behind them.

The sole, notable difference was that instead of oil lamps hanging from the ceiling, globes lit the room. Granted, the metal cages they hung in tarnished Talp's display of wealth, but he must have needed them to keep those who sat below the globes from climbing up on a table and stealing them. The bars of the cages cast stark shadow lines around the room.

Getha walked the room's perimeter searching for a flash of the princess's yellow hair. People laughed and jostled one another as they had in the ale tent, but here the celebration was tinged with something darker. Halfway to the dance floor, at a nearby table, a cackling man with shivering jowls shoved the woman sitting next to him a bit too hard, and she responded with a fisted clout to the side of his head.

He grabbed his ear and scowled at her. "Here, Mee! What's you doin' 'at for?"

"I told you," the woman, Mee, said. "Lay hands on me again an' see if you don't get worse."

The woman sitting across from them watched their exchange through hooded eyes. Despite the heat in the hall, she wore a voluminous greatcoat. She reached into a pocket, and Getha braced herself, but she brought out a stack of cards and started shuffling them.

"Too early for that," she said to Mee and the man. "Let's play."

They both nodded, but the tightness between them remained, tinder just waiting for the next spark.

Getha continued on and made a full circuit of the hall, even dodging between the dancers, before ending up at the bar. In her first bit of luck, Talp himself was nowhere to be seen. She shouldered her way into a gap near the end of the bar and waved down the barkeep, a pert-nosed woman with arms muscular enough to suggest her skills extended beyond tapping kegs and pulling ale.

The barkeep waved back to Getha, and after pouring a thumbcup of clear thorno for a long-haired old man, she hustled down to Getha's end of the bar.

"Lookin' for somethin'?" Her raised eyebrows suggested that anything and everything behind the bar was on offer.

Getha leaned in, and a smile ghosted the barkeep's face as she mirrored Getha's posture. "You seen Natts come in?"

The barkeep's eyebrows fell. "Can't say I have." She shifted back, her shoulders stiff. "Anything else?"

Getha shook her head, and the barkeep left to serve someone else.

A tide of fear rose within Getha, but she refused to let it drag her under. She had run from the Meet, her feet flying over the cobblestones, and because of that, she'd beaten them here.

The group of men to her right wandered away from the bar, and she grabbed one of the empty stools, the one with the most direct view of the main doors. Minutes crawled by, and with every passing moment, with every person who entered and wasn't Natts or the princess, more doubt crept into her mind. The problem was, if they didn't come to Court, they could be anywhere. So she waited. A handful of people came in and went out through a narrow door set into a shadowy space of wall next to the bar, and she prayed.

She'd pricked every finger with her locket, but for one, when Natts and Princess Renn walked in. Getha worried she'd conjured them up in her desperation, but then a woman rushed out of the crowd to embrace Natts, and Getha decided they were real. She slid off her stool, and for the first time in almost a candlemark, took a full breath.

Across the room, Natts said something to the princess, and she giggled, her cheeks flushing a bright shade of pink as she turned away from him. He had quite the reputation, but Getha had never seen the appeal, not with his heavy brow, too small nose, and too square jaw.

Not the sort for hidden weapons, he wore an eating knife on one side of his belt and a short sword on the other, and his sleeves were rolled up over his elbows to emphasize the girth of his biceps.

Getha's worry quieted as she sized him up, and he became no longer a person, but a problem to solve. A fight to win.

Natts pressed a hand to the small of the princess's back and led her through the busy room, keeping to the far wall, stopping here and there to shout a greeting across the room or to speak with someone.

Getha scanned ahead. In the corner nearest them hung a curtain almost the same color as the smoke-greased wood of the walls. Getha had no idea what was behind the curtain and no intention of finding out.

She cut a line through the room, careful to watch where she stepped. Natts and the princess moved farther and farther away from the front exit, but Getha kept in mind the door next to the bar. Her best option was for a quick extraction and a quiet retreat. No fighting, not if she could help it.

She approached the couple just as Natts stopped to exchange a complicated handshake with a string-limbed, silver-eyed Xantish sailor. The princess stood off to the side, her brow creased, a folded piece paper in her right hand.

Natts and the sailor separated, and the princess held up the paper. "I thought you said we were going to—"

Getha arrived at her side. "There you are, Alyse!" she cried out, using the first name that came to mind. "I been lookin' for you everywhere."

Startled, Princess Renn turned to face her, and after an instant, a hint of recognition flitted across her face. Getha guessed the princess thought she looked familiar, but couldn't quite place her.

Natts wrapped a possessive arm around Princess Renn's waist. "Who's this now?"

The princess elbowed her way out of his grip, saying, "She's a friend" at the same instant Getha said "I'm her cousin."

Natts took a step back and put his hands on his hips, near his blades. Getha bit the inside of her cheek and dropped her hands to her sides.

Son of a motherless bastard.

The Xantish sailor watched from the side. One of the shadowy lines from a globe cage crossed his face as he shifted back and forth on the balls of his feet, and on the side of his neck, the brand of a broken spear caught the light. A slaver.

"We have to go," Getha said, not taking her eyes off Natts or the sailor while she eased closer to the princess. "Her ma sent me after her."

Natts opened his mouth to speak, but the princess beat him to it. "I'm not going anywhere," she said with conviction. The princess had placed Getha's face and, for whatever reason, had decided to dig her heels in. Her chin tipped up, the very picture of highborn stubbornness. "You can stay if you'd like, but this man and I have some business to which we must attend."

Getha glanced around. It worried her that, aside from Natts and the barkeep, she didn't know who Talp's people were. She'd been out of the city guard for too long.

"Yes." Natts laughed, hitching up his belt. "Business."

The word dripped with double meaning, and the princess's lip curled in distaste, yet she held her ground. She didn't act like some dozy girl seeking a tryst on the wrong side of the Hedgerow, but Getha had bigger concerns than parsing out the princess's every expression.

Natts's grabbed one of the princess's hands, twirled her in a circle, and linked her arm through his. "She'll come when we're done, cousin." He lowered his voice. "And not a moment sooner, got that?"

"Excuse me?" Princess Renn yanked her hand away from him. "I will go whenever I damned well please. Now, you promised me a chance to speak with Talp, and I demand you bring me to him."

The Xantish slaver chortled, and Natts's neck and ears grew florid. He was a man spoiling for a toss or a tumble, and since the princess wasn't going to give him one, Getha would provide the other.

She faced the sailor and feigned surprise. "What did you say?"

The man's silver eyes narrowed. "What is this?" His thick accent made it sound like "Vas is zis?"

"About him." Getha pointed at Natts. "I heard you say something about him."

Natts's shoulders rose like a dog's hackles, and his biceps rippled as he clenched his hands into fists. "What did you say?"

Now the slaver's eyes widened. "What?" He looked from Natts to Getha and back again. "I... I didn't..."

A wild grin split Natts's face. Getha hooked a hand around the princess's arm and pulled her out of the way just as he threw his first punch.

The dazed slaver hit the wall, and before he could get his hands up, Natts grabbed him by the front of his shirt, spun him around, and tossed him toward a table. Those sitting around it scrambled back, and the slaver landed hard, sending dice, coins, and jacks of ale flying.

Then, like a sudden downpour, the room erupted into a full-on brawl.

In the madness, Getha jerked Princess Renn closer to shield her and headed for the door by the bar. The princess tried to pull away from her, but now that she had her hands on the princess, she wasn't letting go.

A bench flew over their heads. Then a pair of bodies crashed into them, and only Getha's firm footing kept them from tumbling to the floor. When the princess regained her balance, their eyes met, and an unspoken agreement passed between them. The princess would stop struggling against Getha, and in turn, she would get them out. Princess Renn huddled against her side, and together, they made for the bar.

As they wove between the small fights that made up the larger brawl, Getha kept her left arm at the ready and a watchful eye out for bludgeons or blades. A group of men caught in a knot of hair pulling, eye gouging, and throttling stumbled back and forth at the end of the bar, blocking the door. Getha planted her feet, grabbed the eye gouger by his arm, and pulled, sending all of them into a crashing heap away from the door.

She and the princess neared the opening beneath the bar, and the barkeep—as likely chosen for her ability in taking down troublemakers as her skill at pulling pints—came rushing out, a glint of silver in her right hand. Getha shoved the princess back just as the barkeep swung her blade in a wide arc that scythed the air mere inches from them both.

In a single motion, Getha swept Princess Renn behind her and flexed her wrist; a dagger fell into her waiting hand. She blocked the barkeep's next swing, released her other blade, and brought it up inside the barkeep's guard, slicing along her side. The barkeep screamed and crumpled to her knees, giving Getha the space she and the princess needed to get past.

Getha wrapped an arm around the princess's shoulder, and together they scrambled under the bar. On the other side, the door hung ajar, and Getha shoved her way through it, blades at the ready, to end up in an alleyway lit by a single oil lamp, piled high with garbage, and bordered on all sides by high, blank walls devoid of any doors or windows.

After a quick look around, the princess dashed off toward one of the dead ends, leaving Getha no choice but to follow. As they neared a stack of crates, the door slammed open again, and the barkeep, her side dark with blood, rushed out with a gang of six—no, seven—armed thugs spilling out into the alley behind her.

FOURTEEN

*"When an opposing force is too strong, sometimes the best choice—the only choice
—is to retreat."*
-Megg Pagio, *The Defeat at Antoth*

W hich way?" one of the gang asked, her voice rough with
excitement.

"North?" a man guessed, and the group quested down
toward the other end of the alley.

Getha dropped into mountain stance. Shadows hid her and the
princess, but only for the moment. Getha had never faced down seven
armed foes alone before, and she didn't know how many she could take
before they overwhelmed her, but she only needed to distract them long
enough for the princess to get away. With the narrowness of the alleyway
and a wall at her back, she might—

Princess Renn snagged Getha's arm, pulling her off balance.

Getha faced the princess, who waved at the stack of crates. Did she
think the two of them could hide there? It wasn't that long of an alley, and
the barkeep and her friends wouldn't just give up. Getha shook her head.

The princess waved at the boxes with more emphasis. Getha gestured
for the princess to hide—an idea she should have thought of first—then
pointed to herself and down toward the others, indicating she would stand
and fight.

Princess Renn again pointed at the crates, held up her hand, and using her first two fingers, mimicked legs moving.

What in the pathless hells did she want? Were they supposed to climb up the walls? Exasperated, Getha spread her arms out to both sides. *What?*

The princess whispered something too low to be heard.

"South end," cried one of the gang.

Footsteps came pounding their way, and Getha had lowered halfway into mountain stance when Princess Renn huffed, then hissed more loudly, "It's an exit!"

Again, the princess dashed off and Getha was left to follow, which she did, and when she cut around the crates and discovered an alleyway so narrow only one could pass through at a time, heat crawled up her neck. But she forgot her embarrassment as a man came into sight.

"Here!" he called to the others. "Down here."

Getha fell back into mountain stance. *I'll stand my ground and create a blockade so the princess—*

Though Renn had always had an ear for gossip and a head for names, it wasn't until the guard returned to her fighting stance that Renn placed her. Getha Barei wasn't just *a* palace guard; she was *the* palace guard, the one Lead Varo Orli had trounced before refusing her entry into the varo, the forthright guard Renn had conversed with that day along the Sap.

Fury toward Getha boiled beneath Renn's skin, but she had no intention of running away and leaving the woman to taking a beating for her. She grabbed Getha's arm. "Come on," she said. "I'm not going unless you do."

The guard nodded, and Renn took off down the narrow alleyway, trusting her to follow. Her shoulders bumped and rubbed against the walls as she ran, the shouts of their pursuers echoing around her. The alley let out on the same street as the main entrance to the underground pub, and Getha caught up with Renn as she turned away from the doors.

Side by side, they ran away from Talp's Court, the guard's long strides setting a pace that Renn, with her shorter, Transformed legs, struggled to match.

AFTER RUNNING SEVERAL BLOCKS, Princess Renn began to flag. She slowed, and Getha ventured a look back. The late candlemark meant the streets had emptied some, and they seemed to have lost the barkeep's gang, but Getha didn't want to stop until she could be certain, so she grabbed the princess's arm and forced her on until they had left the Tangles and entered the less shabby and more familiar Mire.

A couple of blocks down from Getha's old city guard precinct, Princess Renn stopped and Getha let her. The princess doubled over, hands on knees, gasping for breath while Getha watched back the way they'd come. Warehouses and taverns bordered the road, and the only people about were drunks, sailors, and drunken sailors.

It had already been one of the longest nights of Getha's life, but it wasn't over yet. It wouldn't be over until Princess Renn was safe back in the palace. Thinking of the palace made Getha think of the queen. There was no way she could haul the princess in front of the queen now, not without making herself look like an utter fool.

What a mess.

WHAT A MESS.

Renn pressed a hand to the stitch in her side and dragged in breath after breath as the guard, barely winded, paced back and forth, her eyes everywhere.

Trusting the guard to notice any threat, Renn focused on recovering from their flight. Though she'd been warned about Natts, first by the servants and then by the group of women standing outside the ale tent, she still hadn't been quite sure what to expect of the lowborn man.

What she'd found was the familiar discomfort of an irritating fellow trying to knock her out of kilter with his lingering, appreciative looks and his crooked grin. He resembled some messeros she knew, the only difference being that his charm was wrapped in rough suede rather than silk.

But Natts was the man with access to Talp, and Renn had been determined to find the answers to Parneo's questions, so, when he'd explained they'd find his boss at his tavern, she'd ignored her misgivings and let him lead her farther into the city. She'd probed his knowledge of Talp's business, but had been met with blank stares, so she'd forced laughs at his japes and fought the urge to sidle away from his flirting touches, enduring his presence until he brought her to the man with the answers she needed.

Entering the tavern had reminded her of entering a ball. Except the tavern stank worse than the ale tent had, no one announced her arrival, and instead of everyone's eyes turning to her first, they turned to Natts and then to her.

Even if she had enjoyed her anonymity in the night market, she didn't much care for the dismissive looks that passed over her on their way back to Talp, but he'd been oblivious to her growing impatience as he'd greeted every second person in the packed tavern. In their slow progress, it had become evident they were headed for a curtain in the far corner of the room, and she'd taken Parneo's list out of her purse in anticipation.

Then, less than thirty feet from the curtain, from Talp, from Renn's answers, that palace guard had appeared and ruined everything.

At last, the princess straightened and put her arms up, her clasped hands resting on the top of her head. Getha scanned the road and waited for the princess's gratitude, perhaps even an apology.

"Why did you do that?"

"What?" Getha turned to face the princess, who, with her flushed cheeks and flared nostrils, didn't look the slightest bit contrite or grateful.

"Why did you do that?" the princess demanded, managing to sound both petulant and imperious. "That sailor didn't say anything. Why did you start that fight?"

It seemed the brawl had gotten her blood up, and at her harsh words, Getha's own blood rose in response. She opened her mouth to ask the princess if she had a brain in her head, then snapped it shut again. She had to remember who she spoke with. It would be too easy to forget herself when speaking to the princess's lowborn face. "I started the fight to get you out of there."

"Who asked you to do that? Who asked you to find me there, anyway?" Her eyes narrowed. "How *did* you find me there? Were you following me?"

"I..." Getha couldn't think of another believable reason. "Yes."

The princess's mouth fell open. "You did?" She reared back. "How dare you!"

"Well, someone had to." The response popped out before Getha might stop it. More boiled up in her chest, but she bit the insides of her cheeks. *Swallow it, Barei. Remember who she is.*

The princess laughed without mirth. "Oh, by all means, do speak freely."

Getha brought her hands together and sparked her bloodmark over and over, the tingle of it centering her. But when she didn't say anything, the princess stepped forward and glared up at her. "What if I order you to speak your mind?"

Remember who she is. Through clenched teeth, Getha said, "We should get you home."

"Why did you follow me?" The princess grabbed Getha's arm. "Why?"

How oblivious could one person be? "That barkeep would have sliced you open if I hadn't been there."

"That barkeep wouldn't have done anything if you hadn't started the fight in the first place."

The truth of that struck a raw nerve. "You're right," Getha said. "I should have just let you get on with your important business."

"Yes, you should have. And it *was* important."

Remember who she is. Getha took a deep breath. "Of course."

She meant the words as an appeasement, but they came out sounding dismissive, and Princess Renn's expression darkened. "What I was doing was far more important than anything someone like you could ever hope to understand." She clasped a hand around the amulet hidden beneath her tunic.

Not quite blasphemous, but close enough. A blinding rush of anger, embarrassment, and the dregs of Getha's fear loosened her tongue. "What would you know about importance?"

"What does that mean?"

"Your brother discovers one of the Lost Pillars, and what do you do with it? You use it amuse yourself by fooling servants—"

Confusion clouded the princess's gaze. "I wasn't—"

"—then you skip off into the Tangles with Natts like some empty-headed clacket."

"An empty-headed *what*?"

"For Amma's sake, he found one of the Lost Pillars! He made one of the most important findings in Ombratian history, and you play around with it as if it's a toy. As if it's nothing."

"It is not nothing," Princess Renn said, her ire rising to match Getha's. "My sister is dead, and—"

"And you act as if that one hardship entitles you to such selfishness. Do you ever think of anything beyond the end of your own nose?"

"You don't know anything." Princess Renn put her face in Getha's, and her mouth twisted into a cruel smirk. "You don't even know enough to get yourself into the varo."

A maw of humiliation opened up within Getha, devouring the last of her good sense. "You told Natts you wanted to speak to Talp. Do you know who he really is?" The princess hesitated. "Do you?"

Princess Renn crossed her arms over her chest. "He's a merchant who deals in alchemical specialties."

"He's a slaver," Getha said, relishing every word.

The princess took a step back. "That's not possible. There are no slavers in Ombratos."

Getha stepped in and towered over her. "See, I do know something. I also know that if it wasn't for me, then right about now you'd either be tied up and on a ship halfway to the slave markets in Xanti or off tumbling some tofter in the hopes of forgetting your darling Prince Dallan left you."

A flash of movement and a rush of air were Getha's only warnings before a knot of pain burst over her left eye.

The princess cried out in pain. "Burning pathless hells!"

Getha clutched her forehead and stumbled into the gutter. *She hit me!* Her eyes were open, but colors swam in her vision and further pain lanced down her neck and across her brow. She had learned how to take a blow in training, but that training assumed one had the slightest inkling that a blow was coming, and never, not in a hundred thousand years, might she have anticipated being hit by a Morovide.

RENN REGRETTED striking Getha the moment she did it, and not just because she was almost positive she'd broken a couple of her fingers, though that did factor in. She'd watched plenty of tourneys, had seen lots of traded blows, and no one throwing them had ever given any indication that it hurt so bloody much. She crumpled to the ground, cradling her damaged hand, biting her lower lip to hold in any other cries of pain. Even so, most of her regret came from knowing she'd just broken a promise she'd made to Solena many years before.

For Renn's ninth birthing day, she and Solena had spent a lovely day together, first sailing out in the bay, then shopping along the Chestnut's high street. They had just stepped out of a shop when a man's angry shouts came from across the street. Renn didn't remember what the merchant had been shouting about, but she remembered how his servant had cowered before him and the way he'd cried out when his master hit him.

She also remembered Solena crouched in front of her, asking her to promise she'd never strike anyone beneath her, telling her it would be unworthy of her to lash out at someone who couldn't, or wouldn't, defend themselves.

Clearly Getha could defend herself. But, as she stood there with her hand covering her eye and forehead where Renn had struck her, it was just as clear she wouldn't, not against a member of the royal family.

Renn had failed Solena twice, first in her fruitless journey to find Talp—who, if the guard spoke the truth, was a slaver—and now in this.

A SMALL PART, a very small part, of Getha was impressed by how soundly the princess had hit her.

She blinked until the colors receded and she could make out the shape of Princess Renn writhing on the ground next to her. The princess whimpered and cradled her hand against her chest like a crushed bird. A hateful voice in the back of Getha's head crowed, *"Remember who she is,"* and the full weight of everything that had just happened, of everything she'd just said, struck her like a thunderclap.

She'd never learned where "breaking the hand of a crown princess of Ombratos" fell on a list of punishable offenses, but it had to be near the top. That the princess had broken her own hand with her clumsy punch would matter little in a trial before the queen. Forget joining the varo. Forget even remaining in the guard. Getha would be lucky to make it through this night with her head still attached to her body.

Falling to her knees, she lost the knobby apple and the slice of bread she'd eaten candlemarks earlier into the street. When the heaving ceased, she wiped her mouth with the back of her hand and almost lay on the ground to put her head lower than the princess's. "I am so sorry, Your—"

A stumble-stepped sailor wandered into the street to pass around them, reminding Getha where they were, and she stopped the title before it fully left her mouth. "You look so different that I forgot myself. I—I beg for your forgiveness and throw myself upon your mercy."

Princess Renn's pained cries turned to the helpless, shattered sobs of a child. Leaving aside their difference in rank, Getha just had goaded an eighteen-year-old girl into hitting her by frightening her and taunting her with a departed lover. Had she anything left in her stomach in that moment, she would have lost that too.

The weeping continued. Getha wanted to fix what she'd broken, but she didn't know how. On second thought, the princess's hand required a healing charm. That much she knew.

"If you'll allow me," Getha said, "I'll help you home. Or to the academy." She tried not to think about what might happen to her once they arrived there.

"No!" The princess looked up and wiped her unhurt hand over her sodden, snot-covered face. "We can't"—her breath hitched—"go to the academy. My brother made me"—*gasp, gasp*—"promise I wouldn't tell anyone about the...thing." She touched the amulet beneath her tunic.

Getha fished in her purse. The palace gave those in the guard half a dozen pea-sized healing charms every two moons. If they required any more than that, the cost came out of their own pockets. She trained hard, and had used four of her six in the last moon, one for a shallow cut along her upper arm, another for a scrape along her shin, and two for a dislocated elbow, which left her with two charms for the next moon, but even by torchlight, it was clear to see the princess's face had grown waxy and sweat stood out on her brow.

Getha pulled out a single charm. Her eye had almost swollen shut, but the princess hadn't broken the skin, so she would bear it. "Here," she said, holding the charm out.

Princess Renn looked down at it. "What's that?"

"A healing charm," Getha said, only a little surprised a highborn girl didn't recognize it. "It's for—"

"I know what they're for." The princess's face had taken on a greenish cast. She plucked the charm out of Getha's palm with her good hand and then just held it. "I don't..." Closing her eyes, she swallowed.

Getha edged out of heaving range. "Use, uh, use your prayer locket to prick your finger, and I'll tell you the incantation."

The princess swallowed again. Then again. At last, she opened her eyes. "I don't have a locket." Some of Getha's disappointment or disgust must have shown on her face because the princess averted her gaze and said, "Haven't worn it since...that morning."

She didn't explain which morning she meant, and she didn't have to. A strange, cloying feeling swept through Getha. Pity? *And what good has pity ever done anyone?* She brushed the emotion aside, released one of her daggers, and offered it to the princess.

Princess Renn reached for the blade with her unhurt hand, but in it she already held the charm. Then she lifted her other hand, crying out when she tried to open her fingers.

Getha had never spilled blood for another, but she didn't see any way around it. *Pathless hells.* Gesturing toward the princess's broken hand, Getha said, "Can I?"

Princess Renn hesitated before holding out her shaking, swollen hand. Getha pressed the dagger's tip into the fleshy mound at the base of her thumb just hard enough to pierce the skin. The intimacy of the act made her itch all over.

When crimson welled up around the blade, she removed it and shuffled back, glad for the moment to end. She opened her mouth to instruct the princess through the rest of the process, but the princess smeared the charm through the blood, set it in the center of her broken hand, and hissed the incantation through clenched teeth. Soon the charm gave off a faint glow.

So she has used one before.

Getha stood, walked to the nearest street torch, and poked the tip of her dagger into the flame to burn away any of the princess's blood that might cling to it. Then she returned to Princess Renn, who stared down at her swollen hand. The healing charm glowed, working away, but as small as it was, it would take a while to repair a broken bone. Though Getha had given the princess the healing charm and helped her use it, she steeled herself for even more blame.

"How am I supposed to explain this?" the princess asked, a whine creeping into her tone.

Renn felt raw and exposed after letting the guard spill her blood—had her hand hurt any less, she would have waited until they got back to the palace —but as the healing charm worked, the pain receded enough to allow her to imagine what might happen if the queen found out about her unsupervised foray into the Branches, and she once again tasted bile on the back of her tongue.

"How am I supposed to explain this?"

"Find a use or I will find one for you." The queen's warning echoed in her mind. When Theodora found out what Renn had done this night, she'd

send Renn away and arrange for some sort of political marriage, or force her to join the ductoran, anything to be rid of her once and for all.

A plea was on Renn's tongue, a plea for Getha to keep her secret, when she remembered that the guard had admitted to following her. She'd also made a comment about Parneo's discovery of the Lost Pillar, meaning she knew about his workshop and his alchemical work. Had it been her intent all along to drag Renn and Parneo in front of the queen? Had she chased after Renn in the hopes of bringing her in and being asked to join the varo?

Fear, a little for herself but mostly for Parn, swept through Renn. She could survive whatever punishment the queen concocted, but without his alchemy, Parneo would go mad. Perhaps even mad enough to seek the same refuge their uncle had sought, hanging himself from one of the chandeliers in his rooms.

"Listen," Renn said, banishing her horror. "If you don't tell anyone about Parneo's workshop, then I won't have you brought up on charges."

Getha flinched. After a long moment, she nodded and turned her head away, yet Renn caught the scowl that slipped across her face. She'd struck another blow against the guard, this one metaphorical, but still a form of abuse, especially when Renn had so much less to lose.

Could she do nothing good or correct this night?

GETHA CHAFED at the princess's threat, but at least she knew she'd live to see the dawn. That was something. A big something, actually. A tightness she hadn't even realized was there released from around her chest.

"I'm sorry," Princess Renn said.

Getha whipped her head around. "Pardon?"

The princess stared at the ground between them. "For hitting you. I'm sorry."

For once, Getha found herself at a loss for words. First a member of the royal family had hit her, and now she apologized for it. Had the world turned on its head?

"If it means anything," the princess said, wincing as she touched her swollen knuckles, "I really wish I hadn't."

The world right itself a little. "Because of your hand."

Princess Renn met Getha's eyes, then looked away. "Because it was unworthy of me."

Meaning what? That it was beneath her to even touch a lowborn? The world and Getha's sense of the princess clicked back into place like one of her daggers settling into her vambrace.

The princess sighed. "I'm not certain where we are. Can you lead the way home?"

RENN HAD THOUGHT them farther to the south, but after a few minutes of walking, they came upon the west end of the commons, where the stink of the grazing fields hung in the air.

While Solena had been gone to the Yent Isles, the queen had changed the grazing laws on the commons based on a vote within the convocation. Renn despised the weekly convocations—she had no patience for all the political maneuverings—and in Solena's absence, had ceased going. The law, some boring thing regarding taxation and forfeitures, had passed by a vote or two, and the only reason Renn knew about it at all was because she it was the only convocation in recent memory she wished she'd attended. Apparently, it had been quite exciting. Almost every highborn in Ombratos had been there, and though two moons past, people still brought it up at every gathering.

To take her mind off her throbbing hand, Renn stared out across the dark expanse of the commons and wondered for the thousandth time how the fate of a danky field could be even the slightest bit interesting.

Then, amidst the shadows, she caught sight of movement. Sharp pains radiated from her hand, a bone-deep weariness tugged at limbs. The sooner they returned to Seedfall the better, but her curiosity overmastered her. She could not... No. She *would* not end this night as useless as she'd started it.

WITH THE CANDLEMARK SO ADVANCED, the darkness in the sky gained depth. "We need to return," Getha said. "It will take us longer to get back than—"

"What's happening there?" With that, the princess walked off across the field, headed toward a herd of sleeping cattle, heedless of the piles of shit she might step in along the way.

Glad to know the night's made an impression on her. Getha once again chased after the princess, catching up with her halfway across the field. "Really, it's probably farther than you think, and—"

"Who's there?" a male voice called out.

Getha stopped, as did the princess, but she waved. "Name's...Alyse," Princess Renn said, using the name Getha had given for her in Talp's Court. "Who are you?"

To Getha, the answer to the princess's question was more than obvious. The man's broad shoulders and ragged clothing marked him as a farmer. Except farmers didn't graze their cattle in the dead of night, not unless they did so in violation of the city's new grazing laws. Which made him a criminal.

"I'm Sanger," the farmer said, holding out his left hand. He and the princess touched palms, then separated their hands, and even in the dim light, their bloodmarks stood out before fading away.

"What are you doing?" Princess Renn asked, her tone innocent.

Did she expect Getha to arrest this man? She considered it. At least then she might have something to show for this wreck of an evening.

Sanger's eyes glittered as he looked the princess up and down. "Only reason I came over here is 'cause you didn't look like no guard. But her"— he nodded in Getha's direction—"she looks like a guard."

"I'm Fera," Getha said, trying to mimic the princess's wave so as not to give them away. "Not a guard."

"Sure, sure," Sanger said. She couldn't tell whether he believed her or not. Then he said, "We're grazing our cows out here."

A frank admission of guilt with two witnesses. *You're already in over your head, friend. Keep digging.*

"Isn't that something people usually do during the day?" the princess asked, sounding as if she asked with genuine interest.

"You caught me," Sanger said, taking the question as the sort that didn't require answer. "Messero Cousteau bought the grazing rights right out from under me, but what am I supposed to do? These cows are the only living I have. Should I let them starve?"

Under the statutes of the state and in the name of the crown, yes. That was exactly what he should have done. Getha flexed her wrist and gripped her knife in preparation for an arrest.

"No," Princess Renn said. As with her question, the shock rang true. "Of course not."

"Damned right," Sanger said, warming to her. "Of course not! Anyhow, that's why I'm out here."

Thinking their pointless little trip out into the field done, Getha reset her dagger, but then the princess started asking Sanger more questions, about his beasts, his work, his family.

Getha pressed a hand to her brow, hissing and yanking it away when she touched the lump where the princess had hit her. She wanted to be angry, but how could she be when this was her own fault? During their fight, Getha had accused the princess of not thinking of anything beyond the end of her own nose. *She does this now just to prove me wrong.*

It obviously hadn't occurred to the princess that she kept this man from his illegal work, and every moment they spoke was another moment the city guard might come along and arrest him. She interrogated the man to show her selflessness, but in doing so, she proved her selfishness.

Getha had a lot of respect for the Morovides, but for Princess Renn, given what she'd learned of the young woman in the past few candlemarks, that seemed about right. Summoning the patience required for boring candlemarks spent on guard, Getha stood off to the side and waited for the princess's demonstration to finish.

A sudden rustling sound came from behind her, and she turned, blade in hand. She peered into darkness too dense to pierce with her sight, so instead of trying to look, she narrowed her eyes and listened, but the noise didn't come again.

FIFTEEN

"Though people might wish to change, they cannot be what they are not. Imagine a mouser that's climbed too high in a tree. When faced with such a height, it's not in the cat's nature to suddenly decide it can fly."
-Violaine Morovide to her daughter, Theodora

When Renn ran out of questions, she bade Sanger farewell, then walked back toward the lighted edge of the commons, leaving him to his animals.

She had her bearings leaving the grazing fields and no longer needed the guard's guidance. Good thing too. Getha strode along behind her, in the position her varo always took, and her silent disapproval, so much stronger than when Renn had admitted to not wearing her prayer locket, jabbed like tiny arrows shot into her back.

They'd reached a spot halfway up the commons, where the ground started to rise in a gentle incline, when Renn decided she couldn't take it anymore. "You think I should have arrested him," she whispered, aware of all the dark, silent houses they passed.

"It doesn't matter."

"It does," Renn said, glancing back over her shoulder.

Getha didn't meet her gaze and didn't answer.

Renn sighed, frustrated. Sanger's plight had made her think, and she refused to be dismissed or ignored the entire trip back to the palace. She fell back a step and matched Getha's stride. When Getha dropped back again, Renn followed. They did this twice more before Getha at last held her ground.

"Well," Renn prompted.

Getha sighed. "Yes, you should have arrested him."

"Why?"

"Because what he's doing is wrong," Getha said, as if explaining how water was wet to a half-wit.

Renn, tired of the guard's condescension, said, in the same tone, "It's not wrong. It's illegal."

"Same thing."

"Is it?" Renn asked, surprised to find herself warming to the debate.

"Doesn't matter if it's right or wrong." Getha held her empty hands out and moved them up and down like the pans on a scale. "He's breaking a law."

Renn thought of Sanger's tale, of his inability to match Messero Cousteau's coin and how that had all but lost him his claim to graze. She thought of Cousteau's round belly, then of Sanger's skinny frame, of the hungry wife and son he'd told her about. "But it's a stupid law," she said. "Harmful, even."

From Getha's silence, her opinion was clear, but Renn wanted to hear her say it. "You don't agree?"

Getha shrugged. "Not my place to agree or disagree. It's still a law."

"So we should just follow it without thought?" Renn's impassioned words echoed down a side street.

Getha's expression closed, and she fell back into her guard position.

Renn let her go. But she did have one last question. "Was that thing you said about Talp true?" she asked, over her shoulder. "Is he a slaver?"

A long pause. "When I was in the city guard, we were never able to prove anything."

"But is he?"

Another long pause. Then, "Yes."

A shiver racked Renn's body. How could Parneo have sent her alone after such a monster? She shook her head, dismissing the question. Parn couldn't have known about Talp or he wouldn't have sent her after him.

Besides, more important than that, what was happening to Ombratos? One man ran slaves while another starved due to a foolish law. *Solena will know what to do.* The unbidden thought made Renn's chest ache, as did the realization that she couldn't let herself think like that anymore. She didn't have Solena to watch out for her and neither did the lowborn. But someone had to care for the lowborn. Someone had to champion their interests in the convocations, and the idea that that someone might be Renn frightened her down to her very core.

The walk to Seedfall from the grazing fields was even farther than Getha had made it sound, and it seemed like they had been trudging along for days when they came upon the Meet, where all signs of the night market, even the ale tent, were long gone, and the empty, interconnected islands looked much larger for it.

The earlier part of the evening—walking through the market, stopping to listen to the singer, buying the comb—felt like something that had happened to another person, like a story she'd been told. That Renn had been nervous and excited, floating along like a leaf on the wind. This Renn had a head stuffed with unanswered questions, aching feet, and even with the charm, a broken hand that cried out a little with every step. She dropped her gaze to the ground and concentrated on putting one foot in front of the other.

When next she looked up, the green stone of the Hedgerow and one of the gates into the Bole loomed at the end of the street.

"Have I your leave to deal with this?"

Renn jumped, hissing as the movement jolted her hand. In her stupor, she'd forgotten Getha was there. Yet she'd felt safe enough to pull inward and let her mind wander. "What's that?"

"The guards," Getha said. "Would you like me to deal with them?"

There are things to be dealt with? Renn nodded.

"All you need to do is agree with whatever I say."

The gate they approached turned out to be Balance Gate, the one gate of the three that had a different image on either side, because of the Three Pillars, only Balance had two distinct facets—Creation and Destruction. A city guard stood to either side of the gate. The one on the left watched Renn and Getha approach, his eyes bright, but his partner slumped against his side like a dirty sack of potatoes someone had rested against the wall and forgotten.

The bright one's Creation and potato man is Destruction. Renn bit back a giddy laugh. She'd never been so tired in her entire life.

She and Getha reached the gate, and Getha approached the bright-eyed guard. Renn meant to listen, but the shapes etched into the stone caught her attention. As with the other gates, she'd passed through this one dozens of times, but always in a carriage or on horseback, and it took a long moment before the shapes resolved into recognizable images.

Twisted bodies, heaped in piles or broken and impaled on pikes or swords, covered the gate's supports. At the peak of the arch, a block showed a figure standing on a hilltop, or a mountain's summit, circled by hunched creatures that might have looked human but for their too-long arms and their misshapen heads. The figure in the center, surrounded on all sides, had his or her hands raised to the sky in surrender. Or supplication? Either way, Renn wasn't sure if the side she looked at was meant to depict Creation or Destruction.

"Isn't that right, Alyse?"

The fake name brought Renn back. She turned toward Getha, who, along with the city guards, stared at her.

"Begging your pardon," Renn said.

The potato man, now awake and alert, laughed. "Listen to that fancy talk! No question you work at the palace, is there?"

"Oh," Renn said, "I suppose not."

The bright-eyed guard frowned at her. "Don't start thinkin' you're one of them just 'cause you work for them. There's thems and there's us. Easy to forget that when you're workin' up on the hill."

Getha edged between him and Renn much in the same way she'd edged between her and Natts. "Easier for some of us than others. It's late. Are you going to let us pass?"

The bright-eyed guard handed something to Getha. "Go on." He spoke around her, to Renn. "Make sure you get your chit before you come out again."

"Indeed," the potato man said, scratching his neck and leaving reddened furrows through the sweat and dirt caked on it. "Not everyone's as nice as me an' Ern here." Then, as his partner opened the postern door, he snorted some phlegm back into his throat, sucked it into his mouth, and spat a runny, yellow wad onto the cobbled stones at their feet.

Some measure of Renn's horror must have shown on her face because Getha said, "Fair night, then," and hastened her toward the postern.

On the other side, a block from the gate and under the light of a globe, Renn glanced over her shoulder and said, "That man was disgusting."

Getha pressed a couple of fingers to her lips, then ballooned out her cheeks as if holding back vomit. Crass humor, but also rather amusing, especially in Renn's current state. She giggled, and Getha almost smiled as she said, "No argument here."

No argument. The knot on Getha's forehead had grown quite a bit, and the moment between them broke.

"Here," Getha said, again serious. She offered Renn a flat piece of wood about the width and length of a grown woman's thumb. "To show at the Seedfall gate."

Renn took it, and when they passed under the next street lamp, held it up into the light. Burned into one side of the golden honeywood were three interlaced circles between a pair of columns with serpents coiled up their lengths, and the columns' bases were linked together with an unbroken chain. The Morovide seal.

On the other side was their family motto—*Nan la sanguor i le dofficium reus.* In blood and duty bound.

"Is this the chit that guard mentioned?" Renn asked. How had she never seen one before? "Does everyone at the palace carry one?"

"Everyone outside of your family."

That seemed wrong to Renn in a way she couldn't quite grasp, but her thoughts about it were soon drowned out by the whimpers of her hand and feet and the rising howl of her thighs. Walking up the hill toward Seedfall was proving to be a lot less enjoyable than strolling down it.

As Getha mounted the hill, a sense of being watching prickled the back of her neck, bringing to mind the sound from the grazing field. Pretending to scratch her side, she untied her belt purse. It fell, and she turned around fast, as if to catch it before it hit the ground. She hoped for a glimpse of startled movement in the shadows at the center of the wide, empty road, where the light of the globes didn't quite reach, but none came, and the sensation of being watched disappeared.

"What is it?" Princess Renn asked.

Getha rubbed a hand over her eyes. "It's nothing."

Renn had never witnessed a sight quite as wonderful as the clean, alert guards standing beside the palace gates. She expected one or all of the guards to call out a greeting to Getha as they neared, but none did. An older, broad-shouldered man guarded the palace wall's postern door; a globe hung right above his head, and the fall of the light made it appear like shadows dripped down his face.

"Tumolo," Getha said.

The guard, Tumolo, sneered at her. "Barei." He pointed to the lump on Getha's brow. "Nice one, there. What? I wouldn't give you a battle so you went out searching for one?"

Getha met his stare but didn't answer. After a tense moment, he tipped his head in Renn's direction. "Who's this?"

Renn held out the chit. "I'm Alyse. I'm new."

Without looking away from Getha or so much as glancing at the chit, he cupped a hand to the side of his mouth and said, in a mock whisper loud enough for all the guards standing around the gate to hear, "You really should look for a better sort. If you spend your nights with one of the forsaken, then people might start thinking you're one too."

A guard on the wall above them snorted into her hand. Renn had never met a forsaken before. Was Getha one of them? Her demeanor didn't change with the accusation, but from the way she asked "Can we go in now?" like each word was formed from glass, it could very well be true.

"Sure," Tumolo said. "As soon as you show me your chit."

"I forgot it."

"You forgot it?" He laughed once, a sharp, mean sound. "So much for Waltham's pet!"

There was a quiet *snick*, then Getha reached over and shoved something back into her vambrace. *Snick.* "Please let us in."

"That's fine," he said, smiling. "But I'm going to have to report you."

She glared at him. "You're a motherless bastard."

He opened the door, bowed, and waved them through. "Have a fine night, Barei."

"Eat shit, Tumolo."

Aside from several patrolling guards wandering here and there, the grounds were empty. Renn wanted to ask Getha about the forsaken thing, but if it wasn't true, she didn't want to imply it might be. But she had to know about the animosity between Getha and the other palace guards.

Renn waited until they had moved out of earshot of the gate, then asked. "Don't you work with those people? Aren't they your friends?"

"Are all the other highborn your friends?" Getha snapped.

Renn appreciated everything Getha had done for her, but she was exhausted and in pain, and as a crown princess, had reached her limit for the woman's insolence. "I've forgiven quite a lot this evening, wouldn't you say?"

"Yes, Your Highness," Getha said, her tone soft but brittle. "I apologize."

There's thems and there's us. Getha's contrition seemed both right and wrong, and Renn decided she'd also had enough of her own inadequacies for one night. "I'll be fine from here. You may go."

"Yes, Your Highness."

Renn sighed. After everything, she didn't want to leave their night on that note. "I'm sorry. Thank y–"

When she turned around, Getha had already disappeared. "I have your chit," Renn said to the empty air. She couldn't give it to a servant, not without getting Getha in trouble, so she'd have to find her in the morning to return it.

She crossed the grounds to the row, then stopped at a tree near the fletcher's pen at the end of it to peek around the side. Varo Roher was alone in front of Parneo's door, which meant that her brother had left without her.

A spike of pain drove up her arm. *If he didn't leave the shutters open...*

She waited until Roher looked the other way down the row before scurrying to the far side. All of the shops had long since closed for the night, and everyone had left their windows shuttered, rendering the darkness of the alley complete. Running her good hand along the wall, she counted windows until she reached Parneo's rooms. The shutters were closed, but she gave them a push, and they swung inward. Light from his globes spilled into the alley, and a glance through the window revealed her dear twin had left the stool inside.

She leaned over the sill, and her fingers just brushed the stool when a hand clapped over her mouth and an arm wrapped around her middle, dragging her back into the darkness.

SIXTEEN

*"We are stewards of this land and of these people. They carry us on their backs,
and in return, we care for them."*
-Princess Solena Morovide to her youngest sister, Renn

Renn struggled against the arms wrapped around her. She tried
to cry out for Varo Roher on the other side of the building,
but the hand over her mouth was too tight. She kicked at
the wall and managed to loose one of her arms from her captor's grip.
Lashing out, she slammed it—her hurt hand—against something
hard.

A black cloud of pain swallowed her whole.

SHE WOKE inside her brother's workroom with a narrow-faced, black-eyed
stranger kneeling over her. She opened her mouth to scream, but he again
clamped a hand over her mouth, pinning her to the floor.

"Renn," the young man whispered. "It's me!"

That took a moment to sift through the haze of her fear. When it did,
she stopped fighting and stared up at the stranger, at his upturned nose
and skinny lips. Recognizing him at last, she relaxed her muscles.

"You know who I am?" Parneo asked, his voice deepened by the Transformation amulet around his neck. The one he'd said he'd never wear again.

She nodded, and he removed his hand from her mouth. She sat up and slid back until she rested against the wall and took slow breaths to calm herself. "What in the pathless hells were you doing out there?"

"Coming to find you," he said, rocking on his heels. "I snuck out and went to your rooms, but you weren't there. Why weren't you there? Do you have the answers to my questions? Why weren't you there?"

Gone was the sharp, detached Parneo from earlier in the evening. She had to be careful with this version of her twin or he'd break down and have a fit. She wrapped both hands around his upper arms. Both hands. A healing charm the size of a chicken's egg was tied to the wrist of her broken hand. She opened and closed her fingers, but the hand felt no more than bruised, and even that minor ache was fading.

Parneo looked down at the floor. "I didn't mean to hurt you. I fixed it."

"It's fine, Parn. You didn't hurt me."

His head moved in a couple of jerky nods. "Why weren't you there? Do you have the answers to my questions?"

She needed to break the news to him gently. "Talp," she said, "isn't who we thought he was."

He pointed to her hand. "Did he do that to you?"

Part of her wanted to tell Parneo everything that had happened, but she didn't want to worry him with the knowledge that a stranger knew about his workroom. She also still regretted hitting Getha and didn't want Parn to think less of her for it.

She tucked the hand beneath her leg. "I did it to myself."

"Oh," he said. "Hit her hand herself. No more Talp, then. Good. I'm taking care of it."

"What does that mean?"

Parneo grinned at her, and despite the amulet, it was his smile. It unsettled her to see her brother's expression warped by unfamiliar features. "They didn't want me to use it again," he said.

The hairs on Renn's arms rose. She could handle calculating Parneo. She could handle him during his fits. But when he talked about "they" and "them," he seemed miles away from her. She had no idea whom he meant.

He touched his amulet. "They can't see around corners like I can. They shouted and shouted. Then I stepped around the corner, and now they're happy." He ran his thumb over the bridge of her nose, smoothing her furrowed brow. "You're worried. Don't worry."

"Who are *they*?" she asked, brushing his hand away, hoping this time he might answer.

Parneo sat back on his heels, closed his eyes, and took a deep breath. Another. When he opened his eyes again, they were focused and clear. "I shouldn't have sent you out after Talp in the first place. I'm going to the academy tomorrow, and I think I'll be able to find out a lot there."

"The academy? Parn..."

He held up a hand. "I know I can't enter. But you were right. I'm the one who needs to research the working."

She wanted to chastise him, but she hadn't the heart for it. "Are you going to tell the alchemists who you are?"

Parneo paused, then turned his back to her and climbed to his feet. "No."

"What about your discovery of the Lost Pillar? Will you share that?"

He eased open the shutters and looked out the window. "Dawn is coming."

Renn stood and joined him at the window. Brightness limned the peaks of the Cassedents. "Are you sure about this?" If Parneo had a single fit at the academy, everything would fall apart. They would find his amulet, and if they removed it, which seemed likely, they'd figure out his true identity. Renn's involvement was sure to come out as well. She shuddered to think of Queen Theodora's reaction.

"I'm sure," he said, sounding it. "Please, Renn. Let me go to the academy. Let me find out what happened to Solena."

She leaned against his side, and he stiffened. "Promise me you'll be careful."

"I promise." He edged away from her until she stood unsupported, then he tossed his leg over the windowsill just as she had candlemarks before, clambered outside, and ran off to sneak back into the palace in whatever manner he'd sneaked out. No one knew the secrets of Seedfall like he did.

In the front room, Renn took off Alyse's clothing—that's how she thought of her lowborn self now, as Alyse—and removed her amulet. When she was again dressed in her highborn clothing, she'd reached a point beyond exhaustion. She tucked her amulet into its silk-lined bag, stuck it in her bodice, and opened the door.

"Fair night, Varo."

Roher turned to face her. "Fair night, Your Highness. Or should I say fair morning?"

She heard his unspoken question about what might have kept her in her brother's rooms so long after he left, so long after everyone else in the palace had retired to their rooms. She heard it and chose to ignore it. Between Parneo, Getha, Sanger, Talp, and everything else, she had more than enough to think about. With a jaw-cracking yawn, she trudged up the row toward the palace.

GETHA RETURNED to her quiet barracks, laid down on her bunk, and listened to Hoefen's hitching snores. She needed to rest, her next shift started at sunrise, but sleep was like the little sorrel worms she'd hunted for in tide pools as a girl, constantly slipping from her grasp.

When she had to report for duty, she rose and moved through the day as if in a dream. A few people asked her about the bruise on her face, and Tumolo made a crude remark about stepping out with a servant, but it all felt like it happened to someone else.

After midday meal, she skipped the voluntary afternoon training and returned to the barracks. The next day was her free one, and she couldn't leave the palace grounds without her chit. Intending to think of a solution for getting it back, she rested her head on the pillow, but the moment she closed her eyes, sleep crashed over her.

"GET UP, BAREI," Lead Palace Guard Selm called from the foot of Getha's bed. "You're expected to relieve Guard Beauchen in one candlemark."

No more than half awake, Getha rolled out of bed and to her feet, squinting at the stocky woman silhouetted by the midmorning daylight streaming in through the barracks' open door. Getha estimated she'd slept for about fifteen candlemarks.

"'s my free day, Lead Guard," Getha said, her voice rusty from sleep. Unless... Had she slept through a whole day?

Selm's boots thumped against the floor, and she got right up in Getha's face, close enough to envelope Getha in her sticky peachy fragrance, close enough for Getha to count every dark hair on the woman's upper lip.

"Special request," Selm said. "Beauchen's in the throne room."

The throne room? Getha catapulted into full wakefulness. "What? Why? Why me?"

Selm raised an eyebrow. "I was hoping you might know. Not every day I get one of the princesses telling me where to put my guards."

"One of the princesses" had to be Princess Renn. She'd sworn she wouldn't tell her mother about Getha, but perhaps now it benefited her in some way to do so. Why had Getha trusted her? Why—

"Well?" Selm asked, yanking Getha from her thoughts.

"Well what?"

"Do you know why Princess Renn wants you in the throne room for convocation?"

"I..." Getha sparked her bloodmark. "No."

Selm wasn't a fool. She hooked her thumbs over her belt and grunted. "As you say, Guard." When Getha didn't reply, she turned to leave, speaking over her shoulder, "Be there in a candlemark."

Getha's skin felt too tight, her legs itched to run, and twice she put her tunic on backwards. She imagined Guard Beauchen taking her into custody the moment she stepped into the throne room, hauling her past the high-born and up to the dais to kneel before the queen. She tried to add Princess Renn hurling accusations in her direction, but all she could picture was a yellow-haired girl with a broken hand, a dead sister, and an absent lover sitting in the middle of the street, sobbing.

She'd been so worried about the possible outcomes of her own actions that she hadn't spent much time ruminating on the princess, or the weaknesses she'd bared that night. The truth was, Getha wasn't sure how she felt about the princess having foibles and facets. The royal family always seemed distant from people like her. Unreal, even. To have one break down in front of her...

The only thing she could compare it to was if a statue came to life, only to start crying. How was one meant to deal with something so far removed from the natural order of things? She wanted to dismiss it as a mad dream, but the bruise on her face was a constant reminder that it had been all too real.

Dressed, Getha went to the eating lodge and forced down a mugful of sop. It sat in her stomach like a rock, but if she was going to be arrested, she'd rather do so with a full belly. Aware of how much trouble she might have avoided by going to Waltham with her information about the princess in the first place, she ran to his rooms in the varos' wing of the palace.

The globelit hall was quiet, but as she rushed along, the door next to Waltham's opened, and Varo Meton stepped out of his and Varo Tisko's chambers.

"Fair morning," Meton said, smiling.

She ignored him, knocked once at Waltham's door, then, without waiting for an answer, charged into his office and shut the door behind her.

Waltham's office—with its bookshelves along the north wall, the Althian map hanging next to the room's single window, the ugly carpet, the matching set of chairs in front of his orderly desk—was usually a sanctuary, but not even the sight of his varo blade mounted above the fireplace could calm her.

The door to Waltham's bedchamber opened, and he poked his snowy head into the room. "Thought it might be you. Give me a..." He stepped over the threshold. "What happened to your face?"

"It's a long story." She sat in one of the chairs and stared down at her bloodmark as she sparked it over and over. "There's a chance I'm in trouble."

Waltham didn't say anything, but his silence spoke volumes.

Gritting her teeth, she clarified. "Not *that* kind of trouble."

"Of course not," he said with enough vigor and conviction she almost believed him. Unable to sit still, she leapt to her feet and paced around the room.

He crossed to his desk, following her with his gaze. "How big of a chance?"

"Hard to say." Stopping in front of the hearth, she rested one arm on the mantel and ran a finger from her other hand along his varo blade. She'd never asked him to hold it because the first time she held one she wanted it to be her own. "Can you come by convocation today?"

"Getha, I—"

Her stomach clenched. She couldn't talk about it anymore. If she was in trouble, he'd understand when he got there. "I have to go or I'll be late. Will you come?"

"Certainly," he said, sitting. "But I wish—"

She hurried from the room before he could finish.

Crossing from the varo wing into the palace proper set her pulse racing, and the carved wooden doors to the throne room seemed twice as tall as the last time she'd passed through them. Sunlight streamed through the wall of floor-to-ceiling windows and shone off the polished honeywood floor. Beauchen stood guard just inside the entryway to the already warm room, empty but for Princess Heshiette on the dais, the on-duty guards spaced at even intervals along the wall, and the servant opening the windows on their vertical pivots.

Beauchen raised a bushy eyebrow at Getha as she dismissed him and claimed his post. "Why are you replacing me? Am I to report to Selm?"

"Yes." Getha wasn't sure if he was supposed to or not, but saying yes seemed like the quickest way to be rid of him.

He nodded and left. She sensed the other guards looking at her, sharing in Beauchen's curiosity, but she stared straight ahead. At the far end of the room, Princess Heshiette, black hair pulled back, clad in a gown the color of a stormy sea, wandered around on the dais. First she ran a hand over the larger throne, the one with the gilded likenesses of all the former queens carved into the back, then she slapped her palm against the tufted purple velvet cushions of the smaller heir's throne.

Varo Libran guarded her from the front of the dais, on the side nearest the windows. The varo's squat frame gave no indication of his immense skill in disarming opponents. Getha had hoped to learn a lot from him, but that dream now seemed further away than ever.

The throne room attendant entered and announced, "Presenting Messera Cadice Gallieri."

Princess Heshiette descended the dais and met the painfully slender Messera Gallieri halfway across the room, where they embraced and strolled off to a spot near the windows, heads together. Gallieri wasn't one of the princess' usual set, one of her Spares, but perhaps something had changed. Getha had larger concerns than the ebb and flow of Princess Heshiette's social life.

One by one, the attendant introduced the highborn as they arrived. The women wore colorful gowns and the men sleeveless robes that brushed the floor. Some received attention while others were snubbed as the highborn danced to a tune only they could hear. Soon, about thirty highborn milled around the sunlit room, jockeying for position near Princess Heshiette and waiting for convocation to begin.

"Presenting Esteemed Varo Hillard Waltham."

Most turned—varo didn't often attend convocation outside of their official capacity—and Getha relaxed a little when Waltham walked in wearing his dress uniform. He looked around until he found Getha, then he strode slowly through the room, stopping here and there to speak with one messeran or another. At length, he sat in a chair beside one of the windows in the guise of an old man basking in the sun, but she knew he was ready for whatever might come.

A second attendant appeared on the dais. She rang a small silver bell, its airy peal cutting through the room and bringing a halt to all conversation, and said, "Presenting Princess Linore Belia Violaine Theodora Morovide, eldest daughter of Queen Theodora and heir to the Blessed Crown of Ombratos."

The attendant stopped there, meaning no queen attended the convocation with her. Was that a good sign or a bad one?

Getha and the rest of the guards bowed, and the highborn either bowed or curtsied. Entering through a side door, Princess Linore walked across the dais. Her sandy-colored hair hung limply around her face, and her finely tailored dress only emphasized her narrowing frame.

Varo Kane took his place to the side of the heir's throne, and Princess Linore dropped down onto it, resting her chin on her hand. "Rise," she said, her tone as pallid as her skin, and everyone in the room straightened from their bow or curtsy. "Come forth and be recognized."

A line of highborn formed at the dais, and each one knelt before her in turn. Though the princess spoke the proper words for the rituals of convocation, she did so while staring out the window.

Getha bore no special love for the highborn, but their attendance seemed worth more than the heir's indifference. Thinking of Princess Renn's breakdown in the middle of the street, Getha considered all the sisters had lost with Princess Solena's death, but her sympathy fast gave way to disappointment. True, the princesses had lost their sister and the heir, but they were Morovides, and it was their responsibility to do better. To *be* better.

The line ended, and since Princess Linore offered no direction for the convocation, that freed the highborn to discuss whatever they wished. Near Getha, Messero Orosin and Messera Sciaraperra turned, as they so often did, to gossip. Minutes both dragged on and flew by as Getha did her best to block out the messeran's guesses as to who tumbled whom, and suddenly the attendant was announcing the newest visitor to the throne room.

"Presenting Princess Renn Belia Violaine Theodora Morovide, youngest daughter of Queen Theodora and third in line to the Blessed Crown of Ombratos."

Everyone turned to watch the princess enter, but since Getha stood beside the door, it felt like they stared at her. *Don't look at her. Don't look at her.* But then movement shifted in the corner of her vision, and her eyes moved of their own accord.

The young woman who entered wasn't the girl in riding leathers Getha had spoken to along the river or the sobbing child she'd argued with in the

Mire. This Princess Renn wore a gown of deep blue, with her wild black curls pinned back and a thin silver circlet across her brow.

She looked around the room as she walked in, and for an instant, her grey eyes met Getha's. Getha tried to read the princess's intent, but her face gave nothing away.

Messero Orosin spoke behind his hand to Messera Sciaraperra. "I can't remember when young Renn last graced us with her royal presence."

Messera Sciaraperra sniggered. "Nor can I."

Shoulders back, the princess strode toward the dais. The servant Tomas brought forward a stool covered with a threadbare cushion and set it out for her. Princess Renn lifted her skirts and knelt, and the room filled with the whisper of rich fabrics as the rest of the highborn lowered themselves to the ground.

This is it. Getha bit the insides of her cheeks and held her breath. Princess Linore studied her youngest sister. "Yes?"

"Heir, I come to this place with open heart and an open mind." Renn's voice shook, but it also carried to every corner of the room. "I vow respect in thought, speech, and deed."

"Have you anything to bring before us?"

Getha dug her nails into her palms, and her bloodmark throbbed.

"Not as of yet," Princess Renn said.

Getha's breath came out in burst, earning her dirty looks from Messero Orosin and Messera Sciaraperra. *If I'm not here to be punished, then what is her game?*

Princess Linore waved a careless hand. "Then we bid you go forth and be heard."

Tomas came forward to offer Princess Renn his hand. She took it and stood, and the resultant rustle of fabric as the highborn rose was like a flock of birds taking flight.

AFTER LEAVING Parneo's workroom and traveling back to the palace from Menders' Row, Renn had spent the rest of that night lying in her bed and staring at the chit she'd forgotten to return. She'd turned it over and over, looking first as her family's crest, then at their motto.

She was a princess, a Morovide, but she'd never given much consideration to what that truly meant. Solena had always been mindful of how she was perceived, yet Renn, even in listening to Solena speak of their stewardship to the people of Ombratos, had mistaken that mindfulness for a necessity of Solena's position as heir when, in truth, it was an admirable facet of her personality.

Of course, Renn was an heir, too, but as the fourth in line behind three perfectly healthy and capable sisters, she'd never once imagined a world in which she ascended to the throne.

She'd eventually lapsed into a fitful sleep and only to be woken by the return of her blood-soaked nightmare a few candlemarks later. Calling on her maids, Renn was struck by the care and attention the women gave to her and their jobs.

When Nessa and Editi offered their hands to assist Renn into her bath, she squeezed Nessa's. "Thank you. For all that you do."

Nessa's watery hazel eyes went wide. "Yes, Your Highness."

Renn turned to face Editi and squeezed her hand. "You too."

Editi's cheeks flushed red under the freckles, but she smiled. "It's my pleasure, Your Highness."

In the bath, Renn resolved to thank her servants more often. *That's not enough,* said a small voice in her mind. She knew that, but what next?

She'd finished bathing, and her maids dressed her in riding clothes, but on her way to the stables, she'd passed the library, the walls of books and the knowledge they contained beckoning to her. Inside, she'd discovered a bespectacled woman surrounded by stacks of books and piles of papers, all covered in notes written in the same hand, bent over another page already half-covered by her flowing script.

She glanced up as Renn neared her table, then leapt to her feet, knocking over a stack of books. She reached for them, but the top two slid off the edge and she winced as each fell—*slam, slam*—to the floor. "I'm terribly sorry, Your Highness. I didn't see... I should have seen... I mean, I should have looked to have seen—"

I should have worn the amulet. "It's all right," Renn said. "Please, what can you tell me about the grazing laws?"

After a long day of studying, she'd slept through the night and woken with the dawn to summon her maids.

"I'd like to dress for convocation," Renn said, as Editi and Nessa entered, hoping she sounded much more confident than she felt.

The maids hid well any surprise they might have felt at such a request. Editi readied the washbowl while Nessa sorted through Renn's jewelry at her dressing table. Renn left it to her to choose the right dress for the right occasion.

Nessa held up a pair of delicate gold and amethyst earrings. "It's going to be a warm day. Might I suggest the lavender silk?"

Dallan had once complimented Renn in that dress, telling her she was radiant and then asking her to dance despite a lack of music. They had whirled around the room together until she was fall-down dizzy and they were both laughing. What would he make of her intent to attend convocation? If he had stayed, would he have gone with her?

If he had stayed, would I be going at all? With that uncomfortable thought, Renn sat at her dressing table. "I think the cerulean linen."

"As you say." Nessa set down the earrings and picked up ones of sapphire and silver, laying them on the table in front of her, next to the small collection of powders and creams.

She'd requested Getha's presence in the throne room because she'd needed to return the woman's chit. Or that was what she had told herself, not understanding why it was important to her for Getha to witness her efforts on Sanger's behalf, only that it was.

Despite their awkward farewell, it had bolstered Renn to enter the throne room and see Guard Barei on duty. Especially since her face lacked the shock present on everyone else's.

When Linore gave her leave to, Renn rose from the bench, thanking Tomas for helping her up, and a glance around the room sent her in the direction of Messero Orosin and Messera Sciaraperra. Both from the queen's birth cluster and more interested in marriage contracts and trysts than politics, she considered them prime candidates on which to try out her arguments. They also stood on the far side of the room from Messero Cousteau. With the grazing fields as part of his district, giving him the most to gain from its increased taxation, he was sure to be her staunchest opponent, and Renn wanted to strengthen her arguments before facing him.

That Messero Orosin and Messera Sciaraperra tittered about near Guard Barei... Well, should the guard happen to overhear Renn's plan to help the lowborn, so be it.

The messeran greeted Renn with false smiles and open arms.

"What a lovely surprise," Messero Orosin said, bowing to kiss the air above the back of Renn's hand, raising it just high enough that he didn't expose the balding spot on the crown of his head. "It's not often we see you here."

"Indeed." Messera Sciaraperra also kissed her hand, her dry lips actually brushing Renn's knuckles. "To have all the princesses at convocation is quite the treat. If only there was something on the agenda."

Renn bit the end of her tongue. Even Getha would be able to understand the far-from-subtle barbs the messeran shot her way, their comments that proved that even Renn's peers thought her silly and vain. She took a deep breath. No one could change that but her.

"I wonder," Renn said, touching Messero Orosin's forearm, "if you've given any more thought to the grazing law."

"The grazing law?" Messera Sciaraperra's brows came together for an instant before she shook her head and visibly relaxed her forehead. She feared wrinkles the way most feared a plague. "That passed moons ago, darling. Whyever would I think about it these days?"

Renn explained to the messeran about Sanger, not about her direct experience with him but about his predicament, about her newfound knowledge as to how closely the lowborn lived to the edge of existence, and in pairs and small groups, other highborn began wandering over from other parts of the room. All the attention made her cheeks warm and her palms sweat, but the importance of her subject drove her on, and as she spoke, as the messeran listened, her nervousness lessened.

Outside the circle, Getha stood against the wall and stared out at whatever guards stared at while doing their jobs, and Renn kept glancing up, searching her blank expression for any hint of approval.

"Sister," Heshi crowed, startling her. "You seem to be stirring up something over here. Whatever could it be?"

A smile creased Heshi's face as she approached, though the expression didn't extend beyond her mouth. Then she neared, grabbed Renn's upper arms with claw-like hands, and kissed her on both cheeks, an act hostile for its strangeness. Renn and Heshi hadn't discussed her brief betrothal to Dallan or the part Renn had played in ending it since Heshi had never seemed to care two licks for the prince, yet the viciousness of her grip suggested some feelings on the topic.

But this wasn't the time or the place for that conversation. "I wanted to revisit the grazing laws," Renn said, pulling out of her sister's bruising grip.

"Oh, Renn," Heshi said. "It's such a beautiful day. I'm sure you'd much prefer to be out riding."

The highborn surrounding them tittered, and Messero Cousteau strolled over, leading as he always did, with his rounded gut. "What's this about the grazing laws?"

Renn again spoke of Sanger, but instead of aiming for Cousteau's heart, she went for his purse, arguing how it hurt them all to widen the already massive divide between the highborn and the lowborn.

She knew what she believed, but her arguments sounded simplistic even to her own ears. Cousteau listened for a while, then smiled at her as if she was a precocious, but tiresome, child. "That's a charming notion, Your Highness. If only the matters at hand were so easily solved."

Heshi chimed in to lecture Renn on the costs of animal transport and falling grain prices, and Renn tried to follow along, but she'd only studied for a day, and they soon ranged out of her depth. Embarrassed, she shifted her back to Getha and waited for a chance to excuse herself.

When Heshi at last paused for breath, Renn thought she'd found her opportunity, but Heshi dropped into a curtsy, and the other highborn lowered to the ground, which meant Linore approached. Renn dipped her own curtsy, then faced Linore, certain she was the reason her sister had left the dais.

"Why are you here?" Linore asked, sounding as impatient and weary with Renn as the queen usually did.

Everything was moving so much faster than Renn had planned. She'd thought to come to convocation more than once before presenting anything to the throne, but here Linore stood, asking her a direct question she had to answer, and an alternate topic, a decoy, eluded her. "I, uh, would like to make a formal petition to revisit the issue of the grazing law."

Linore sighed and pinched the bridge of her nose. "The matter has been decided, and it is closed for discussion."

"I understand. That's why I'm petitioning to reopen it. I also wish to address Talp—"

Linore, eyes wide, leaned in, pressed her cheek to Renn's, and whispered harshly, "You do not ever say that man's name here."

Renn jerked back. "Why not? Solena once told me—"

"Amma's eyes, Renn," Linore cried, and Renn's stomach dropped. The old Linore had never blasphemed. "Solena is dead!"

Her words echoed through the room, and the highborn stared at their feet. "She's dead, and she left me quite enough to deal with without you adding to it." She narrowed her bloodshot eyes. "I don't need this. Not now. Not from you. Stop whatever you're playing at, and go back to doing what you do best."

"And that is?" Renn asked, before wondering if she really wanted to know the answer.

Heshi stepped forward. "Not caring about anything that doesn't concern *you*." Her voice cracked on the last word.

Renn finally allowed herself to see the full impact her tryst with Dallan had had on Heshi. Although Heshi never cared a whit about Dallan, a marriage of such high political importance would have raised her standing at court. Instead, her little sister had slept with her betrothed, forcing a scandalous and very public breaking of the engagement. Renn had considered the damage she'd done to her own reputation, about which, until recently, she'd cared very little, but she hadn't only hurt herself, had she?

"I'm sorry," Renn said. "I'm so sorry. I—"

A tear fell, and Heshi dashed it away, her face, neck, and chest turning crimson. She ducked her head and ran out through the main doors. A grouping of Spares smirked and pointed after her but none followed, so Linore followed her, with both of their varos at her heels.

Their exits brought an abrupt halt to the convocation, and while people whispered to one another and wandered out, Renn stared down at her feet, waiting for everyone to leave, the humiliation coursing through her veins a poison of her own making. Why hadn't she apologized to Heshi sooner? She was right. Renn had been so wrapped up in her own broken heart that she hadn't considered how much her sister's standing among her peers meant to her. She added Heshi's reputation to the list of problems she didn't know how to fix.

When she finally looked up, the highborn had left, but the guards, including Getha, Renn's varo, Adeliana, and Esteemed Varo Waltham remained.

Renn's pain was a sore tooth she wanted to poke. She'd failed in a dozen different ways, and a bit more abuse seemed due. "Dismissed," she said. "All except for Guard Barei."

The palace guards left without question, but the varo were more reluctant to comply. Adeliana was on duty, and from the way Waltham stared at Getha, she had at least one friend in the guard.

"Dismissed," Renn repeated to Adeliana, "You may wait outside the door."

Varo Adeliana allowed Varo Waltham to walk out first, then followed him and closed the door behind her.

Alone with Getha, Renn pulled out the chit. She ran her fingers over the Morovide seal, over the motto. Solena would be so damned disappointed in her. "Don't you find this unbearably heavy?" she asked, expecting a curt answer or a derisive silence.

"No, Your Highness."

Renn held out the chit. "No?"

Getha took it and slipped it into her pocket.

"Why not?"

"I don't know." Getha rubbed her right thumb back and forth over her left palm, sparking and resparking her bloodmark. "I suppose because I asked to carry it."

The profoundness of that struck Renn to her core as she watched Getha's bloodmark rise and fade. "Are you really—" She stopped herself before she said *forsaken*. "Did you really grow up outside the Gift?"

Getha pressed her lips into a hard line. "Yes."

"Then how did you get your bloodmark?"

"I decided I wanted one, and I didn't give up until I had it."

"Was it hard?"

Getha resuming her guard stare. "It wasn't easy."

Renn ran her thumb across her palm, and as it always had, her bloodmark flared crimson. She looked up and tried to imagine how the throne room appeared to Getha, through the eyes of a lowborn. She saw abundance. She saw inherited wealth and unearned privilege. *I asked to carry it.* That Renn hadn't chosen the circumstances of her birth meant nothing. She was a princess, a Morovide, and it was up to her to decide what that meant.

She stood and faced Getha. "Will you help me?"

Getha met her eyes. "With what?"

"I want to be worthy of my name," Renn said, removing the pins from her hair, releasing her curls from their confinement.

ABOUT TO REFUSE, Getha watched the princess pull the pins out of her hair.

As with their talk by the Sap, as with their night out in the Branches, not a moment of this afternoon had gone as she'd expected. Princess Renn had endured much in the past couple of days. She'd been knocked down and knocked down, but here she stood. That Getha had misjudged the princess was clear. The young woman was a fighter. The princess winced as she yanked a pin out from behind her ear. One who sought to be worthy of her name.

"What does that mean?" Getha asked, startling herself with the question. "What would it take for you to become worthy of your name?"

Princess Renn dropped her hands and seemed to think about that. Half of her hair was loose, the other half still pinned into place. Absently, she ran a hand through the free side, allowing her wild curls to reclaim their true form.

The sight of her unruly hair side-by-side with her severe coiffure seemed right for the princess, an impulsive, wayward creature intent on escaping her cage.

"I'm not sure yet," the princess said, answering Getha's question about what it would take for her to become worthy of her name. "But I think it might require future trips into the city, if you're up for it."

"I won't do anything illegal," Getha said. She wouldn't break her promise to Waltham, not even for a princess. "We can't ever return to Talp's."

"Nothing illegal," Princess Renn said. The corners of her mouth fell. "And, I suppose, no more dealings with Talp."

"What if I have a bad feeling about something or don't think it's safe?"

"Then I won't do it," the princess said. "I want to help people, not put us danger." She held out her left hand. "Will you help me?"

Getha stared down at the outstretched hand. The princess offered her all the responsibilities and leeway given a varo, but what did that mean without the title? With Princess Renn involved, Getha had no idea what might happen next. But there was only one way to find out.

Blood whishing through her veins, Getha clasped hands with Princess Renn, and her palm tingled as their bloodmarks sparked against one another. "I will."

SEVENTEEN

*"Every major working requires a framework, and upon said framework, the
results will return tenfold."*
-Law of Returns

The campus of Galathar Morovide's Alchemical Academy of Higher
Learning and Purpose—more often referred to as the Academy—
occupied an area in the Branches that butted up against the Gift
on one side and the Hedgerow on another. High, alchemically warded
fences protected the rest of the land, what there was left of it. The Academy
had long outgrown its original structure, and former high alchemists had
chosen to build out before building up, leaving scant gardens, lawns, or
paths for the students and alchemists to enjoy. That was not so great a
sacrifice since the rest of Ombratos was on the other side of the fences and
a rooftop garden had been built and rebuilt with each upward expansion.
Even so, few visited the garden without purpose as the Gift, close as it was,
seemed to loom over anyone who visited.

High Alchemist Kitra Rande rubbed her closed eyelids and tried to
remember her last good night's sleep. When she pulled her hands away and
opened her eyes, bright stars danced in her vision, so she sat back in her
chair and waited for them to fade.

Unlike most of the alchemists who had been there the morning of the
accident, Kitra wasn't plagued by nightmares. Not that she blamed those

who were. As ugly as things had turned out on the observation floor, the scene in the preparation chamber had been that much worse.

Every student learned the Law of Returns on her or his first day at the academy, and while Princess Solena's blood had been the catalyst, High Alchemist Marcal's had served as the framework. A successful working would have provided him with the tremendous boons of heightened health, strength, and intelligence. But a calamity of the sort they had experienced…

Princess Solena's death, awful as it was, had been peaceful in comparison to Marcal's. While the Morovides burned their eldest daughter, the alchemists had incinerated a pile of body parts. But the memories of Marcal's death, of being ushered from the palace and back to the academy covered in blood and unidentified bits of her former friend, were not what kept Kitra up at night.

There was another lesson taught to the alchemists in their first tenday about how one must place his or her own feelings behind the needs of their work. *An emotional alchemist is a careless alchemist, and a careless alchemist performs failed workings.* Grief and horror had no place in alchemy. She might have spent an evening or two at a tavern out in the city weeping into her ale, but she left that at the door whenever she returned to the academy.

Silent, briny breezes swept through the open office window, fluttering the papers on her desk, and the stars faded from Kitra's vision, replaced by fuzzy colors and indistinct shapes. She picked up her gold-rimmed spectacles from the desk and put them back on. The weight of the thick disks of glass rested heavy on her cheeks, but the colors and shapes of her office jumped into focus, and she squinted in the unrelenting brightness of the twelve unshuttered globes. The globes were Marcal's. He had abhorred shadows and darkness, and whenever she'd complained about the glare, he'd stand and say, "Truths, my dear, are revealed in the light!"

Instead of returning to the maddening, flapping pages on the desk—*my* desk, Kitra reminded herself—she plucked a globe from its wooden frame and rolled the cool glass between her hands. Though the overabundance of light gave her headaches after too long, she'd yet to have the globes removed.

Sentimental carelessness.

She stared at the globe, which made her think of Marcal, which made her think of the palace, which brought her back to the Morovides. Not for the first time, Kitra begged Amma for a chance to speak with Prince Parneo.

For a day, Blessed Amma. Even just a candlemark.

The globe in her hand proved the prince exceeded even the remarkable alchemical skill for which the male twins in his family were so well known, and she hungered for a glimpse into his process. That returned her thoughts to Marcal. Few had seen him seethe with envy over Parneo's brilliance, and more than once it had been up to Kitra to remind him the prince's talent was a gift of his bloodline and one that came with far too high a cost. Those who didn't go mad and kill themselves ended up victims of their ambition, dying in alchemical experiments or workings gone wrong.

Kitra had sought an audience with the prince since ascending to the position of high alchemist, but Princess Linore had refused every request, no doubt at the instruction of her mother. Queen Theodora remained in almost total seclusion since the announcement of Princess Heshiette's betrothal and Prince Dallan's disappearance. There were several rumors regarding these events, but only two that seemed likely to Kitra; either Prince Dallan had jilted Princess Heshiette in anger over his broken engagement to Princess Solena, or the prince had done something to displease the queen and was sent away. Kitra, having seen the obvious attraction between Prince Dallan and Princess Renn, leaned toward the latter—a secret affair followed by banishment appealed to the romantic streak she kept well hidden—but, being the subject of much gossip at the Academy both throughout her studies and her career, she refused to discuss the matter.

Regardless, in the wake of Prince Dallan's abrupt departure and Princess Solena's death, it seemed the queen had given up on everything, save for Kitra's final word on the disaster that had claimed the heir's life, about which she sent messages daily. Kitra itched to tell her it was an accident, to say she was certain and be done with it, but the queen trusted her to find the truth, and Kitra owed that to Marcal as well.

Besides, it wasn't as if Kitra looked forward to the coronation. For most occasions, Queen Theodora wore the crown made for her when she ascended to the throne, but the true crown, the one forged by Galathar's hand, was kept in an alchemically locked iron box hidden under the floor in Kitra's office. The act of ensuring Princess Linore was fit for the throne had been as simple as wiping a drop of her blood on the crown, and when Kitra had smeared a drop of Linore's blood on the knobby circlet of raw gold, it had absorbed the crimson, drinking it up like a patch of dry dirt soaking up a raindrop. If the Yentish prince lived, then the act of Binding Princess

Linore to the throne would be almost as simple. The ceremony would succeed, and all would be well.

But if the prince died...

With everything in her, Kitra hoped the prince stayed alive and that the Binding held. Marcal had told her of his failed attempt to Bind Lead Varo Orli and Queen Theodora. Though, when he'd tried the Binding, of course, they had been Messero Orli and Princess Theodora.

Marcal had detailed the signs to watch for—*"First the nail turns blue, then the skin will start to gray."*—and had emphasized the speed with which one had to act—*"You cannot hesitate. You must make the cut before the darkness spreads any farther."*—and had shown her the results on his own body. After seeing Marcal's deformed foot, the missing toe, the jagged scar, and knowing Orli and the queen bore similar wounds, Kitra had dreaded the possibility of ever participating in a royal marriage Binding.

At least she needn't worry about the Binding holding. As long as the prince lived, the Binding would hold, of that Kitra remained certain. Based on Kitra's suggestion, Marcal had sent Alchemist Claudine Virey, one of their best, with Princess Solena. Marcal and Princess Solena's deaths meant Claudine was also dead, but she well knew to tie off a Binding so that its effects continued after one's death. Of course, that only worked for the grounding alchemist. If the prince died, or was already dead, then Princess Linore needed to be Bound to someone else, and that would require Kitra, a fear that sometimes kept her up at night.

However, nothing was certain until the coronation, and the coronation wouldn't happen until the matter of Princess Solena's death was settled.

The brass bell that hung above the office door rang, startling Kitra from her thoughts. The major structures of the room—the walls, the floor, the ceiling, the door, the window—were Bound to catch noise; a person outside could knock for a lifetime and never be heard within. She tugged the rope hanging against the wall behind her desk. The rope led to a bell on the outside of the door since the person inside could shout for the knocker to come in until her voice gave out and anyone outside would never hear a thing.

The door swung open before the outside bell finished ringing, and Alchemists Myka Berren and Ithan Virey entered, the former carrying a rustling sheaf of papers in her hands, the latter closing the door behind them.

Because Marcal had named Kitra his successor, she had been forced to pass the investigation of the accident along to avoid any suggestion of impropriety. Kitra hadn't killed to reach her position, but if she had, she wouldn't have been the first, and this abdication of responsibility was another thing that kept her up nights. Her friend was dead, and because she now served in the position she'd spent her life coveting, she couldn't so much as lift a finger to find out why.

She hadn't even assigned the various tasks of sifting through the aftermath. Alchemist Tusson had performed that duty and with a fair amount of bitter glee. Kitra was, however, aware Myka and Ithan had been set to work together, so their combined presence alarmed her.

Tall, thin Ithan crossed the room to stand before her, one shoe sole *slip-slapping* as he walked, his sweaty, balding pate gleaming in the light of the globes. The hood of his crimson robe hung in worn tatters down his back and a large stain marked his left sleeve. Myka trailed behind him like a shadow, but her ample weight, thick curls, and tidy personage formed her as a shadow of opposites. But even with their differing appearances, both seemed harried, and Kitra's alarm deepened into a stomach-churning disquiet.

From what she'd heard, all of the materials used in the working had proven clean, the only difficulty being the working itself. It seemed the princess's blood had hardened over the formula like a sheet of ice, and though people had tried breaking it or dissolving it with cleansers, it remained untouched. Kitra had performed a bit of secret research, but had yet to find anything to explain the phenomenon.

Myka stopped before Kitra's desk, and, without leave, Ithan slumped down into one of the two armchairs across from it, his weak, chinless face taking on a hard cast as he stared out the window behind her. He treated her with such disdain because he, like so many others, thought Kitra had slept her way into Marcal's position. That was her theory anyway, since only Marcal had known it was Kitra's recommendation to send Claudine Virey, Ithan's wife, to the Yent Isles. But sometimes, when Ithan looked at Kitra in a certain way, she wondered if he knew it was her suggestion that had sent his wife to her death. An extension of her own guilt, no doubt.

Myka cleared her throat. "We have completed our study of Marcal's formula and the vial of the Yentish prince's blood."

Kitra straightened in her chair. "Should Alchemist Tusson be here for this, or have you already spoken with him?"

Ithan and Myka shared a look that spoke of a well-trod disagreement between them. "Not yet," she said. "We thought you might wish to see this first." She hesitated, the silence growing larger and more looming until Ithan broke it.

"From what we can tell," he said, "the failure was due to a small error."

"What?" Kitra's mouth went dry. "That's impossible. High Alchemist Marcal never made errors."

Everyone in the academy had respected Marcal, but few had been capable of working beside him for long. His brilliance, his unrelenting scrutiny, had driven most of them to distraction. Marcal had insisted on checking and rechecking his partners' formulas, and more often than not, he'd found mistakes. But unlike the more skilled alchemists, Kitra had always expected to make mistakes and had welcomed his eye. In turn, she'd provided a shield between him and the highborn, thereby allowing him to pursue his lifetime goal of reclaiming one of the Lost Pillars.

And yet, consumed as he had been by his pursuit, Kitra spoke the truth —Marcal had never, not once in the fifteen years she'd known him, made a mistake. "Where was this error?"

"We went over the formula a hundred times," Myka said. Ithan seemed lost in his own thoughts and content to let her explain for them both. "It was sound, but only in relation to the information High Alchemist Marcal was provided."

"Meaning what?"

"Two nights ago, I noticed the Yentish prince's blood had separated from the sand."

The hairs on the back of Kitra's neck rose. "You must take this to Alchemist Tusson. I can't—"

A bead of sweat rolled down Ithan's brow to the tip of his nose, belying his disinterest. "He said we shouldn't report our findings until they were complete." The drop fell to the floor.

Kitra shook her head. "That might be the case, but speaking to me before—"

"I understand," Myka said, dropping the papers on Kitra's desk. "But what we found absolves you."

Relieved but still on tenterhooks, Kitra waved for her to continue.

"Because of the separation, we divided the properties and tested each one on its own." She paused again, and Kitra flapped her hands at her and Ithan.

"Well," Ithan said, wiping his face with his sleeve, "the blood was as we expected, but the sand wasn't. The stone content was much higher than what Marcal calculated for."

Kitra's thoughts scattered. "But where was the mistake made? Did Marcal transcribe the wrong numbers from his notes, or did he mistake his assessment of the sand's individual components?" Both possibilities seemed equally absurd, equally unlikely.

"Neither." Myka pointed to a line on the top page. "As you can see in the high alchemist's notes, he based his numbers on a visual assessment, and in the course of his assessment, he mistook some of the salt for stone."

Kitra examined the note, which was plain enough for even her to read. It did indeed absolve her of any culpability in Marcal's death, but it didn't account for such an egregious error on his part. "How...?"

Myka shuffled to the next page. "Based on the information, he made a very reasonable supposition, and his expected margin of error should have been well within the limits for a successful working."

So it said on the page before her. Marcal's assumption, based on a lifetime of knowledge, should have been correct. Myka turned to the last page. The notes on this one were in a different, neater hand, and the initials at the bottom were C.V. *Claudine Virey*. Ithan's dead wife. A sum next to the initials caught Kitra's attention. She struggled to do the math in her head, wishing she could write out the numbers but not daring to so in front of her new subordinates.

Hoping her calculations were correct, she said, "If the sample was properly catalogued before being sent to us, there is no natural way for the sand to have such a high salt content."

Ithan bristled. "Do you doubt Claudine's cataloging?"

"No." Claudine's care was one of the reasons Kitra had suggested she be sent to the Yent Isles. With some effort, Kitra set aside her guilt and focused on the facts laid before her. Her scattered thoughts came together and sharpened into a hard point. "Someone spoiled the working on purpose."

"That was our conclusion as well," Myka said, her voice shaking.

Kitra thought to reprimand the young woman for allowing her emotions to master her, but then she recalled Myka was highborn, a member of Solena's birth cluster, and a spoiled working meant someone had meant to kill her former peer. Or the Yentish prince. Possibly both. So was it any wonder Myka acted as if someone had just shoved her from a great height?

Sharing in Myka's distress, Kitra sat back in her chair, her heart pounding. As high alchemist, she was under every obligation to bring her news to the queen. Closing her eyes, she imagined herself on Ithan and Myka's side of the desk. What might Marcal have said if she'd brought this to him?

That, at least, she had answer for. He would have said, "Check your work again, Rande, and don't bring it back until you're certain."

Forget Tusson and forget impropriety. This went beyond that, and Kitra wouldn't bring such sensitive information to Seedfall until she'd been over and through it all top to bottom, forward and back. After all, one didn't go throwing about words like "treason" or "regicide" until one was absolutely certain.

Another silent breeze rustled the pages on Kitra's desk. Opening her eyes, she slammed her hands down to keep them in place. "Who else knows about your findings?"

Ithan glanced at Myka, then back to Kitra. "Just us."

"Fine." Kitra met Ithan's gaze and held it. "Then you must tell Alchemist Tusson you've completed your study, but that you didn't find anything out of the ordinary."

He frowned.

"If someone..." The word "assassinated" caught in Kitra's throat. "If someone did something and they have reason to fear they're on the verge of getting caught, then we might drive them away or force their hand toward the queen."

"Yes," Myka said. "That's what we thought. That's why we brought this to you."

"You did the right thing, but now you can't tell anyone else." Kitra held Ithan's gaze. "You can't even discuss this with one another outside of this office, understood?"

Ithan nodded, but that wasn't enough.

"Swear to me," Kitra said. "Swear to me on your bond with Amma." To an alchemist or a member of the ductoran, there was no promise more sacred.

"I swear on my bond to Amma," Myka said.

"I swear," Ithan said, not looking away from her. He didn't respect her, but she trusted his oath.

Their promises made, she dismissed them. Myka bowed, Ithan stood and bowed, and they left together, Myka once again closing the door behind them.

Treason. Kitra leaned forward and set her brow on her desk. *Amma save us all.* On top of that, if those in the Academy found out that Tusson's study had uncovered the betrayal, the argument for him to replace Kitra as the head alchemist, despite Marcal's instructions, would grow from their current whispers to shouts.

The bell over the door rang, and she shot back into an upright position. Hoping it was Ithan or Myka returning to reveal their findings had been a mistake, she rang her own bell. But neither of her previous visitors opened the door.

Instead, Fost, her industrious secretary, peered inside. "Alchemist Lirra says we're low on flowering charms, and there's a young man here to petition for entry into the academy."

Of all the days... "Tell Lirra everyone proposes in spring, so of course we're low on charms. Give her leave to produce another fifty, and ask the young man to return tomorrow." Could her current problem really be solved in so short a time? "Better yet, ask him to return next tenday."

Fost ran a hand through his hair, causing the fluff to stand on end. "I'm afraid he's rather insistent." He darted inside and shut the door partway behind him. "I think he's highborn."

She sighed. Since the highborn were the ones who could afford the alchemists' services, their payments and patronage funded the academy, and refusing to speak to one would only add to her troubles.

Again mastering her emotions, Kitra adjusted her spectacles and straightened her shoulders. "Send him in."

Fost scampered out and returned with an unfamiliar young man with a tiny, upturned nose, a heavy brow, and lips like worms that had dried up in the sun. He towered over Fost and wore strange clothing. Well-constructed and made of the finest wools and linens, it was also quite ill-fitting. The cloth billowed around his narrow frame, but the hems of his sleeves and breeches were far too short.

Fost left the odd young man in the center of the room and retreated, closing the door behind him. Kitra stood and offered her left hand. "Well met. I'm High Alchemist Kitra Rande."

The young man came forward, pressed his palm to hers, and sparked both their bloodmarks. "Hale Enfoi," he said. "Well met."

Enfoi. She didn't recognize the family name, which meant he wasn't a member of the highborn, which meant their meeting could have waited. *Damn it, Fost.* Her secretary didn't know it yet, but he had several evenings' worth of studying peerage volumes in his very near future. As for Hale Enfoi, she guessed him to be a merchant's son, a recent transplant to the Chestnut. She thought to dismiss him, but the intelligence behind his eyes stopped her. Even in these troubled times, or perhaps because of them, they could always use another bright mind.

"Please," she said, gesturing to the chair Myka had recently vacated, "have a seat."

Hale took the proffered chair, and Kitra also sat, studying him as Marcal had once studied her. He bore it well, another point in his favor.

"I understand," she said, "you're here to petition the academy for entry."

He reached into his tunic and pulled out a charm attached to a chain around his neck. "In a way." With that, he let the charm fall against his chest. But it wasn't a charm. After candlemarks of listening to Marcal go on and on about the Lost Pillars, after being shown drawing after drawing, she recognized Hale's object for what it was—a wonderful copy of a Transformation amulet. She knew this because charms were either plain stones or stones wrapped in fabric, and amulets required metal. No one knew which materials were required to produce the foci for Balance workings.

At any rate, this Hale knew his history. Another point for him.

She squinted for a better look at it. "A friend of mine made one of those once. Did you use Rengalda's formula?"

"Of course not," he said. "That formula is incomplete."

Did he think her unaware of that fact? "I'm not a fool, boy." He slipped the chain off over his head and set the amulet down on the edge of her desk. "They're all incompl—"

Kitra's insistence that all of the Transformation formulas were incomplete died on her lips as the young man's features shifted and changed right before her eyes, overturning her entire world for the second time in a candlemark. This young man, whoever he was, had discovered one of the Lost Pillars, solving a mystery four hundred years in the making. She wanted to laugh, to cry, to fall on her knees at his feet. He was a genius, an alchemist without parallel. He was...

When the young man's features settled, the answer to her earlier prayer sat before her, and the only thing she could think to say was, "But all the formulas are incomplete."

Prince Parneo, looking every inch as arrogant as Marcal ever had, set his elbow on the arm of his chair and rested his chin on his hand. "Well," he said, "not quite *all*."

EIGHTEEN

"There is no romance to the mystery that is the Karskil Forest. People speak of its darkness, and we nibble away at its edges, ignoring when it bites back, but that fell place is not worth wondering or, indeed, writing about. It is better off forgotten."
-Complete entry on "The Karskil Forest" in Danlan's *Histories of the Known World, Vol. 4*

For the first few days after leaving Derlest, Jos spent every moment on the road certain his father was right behind him. One night he would go to sleep in the back of his wagon and wake surrounded by the caravan.

Not that it would be difficult to track him down. Oveno knew Jos's destination, and Jos's wagon limited his traveling options. He invited every sort of trouble, from broken axles to bandits, if he strayed from the main roads, and the choice of whether to take the Sea Road or the shorter route along the dark, wild Wood Road wasn't really a choice, not for a lone traveler. No, circumstances dictated the Sea Road, with its guards and stunning views of the coast, as his path.

Besides, it wasn't as if Oveno hadn't tracked Jos down before. He found Jos and Rahel the first time when Jos was a babe. His mother had told him how Oveno had begged her to join his caravan, but she'd refused, preferring the obscurity of a woman and her child living alone.

Oveno had next hunted Jos down in his in twelfth year, after two and a half hard moons spent avoiding slavers on the streets of Bilbago in Xanti. He still wasn't sure how his father had known to come for him, but he'd always suspected his mother had written to Oveno in the moons leading up to her death. The disease that had robbed Rahel of her appetite, her hearing, her movement, had overtaken her slowly, stealing her from Jos in pieces.

But Leader Oveno and his caravan never appeared, and once it became clear Jos didn't face pursuit, he slowed and discovered his own traveling rhythm. Some days the urge to create came over him, and when that happened, he hit the road late or stopped early for the night. He took a full afternoon to paint the inside of his wagon the same way he'd painted the walls of the last tenement he and his mother had shared. He also passed two nights camped alone on the outskirts of Glarken building a false bottom into his wagon. All of the Wandering Fallen's wagons had them, and though he'd left his copies of the sacred texts back in his father's wagon, he felt exposed without the secret compartment.

In truth, he often missed the people of his caravan, especially his best friends, Gent and Nora, and little Anell, but without the daily arguments and struggles with his father, his mind quieted, and he slept better than he had in ages. The notion he might have "failed" his Tempting continued to nibble at him, but he put his faith in Amma and trusted in her not to let his heart lead him too far astray.

Some days, he painted or drew the things he saw. He sketched the muddy stone houses of Glarken and a few of the hard, mistrustful souls who lived there. Farther south, he captured the sunnier disposition of an old man who lived alone in his hut on the beach. He sought out natural subjects too, though the truth in nature was fixed and therefore much less of a challenge. He painted a sunset, then the following sunrise over the fishing village of Calib. He even sketched the asses he'd bought back in Derlest to pull his small wagon. He named the one with the white belly and the inclination to fart Thunder, and as the full gray tended to pull ahead of Thunder whenever given the chance, Jos named him Lightning. They were stinky, stubborn beasts, but they were his.

Other days, Jos worked from his imagination. One such painting depicted the war-torn crossroads where the Sea Road split in two, one road leading into East Baltwull, the other into Caskius. While the Baltwullian soldiers laughed and gamed, the Caskian soldiers, most too young to have fought in the civil war that had ended twenty years ago, still guarded their side with vigilance and pride, as if they might be called to battle at any moment.

Mile by mile, he made his way farther and farther south, until he neared Sander, a port city, the largest along the Sea Road, and the waypoint for many a traveler.

For reasons known only to him, Oveno didn't care much for Sander, which meant his caravan had never stopped there for long, but Jos had always liked it and wished they might stay for more than a day or two. He and his mother had lived there when he was four and five, and his shadowy and disjointed memories were tinged with warmth and comfort. So, on the morning Jos set out for Sander, he decided to camp there for a couple of days. Maybe even a full tenday.

To the east of the city, a swath of land a half-mile square had been cleared from the Karskil Forest to make room for those with wagons or those without the coin or desire to pay for lodgings. After entering through Sander's northern gates and traversing the wide roads made to accommodate the large volume of traffic that passed through the city every day, Jos arrived at the clearing around midmorning.

Lines of weather-grayed wooden standards broke the field into rows, and Jos, not wanting to inflict Thunder's stench on others, parked well away from the travelers already camped there, close to the palisade that blocked the clearing off from the forest.

Signs of wear marked the fence—some teeth or claw marks here, a few fresh stakes there—but it remained standing, and Sea Road guards walked it day and night. The Sea Road Guard served the Sea Road Council, a group of elected officials, one from each town along the road, who worked toward their collective interest. Amongst other responsibilities, the council levied the taxes needed to maintain the road and hired the guards to patrol it and keep it safe. As the seat of the council, the guard also worked in Sander.

Jos saw to Thunder and Lightning—releasing them from their traces, hitching them to a standard, bringing them water—then he gathered some supplies, locked up his wagon, and headed into the city, where the streets of Sander teemed with a mishmash of people from every corner of Althea, from tattoo-faced Tithen mercenaries to silver-eyed Xantish sailors. He even encountered a pair of Rhyllexie men in a tavern. They sat at a table in the corner with their full beards and their scarred forearms bared. When Jos drew them, he expected to sketch them as hunters wrapped in furs, stalking some beast through a snowy forest. Instead, the men stood tall and proud outside a stone keep while dozens of white-haired men, women, and children stared out from the windows.

Jos wanted to ask the Rhyllexie what sort of mission they were on, but the way they hunched over their ales and spoke only to one another suggested his question wouldn't be welcome, and so he was left to wonder.

His first morning in Sander, Jos sought out the Sea Road Council's meeting hall, a blocky, two-story structure in the center of a square at the heart of the city. A series of fifteen short but deep stone steps ringed the building, and every morning of the year at dawn, the council opened the doors on all four sides of the building and invited anyone with desire or cause to enter and be heard. Just as Jos remembered it, dozens of artists—from singers and jugglers to fiddlers and sculptors—peppered the stairs. As long as they didn't block the doors or stop anyone on their way in, they were welcome to stay.

Those with canvases and easels clustered on the eastern steps to take advantage of the morning light, but Jos set up on the western steps, and while he sat in the shadows and waited for the sun to come to him, he watched the parade of anonymous souls wandering by and reveled in the comfort of his solitude.

For the next few days, he set up in the exact same spot, yet every day brought something new. He sketched Sea Roaders and Caskians and Baltwullians, sailors and merchants and beggars, men and women, young and old, those weighted down with pain or secrets, or those light with joy. He drew anyone who asked, and charged whatever he thought his subjects might afford.

Jos's father had never let him focus so hard on his gift, and as if it was a muscle, the more he used it, the stronger it grew. Some liked his depictions, others looked as if they hated them, but all seemed to sense the power behind his skill, and many walked away from him thoughtful, their eyes fixed to the sliver of their truth he'd captured on the page.

His skill proved to have other benefits as well. His drawing of an exuberant, yellow-haired woman named Danni led to ales at a nearby tavern and a very pleasant evening in her bed. He had a few extra flowering charms on hand for just such occasions, but their usefulness had spread beyond the Gift, and Danni wore her own. As he lay there after, with her body pressed to his and her soft snores in his ear, he thought he might just pass the whole of the summer in Sander.

In the morning, Jos walked Danni to the butchery where she worked, and they parted with a kiss. She tried to peg down a place or a time in the future where they might meet, but he kept his promises vague. Though he liked her well enough, he risked too much with a more permanent connection.

He left her and returned to his wagon to see to his asses, then to his place on the steps, finding it claimed by a whittler surrounded by wood shavings and a small army of inch-high carved deer. Jos bought one—the detail the man achieved with his large knife was astounding—and found a new spot on the southwest corner. After a slow morning and a midday meal in a tavern off the square, he chose another new spot and business picked up.

Around the third candlemark of the afternoon, a pair of Tithen merce-naries asked him for a drawing of the two of them together and then refused to stand closer than two feet apart. Not wanting them to appear as bookends, Jos considered the composition of the piece for several minutes, yet the moment he started, the mercenaries came together in the center of the page, their naked limbs entwined, their eyes closed and their mouths open in shared ecstasy.

Though it bothered him to do so, Jos stopped halfway through and showed the mercenaries his work. The man, his cheeks flushed, ran off, and the woman reached for the half-finished drawing.

"May I have it?" she asked, her voice deep and rich with its Tithen lilt.

Jos handed it to her. "I can keep it or...destroy it."

She shook her head, folded the page, and tucked it into her tunic. "Said he would send me to another company if anyone found out. I'd rather remember this than that."

When she left, another woman came along, and he went back to work. Every so often, people stopped to watch him, but on this day, a man in a violet tunic with dark hair stayed for the better part of the afternoon, hovering over Jos's shoulder and making him more and more nervous with each passing candlemark.

Bloodhunter.

Once the word jumped into his mind, it repeated with every thun-derous beat of his heart, and by the time the sun touched the tops of the buildings, sweat soaked his tunic. He rushed through his final sketch of a merchant man with dozens of portraits of himself on the wall behind him and refused to charge him. Then, while the man who watched him seemed distracted by the wit telling japes two steps up, Jos gathered his things and sidled off.

When he looked back four blocks later, the dark-haired man followed some fifty feet behind. Jos lengthened his strides and the man matched pace; he slowed and the man neared to forty feet, then thirty. A narrow gap opened in the road traffic, and Jos darted across the street, breaking into a full-out run, turning corner after corner and soon becoming lost in a part of the city where he'd never ventured.

Then his panic took him down a blind alley, and before he could turn around or climb the wall at the end of it, a shadow darkened the alley's mouth, stretching out long to meet Jos's.

"As a member of the Sea Road Guard, I order you to stop."

Jos froze, his heartbeat racing. Keeping his expression mild, he turned and faced the supposed guard. The man wore a deep violet tunic with a Sea Road Guard patch sewn to the left breast. He stood less than half a foot shorter than Jos, and with the cragginess of his tanned features, Jos guessed him to be in his late thirties.

"Why did you run?" the guard said, his pale gaze unwavering.

A truth seemed better than a lie. "Because you were chasing me."

The guard frowned and stepped closer. "I saw what you did back there."

Bloodhunter! "What do you mean?" Jos waited for the man to reach out and touch him, to reveal them both.

"The drawings," the guard said.

Jos flinched as the guard raised a hand. But then he took a step back and ran that hand through his hair, causing it to stand on end, and all of a sudden he appeared much closer to Jos's age. "There's something about your drawings."

The guard had noticed Jos's skill, nothing more. He coughed to cover the relieved laugh that burbled out of him. "What's that?"

The guard shook his head. "Damned if I know, but I've never seen anything like it. Take that drawing you did of the ink faces. How did you know they were together?"

If the guard had been there while Jos sketched the Tithen mercenaries, then he'd been watching much longer than Jos thought, and that meant living with his father's caravan for so long had softened his edges even more than he'd realized.

"I'm an artist," Jos said. "I notice details other people might not. Now, if you'll excuse me..." He started to walk away.

"Wait." The guard chased after Jos until he turned back. "I think you can help me. Well, I think you can help the guard. And maybe a woman. Or not the woman, but someone else." Jos's confusion must have shown on his face because the guard smiled, ran his hand through his hair again, and said, "I'm not making much sense, am I?"

Jos knew better than to insult a member of a guard, any guard, but this man was unlike every other guard he'd ever met. "Not too much, no."

The guard laughed and then hit himself on the forehead, and Jos dropped his age a few more years. "Fool, me," the guard said. "I haven't even introduced myself." He held out his right hand. "I'm Lathan. Sea Road Guard Lathan Cyon."

Jos held up his own right hand, still streaked with charcoal, as an excuse. "Sorry," he said. "Haven't had the chance to clean up."

"I don't mind," Lathan said, and before Jos could drop his hand, Lathan reached out and grabbed it. Jos tensed, but his bloodmark remained dormant and hidden. Bloodhunters usually stalked Wandering Fallen, only because they ventured far from the safety offered by the Gift. However, they would happily kill a lone Fallen if given the chance. Between Jos and Lathan, however, nothing happened beyond an awkwardly angled handshake.

"Josiah Porthain," he said as Lathan let go. "But most call me Jos."

"So," Lathan said, sticking his hands in his pockets, "what do you say, Jos? Want to help?"

THE GUARDHOUSE TURNED out to be a few blocks north of the meeting hall, a squat, plain-faced building with a sign marking it as *Sea Road Guard—House 12*, and Jos walked through the open door still uncertain as to how Lathan had talked him into doing so.

The man just had a way about him, and though Jos hadn't been able to sketch him as they walked along, all his chatter about Jos using his ability for a larger, if mysterious, purpose rather than to make coin, appealed to him on a profound level.

What if Amma put Lathan on my path for a reason?

Jos followed Lathan through the front room of the building, an open area with people waiting on benches along the walls and a guard standing behind a podium, stifling a yawn as she listened to a man ranting about goats. Or stoats. It was hard to tell with all the yelling.

With a wave to the bored guard, Lathan guided Jos down a short hall to another open room, this one filled with desks and a dozen guards seated at them or standing around. Two closed doors marked the far wall and a hall between them led farther off into the building.

"What's this, Cyon?" asked a pert-nosed guard. "Find the man who did it?"

The man who did what? The guards all turned to face Jos, and regret gripped him far too late. He hadn't done anything, but if he ran now, the guards would assume guilt of some stripe or another.

Lathan clapped his hands and rubbed them together. "Get ready to pay up, Frith."

Frith laughed. "Not in a hundred years."

"Go get her." This came from a guard at a desk in the corner. Dimples dented her round cheeks and her heavy arms at the elbows. "If we don't settle this soon, the captain will have all our hides."

Frith sighed, but then he disappeared off down the hall and returned with a slip of a woman. He guided her to a desk in the center of the room, and Lathan gestured for Jos to sit across from her.

"What do you want me to do?" Jos asked, happy to do whatever it was as quickly as possible so he might get out.

"Just draw her," Lathan said. "Like you did with the others."

Jos sat. The woman held her hands in her lap and kept her chin down; her shoulders bowed inward, her dirty hair hung around her face like a curtain, and mud clung to her tunic. She glanced up as he sat across from her, and her hair fell back. Four scratches furrowed her left cheek, the jagged cuts caked with dried blood.

Jos hesitated before putting his charcoal to the page, nervous about discovering whatever horror this woman had been through. But if his drawing helped her in any way, then he had to do it. He expected the first line to be soft, as timid as the woman sitting before him, but it came out hard. Dark. He slashed the charcoal across the page, and as the image grew, the heavy lines devoured first one stick and then another.

With angry line after angry line, he revealed a much different story than the one he'd expected, and when he ran out of charcoal, he sat back and clenched his hand into a fist, ignoring the itch compelling him to complete what he'd started. The picture in front of him was more than enough. In it, the woman cowering before him stood in a featureless room over a dead man's body with a knife in her raised hand and look of frenzied satisfaction on her face. Pools of black covered her, the man, the floor, and the walls around her. Blood.

Lathan took the drawing from Jos and held it up so the guards around him could see. Then he walked over to the woman and held the picture under her nose. "What do you think about this?"

The woman's head flew up, and her wide eyes met Jos's. He waited for her to cry, to deny the image before her, but she screamed, knocked the drawing aside, and leapt to her feet. Like Jos, the guards took a few precious seconds to respond, and the woman managed to climb over the desk and wrap her hands around his throat. He pried at her fingers and kicked at her frail body, but her rage gave her strength, and she clawed at him like a thing possessed. The guards, at last reacting, piled on her and pried her away from him as she continued to snarl and thrash.

"What in the sweet fancy fuck is going on out here?"

The words barely carried above the noise of the uproar, but they demanded attention and everyone, even the mad woman, stilled. One of the closed doors now stood open, and framed in the opening was a woman wearing a coat of the same deep violet as the guards' tunics, her hair pulled back in a tail so tight it warped her otherwise regal features. She bore the sort of presence that filled an entire page.

A skinny guard with pox scars on his face was the first to speak up. "Lathan was right about that woman, Captain Jensen. She killed her husband."

Captain Jensen walked over and picked up Jos's drawing from the floor. "Who did this?"

Several of the guards pointed at Jos, and the captain turned her attention on him. From the way she stared at him, he didn't think she missed much. "Were you there?" she asked.

"No." Jos's mind went blank. "I didn't... I wasn't..."

Lathan stepped forward. "He's an artist, Captain. I found him drawing on the street and asked him to come in."

The captain eyed Lathan, then she turned her attention back to Jos. "How did you know what this woman did?"

"He sees things, Captain," Lathan said. "Details, I mean. There were these mercenaries wanting..." Captain Jensen's nostrils flared, and he stepped back. "Sorry, Captain." She opened her mouth to speak, but before she could, Lathan held out his empty hands and added, "But he didn't know a thing about this till I brought him here."

The captain closed her eyes and tipped her face up to the ceiling, as if silently beseeching whatever god she believed in for strength.

Lathan frowned, baring his teeth, and tucked his hands behind his back. "Sorry, Captain."

She took a deep breath, opened her eyes, and looked at the picture. "So you weren't there."

She didn't phrase it as a question, but Jos answered anyway. "No, madam. Between the scratches on her cheek and the amount of blood on her dress—"

The murderous woman came to life again, struggling against the guards who held her. "While I was out working, puttin' food on our table, he swived half the women on our block." She spat at the picture, splattering the captain's face in the process. "Lazy pig was asking for it!"

Captain Jensen took a handkerchief from her pocket and wiped the flecks of spittle from her cheeks. Then she gestured for the guards holding the woman to take her away, and they dragged her off, kicking and screaming, down a hall.

The captain looked at the picture again, and Jos was glad he hadn't drawn more details of the room. He had no idea how he might have explained that.

"Want me to give that to the magistrate?" the skinny guard asked.

"No need," Captain Jensen said. "She just confessed in front of everyone here." She turned to Lathan. "Nice work, Cyon." Then to Jos. He braced himself for a threat that he would be watched, and in his head, he already packed for the road. "If we need your help again, can we call on you?" she asked.

She knows. Like Mutta Kirsch, Captain Jensen recognized his gift. How were so many people aware of this ability that, for most of his life, he hadn't even known he possessed? His small life, first with his reclusive mother and then in the close embrace of his father's caravan, seemed even smaller.

He wanted to say yes, to reach for the wider world with both arms, but in that moment, a lifetime of caution reasserted itself. "I, uh, I'm not sure how much longer I'll be in Sander."

"Hm." Captain Jensen gave him one last appraising look, then spun on her heel, went back into what Jos presumed was her office, and shut the door.

With her gone, the other guards returned to their business, some eyeing Jos with suspicion, others with admiration or concern. He needed more space and fresh air. Taking the captain's leaving as his own dismissal, he went back the way he and Lathan had come, passing through the hall, the front room, and walking out into the early evening. He'd missed the sunset, his favorite part of the day.

Lathan came out right behind him.

"Why didn't you tell me?" Jos asked.

"About what the woman did?"

Jos nodded.

"I thought if I told you that might affect how you saw her." Lathan ran his hand through his hair. "Also, I didn't know if you would come."

The deceit bothered Jos a little, but when he thought about it, he wasn't sure if he would have come either. "What will happen to her?"

Lathan shrugged. "She'll hang."

Jos leaned against the wall of the guardhouse, not sure how he felt about using his gift to put a woman's neck into a noose. But Lathan hit his shoulder and jarred him from his thoughts.

"Listen here," Lathan said. "Sounds like that guy was a right bastard, and maybe he did ask for it, but that doesn't let her off for giving it to him. She took a life, and that's a life owed."

Though Lathan spoke of it in terms of black-and-white, Jos wondered about the shading, the contours of the issue.

But again, before he could fully gather his thoughts, Lathan hit him and said, "Let's go find some ale. You earned a pitcher or two."

Jos liked Lathan, and the ale sounded great, but his fear held him. "I don't know."

Lathan's cheer dimmed. "Oh." He glanced down the road. "Well, I'm going for a drink, and I suppose you can come or not." Showing Jos his back, he strode off.

Jos willed his feet to move, but it was as if they were nailed to the ground. *Why did you leave the caravan if not to take risks?* That did it. He took one step, then another. Unsure of the path he now walked but excited to see where it might lead, he tossed the last of his caution into the sea and hurried to match pace with Lathan.

MUCH LATER THAT NIGHT, Lathan stumbled home to write a letter about his new friend and that friend's remarkable skill. When he was done, he pressed a scribe's ring into the blue wax seal, addressed the letter to someone in Dawskellio, and set it by his door. The next morning, he checked inside a locked box mounted on the wall outside the door of some stranger's tenement, where a fat little purse waited for him. He wasn't sure who he worked for or what their goals were, but they paid so well that, in truth, he didn't much care. He took his coin, dropped the letter in, relocked the box, and continued on to the guardhouse.

The sound of the box opening and closing woke the man who lived behind the door, and he rose with an aching head and a sour stomach. Swearing off ale for the fourth time that tenday, he checked the box, and finding the letter, walked it to the door of his downstairs neighbor, where he paid a harried woman's daughter a full silver to deliver it to a sailor on the *Blithe Reckoning*.

The nine-year-old girl, glad to be away from her six siblings, especially the screaming infant twins, hurried to get the letter to the ship before it set sail. She dashed through the streets and made it to the docks in less than half a candlemark, where, as it turned out, the *Blithe Reckoning* wasn't to leave until the next day. Even so, the white-haired sailor she gave the letter to tipped her a copper for her trouble, and she strolled home rubbing the coins in her pocket, dreaming of the day she might leave on her own voyage.

The letter joined two others in the sailor's pack, and stayed there for the five days it took for the ship to reach Keecoe, a tiny port town on the southern coast of Tithen. There the sailor stopped in at the town's sole tavern, dropped the letters off with the one-eyed barkeep, and spent two coppers of his payment for the delivery on a dram of thorno. Though he was too old to earn his tattoos and some faulted him for it, calling him "barefaced" or "coward," he loved his adopted home as if born to it. More so, perhaps. How many of those who insulted him could say they risked life and limb for a greater Tithen? Another dram of thorno, and he set off for home with a warm belly and an even warmer heart.

Over the next several days, the letter worked its way across Tithen, passed from the one-eyed barkeep to a young tinker, from that tinker to a farmer, from that farmer to her lord, from the lord to a seamstress, and from that seamstress to a maid. The grubby, travel-stained letter ended its journey on a polished honeywood desk in a study in the finest manor outside of Tithen's capital of Galleford.

There, Mayve, former queen of Tithen and current duchess of Morleon, plucked it from amidst its brethren and cracked the seal. She read about the artist with the remarkable talent, then sat back, closed her eyes, and pictured a map of Althea. In her mind, her agents—scattered from Rhyllex all the way down to Xanti and beyond, everywhere except the Karskil Forest—shone like stars, with thin lines of light stretched between them, a glowing lacework almost forty years in the making. She thought of the lacework as her net, a net that reached farther and wider than anyone knew, and she longed for the day she would be able to snatch it closed, all for the glory of Tithen.

If that meant rising up and knocking Adameth from his throne as well, then so be it. For now, she burned the letter from her Sea Road guard and wrote a message of her own, short and to the point.

Use it for a moon, make certain it's reliable, then send it to Calyn.

She didn't yet how she might use the artist in Ombratos, especially since she still wasn't certain why Helenia and Dallan had returned to Tithen, but her instincts said to place him there, and so she would. She sealed the page, drew a symbol in the corner, and set it on the stack of other letters bound for the mainland.

NINETEEN

"Love is a weapon. Givin' your love away is like handin' someone your staff or
blade; the moment you do, they can use it against you."
-Podriach OcNessa to his daughter, Helenia

Tithen's green and rolling hills soothed Helenia's bruised spirit. She hadn't realized until they'd driven past Galleford's gates and out into the countryside how much she'd missed everything about the land, even the sudden showers and the clinging mists.

Along the road, watchtowers appeared in the fog like moss-bearded sentinels, and herds of shaggy cattle and black-faced sheep grazed around the stunted, wind-swept trees in the fields. Houses built with chalky stone and roofed in sod dotted the landscapes like rock formations that had pushed up from beneath the soil.

Earth wives served where they were needed, with their backs bent and their hands buried in the ground, and farmers worked with dedication and fervor. Theirs was a land rich with beauty and laden with promise; the very air smelled fertile. No wonder so many had claimed and tried to keep it for their own. But as the tattoos marking the faces of those they passed vowed, Burk had set his people free, and neither they nor their land would ever be taken again.

"Do you think she'll still love me?" Dallan asked. "After?"

Helenia tore her attention away from the view of Tithen passing by the coach window and focused on her nephew. He was keeping to the darker items in his wardrobe, though some deep blues and purples had crept in. Those hues broke up the black, further enhancing the coloring of his eyes and hair.

"Do you?" he asked again. "Because I don't think I could stand to lose her again." He sat forward and pressed the princess's flowering charm to his lips.

His earnestness drew a smile from her. "It's hard to stop loving someone once you've started."

Not quite an answer, but he seemed to accept it as one. He returned her smile, leaned back on his bench, closed his eyes, and within minutes, fell asleep, leaving Helenia to return to her thoughts.

The evening after their encounter with Adameth, she and Dallan had spent the night in Galleford before pressing on to Morleon. Upon her release from prison, she'd promised herself she'd never pass another night in the palace, but as prince, Dallan had little choice but to stay there, and he'd offered her a room in his suite. Not wanting to risk their fragile reconnection, she'd accepted. Though she'd feared she might be haunted by her moon spent in the dungeons, something else had kept her awake.

Adameth's accusation, that Mayve had been the one to offer a divorce in exchange for Morleon, had gnawed at her, and whenever she'd closed her eyes, she'd heard Adameth's spiteful whisper, *She offered it to me.*

But that couldn't be true. If it were, it would cast a pall over twenty-seven years of friendship because Mayve knew Helenia's past. Mayve knew how hard Helenia had worked to become a worthy duchess, knew how much Morleon meant to Helenia, and that, if or when, Carhal passed before Helenia, Morleon would be her solace. In short, Mayve was well aware of how very much the duchy meant to Helenia; next to Carhal, it had been everything. And yet, how could Helenia throw her relationship with Mayve away based on the words of her hateful ex-husband?

In the morning, she and Dallan learned King Adameth had ordered Seifan and his Wolf Company to serve as Dallan's honor guard. As expected, neither brother welcomed the arrangement, and Helenia had suffered a candlemark's worth of complaints as they rode from the city, her and Dallan in one carriage, their servants and baggage in the next, and Seifan and his mercenaries riding in formation around them. Though her head had ached from lack of sleep, she'd endured it in silence for the sake of keeping Dallan on her side.

When his tirade had subsided, he'd stared out the window for almost a mile before, "On the *Forweary* you said you had an explanation for why you demanded Queen Theodora betroth me to Heshi instead of Renn." He made a gesture as if beckoning her forward. "Tell me, then. Explain."

Despite the throbbing at her temples, Helenia had been glad to delve in. She'd taken a deep breath, then done just that. Or, rather, she'd explained the parts of the plan he needed to know, mapping things out for him in broad terms, softening where she thought appropriate.

When it came to the Morovides, she told him a half-truth. She explained that their Tithen forces would imprison the queen and her two older daughters. Of course, the truth was Theodora, Linore, and Heshiette had to die. There was no way around that. But Helenia meant it when she promised to keep Princess Renn, her twin, and the prince-consort alive.

Having thought it through, young Renn's life would ensure both Dallan and Orli remained on her side. True, Orli had loved Theodora when they were young, but that love had curdled into a bitter, rancid hatred. So, while he insisted that at least one of the female Morovides remain alive, Helenia imagined that he'd welcome the chance to be rid of Theodora once and for all. He might even commit regicide himself, given the opportunity.

After that, having a Morovide on the throne might help the Ombratians accept their new Tithen leadership. Along those same lines, saving Corlin and Parneo would garner the princess's compliance. She would mourn her mother and sisters, perhaps Theodora less so than Linore or Heshiette. However, from what Helenia had seen, Renn's closest ties were to her father and brother, and the flowering charm around Dallan's neck suggested a very strong, very deep attachment to him.

Helenia had laid out the plan to Dallan, but she didn't bother with the larger picture, the issue of expansion. Why bother when his part centered on the princess? Politics would simply muddle things.

Dallan had listened, and when Helenia finished speaking, he sat forward and put his head in his hands. "We'll be married, then?"

"Yes."

"But after all that, how will she ever forgive me?"

"Love forgives much," Helenia had said, the answer coming without thought. "Sometimes more than it should."

She still wasn't sure where that bit of advice had sprung from or if it was true.

True or not, Dallan had looked up at her, his eyes wide and hopeful, and she'd known it was done. He'd believed her because he wanted to, because he trusted her, and though it had been to her advantage, she'd rubbed a hand over her brow to hide her contempt. Shame on him for trusting her—for trusting anyone—so blindly. After all, it was the rarest sort of person who never let anyone else down.

Love forgives much.

She offered it to me.

With the matter of Dallan settled, Helenia's mind had been free to wander back to Adameth's accusation, and she'd gritted her teeth against it. He had already taken so much from her. She would not allow him to take Mayve too. She returned to the view outside the coach window, and, with her thoughts, urged the horses on.

THE GOOD WEATHER held for the duration of their trip. For Tithen, that meant they faced no more than light rain. Helenia and Dallan stayed at the finer inns strung along the road for the gentry travelling between the capital and the country's largest inland city. Along the way, they spoke little about the plan, and he spoke a lot about Renn, enumerating her every virtue before discussing them in exhausting detail. He even wrote her a letter, one closed by verdigris sealing wax the color of Tithen grass in spring with the princess's name and title written on the front in his fine, flowing script, promising his soon return.

After resolving the Dallan issue, Helenia hoped she might relax, but with each passing mile, she grew more and more anxious, both for her reunion with Mayve and for her return to Morleon, and so, grateful for any distraction, she listened to Dallan prattle on. But the trip proved both brisk and uneventful, and sooner than she felt ready, they neared the border of the Morleon holdings.

Nothing marked the transition from one holding to the next, but Carhal had insisted on Helenia riding every inch of their land, and to please him, she had. After almost thirty years of marriage, she knew it as well as Carhal ever had, and the moment they passed the invisible line of demarcation, grief battered against her, clamoring for release.

Dallan placed a hand on her arm. "You've gone pale. Are you well?"

Was she? She'd expected this visit to be difficult, but she was beginning to wonder if she could even stand it. "Fine."

Dallan, in one of his moments of insight, didn't pursue the issue further. He even turned away from her, allowing her as much privacy as he could in their tight quarters.

The coach rounded a gentle curve and entered Gilly's Thicket, a wood that covered almost two full acres at the city's edge. Adameth had repeatedly asked Carhal to divvy it up among Carhal's lords, but Carhal, who'd loved to hunt coneys there, had resisted just as often. Adameth wouldn't have accepted such behavior from anyone else, but with Carhal he'd always laughed and said, "That's my brother!"

They rode beneath the shadows thrown across the road by the leafy canopy, rushing past the tangled briars lining the verge. She and Carhal had often left the city to walk the deer trails in those woods. Once they'd even brought a midday meal to share in a well-hidden clearing to the north.

The memory battered at her wall with remarkable force, creating cracks with its very first blow. She tried to shore up the damage, but the harder she worked, the more it crumbled. The scent of new growth and wildflowers entered the carriage, and visceral memories—the taste of mutton pie on Carhal's lips and tongue, the sunlight beating down on her bare breasts—brought the day back to her in full.

That night, after she and Carhal had ridden home and climbed into bed, he had started itching, then she had, and they discovered on one another dozens of midge bites where no one should ever have to endure them. A laugh burbled up from her chest, and a tear spilled down her cheek.

With a glance, Dallan reached out and grabbed her hand, then returned his attention to the passing scenery. Helenia, surprised and touched by the gesture, squeezed her nephew's hand before letting go to pat her face dry.

Driving out of Gilly's Thicket, the coach tipped back as they reached the last hill before the city. At the rise, they would be able to see Morleon. Helenia's first look at the city had been from that very hill. Eighteen and newly orphaned by her father's death, she'd ridden into Morleon with little more than a purse full of coins, the clothes on her back, and the fear in her heart. No stranger to cities in general or Morleon in particular, she hadn't felt afraid of the place itself, more what the place represented—a life without her father and a fresh start. She'd thought to remake her life in Morleon, never suspecting how high she would fly or how hard she would eventually fall.

Today, she approached the city in much the same way. She had more coin to her name and wore finer clothing, but fear had once again taken root. Yet, unlike the fears of her youth, which had been formless with inexperience and laced with anticipation, hard-earned knowledge and loss had formed a knot of dread in her belly. Only her doubt remained the same.

Part of her longed for the sight of the city as it had always been, a steadfast island of strength amidst a sea of farmland, a noble and lasting tribute to Carhal's name. But another part of her hungered for the sight of a burned-out hulk, a city devoid of life, the buildings skeletons of charred wood and smoke-stained rubble, a damning testament to Mayve's failure. To see her, just once, not come out on top... Helenia knew this to be a selfish, petty desire, but a small part of her longed for the sight nonetheless.

The coach attained the top of the hill, and Morleon sat before her, a large collection of steep-roofed buildings ringed by an ivy-covered stone bulwark. Ribbons of smoke did drift through the air, but they came from chimneys, not ruins, and the ducal manor sat at the city's heart, its towers and spires unbroken.

Helenia wondered at her momentary desire to see her friend brought low but didn't linger on it. Adameth's words festered in her heart like an infected wound. One discussion with Mayve would lance it and allow Helenia's rancid suspicions to ooze away.

With Mayve aware of their impending arrival, the coach rode into the city to much fanfare. The people of Morleon lined the streets leading to the ducal manor, clapping and cheering. Tossed flowers littered the street. Dallan leaned out the window to smile and wave, and even Seifan rode with his head held high.

Carhal had hated venturing beyond his holdings, and Helenia had hated travelling without Carhal, so the two of them had left Morleon as seldom as possible. But she had made the trip to Galleford on four occasions without her husband, one trip for each of Mayve's sons, and when she'd returned to the city, it had been to a similar welcome. Unsure of what sort of response she might elicit now, she sat back against the bench, and from the shadows, took in the familiar sights.

Riding past Nearson Street, Helenia pictured the sign for Tommel Tailor hanging above a shop door halfway down the street, even though they'd closed up years before. Tommel's was where she'd found an apprenticeship, where she'd first met the unattractive and blunt Duke Carhal, and where, over the course of almost a year, they'd fallen in love. In his wedding toast to her he'd called it "a mile-long courtship traveled by inches."

Their small retinue continued to wind through the city, their progress slow, and it was almost a candlemark before the ducal manor returned to view.

It was a modest building, less than half the size of the palace in Galleford and less than a third the size of Seedfall, but a pretty one, with a face of pale stone and curls of ivy that framed the windows like long eyelashes.

Carhal had referred to the manor as his "coquette" since she flirted with everyone who walked by, and Helenia had loved it from the instant she saw it, long before she had any inkling it might one day be hers.

Later, when she'd first rode through the iron gates and first heard the stones of the drive crunch beneath the wheels of a coach in which she sat, the first time she walked beneath the portico held aloft by marble pillars and through the open double doors, she did so do on Carhal's arm, as his betrothed, and with the knowledge it was to be her home. Their home.

Actual, physical pain gripped her chest, squeezing the air from her lungs. She closed her eyes and concentrated on drawing in her next breath. Both her grandmother and her father had died from heart storms, and if Helenia's heart didn't fall numb from all this abuse soon, she might not have to worry if the plans for taking Ombratos would succeed or not.

The coach jostled as the wheels moved from the cobbled road onto the gravel drive leading up to the manor, and a breath came as a sudden calm washed over her. Death changed nothing. She was the daughter of Podriach OcNessa, one of the cleverest mountebank's Tithen had ever known, and the wife of Duke Carhal Briain, a powerful man who had borne a gift from the Unknowable Beyond. She was theirs. And their strength was hers.

She opened her eyes.

Servants stood in a line near the open front doors, and as the carriage approached the circular turnaround, Mayve stepped outside to meet them. At their initial meeting, it had been Helenia coming out to greet Mayve. Queen Mayve, in those days. Helenia, rebuffed by the nobles of Morleon, had expected more of the same from Carhal's brother and sister-by-law, and Adameth hadn't disappointed, but Mayve had bypassed Carhal for Helenia, kissed her on both cheeks, and whispered in her ear, "I've always wished for a sister."

Almost thirty years had passed since that day, but Mayve appeared somehow younger today than she had then. If her ex-husband looked to be chiseled from granite, then she, with her rounded cheeks and heavy-lidded eyes, was carved from soapstone. Born the daughter of a country lord, the blue lines of her tattoos were thicker and more prominent than most of her station, but they suited her just the same.

Excitement and relief gripped Helenia at the sight of her oldest and dearest friend—*She offered it to me*—and she did her best to ignore the echo of Adameth's words.

Dallan, as eager to see his mother as he had been reluctant to see his father, jumped from his seat, threw open the door, and dashed from the coach before it came to a full stop. Seeing him, Mayve opened her arms wide for her youngest son, and heedless of propriety, he swept her up into an undignified embrace. Smiling, she cried out as her feet left the ground.

When he set her down, she grabbed his shoulders and held him at arm's length. "You should be ashamed of making your mother wait six long years between visits. I hardly recognize this dashing gentleman standing before me."

A servant Helenia didn't recognize approached the coach and offered a hand to help her out. She took it and stepped down onto the crushed stone of the drive as she had a thousand times before. Helenia started toward Mayve, yet stopped as Mayve crossed the drive to her, a generous act, one that told the servants Helenia was to be treated with the utmost honor and respect on her visit. She forced a gracious smile, opened her arms to Mayve, and allowed herself the solace of their embrace.

Mayve kissed Helenia's cheek and said, loudly enough for the servants to hear, "Welcome back, dear sister."

Then she squeezed Helenia tighter, and her smile became less forced. Here was the woman who had never treated Helenia as an upstart, who had gently guided her along the path to becoming a noblewoman, who had held her hand through two stillbirths, and who had sacrificed the leverage of her marriage for Helenia's life. How could she have doubted this, their friendship?

They had been apart for too long, and Helenia had forgotten too much.

Mayve pulled back, the scent of her perfume so delicate and subtle Helenia didn't notice it until it was gone, and so close, the youthfulness of her appearance grew clearer. The lines around Mayve's mouth were softer, the wrinkles around her golden-hazel eyes less pronounced. Her freedom from Adameth had returned to her some of the years he'd stolen.

She touched Helenia's cheek and lowered her voice. "We have much to speak of, don't we, Helly?"

She offered it to me.

"We do."

Hoofbeats crunched on the gravel behind Helenia, and Mayve glanced up, her jaw tightening. "Ah. Fair morning, Seifan."

Helenia stepped back to take in both mother and son, feeling adrift as she broke contact with Mayve.

"Fair morning, Mother." Seifan, almost handsome astride his horse, stared off over her head.

"I didn't know you were coming too." She gestured toward the manor.

"Come inside when you're finished seeing to your soldiers. I'll have the maids prepare—"

"Thank you, but I'll stay with my company." Still staring somewhere above her head, he bowed in the saddle, then turned and rode in the direction of the stables.

"Of course," Mayve muttered to Helenia. "Adameth takes every chance to drive that wedge a little deeper." She clapped her hands and spoke again so everyone might hear. "How lucky I am to have two of my sons here at once? Let's go inside."

Dallan bowed, rose, and offered Mayve his arm, and she giggled like a girl being asked to dance at her first ball as she took it. She instructed her secretary, another unfamiliar face, to see to Helenia and Dallan's servants and baggage before starting in. Helenia followed, though at a lingering pace. She examined the maids and footmen scurrying about, not recognizing a single one. Had Mayve replaced the manor's entire staff? That distracted Helenia as she walked through the open double doors into the vaulted entryway. The hem of her white skirt brushed against the square tiles of evergreen and lavender that extended from the entryway into the main foyer, and it was as if her thoughts splashed out around her, creating a puddle on the floor.

A puddle on the floor. The last time Helenia had stood in the foyer was with Mayve while muddy rainwater had dripped from the brim of Mayve's hat and the cuffs of her riding coat. The memory was so strong Helenia could almost feel Mayve's hands clenched around her forearms.

Oh, Helly. I've gone too far. Adameth is going to kill me.

"Helly?" Mayve called from foot of the grand stair. Above her, Dallan disappeared around the sharp curve in the staircase. "Shall I show you to your rooms?"

How often had Helenia stood in that exact spot and asked Mayve that exact question? *She offered it to me.* Mayve started up, and Helenia followed. Not much in the manor had changed. Unsurprising since, in the not too distant past, Mayve had helped Helenia redecorate it.

Years before, Helenia had walked through the manor as Carhal's betrothed, and he had watched her as she'd passed from room to room, running her hands over the bare walls, the heavy wooden furniture, the thick brocade curtains, and when she'd stopped in what was to be their bedchamber, a dark, sparsely decorated cave, he'd asked her opinion. "It's beautiful," she'd replied, and Carhal, hearing her lie, had called her a wicked minx and tossed her to the bed. As someone with the ability to pick truth from deception just by listening, he'd hated being lied to, but with Helenia, her lies had been their game, their secret lovers' argot.

Despite how much she'd disliked the furnishings, she'd kept them for almost twenty-five years because she'd known they pleased him. Only at Mayve's repeated insistences, and with Carhal's eventual agreement, had Helenia changed them. Over a few too many bottles of wine, Mayve had convinced Helenia to at last stray away from the thick fabrics, dark colors, and heavy woods Tithen inlanders preferred, steering her toward the floral hues and intricately carved pieces like those with which she had decorated her rooms in the palace at Galleford. And here Mayve was, a few years later, living amidst her own designs.

Feelings toward Mayve, long held and long hidden, shook loose somewhere deep inside and began rising to the surface.

A strange maid—strange to Helenia—stood on the second-floor landing with her hands pressed to her sides, her eyes and chin lowered as she waited for the duchess to pass.

"Did you keep no one from my staff?" Helenia asked.

Mayve glanced back but continued walking. "I'm afraid not. I offered them all a place, of course, but with…everything that happened, they moved on. From what I heard, most even left the city."

Then their mistress' disgrace had rubbed off on them. Helenia supposed she should harbor some guilt for dragging those poor men and women through the mud with her, and she might have, had she actually done anything wrong.

They went by Carhal's study, and Helenia returned to that night, the one when Mayve had shown up drenched in her entryway.

MAYVE KNELT in front of the fireplace and held her hands out to warm them. "Adameth is no more than a day or two behind me."

Helenia stifled a sigh. With every year that passed, Mayve and Adameth's marriage crumbled further, and she made it worse with her steadfast refusal to divorce him.

"What can he do?" Helenia asked. She knelt next to Mayve and laid a hand on her sodden shoulder. "He's not going to try you without reason, not again."

"And if I have given him reason?" Mayve closed her eyes. A flash of lightning lit up the room, and the crack of thunder that followed shook the whole manor. She opened her eyes and stared into the fire. "I made my move on the Yent Isles."

Helenia felt as if she had stepped out into the freezing rain. They had talked of Mayve's newest plan for a Tithen revolution, but Helenia had assumed that discussion was what they always were, just talk. "You..." She swallowed hard. "You assassinated their king?"

"No, but I don't know why it didn't work." Mayve slapped her hands against her thighs. "It should have worked."

Helenia struggled for breath. "So we are at war?"

Mayve's lips curled in a moue of disgust. "Give me some credit. They will not be able to trace my agent back to Tithen." She tossed her head back, spattering the carpet with rainwater and reminding Helenia of their most imminent threat.

"Then how does Adameth know?"

"I did something foolish."

Helenia mind raced. All that mattered now was protecting her dearest friend. "If the Yents can't trace your agent back, then Adameth can't try you without exposing Tithen's involvement. He's not willing to start a war to rid himself of you, is he?"

"Of course not," Mayve said. "That's why he's going to haul me before a closed triumvirate."

"And he'll execute you? The people will riot."

Mayve slumped down. "He chose his judges too well. They'll swear to my guilt, and the people will forgive him."

"Are you sure they'll find you guilty?"

"With the evidence he has, I don't see how they couldn't." She shadowed her eyes with her hands. "Burk help me, what have I done?"

When Adameth had arrived with his triumvirate, Helenia had taken the blame for the failed assassination attempt, secure in the knowledge that as long as Carhal lived she was safe.

Four days later, Carhal had died.

"Here we are," Mayve said, stopping before an open door and waving inside, into her old rooms, the ones where she'd stayed whenever visiting Helenia in Morleon.

Carhal had returned from his trip to find his wife had been arrested by his brother. For days, Helenia and Carhal had fought over her taking the blame for Mayve's actions. On the third day, he had stalked out onto the grounds "to get some air" and a short while later he'd collapsed in the kitchen. Helenia hadn't been allowed to attend his funeral. The day after it happened, she'd been shackled in a wagon and headed for Galleford.

Helenia entered the bright bedchamber and stood in the middle of it with her back to Mayve. The choice of rooms might have meant something or Mayve might have chosen them simply because the windows faced the front grounds and the road rather than the back grounds, the stables, the cemetery. Another kindness. Even so, the question of whether or not Mayve had been the one to offer a divorce in exchange for Morleon rested on Helenia's tongue. She only need ask it, and all the doubt Adameth had sown in her heart would wither and die.

And if it doesn't? What then?

"You're still in white," Mayve said, reaching out to touch Helenia's sleeve. Then, "I know how much you must miss him."

Helenia wasn't able to hear lies as Carhal had, but even a deaf woman could hear this one. Mayve had never loved Adameth, she'd confessed as much to Helenia over and over, and that made her incapable of knowing how much Helenia's loss meant to her. The murky feelings continued to rise.

Mayve, in the way that only she could, pivoted straight from friend to revolutionary, dropping her friendliness for the business at hand. "Shall we discuss why you're back? That wasn't part of the plan."

Suddenly grateful to put her question off, Helenia explained her return and more, discussing her arrangement with Lead Varo Orli, her manipulations of Theodora and her encounter with Adameth, framing her disagreement with Dallan as a bit of miscommunication and skipping Adameth's accusation. Mayve requested clarification here and there, but for the most part, she let Helenia speak and listened with a hard, calculating expression.

When Helenia was finished, Mayve thought for a few minutes, then said, "Talk to me about Princess Renn."

Helenia had expected some resistance to that part of her plan, but Mayve trusted her. "She has to live," Helenia insisted. "I've thought it over from a dozen different angles, and this is the way through."

"Will she come around once you've executed her whole family?"

"That is a minor risk. But she loves Dallan, and Orli and the Ombratians are devoted to the Morovides, so we can use her in whichever way is best to secure their loyalty."

Mayve considered this for a short moment. Too short. "Perhaps is not good enough. Kill her. We'll find someone else for Dallan to marry and some other means of manipulating the Fallen."

"But he loves her," Helenia said, unsure why she pressed this point and not the others. "If she dies, he'll be devastated."

Mayve shrugged as Dallan often did. "Let it harden him."

Those words carried Helenia back to almost a year earlier. She had spent her first moon as a widow in a stinking dungeon, and she had fully expected to die there. With her Carhal gone, some small part of her had welcomed the notion. But then...

THE LOCK CLANKED, waking Helenia.

Candlemarks inched by in the darkness, and sleep had become her refuge. As always, there was a perfect moment when she hadn't yet remembered where she was, hadn't yet remembered what had happened. Then cruel reality reasserted itself as someone opened the door to her cell.

Helenia stood and squinted in the flood of light from the hall, but instead of a guard with her daily meal, a more familiar shape entered.

Mayve.

Helenia, desperate for a kind touch, flew into her arms. Mayve returned her embrace, but after a moment, pulled away, touching her nose. Helenia, who had grown inured to her own stench, recognized it anew. Embarrassed, she stepped back, and Mayve let her.

"We came to an agreement," Mayve said. "I'm giving Adameth his divorce."

After everything? "Why?" Helenia asked. "In exchange for what?"

"The most important thing is, he's sparing your life. And no matter what happens, you'll always have a place with me."

Helenia stumbled backward. When her knees hit the bench on which she slept, she dropped down hard. "A place with you where?"

"I'm so sorry, Helly." She sat next to Helenia and took her hands. "But this is for Tithen. And you can use this too. Let it harden you."

"YOU SEEM TIRED," Mayve said, wrenching Helenia back to the present. "I'll leave you wash up and rest before supper."

She left, closing the door behind her, and Helenia found her way to a chair by the window, where she sat with Mayve's words, her apologies, her promises echoing in her head.

THAT EVENING, they supped in the small dining room rather than the great hall. Mayve occupied Carhal's seat at the head and offered Helenia her usual position at the far end of the table. As Mayve's elder son, Seifan should have been seated to her right, but he sat at her left, with Dallan to her right. A few local nobles joined them, and for the most part, they snubbed Helenia, who was happy to be ignored. She didn't touch her food, choosing instead to watch Duchess Mayve.

Helenia had spent the past several moons despising Adameth, blaming him for every loss, every humiliation, every bad thing that had happened to her.

She offered it to me.

At the other end of the table, Mayve laughed at something Dallan said and touched his cheek. Her insistence on killing Princess Renn made no logical sense. Not if her true goal remained Tithen expansion.

Let it harden him.

Mayve glanced down the table toward Helenia and winked. It only made sense if her truest desire was for control.

Let it harden you.

Helenia stared at her friend, her heart pounding as hatred broke the surface and nearly choked her with its strength. Here was the woman who had always cared more for her plans than for any of the people in her life, who had ordered the deaths of dozens without so much as a second thought, who had divided houses with discord, and who was willing to sacrifice anything and anyone for her beloved Tithen.

They had been apart for too long, and Helenia had forgotten too much.

"Helenia?" Everyone along the table stared at Helenia because she was on her feet, though she didn't remember standing. Mayve feigned concern, and Helenia fought the urge to crawl down the table and pluck out her eyes. "Are you well?"

"Excuse me," Helenia said, surprising herself with how normal she sounded. "I'm afraid I have a headache."

She left the dining room, rushed through the manor, out a back door, and into the gardens. The moon illuminated her way as she ran along the paths and past the Wolf Company's encampment, toward the iron-picket fence around the manor's tiny cemetery, and through the cemetery to Carhal's grave. She'd never been there, but she passed beneath the shadows of an iaradann tree as old as the city itself and headed for the largest and newest headstone, a giant white stone eagle with its wings extended.

Helenia knelt in the grass before it. The engraving said Carhal's name, the dates of his birth and death, and below that, *Honored Brother and Son of Tithen.* Battered and abused beyond reason, she didn't even feel the blow.

It didn't matter if Mayve had offered the divorce to Adameth, although Helenia was now certain she had. The real question was, what else had Mayve done? How many other ways had she betrayed Helenia? Had she killed Carhal? That thought should have devastated Helenia, but she realized anything seemed possible now. Whether or not Mayve had played a hand in Carhal's death, when he died, Morleon, the manor, the engraving on Carhal's headstone, Helenia's memories of her husband and their life together should have been hers to control, hers to linger over as she wished. And they would have been, if not for Mayve.

Mayve, who Helenia had thought of as a sister. Mayve, who claimed to fight for Tithen but who truly cared for no one and nothing besides herself.

Helenia knew now she had been right when she told Dallan love forgave much. But it didn't forgive everything. She touched Carhal's headstone, the face of it cold beneath her hand. For all his good qualities, Carhal had never been a man to lay down a grudge. Had their roles been reversed, he would have said Mayve's actions demanded reprisal. Revenge.

Murder and sabotage were the quickest routes, but killing Mayve would be too quick, and Helenia had no desire to destroy her homeland.

Footsteps *shoosh-shooshed* through the grass. Helenia looked over her shoulder to find Dallan walking toward her.

"What are you doing out here?" Helenia asked, her voice ragged.

Dallan shrugged. Careful of his clothes, he crouched beside her. "You were obviously upset when you left the dining room."

Yet he had come after her. Not Mayve.

Helenia examined her nephew's kind expression, then turned back to Carhal's headstone, an icy chill washing through her veins. Could she? Mayve's actions demanded retribution, yet it didn't seem fair that sweet Dallan should pay for his mother's actions. Helenia reached out and traced the words that weren't there because she hadn't been there to add them —*Beloved Husband.* No, it wouldn't be fair. But neither was it fair that Helenia's life had been destroyed by her closest friend.

Her father had insisted the world was an unfair place. And so it was.

Helenia dug her hands into Tithen's rich earth, and when she pulled them out, black soil clung to her skin and made dark half-moons beneath her nails. "I think I'll be going back to Ombratos soon."

Dallan stood and offered her his hand. "Not too soon, I hope."

She ignored his hand and used Carhal's headstone to find her feet. "As soon as I can."

For the next few days, Helenia avoided Dallan, pretended to Mayve nothing had changed between them, and spent most of her days at Carhal's grave doing as Mayve had suggested, letting his death harden her.

When she couldn't stand it any longer, when she'd said her last farewells to Carhal and Morleon, she joined Mayve at her morning meal and announced her departure.

Mayve lifted her cup and blew on her tea to cool it. "Already?"

"Yes." It would take a while to plan her retreat into Ombratos after Dallan was killed. She already regretted the boy's death, but that wouldn't stop her from carrying it out. "If I leave Lead Varo Orli alone for too long, I'm afraid he'll lose his nerve."

"Then go you must." Mayve set down her cup and laid a warm hand over Helenia's. "I'm sure it's been hard to be back. I expect your next visit will be easier."

Helenia, knowing she would likely never see Morleon again, plastered on a false, brave smile. "As do I." She pulled her hand away and rose to leave.

"One last thing before you go," Mayve said. "There's this artist who should be in Ombratos before long and might be of use to you."

TWENTY

"It is at the blind curves in the road where our faith is most sorely tested."
-Leader Oveno Porthain in a sermon to his caravan

Jos met Lathan at what had become their regular tavern, The Night and Oar. People spilled out the door, and inside, jostling, boisterous souls crowded around the tables and bar, yet, by some luck, a pair of women at a table near the door stood just as Jos and Lathan entered. The men descended, snatching up the seats before anyone else might. They waited and talked for a while, but no barmaids or grooms came to their table.

Lathan declared himself parched and jumped up. "Save my seat. I'm going to the bar."

Jos nodded his agreement, and Lathan set off, wending his way through the crowd with ease.

Jos admired his friend. Lathan had refused every one of Jos's offers to draw him, but Jos had done so anyway one afternoon, sketching his features from memory. In the picture, Lathan stood in the library of some manor dressed as a noble. The manor resembled Mutta Kirsch's, Jos's sole reference for such a fine place, and Lathan's clothing was far nicer than any Jos owned. Lathan's truth was that he had visions of wealth, dreams of luxury, and enough charm to marry his way into both, but he worked in the guard, as a protector of the people.

Jos fended off several people seeking Lathan's chair, including a sable-haired woman with a charming Caskian accent, before Lathan at last wound his way back through the press of bodies with two dripping flagons of ale. He set them down in front of Jos, and even more spilled over the sides, soaking his hands and the tabletop. He looked at his hands, then flicked them in Jos's direction, splattering him with ale.

Jos laughed and wiped the droplets from his face. "You are a shit bargroom, you know that?"

"Guess I'll stay in the guard, then." Lathan sat across from Jos and slurped from his flagon without lifting it from the table.

Jos wished he could introduce Lathan to Anell. Anell, funny little creature that she was, would love Lathan's antics. A fierce longing to be with her and the rest of his caravan struck him, but he rode it out. Amma had led him to Sander, to Lathan, and he did important work now.

Though Lathan had never asked Jos to return to the guardhouse, he had asked for Jos's help on four more occasions. He had devised a system where Jos would go somewhere with his materials, to a tavern or a near a shop, and wait there until a man or woman matching the description Lathan gave him came by. Then he drew them and revealed their truth. Thrice Jos had proved a man or woman's guilt, and once a man's innocence. Jos wasn't sure how Lathan lured the people in, and after the murderer, he didn't want to know their sentences, but Lathan had assured him they all met just ends.

Jos had even uncovered two criminals on his own. The first, a thief, saw Jos's drawing before Jos could alert the guard and ran off. Jos caught the other one himself. A smiling, japing man had asked for a portrait of himself for his wife, and Jos had been happy enough to do it. Until he'd started.

Fractured pieces of images had spilled across the page, and he'd struggled to bring forth more than shadows. Later, he'd wondered if his mind had been trying to protect him. At the time though, he'd fought for mastery, focusing all of his efforts on a single shard, and when the shadows had resolved into recognizable shapes, an anger unlike any he'd ever known had washed through him, and he'd leapt on the man, striking him down before kicking him over and over until some guards came to pull him off.

The guards, one the skinny man with the pock-marked cheeks, had brought both Jos and the man back to the guardhouse, but a glance at the drawing was enough for Captain Jensen to set Jos free with a warning not to beat the next one.

"No matter how much he deserves it," she'd said, Jos's drawing crumpled in her fisted hand.

With Lathan's help, Jos drank himself into a stupor that night, and he didn't draw for a couple of days after that. But then Lathan had reminded him that he'd freed that man's poor children with the truth he had uncovered, and he'd returned to his art with a renewed fervor.

It was odd work, hard at times, and it left him exposed, but his mother would have been so proud of him. Pathless hells, perhaps even his father would find his efforts worthy of praise. He had left his father's caravan unsure when, or even if, he'd ever return, but he found himself thinking more and more of the next convocation. He imagined sitting around the fire and spinning out the tale of—

"Jos!" From the way Lathan said Jos's name, he'd already called it more than once.

"Sorry." Jos grabbed his flagon and slid it over so as not to spill, but the ale sloshed around half an inch below the rim. "Did you...?"

Lathan grinned. "That's what you get for dreaming with your eyes open."

On the other side of the tavern, a group of Xantish sailors broke into song. A sea chant, from the sound of it. They had just reached the chorus when, at the next table over, a ragtag collection of men and women with no discernable ties began singing their own song, a popular tune Jos had already heard about seventeen times that day on the steps of the hall.

Lathan leaned over the table and shouted, "I mentioned you in a letter to my aunt, and she could use your help."

"Where is she?" Jos asked, straining his voice to be heard. "I don't know if I can, but I'd like—"

The singing cut off all at once. Jos turned to see what had stopped it and found the barkeep trudging back to his post behind the bar with a hinged flail swinging from one meaty paw.

"That's better," Lathan said.

Jos rubbed his ears. "It is."

"What were you saying?"

It took Jos a moment to track back to his thought. "Oh. I don't know if I can help your aunt, but I'd be happy to meet her."

"Good man." Lathan clapped Jos on the shoulder. "Aunt Calyn used to work for the guard, but then she broke her leg and it never healed right. She does well enough, though. I think her daughter farms salt or some mad thing."

Jos, well used to Lathan's ramblings, sipped from his ale until he was sure his friend had finished. When Lathan didn't continue, Jos said, "I didn't know people farmed salt in Sander."

Lathan's brow furrowed. "What are you on about? There aren't..." His brow smoothed, and he slapped a hand to it. "Fool, me. Did I not mention she lives down in Shade's Rest?"

"Outside Ombratos?" A shadow dimmed Jos's good mood.

"Only Shade's Rest I know of."

Jos picked up his flagon and stared down into it. "Right."

"Heyla." Lathan hit Jos on the shoulder, stirring him from his sudden gloominess. "What's your trouble? You're headed that way, aren't you?"

"I was." Jos drank from his ale, surprised he hadn't said "I am."

Lathan, ever the sly one, noticed that too. "You *were*? Since when? You told me you wanted to go down there not two tendays ago."

Jos shrugged, a gesture he'd picked up from Lathan. "I'm not certain."

"But what about Ombratos?" Lathan asked. "Think about how much larger that place is than here. Think about all the people there are to draw, all the good you could do. And your father. Think about him, and how he..."

Lathan chattered on, moving through all of Jos's reasons for wanting to go to Ombratos. He had shared a lot with Lathan the night he drank himself out of his head. He hadn't gone so far as to reveal his Wandering Fallen heritage, but he had talked about his relationship with his father and his desire to return to Ombratos.

Everything Lathan said was true, but Jos wanted to stay in Sander. Why? *Because you put down roots.* He'd expected to do that in Shade's Rest, but his gift, now wielded with a knowing hand, had lent him more freedom than he'd ever had before. Yet, Amma had led him to Lathan, and Lathan...

"Think about the Ombratian women."

...pointed him toward Shade's Rest.

"I'll go," Jos said.

Lathan seemed startled by the abrupt reversal, but he recovered well enough. Lifting his ale, he knocked it against Jos's and then held it aloft. "To Ombratian women!"

This earned them some looks from people at the nearby tables, and the barkeep reached for his flail. Jos rushed to pick up his flagon. "And to Sander!"

A cheer went up, and many more drinks were lifted into the air. "To Sander!"

THE MIDDAY SUN beat down on the wide brim of Jos's straw hat. He rode around a curve in the coastline and there, off in the distance, stood Ombratos. He tugged on the reins and Thunder and Lightning slowed to a stop.

To the west of the city were the deep blue waters of Crown Bay, where white-capped waves dashed against the stone breakers, sending plume after plume of foam into the air. A two-masted ship passed through the gap in the breakers, the ivory-colored sails billowing as the ship eased out toward the open waters of the Farouche. To the east loomed the Cassedents, dark and solemn, the snowy peaks like the hair atop the heads of craggy-faced old men, and several mines blighted their feet. From this distance, the miners looked like ants crawling in and out of their hills.

Between the mountains and the sea, Ombratos filled every inch of the valley, limned by the bright, unbroken starkness of their wall. The Gift.

The road from the mines—Miner's Trace—ran along the base of the wall like a smear of too-dark shading added by an unskilled hand, and the shading led to a black smudge radiating outward from the wall's North Gate. Jos hoped to reach that smudge—Ombratos's sole faubourg, Shade's Rest—by sundown.

He clucked his tongue and gave the reins a good snap.

THE FALLING sun kissed the horizon's edge as Jos drove his wagon through the packed streets of Shade's Rest, keeping pace with the crowds of miners, merchants, salt farmers, and the visitors who'd come to Ombratos but didn't have the bloodmark that allowed them to spend the night within the city's wall.

Dusk leant a softness to Shade's Rest's edges, but Jos knew better than to be out in certain parts of the faubourg once night fell. It was particularly ill-advised in the Amma-forsaken neighborhoods where the foreign miners lived.

According to Lathan, his aunt lived on the western end of town, near the coast. The directions from Lathan were precise, and Jos rode straight to a well-kept, two-story building down near the docks. It seemed like a nice enough place, but it didn't appear to have anywhere to keep his beasts. Selling them off was the more practical choice, but his mother had always kept a wagon, and unless circumstances forced him to do otherwise, as they had near the end of her life, he would pay to keep his and the animals for as long as he was able.

He climbed down from the driver's bench, knocked, and waited. Before long, an old woman flung open the door. She was tall, though her bowed back robbed her of at least four inches, and a cloud of bluish smoke—jayberry, from smell of it—wreathed her lined face and wispy white hair.

This woman was in the guard? "Are you Calyn?"

"Last I heard," she said, speaking around the pipe hanging from the corner of her mouth. "Who's that, then?" She wore a tattered, crusty dress, and the smell of rot came from the dark hall leading to the front door, suggesting the inside of the building wasn't anywhere near as well-kept as the outside. He saw no sign of the woman's salt farmer daughter.

"I'm Josiah Porthain."

"Who?" she asked, peering up at him with deep brown eyes, the whites more of a yellow.

Jos struggled to find a familial resemblance between this woman and his friend. "I'm Jos Porthain." She stared at him. "Lathan sent me." Still nothing. "From Sander?"

"From Sander, eh?" She plucked the pipe from her mouth, touched her palm to the bowl, then tapped it out on the doorframe, sprinkling his boots and her bare feet with charred bits of jayberry leaves. "Why didn't you say when I opened the door 'stead of keepin' me standin' here like a tofter?"

It seemed neither looks nor charm ran a wide streak in the Cyon family. Perhaps Lathan had gotten all they had to spare. "Your nephew said you could use my help."

She eyed him sharply, at last revealing some facet of the guard she'd once been. "You're the artist, hain't you?"

"That's right."

She pulled a pinch of dried leaves from a pocket of her dress and stuffed it into the pipe. "I suppose I'll have use for you sooner than later. Where you stayin' at?"

Sooner than later? Lathan had made his aunt's issue seem more pressing than that. "I'm not sure."

"I hain't got no rooms, if that's your thought." She pointed toward the wagon and his asses. "I hain't got no place for them neither." Thunder made his opinion of her statement known, and she waved away the resultant stench. "'Specially not that one."

Thank Amma. Except that left him without anywhere to spend the night. Shade's Rest didn't have a traveler's field like Sander, and darkness was falling fast.

Calyn gnawed on her pipe stem. After a long moment, she took it out of her mouth and pointed it at him. "Here's what. There's a man up the street what owns a bakery, and he lets his barn out when he's of a mind to. Don't think they need the coin, but Amma knows they got the room. We'll see if they're in the mood to take you in."

Her invocation of Amma calmed him. If she lived out in Shade's Rest, chances were it was because she didn't have a bloodmark, but there were some Fallen beyond the wall and those who worshipped her anyway, adhering to her tenets rather than suffering some godless existence.

She stepped outside in her bare feet, closed the door behind her, then waited by the wagon for him to hand her up. Her dry skin rasped against his, and the bottoms of her feet had the look of hooves.

He climbed onto the bench beside her, and she directed him around the block, to a shop with a sign above the door depicting a sheaf of wheat lying in front of a basket filled with different types of bread. The amount of detail in the woodworking gave the impression one could pluck the basket right off the sign, and the rich, homey smell floating out into the street through the open door only enhanced the sensation.

He handed Calyn carefully to the ground, and when she told him to wait outside and entered the shop alone, he stood and jumped to the street as well to stretch his legs. Amber light drained from the crimson sky, and not too long passed before she returned with a man soft and round enough to have been made from his own stock.

"This here's Ysobello Dufore," Calyn said, again speaking around a lit pipe. She gestured toward Jos. "Ysobello, Josiah Porthain."

She'd remembered his name. That was something. He held out his right hand. So close to Ombratos, he had nothing to fear if someone revealed his bloodmark. "Most call me Jos."

Ysobello shook his hand. "What do you do?

"I'm an artist," Jos said. "I sketch and paint."

"Can you pay rent with that?" Ysobello told Jos the rate of the room, a fair price. "Due at the start of each tenday, and you care for the animals yourself."

"I can do that." Even if Jos made just half as much every day as he had in Sander, he would be fine.

Ysobello looked Jos up and down, then he clapped his hands, tensing the large muscles in his forearms and sending a cloud of flour up into the air. A smile creased his doughy face. "You seem trusty enough. But if I decide this hain't a good arrangement, then I return your coin and send you packin.' How's that?"

Jos agreed to the terms, and Calyn took a couple of hard puffs on her pipe. "Whisper your wishes and Amma will provide." Above them, Amma winkled, as if to prove her point.

As the last of the day's light faded, two girls came running down either side of the street, stopping every twenty-five feet to light the street torches from the ones in their hands. They seemed to be racing, and the shorter of the two tore past just as Calyn turned to leave, almost knocking her off her feet.

Ysobello steadied her before she fell. She pulled her pipe from her mouth and jabbed her stem after the girl. "Forsaken shit!"

Jos winced at the slur, and Ysobello stiffened.

"Sorry," she said, not sounding sorry at all. She jammed the pipe back into her mouth, then wandered back toward her home, muttering under her breath.

Ysobello shook the stiffness off like a dog shaking water from its coat. "How about you go around and meet me in back, and we'll see you settled."

WHILE JOS WAITED for Calyn to have use of him, he stayed in Ysobello's barn. After his first night in his wagon, he dragged his mattress up into the loft, where he slept with the loft doors open, as a reprieve from both Thunder's stench and the rising heat of summer. Most days he woke around dawn to the scent of baking bread, a mighty smell that overpowered even Thunder's wretched stink.

He drew Calyn and, as with Mutta Kirsch and her Alric, revealed the part of life she returned to most often. In the picture, a stoic-faced Calyn in her middle twenties stood in the front doorway of the house where she still lived. She held a weeping infant in her arms, and at the edge of a drawing, the boot of whomever had walked away from them. He guessed the girl to be the salt farmer, the daughter Calyn had raised alone.

Since he had been thrifty with his coin and paper cost even less here because it was produced at the mills inside the city, he spent his first tenday walking the streets of Ombratos not working but just watching people, drawing them, speaking with them.

He sketched the taut-limbed dock workers of the Mire, the hungry children in the Tangles, the haughty, well-dressed merchants strolling the avenues of the Chestnut. He drank with some artists from the Blossom and almost tumbled a stunning dark-haired, dark-eyed quilter named Leira. Fortunately, after a few kisses, she insisted on him drawing her before they did anything else, and his sketch revealed the beautiful woman's ugly heart. When she saw his work, she tossed him out, and he happily returned to his barn alone.

The next morning, he rose, walked around the block, and joined the stream of customers flowing into Ysobello's bakery. He ate many of his meals from Ysobello's shop, often starting his mornings with a tart or a dark brown trencher and supping on hot meat pies. He loved the small bakery. With the warm colors on the walls and the curtains hanging in the front window, the shop was as comforting and inviting as its owner.

Ysobello and his youngest daughter, a quiet girl called Bibi, bustled around behind the counter, serving the people and stuffing the coins into their bulging apron pockets. Their success had turned out to be why they charged Jos as little as they did.

"Heyla, boarder," Ysobello crowed as Jos made it to the counter. "What'll you have this morn?"

As always, everything on the rapidly emptying shelves looked delicious, but a glistening roll with nuts sprinkled over the top caught Jos's eye. "I think I'll try your honey roll today."

Ysobello grabbed that very one and brought it back to the counter. "Near forgot. Calyn's daughter stopped by, asked me to tell you Calyn wants to talk to you."

At last. Thinking of his drawing of Calyn, Jos asked Ysobello about her favorite of his baked goods.

"She likes the apple tarts," Ysobello said, his eyebrows high on his forehead. "You take a shine to our Calyn? She's a hard one to like."

Jos shrugged. "A hard life takes its toll."

He bought the tart and walked down to Calyn's, devouring his own sweet, sticky honey roll along the way. She answered the door in her same gruff manner, with the same bluish aureole of smoke around her head.

"What's this for, then?" she asked when he handed her the tart.

He put on his most charming grin. "Eating, I think."

"Piss off, tofter." She frowned at him even as color rose to her sallow cheeks. "Be near the crossing of Thate's Road and Breaker Way at the fourth candlemark of this afternoon, and draw the man waiting on the northeast corner."

"Any idea what the man did?"

She took the pipe from her mouth and sniffed at the tart. "Hain't that what you're meant to tell me?" Stepping back inside, she said, "Ta for this," then she used her elbow to slam the door closed.

For the first time since his arrival in Shade's Rest, the day was cool. A brisk wind came in off the ocean, and clouds blanketed the sky to every edge of the horizon. With one good deed under Jos's belt and another to come, he spent much of the day down at the rocky beach, sketching the strange creatures caught in the tide pools.

At about half past the third candlemark, he went to the crossing of Thate's Road and Breaker Way. A tea shop with outdoor tables stood on the southwest corner, giving him a spot from which to work unnoticed. Jos had learned in his time with Lathan that guards saw the world from a slightly different perspective. The tea shop was a prime seat from which to watch passersby without seeming to, and in his mind, that proved to him once and for all Calyn had been in the guard.

Choosing the table he thought Lathan would be most likely to pick, Jos sat, asked the server for a full pot of peltoi tea, and waited.

Some men lingered on the opposite corner, but none for long. Not until right at the fourth candlemark, when a man charged up to the corner and stopped at its apex. He had shaved his whole head down to the scalp—a shadow darkened his jawline and showed where his receding hair started far up on his forehead. His plain features seemed mismatched and bland, as if someone had drawn his face with the intention of going back in and adding more detail later and had never gotten around to it. But an aura of command radiated from him, and the way he wore his plain linen tunic and breeches gave them the look of armor, the eating knife on his hip the look of a sword.

He stood there without any clear purpose, so Jos, deciding this man was his subject, concentrated on bringing out the darkest part of him and began sketching.

In the drawing, the man knelt between two women, all three of them stark against a field of grey. On his left loomed a woman of monstrous proportions. Ebony curls ringed the tiny head, and a disfigured face sat atop mounded shoulders and a fleshy, shapeless body. To his right stood the horror's opposite, a striking woman clothed in a pure white gown, and the man reached out for her, though she kept her hands clasped at her waist. The man was Jos's target, but he struggled for a bit with the woman on his right, certain he missed something of her essence. It took him a few moments, but he finally placed the source of his dissatisfaction—her hair. No matter how he shaded it, he longed for color, for reds, oranges, and yellows to bring the tresses to life.

The man glanced up and down both crossroads, then up into the sky, where the lingering clouds obscured any view of the sun. He wouldn't wait much longer, so Jos returned his focus to the man, capturing weariness around his eyes and mouth and stiffness in his bearing, but nothing more about his truth. Would Calyn be disappointed with Jos's work? His subject seemed torn between two women, perhaps he even cheated on one with the other. Was that wrong? Of course, but far from a crime.

Across the way, another man, this one wearing silks and a peacock-plumed velvet hat, walked past the corner, glancing at Jos's subject. Then, halfway across Thate's Road, he stopped, turned around, and came back.

"Orli!" the behatted man called out. "Is that you?"

Startled, Jos's subject spun around, but he recovered fast, expressing his own greeting and shaking the man's extended hand. Then they both held their hands out to expose the fading bloodmarks on their palms. Fallen. Did the Shade's Rest guards have any authority over those who lived inside the walls? A question for Calyn.

Jos's subject, Orli, spoke with the man in the hat, but he kept looking around, as if concerned someone else might come upon them. So the man wasn't the person Orli expected to meet. An interesting detail, if not too relevant for Jos's purposes. Except...

As the man with the hat chattered away, Jos pulled out a fresh page and sketched him. In the picture, he stood on a rock, staring down with an uncaring expression at the line of bowed-back men, women, and children linked by shackles and parading before him. The man at the end of the line lay on the ground, dragged along by the chains around his wrists.

Jos looked up. The man speaking to Orli worked his miners like slaves and perhaps even kept them as such. Surely Calyn and the guard would do something about that.

The cruel taskmaster babbled on for another couple of minutes, and Jos listened as well as he could on the busy street, hoping to catch the taskmaster's name, but they spoke of nothing—the weather, their health—and Orli never said it. After another handshake, the man walked off.

Jos sat there while Orli waited for another five minutes or so, but no one else came to meet him. After he stalked off, Jos finished his tea, then headed back to Calyn's. His image of Orli was useless, but even without a name, she might make use of the drawing of the other man.

When Calyn answered her door, this time with a touch more civility, he handed her the rolled-up drawing of the man with the hat. Pipe clenched in her teeth, she looked down as she unfurled it.

"Do you recognize him?" Jos asked.

"I do," she said, her expression grim.

"So you can use this?"

She met his eyes. "I'll make sure this finds its way into the right hands."

Her promise soothed his troubled conscience, and he presented the other drawing with a flourish. "As requested, one drawing of Orli the Romantic."

Her head snapped up, and the pipe dipped. "What did you call him?"

"Orli the Romantic?" She unrolled the second drawing, and he pointed at the picture. "Look."

She did. "How did you come up with the name?"

"The man in the hat called him Orli. The rest..."

She barked a laugh. "Yes, I see." Reaching into her pocket, she pulled out a silver with pieces of dried jayberry leaves clinging to it. She brushed it off, then handed it to him. "That's fine work, that is."

Her compliment surprised him. "Does that picture help you?"

Calyn's pipe rose as she smiled. "More than you know."

That evening, to celebrate a job well done, Jos decided to visit a tavern Ysobello often mentioned, one he said served ale to rival any on the other side of the wall. As Jos walked the few blocks to the tavern, he imagined Calyn carrying his picture into a Shade's Rest city guardhouse that looked much like Lathan's House 12, back in Sander. He also wondered if Orli the Romantic was with his beloved, kneeling at her feet as he showered her with praise.

The thought brought a smile to his lips, and he crossed the threshold into The Red Dawn in a convivial mood. The tavern turned out to be a clean, well-lit place, with a singer warbling away in one corner and a healthy amount of trade populating the booths and tables.

The patrons appeared to be a mix of Shade's Rest guards and local sailors, an odd combination, but one that seemed friendly enough. At least at this candlemark. Ysobello had warned him to leave before either group fell too far into their cups.

He cut through the crowd, his size lending him an advantage, and went up to the bar, where a pert bargroom filled a rented wooden jack with the house ale. The first sip proved it as smooth and rich as Ysobello had claimed, and Jos, his elbows back on the bar, nursed his drink as he scanned the room. For the most part, the sailors kept to one side and the guards to the other, but a bit of overlap muddled up the center.

Jos emptied his jack, and was deciding whether to stay for another one or go, when the door opened and a tall, plain woman close to his age entered. Plain, yes, but there was something more about her. Then she started toward the bar, transfixing him.

Right around Jos's fifteenth birthday, his Aunt Bosk had taken him hunting along the southern border of Rhyllex, and while they were out, they'd stumbled across the path of a cat-a-mountain. This woman's lithe movements and the cold fierceness of her gaze as she prowled through the room reminded him of the animal's savage beauty. She strode up to bar and stood next to him to wait for the bargroom's attention.

"Heyla!" he said, trying not to wince at how overeager he sounded.

She had to look up to meet his eyes, but only a little since he topped her height by a scant few inches. "Heyla," she said. She glanced away, but he sensed he had her attention for the moment.

Jos didn't often struggle for idle conversation, but he didn't know what to say to this woman. From her bearing, she was a guard. Propping her elbows up on the bar, she rubbed her thumb across her palm, sparking and resparking her bloodmark. So a Fallen guard at that, and there was something else about her too. He didn't need to draw her. Not that he didn't want to capture the essence of her strength, her feral allure, on the page. No, he would love to, but unlike with most people, he sensed he didn't need to in order to know her truth. Sincerity outlined every inch of her body, darkened every shadow, shone from the gleam of lamplight on her chestnut-colored hair down to the dull leather sheen of her boots, and he sensed that any drawing of her would depict nothing more the woman who stood before him.

The bargroom came to their end of the bar. The woman handed him the leather jack from her belt, and he pulled her an ale. With a start, Jos realized soon she would be gone and his opportunity past. Heart pounding, he leaned in and said the only words that came to mind. "I'm Jos."

She picked up her jack. Meeting his eyes again, she said, "Getha." Without looking away, she sipped from the foam on her ale, then she cocked her head to one side and bit her lower lip. She reached out, touching his biceps, which he instantly flexed. She squeezed it and raised one of her eyebrows in...appreciation?

A sailor at a nearby table shot to his feet and shouted something incomprehensible. Getha straightened, stepped partially in front of Jos, dropped a hand to her side, and all of a sudden, a dagger protruded from her clenched fist. At the table, the sailor shouted a few more unintelligible words, and everyone around him began slurring their way through a drinking song about a bunk and pail. Or a drunken whale. Perhaps a broken rail...

Getha, not taking her eyes off the revelers, set her jack on the bar and tucked the dagger back into her leather vambrace. That she went around armed with hidden knives should have put him off her, but for some reason it made her even more appealing. Especially since she'd seemed ready to defend him. There wasn't any cruelty to her bearing, just the simple ability to protect herself, and the instinct to protect others, from harm.

Mustering up his most charming smile, he tried to draw her back in. "Want to find a table and talk?"

"Not really," Getha said, still staring at the singers.

Jos's stomach sank as she picked up her jack and drained it in several large gulps. He expected her to leave then, but she remained and turned to pin him down for a third time with her direct gaze. This was his last chance —if he looked away, he'd never see her again—so he stared back, bearing up under the weight of her attention as best he could, and little by little, the scents, sounds, and sights of the tavern fell away, until all that remained was him and her and the heat growing between them.

Hoping against hope he hadn't conjured up that last part, he said, "Do you live nearby?"

"No." She stepped forward, leaving less than a hair's breadth between them, and peered up at him. "Do you?"

Jos never took women back to his home. Safer that way. But Getha... She held his gaze with an intensity that stole his breath away, and desire trampled down the last of his good sense.

"I live not far from here," he said.

Getha didn't go so far as to smile, but her expression shifted the tiniest bit toward amusement. "Lead the way."

Jos dozed in Getha's arms, but she jostled him awake as she disentangled her limbs from his and rose. First thing, she buckled on her vambraces, then she cast her arms wide and stretched. After two tumbles, he'd thought himself spent, but the sight of her naked, muscular form clad only in weaponry forced him to reconsider. She headed toward his chamber pot, and he rolled over to give her a little privacy, stretching out on his mattress, his limbs and muscles loose like unformed clay. What was it going to be like to wake up next to her in the morn? What would her chestnut hair look like in the sunlight? Would she join him in breaking his fast? Would it be too odd to take her to Ysobello's shop?

Dozens of thoughts cascaded through his mind about how the next day might go, but when he rolled back, Getha hunted out her clothing on the floor.

"You don't have to go," he said.

She grabbed her breastband from near the foot of the mattress. "Why do you live out here in Shade's Rest?"

He'd formed a story to explain his bloodmark on their way back to his loft and struggled to remember it now. "I, uh, it's cheaper. Spent all my money on the wagon and the asses." He didn't like lying to a woman who seemed so forthright, a woman—he had to admit—he wanted to see again, but at least in this, his caution won out.

"What do you need the wagon for?" she asked, putting on her breastband and adjusting it.

"I'm an artist. I want to travel, see things."

She grunted, a sound either of acknowledgment or derision. Finding her tunic under his drawing table, she slipped it on over her breastband.

"You don't have to go," he repeated.

Her breeches hung from the top rung of the ladder. "I do."

"It's because of the smell, isn't it?" He'd left the loft doors cracked, and Thunder had been on his best behavior, but even so. And thinking it was Thunder was better than—

"It's because of you." Grabbing her breeches, she sat on the edge of the mattress and pulled on both legs together.

He sat up, now feeling like brittle clay that had been fired too fast. "Because of me?" He scooted back and slumped against the headboard.

Their first tumble had been rushed and awkward, as first tumbles so often were, but with the second he'd held off on finding his release until she'd found hers. Unless... What if she'd tired of his efforts and had pretended to hurry him along? Mortified, he didn't know what to say, so the silence stretched out until she turned to face him.

His discomfiture must have shown because she sighed and said, "Oh, for Amma's sake. I don't mean *you* you. You were fine."

"Fine?" Jos hadn't thought it possible, but he felt even worse.

"No," she said, exasperated. "You were more than fine. Good." A smirk curled the corner of her mouth. "Great, even." She seemed startled to have said that last bit. Her cheeks reddened, and that paired with the compliment—which, he guessed, she did not often give—restored much of his fair humor. "It's just…" She reached out, as if she might pluck the word she sought from the air. Then, seeming unable to catch it, she clenched her hand into a fist and dropped it to her side. "It's you."

"Well, that clears things up." He had no idea what she meant, but he wanted to. Spying one of her boots on the far side of the mattress, he reached over and picked it up while she laced her breeches. "We should do this again."

She found her other boot, jammed her foot into it, and adjusted the buckle just below her knee. Then she looked around. He let her search for a moment before lifting her boot and waved it back and forth. She came over and tried to take it from him, but he held tight. She tried again, and he held fast. She tried for a third time, then, as it had at the tavern, her expression shifted the tiniest amount, but toward irritation rather than amusement. Not wanting to send her sprawling, he waited until after her next tug and let go.

"Is that a no?" he asked as she pulled her boot on, fastening the buckle.

She finished and straightened. "Fair night, Jos."

He wanted to kiss her farewell, with any other woman he would have, but he held the urge in check, suspecting that, in this case, his aloofness would win him more points rather than less. "Fair night, Getha."

Turning away from him, she made for the ladder. The loft shook as she climbed down, but he waited to hear the barn door close before he went for his charcoal and paper. Getha's lines settled on the page without embellishment or artifice because she was, by nature or design, exactly who she appeared to be.

When he finished, she stared up at him from his drawing and he wondered if he'd ever see her again.

TWENTY-ONE

"Don't ever enter a room without knowin' how you're gettin' out."
-Podriach OcNessa to his daughter, Helenia

S ummer had clamped its sweaty hand around the city of Ombratos early. It never grew so warm on Tithen, but the Gift seemed to trap the heat and hold it, making the city like a bowl filled with hot soup. The sun beat down at the hottest part of the hottest day so far, and Helenia walked through the streets of the Mire naked.

Or that was what it felt like. Helenia's mourning whites stood out in Ombratos, where women wore full white when they were with child. She'd enjoyed the attention when she lived at the palace, but since she now sought to blend in, she'd left her dresses behind. Giving up her whites while she still mourned her husband bothered her deeply, but her dearest Carhal would have understood.

Today she wore a lawn tunic and loose-legged breeches tucked into a pair of well-worn boots that had been new when she'd left Tithen, and she'd tucked her pride and joy, her hair, beneath a cap, the tattoos over her brow shadowed by its brim. So disguised, she strolled toward her meeting, nervous for it to start yet anxious to have it done.

Upon returning to Ombratos, she'd made immediate contact with Orli, and in the ensuing tenday, they'd forged a new plan, a plan that would serve her better than it did Mayve.

For a start, Orli and his varos would take down the Morovides and anyone at the palace who opposed them. She knew from living at Seedfall that many of those who served were loyal to the crown and that meant the initial attack would be a slaughter. Judging from the way Orli spoke of that part, with downcast eyes and his hands in fists, he understood as much, but he would carry it out because that was what he'd sworn to do.

Sweat trickled down Helenia's cheeks and neck, and she stopped at a vendor's cart for a dram of fresh-pressed cherry juice. Two young women worked the cart—one cutting cherries, removing the pits, and tossing them into the gutter, the other pressing the juice in a wooden contraption. Helenia gave the girl at the press two coppers and, after a moment's thought, handed her the leather jack from her belt.

The girl cutting cherries reached into her basket for more. "How much?"

"More than a little, less than a lot," said the girl at the press.

"Well, that's helpful." Cherry girl grabbed a handful of the almost black cherries, put them on her board, and sliced into them. "Say, weren't that how you described the guard from t'other night?"

Press girl cackled and cherry girl joined her, and they kept it up, tossing japes back and forth, amusing one another as cherry girl dropped the fruit into the contraption, and press girl set Helenia's jack at the sluice and turned the crank, releasing a few mouthfuls of liquid.

Helenia decided she hated them, these girls who worked so well together, jesting and laughing despite the heat, their hands stained the exact same red.

The warm and jaw-achingly tart bloodred liquid slid down Helenia's throat, and even though she had coated the inside of her jack with kreasoe herself, she couldn't taste it. Good. That meant she'd prepared it correctly.

Kreasoe, a stubby plant with shriveled purple leaves, had been native to Tithen until it was all but harvested out of existence. Her father had kept a small kreasoe plant, just as his mother had and her father before her. It was their only family heirloom.

The benefits of kreasoe were two-fold, Firstly, the small, violet blooms, which thankfully only came once a year and remained for less than a week, stank like a pile of manure. That said, the rancid blooms were edible, and the affects were extreme relaxation and stunning hallucinations. This was the primary reason people had sought it out.

Her father, however, had kept it mostly for its second use. When kreasoe was burned or boiled, it produced a colorless, scentless liquid that, once imbibed, prevented liquor from making one drunk. Her father had often used it on the nights he ran his games because it allowed him to match his marks glass for glass and remain sober enough to relieve them of their coin.

Helenia couldn't be certain they'd offer her a drink at her meeting, but if they did, she wanted to keep her wits about her. Securing her jack back on her belt, she continued on toward the Tangles.

After Orli and his varos dealt with things at the palace, he would signal her and the Tithens out on ships in the bay that it was safe to approach the docks. Then the varos would lie in wait inside the city, and when the Tithens entered, they would attack.

Orli had offered little resistance to the notion of assassinating Prince Dallan. "A nice enough boy," Orli had said, standing in the tiny room he'd rented for her in the Mire, "but I suppose he never was worthy of a Morovide. I'm sure we'll find Princess Renn someone much more deserving."

His words had reassured her even as he'd disgusted her with his readiness to murder her nephew. She comforted herself with the knowledge that Dallan was too good for this world, and in killing him, she would set him free from the betrayals his mother had planned for him. Once at Burk's side, Carhal would watch over him, and Mayve would have to live knowing she'd sent her beloved son to his death.

Let that harden *her.*

Helenia reached the edge of the Tangles, and there, at the corner of Tarner and Stroud, leaning against the wall in a narrow strip of shadow, stood the man she'd set out to meet. He wore a sleeveless tunic, short pants, and a stone-headed mallet hung from his belt. She appreciated the muscles on his bared arms and calves and supposed she found him attractive in a primal, menacing sort of way. He might have tempted her in her youth, but those days had long since passed. Most handsome men weren't worth even half the trouble they caused.

He looked up as she neared, a half-smile quirking his lips. "Heyla, my lady."

She stifled a sigh. He called her "my lady" because he seemed to have guessed how much it irritated her. She stepped into the building's shadow next to him. "Heyla, Natts."

He glanced down at her. In true Ombratian fashion, he towered over her by several inches. "Ready to meet the man hisself?"

"I am."

He pushed away from the wall and waved down Stroud Road, into the Tangles. "Then let's be off."

Helenia started walking, and Natts fell into step beside her.

She might have worried that by "someone more deserving" Orli meant himself, but she had the drawing to ensure her of his devotion. She hadn't intended to make use of Mayve's artist, though she'd told Mayve she might. Yet the idea of a young man with a gift like Carhal's had picked and picked at her, overlapping in her mind with Mayve's betrayal, and after her reunion with Orli, she'd decided she had to know if his loyalty ran as deep as he claimed. So, through a dock worker she found at a tavern in the Mire, she'd made contact with Mayve's agent, setting up a time and place for the artist to capture Orli's truth, and the picture, vibrant and almost throbbing with verity, had shown her what she'd needed it to.

The one wrinkle had been the agent. Helenia still wasn't sure how that damned agent had found out who Orli was, but no one got the chance to blackmail her twice. For a few more coins, the dock worker had dealt with the agent and made it clear to her daughter that she was both expected to take her mother's place and that any further…curiosity would bring her to the same end.

Having Orli and his varos in place against Dallan and the Tithen was good, but there remained the matter of Princess Renn. Natts rounded a corner, and Helenia followed.

Her father had taught her every city had two rulers, "the official lordy or lady what runs things above the surface, and the kingfish what runs things below it." And if Queen Theodora was Ombratos's official lady, then, by all accounts, Talp was its kingfish. What Helenia's father hadn't realized, and what she had learned, was that things above and below the surface were actually quite similar. Flattery, deference, greased palms, oiled jaws— people were people regardless of station. Identifying Talp as Ombratos's kingfish had been easy enough, as had been making contact with his top lieutenant, but arranging for a meeting with Talp proved more difficult. Though not as difficult as it would have been for someone without Helenia's unique background.

Several blocks into the Tangles, the neighborhood's stench grew thick enough to taste. In the narrow alleyways of the Tangles, refuse rotted, and filthy men and women, those too old or too crippled to work, sat in the shade on the west side of the street, sweating, fanning themselves, and gossiping. A flock of screaming children, most of them half-naked, came rushing down the street toward Helenia and Natts. As they neared, he stepped in front of her and raised his hands so the children might reach out and slap them as they passed.

Helenia had been one of those children, and at seventeen, when her father had died, she'd made the decision to reinvent herself. She'd wanted more than a life of gambling and lying and grifting, more than a life of running wild in the streets. That decision had led her to Morleon, to Carhal, to Mayve and her betrayal. In its roundabout way, that decision had led her here, right back to where she'd started. A chuckle escaped her.

"What's that?" Natts asked over his shoulder.

The last child, a skinny boy wearing nothing other than short pants, jumped up, hit Natts's palm, then, screeching his triumph, scurried off to catch up with his friends.

"This place," Helenia said, not bothering to explain further. "Life is strange sometimes, isn't it?"

Natts slowed to match her pace. "More often than not, I'd say."

They walked a few more blocks in silence, then he stopped at the mouth of a dark alley. He'd taken her to several different taverns—once he'd even met her at the ale tent in the night market—but this place was new.

"Where's this, then?" she asked.

"Welcome to Talp's Court."

The dark alley rendered her blind for a moment after the glare of the street. She placed a light hand against the wall and took small steps, giving her eyes a chance to adjust. At the end of the alley, they went through a door, and then down a narrow hall, a kill hall replete with murder holes overhead, that let out into the tavern's main room. Fewer than a dozen people sat at the tables, each at their own, some with jacks in hand, others with their heads lowered. A mirror lined the wall behind the long bar, and the barkeep diced with a patron, a man whose arms barely reached halfway across the bar and whose legs swung miles above the floor, begging the question of how he'd gotten up on the barstool in the first place.

Natts wove a path through the empty tables, leading her toward a curtain in the tavern's darkest corner, and when they reached it, he pulled the curtain back to reveal a door. He wrapped his hand around the handle, holding it until something inside the door clicked. A clever mechanism or Fallen blood magic? Helenia tried to examine the latch as he opened the door, but the deep shadows hid much of it. A cool, musty breeze rushed out to meet them.

He reached into the dark, unshuttered a globe, picked it up, and held it high to show her a set of wooden steps leading downward. He clomped down, and removing her hat, she descended after him. As she did, she grew very aware of the huge tavern above their heads, the tavern that could come crashing down and bury them at any moment, but she forced that awareness from her mind. Instead, she appreciated the underground chill that seeped through the walls and raised gooseflesh along her arms. Thirty steps later, they reached the bottom and another door, this one with a muscular woman standing guard.

The woman nodded to Natts, he nodded back, and the woman opened the door to a root-cellar small room. The walls, ceiling, and floor were no more than packed dirt, but a thick rug lay over the floor, a painting of a man fishing off the end of a pier hung on one wall, a liquor cart stood below it, and a gold-wrought tree bearing two globes sat atop a six-sided honey-wood table with a chair on each side.

Of course, for all its comforts, the room had only one door—one way in and one way out. Her father had taught her better than to trap herself in such a place, but in this room laid the potential for her reward, and her hunger for that reward, for Mayve's reward, made any risk worth it.

"Lady Helenia, I presume."

She started as a man she somehow hadn't noticed stood from one of the chairs and held out his hand. Such an odd man—neither short nor tall, neither handsome nor plain, with clothes made from cheap fabric yet stitched well, and hair, eyes, and skin all the same dried-mud brown. He was a sparrow in human form, remarkable only for his profound un-remarkableness.

"I'm Talp," the unremarkable man said in a voice neither low nor high, "and it's a pleasure to finally meet you."

He offered her the seat across from him, and she took it, determined to regain her footing after her startlement. "Thank you," she said. "What has Natts told you of our discussions? Where should we start?"

"I'm parched with this weather," Talp said. "Let's drink first."

Helenia reached for the jack on her belt, but Natts set two glass tumblers on the table before her and Talp, making her glad she'd consumed the kreasoe while she had the chance. Talp smiled, the expression not cruel or kind, as Natts poured two drams of thorno into both their glasses. That they were drinking thorno made Helenia doubly glad for her forethought.

Lifting the glass, Talp rolled it between his hands before holding it up to the light. "Fine craftsmanship, don't you think?"

She lifted her glass to join Talp in admiring the beveled artistry, the way the liquor danced and sparkled in the globelight. "I do."

She expected Natts to join them, but he took up a post behind her, near the door, and she allowed Talp to set the cadence of their meeting. She drank when he drank and waited for him to speak before she spoke. Since the kreasoe kept her sober, she pretended to drunkenness, loosening her joints, laughing and touching his hand more and more often, and over the course of two candlemarks, they chaffered out a deal: in exchange for the city's mines, Talp agreed to seek out Princess Renn and kill her while Orli and his varo fought the Tithens down at the docks. Then Talp's crew would protect Helenia from Orli and his remaining varos.

Talp warned her at this. "My crew is skilled, but they are not varos."

"They aren't," Helenia said, slurring her words the tiniest bit. "But the varos will have been fightin' for many a-candlemark, and they will be tired when they reach you."

A lie. She had watched the varos train, and even after so much fighting, Talp's crew would fall. The truth of it was, she needed someone to kill the princess and for Orli to believe she played no part in the death, but if the impossible happened, if Talp's people won out over Orli and his varos, Talp had to think she favored him. Either way, with Dallan dead, Mayve would be coming for her, and so she required fighters to help her defend the city.

"Indeed," Talp said. "So"—he drained the last of his glass—"when will this uprising take place?"

"Before the moon is over," Helenia said as she climbed to her feet. She wanted the chance to employ that artist again. "I'll send word through Natts."

Talp said a name Helenia didn't quite catch, and the muscled woman who had let her and Natts into the room came through the door. "Please see our guest out," he said as his mud-colored eyes met Helenia's. "I look forward to a long and productive alliance."

"As do I," Helenia said. She turned to Natts. "I will be in touch."

He smiled his wicked smile at her, and she followed the woman from the room, up the steps, and into the stifling heat of the tavern, now bustling with patrons.

Fighting the urge to walk with her head held high, Helenia let the woman guide her. Talp was the final piece; once she had her picture of Talp's truth, all that remained was to notify Mayve. With that, Mayve would set her plan in motion, Helenia would set hers, and atop the pile of bodies, someone would emerge the victor.

TWENTY-TWO

"Learn to adapt and you'll never go unarmed."
-Waltham

J os sat in a divot in the seawall near one of Shade's Rest's salt farms, sketching the workers and enjoying the breeze coming in off the Farouche. He spent the whole of the afternoon on a single image, drawing the bucket carriers and the fire tenders, and the plumes of steam rising from sea water poured into shallow lead pans. He caught the curved lines of the rakers sifting through their grainy field with backs bent, and beyond them, the frenetic breaks of the seed for their crop that never ceased to wash ashore, all while the sun crept down toward the horizon.

When the bells rang to announce the closing of the city gates, he set aside his chalk and cracked his stiff finger joints. Sundown meant the time had come to return to his loft and wait. He jumped off the wall, and pins and needles shot through his thighs where they'd fallen asleep. He packed his supplies and stomped his feet until the tingling abated, and then, after carefully rolling his drawing, he joined the throng of crusty salt farmers headed for the taverns or their homes.

As always, he stopped by Ysobello's bakery for his dinner. When he reached the head of the long line, Ysobello pointed at the drawing, and Jos held it out for him to see.

"Well, now," Ysobello said, "that's not half bad."

Jos smiled. It was a far sight better than "not half bad," but he'd learned Ysobello hadn't an eye for such things.

"You know"—Ysobello slipped into the kitchen, then returned to place a basket with a steaming meat pie on the counter—"you should be an artist," he said, winking.

Jos laughed as he rerolled the drawing. "I'll give it a try and let you know how it goes." Then he paid for his food, and Ysobello sent him off with a hearty, "Fair night!"

Outside the shop, gold-orange sunlight streamed down the road, the sun taking its last chance to show off before night fell. He walked around the block to his loft, and after caring for Thunder and Lightning, he sat on the back steps of his wagon, savored every bite of his delicious pie, and waited.

He'd finished his pie and was considering climbing up into his loft when footsteps entered the alley behind the barn. His heartbeat leapt to a trot.

"Who is it?" he asked Lightning. The ass just stared at Jos from over his stall door. Jos scratched between the ass's ears. "A lot of help, you are."

Jos seemed overdue for a message from Calyn—they hadn't spoken since his delivery of the pictures of the feather-capped man and Orli the Romantic—but he hoped for a different visitor all the same. When the shadow of feet darkened the gap under the door and their owner knocked, he wasn't disappointed.

"THIS IS THE LAST TIME," Getha said, as she dressed.

Jos didn't reply, but he couldn't help the smile that crept across his face.

Getha stared at him, trousers on but unlaced, hands on her hips. "You don't believe me."

"It's not that."

"Then why are you smiling?"

"Because you said it's the last time." He stood. "But you said that last time." He walked over to her. "And the time before that."

"Are you calling me a liar?"

"No." She let him remove her hands from her waist. Then he replaced them with his own and pulled her closer. "I'm simply saying that your recent actions contradict that statement."

"I really mean it this time," she said, her voice laden with conviction.

He leaned in and spoke with his lips brushing against hers. "I believe you." Then he gave her a gentle kiss and released her. Returning to his mattress, he flopped down onto it and watched her as she bent down to pick her tunic up off the floor. "But I'm here if you need me."

She froze for a moment, her hair hanging in her face, concealing whatever expression she wore. Then she unfroze and continued dressing with her back to him.

Had he said the wrong thing? Sod it. So what if he had? He didn't know what he and Getha had, but he did know he had no interest in seeing it end. Considering the growing frequency of her visits, it seemed she might feel the same way.

The question was on his lips, but she finished dressing and headed for the ladder, and he sensed it wasn't a good idea to push her so far quite yet. *I'll ask her next time.*

The loft shook as she climbed down the ladder, then light, almost inaudible footsteps crossed the barn floor. *If there is a next time.* The door latch rattled, and moonlight spilled inside as the door opened.

"Fair night," he called. "Get home safe."

Another pause. Then a "Fair night" floated up from near the door, and Jos, certain now there would be a next time, let his full smile loose.

A FEW DAYS LATER, Getha followed Princess Renn—or Alyse, since she wore her amulet—though the Branches. As with most of the shops, taverns, and homes in the neighborhoods through which they had passed, the door to The Lost Waif stood open in the hopes of catching an errant breeze. A futile hope. Up on the Gift, banners snapped, but with the tavern so close to the wall and so far from the West Gate, none of the sea winds reached it.

Getha and Princess Renn walked down the road in the Mire side by side, but as they neared The Lost Waif, the princess slowed, allowing Getha to overtake her and enter through the door first. The lamplit tavern seemed very dark after the dazzling glare of the sun, but Getha, using a trick Waltham had taught her, covered one eye with her hand so that both might adjust to the change in light faster, and soon the details of the room grew clear.

The usual barkeep, a stocky man with a lush, full beard the length of a child's arm, sat behind the bar, holding his beard up with one hand and fanning his neck below with the other. His club for troublesome customers hung from a nail on the wall behind him. A man stood on the other side of the bar sipping a drink, his black hair tied back in a neat tail. A sailor, judging by the tattoos up and down his arms and the open backsword on his belt, and from the way he leaned, he wore an additional blade hidden beneath his tunic at the small of his back.

The only other patrons were a trio of men playing a heated game of square bones at a table in the center of the room, all far too old and slow to worry about, and the unarmed bargroom wiping tables on the far side of the room. He glanced at Getha and seemed to decide she could wait while he finished his work. She signaled for the princess to enter, and she did, blinking in the darkness. The bargroom looked up again, and Getha rolled her eyes when, quick as quick, he dropped his rag and smiled.

"Heyla," he said, swaggering over to them. "Welcome back! Hotter than a sinner's pyre out there, isn't it? Let me fetch you a drink."

Princess Renn removed her jack from her belt and held it out in the direction of his voice. "Have any cider?"

"Always," the bargroom said, brushing her hand with his as he took the jack. She blushed a pretty pink, and he preened.

"Hain't cold," one of the old men warned without looking up from his game.

"Shut yer damned mouth, Pallie," the barkeep said. "Everyone knows the academy ran out of cold charms last tenday."

Getha gritted her teeth. The academy did have cold charms; they'd just stopped selling them in the Branches so the highborn could have them all.

"That's fine," Princess Renn said. "Mouth's still dry and cider's cider."

The bargroom's grin widened. "Sure is."

Getha removed her jack from her belt. "I'd like some too."

When the bargroom, still smiling at the princess like an idiot, didn't answer, she held her jack up in front of his face. Irritated, he reared back from it before snatching it from her hand.

"Fine," he said. "Two ciders."

"I'd watch him," the princess said as he walked away. "He might spit in yours." Then she wandered off toward what had become their usual booth.

Getha followed her and tried to keep an eye on the bargroom. Sure enough, after the barkeep pulled her cider and handed it to the bargroom, he snorted and leaned over it. But then he looked up, saw Getha watching him, and thought better of his nasty little plan.

Princess Renn slid onto the bench on one side of the booth, and Getha slid in after. It was awkward sitting on the same side with no one else there, but it put the princess in the most protected position and that mattered more.

They sat in silence, and Princess Renn fiddled with her replacement flowering charm, the one she'd procured for keeping up appearances. It still bothered Getha that the princess didn't wear a prayer locket alongside it, but in light of her good works, Getha did her best to stem her irritation. After all, the princess now spent most of her days either in the palace's libraries or out in the city. She might have done more were she less reluctant to return to convocation or face her peers, but beggars couldn't choose, and the princess had gone to the trouble of setting up a system through the very contact they'd come to meet to collect messages from the lowborn, wishes to be granted. Getha had no idea what would become of the system once the princess' grief, and her interest, waned, but until then, she was making an effort.

Princess Renn tucked her charm beneath her shirt, where it clacked against her Transformation amulet. Then she pulled a heavy something from her satchel and set it on the table in front of Getha with a *thump*. About five inches tall, the bust had been carved from some greyish-white stone. They looked familiar—the bust itself and the face carved into it—but Getha couldn't quite place either.

"Who is that?"

Princess Renn took a kerchief from her pocket and brushed the face with it. "Queen Elissianne."

Because the cost of granting the wishes of the lowborn far outstripped the princess's allowance, she had promised Getha they would only sell items no one would miss, items the princess swore had been packed away in storage for decades, like those eight silver spoons with curled handles or the collection of gilded thimbles or the engraved spit pot. But this. The face was familiar because it resembled the princess's real one, and the bust because it sat in the palace's main hall.

"Don't worry," the princess said. "*A bust of her does sit in the main hall.* It's still there."

Getha frowned. She didn't much care for the princess' uncanny knack of guessing what she was thinking. "So this is a different one?"

"Yes. One of many."

The princess wanted Getha to ask one of how many, but she refused to be strung along any further. She sat back in her chair and scanned the tavern. No one had entered or moved, aside from the bargroom, who fetched drinks for the old men and smiled at the princess every time he walked past.

This practice of taking things from the palace and selling them strolled right up to the edge of what was legal, but as Princess Renn had pointed out, the items did belong to her family and, therefore, her. She had been putting the profits to use in big ways—buying and distributing healing charms to the lowborn, funding a new roof for a temple in the Mire—and in small, like the day they'd rented a room and bought a bed for a crippled quilter in the Blossom. The princess had also helped Getha wrestle the bedframe up two narrow flights of stairs.

"Sixty," Princess Renn blurted out. "There are sixty busts, all identical. And I don't know if you've noticed, but there are also almost twice as many portraits of her than there are of any other queen."

When Waltham became Getha's patron, he'd taught her much—reading, sums, history—but the lesson that came to mind was a few lines from a child's rhyme about the Ombratian queens she'd learned back in the surplus home. *O'erseeing her mother's stores, Elissianne the Plenty. The city was rich and bountiful, and she bore the love of many.*

"Elissianne the Plenty, indeed."

Princess Renn laughed. "Oh, you don't know the half of it. The story is that she had a bust made for every lover she took." She traced one of the bust's stone curls. "I wonder what her prince-consort thought of all that."

The princess furrowed her brow, perhaps thinking about her father or her Prince Dallan. *Since when do I care?* Getha shook her head. *You're her guard, not her friend.* Whether or not the princess worried for her father or still pined for the Tithen prince was none of her concern.

Sixty lovers, though. An impressive number. One Getha would never reach if she kept returning to that daft artist in his damned, stinking barn. That fool and his bloodmark, who wanted to leave Ombratos for the road. That man, with his broad shoulders and strong hands, with that mouth...

She sparked her bloodmark, bringing herself back to the present. Thoughts of Jos plagued her, and she kept returning to him with the intent of silencing them once and for all, but with every visit, the thoughts multiplied, distracting her during the day and keeping her up at night. The comely sailor at the bar caught her eye and smiled. Perhaps the answer lay in tumbling someone else. She didn't smile back, but she held his gaze and considered him not as a potential threat but as a prospect. He, too, had broad shoulders, and she tried to stir up a bit of lust by eyeing his muscular legs and the tight, round curve of his ass, but none came.

The bargroom brought their drinks, and Princess Renn fluttered her eyelashes at him, made little japes, and tittered when he touched her hand. The barkeep called him away, and Getha found herself wanting to confide in the princess, to ask her questions about what she should do about Jos.

She shifted in her seat. Perhaps the strange impulse came from her avoidances of Waltham. This very morning, he'd tracked her down at the practice yards and asked her if she wanted to have her midday meal in his office. She hated thinking about how his face had fallen when she'd begged off, but she'd sworn long ago she'd never lie to him, and truth was, she didn't know if he'd entirely approve of what she was doing. So keeping her promise meant not talking to him at all, even if she did miss his companionship and his shrewd counsel. Such was the price of making her own way.

So her desire to speak with the princess stemmed from her lack of further companionship. That worked for her, and she preferred that answer to the simple, if maddening, desire to say Jos's name aloud.

Just then, a pair of familiar silhouettes walked through the open door, and Getha didn't move, but she forgot everything else as she fell into her mental guard stance.

Beside her, Princess Renn stiffened. "They're here." She tossed her kerchief over the bust.

"I see them."

A man and a woman stood inside the doorway for a moment, likely letting their eyes adjust to the darkness of the tavern. The tall, skinny man was the buyer, Guissand Serrimandier. He wore a thin, white cotton tunic without sleeves and perched his hands on his narrow hips. Armed with nothing more than the eating knife on his belt and maybe a boot dagger or two, he was of no worry to Getha. But his partner...

Serrimandier's partner was a rare creature, a woman of about thirty-five with the tattoos of a Tithen and the bloodmark of an Ombratian. A bit thick around the middle, she still moved with the sureness of a fighter and wore two shortswords. Getha itched to try her skills against the ex-mercenary's, but she wasn't about to provoke the woman while guarding the princess.

"Alyse!" Serrimandier waved and started toward the booth. "There you are." His guard trailed along after him, examining the room much as Getha had before.

Princess Renn edged Getha from the booth in order to stand to greet the buyer, and while the princess and Serrimandier embraced and kissed one another's cheeks, Getha and the Tithen exchanged nods.

Guissand Serrimandier rubbed his palms together. "What fine oddment have you liberated for us this day?"

His educated words and their clipped edges gave his highborn heritage away, not that he made much of an effort to hide it. Everyone, even Alyse, Renn's lowborn persona, would have heard the gossip about the former Messero Guissand Serrimandier. It just so happened that the princess knew more about the buyer of rare antiquities than most.

Though closest in age to Renn's oldest brother, Dace, Serrimandier was considered one of Solena's birth cluster since no one marked clusters by the princes. Regardless, he'd grown up in the Bole, and until Dace left for Rhyllex, the two had been quite good friends. With Guissand being so much older that Renn, they hadn't interacted much, but on the few occasions they had, unlike many of her peers, Guissand had shown her the appropriate respect and deference due a girl of her station. He had been set to take his mother's seat in the convocation, but less than a year before Solena left for the Yent Isles, he had somehow crossed paths with an slightly older Tithen woman for whom he was willing to give up his family, his inheritance, and his one bloodmark—the woman who now sat beside him.

Renn wanted to tell Guissand how much she admired his bravery, but he thought Alyse a maid who worked up at Seedfall, and she didn't think a maid would dare say such things to a messero, even one who had fallen so far.

The pretty-eyed bargroom came to their table to ask if he and his Tithen wanted drinks. Though they refused, the bargroom attempted to reengage Renn in their flirtation, but she sent him on his way and focused on Guissand.

"How are things at the palace?" he asked. "Has there been word about the Yentish prince? Does he yet live?"

"That's what they say," Renn said. As it happened, the queen had received word of the prince's continued survival at a family dinner not four days prior. Linore had shattered her wine goblet against the wall and run from the room in tears. "They also claim the heir is not very happy about it."

"No, I can't imagine she is."

Frowning, he glanced at his Tithen lover. The Tithen didn't look back, but her arm shifted, as if she touched his leg beneath the table, and his face and shoulders relaxed. The display of intimacy drove a spike of loneliness into Renn's heart. She missed Dallan so much it hurt. What if they never found a way to be together? What if his mother and aunt convinced him she wasn't worth the trouble and he stayed in Tithen? What if—

She curled her toes up tight in her boots, then relaxed them. At this moment, she needed to get the most she could for the item sitting on the table before her. Her other troubles would wait.

She put her hand on the top of the bust. "Let's get to it, then."

Guissand rested his elbows on the table. "By all means."

Watching his face, Renn whipped the kerchief off with a flourish. She risked the small chance that he knew about the sixty other busts—she had almost sought out another buyer for just that reason—but doubting anyone else's ability to recognize the piece's importance, she'd decided to roll the dice.

Though too practiced a buyer to give anything away in his expression, his breath hitched the tiniest bit, proving her gamble had been a wise one.

"If I'm not mistaken," he said, "that's Queen Elissianne."

"Is it?" she asked with deliberately false innocence. "I thought it mayhaps be one of the queens, but I weren't sure which one."

"This sits in the main hall." He looked at her. "How did you sneak it from there without getting caught?"

She had dreamed up a story for Alyse's life, imagining her as clever thief who took much pride in her skill. Sitting back in her seat, she laced her fingers on the table; her bloodmark sparked and tingled as she brought her palms together. "Very carefully."

He chuckled. "I see. Well, what would you like for it?"

They chaffered over the price for close to half a candlemark, but he had exposed his weakness the moment she had revealed the bust, and she, having learned much in her earlier negotiations with the buyer, started high, eased off only in the slightest, and then refused to relent further.

When they reached their agreement, Guissand gripped Renn's hand harder than necessary to shake it.

Renn sympathized; Alyse rejoiced.

He counted the agreed upon amount of coin out on the table, snatched up the bust, and with a curt farewell, he and his Tithen slid from the booth and left the tavern.

"Serrimandier didn't want to pay anywhere near that," Getha said. "Well done."

Renn bit down on the insides of her cheeks to hide her smile. Receiving a compliment from the laconic guard felt like unearthing the rarest of gems. On top of that, she had enough coin for her current purposes, with enough left over to buy a few cold charms for The Lost Waif. Getha slid out of the booth, took one last gulp of her cider, then emptied the rest into the sludge bucket on a nearby table.

Renn quaffed the rest of her cider and slammed down the jack, crying, "Onward!"

Everyone in the tavern turned, including the pretty-eyed bargroom. She winked at him, a saucy, lowborn gesture she'd never tried before, and the old men playing square bones cheered. She expected a censorious glare from Getha for how she'd called attention to herself, but Getha waved for Renn to lead the way and bowed her head, and as Renn passed the guard, she thought she glimpsed the corner of a smile.

WHILE THEY WALKED through the city, moving out of the Mire and into the tiny Acorn neighborhood where most of the Fallen talc miners lived, Getha's thoughts kept returning to The Lost Waif.

One moment the princess flirted with the bargroom like a daft chit and the next she bargained with Serrimandier like her life depended on it. Getha had seen mothers from the Tangles with a bare two coins in their pockets chaffer with less ferocity. And then that wink. Getha liked having people sorted out in her head, yet the princess refused to be sorted.

A block into the Acorn, they passed a sweating, downcast man standing beside a meat cart. The heat had slowed his trade to nothing. "Roast scrimple," he called without much interest. "Cooked fresh this morn."

"Those look vile," the princess whispered, nodding at the man's stock. "What are they? What's scrimple?"

The roasted creatures had large front teeth and long, pink tails curled around the spits on which they were impaled. *Isn't it obvious?* "Rats."

Horror settled on Princess Renn's face. "And people eat them?"

"Sure." Getha detested rat—it stank like piss and tasted foully gamey—but the princess's disgust irritated her. Who was this girl masquerading as a lowborn to look down on their fare? "They're delicious."

"Are they?" Princess Renn seemed to consider that for a moment, and then, further confounding Getha, she went over to the man and bought two. She carried them back, handed one to Getha, and said, "Here goes."

The princess took her eating knife from her belt and sliced through the tough, roasted flesh as if it were the softest of cheeses. There had been a brief discussion about the princess learning combat, but she'd refused outright, and so Getha had told her she had to at least keep her eating knife sharp. If the princess was ever in a situation where she had to defend herself with her eating knife, then things would be very dire indeed, but a well-honed eating knife was better than nothing at all, and it pleased Getha to know the princess had followed her instruction in this.

Pinching the bite of scrimple between her thumb and the blade, Princess Renn took a deep breath, followed by another. Getha waited for her to refuse or to take the tiniest of nibbles, but after one last deep breath, the princess slipped the entire piece into her mouth.

Getha was half startled by the princess's trust in her and half baffled at her fearlessness, but as she chewed and chewed, the bafflement won out. How could a person live like she did, constantly hurling herself headlong into the unknown?

At long last, Princess Renn turned her back to the seller and swallowed with some effort. "I do not wish to insult you or that kind man, but scrimple is revolting." Then there, in the middle of the street, one of the crown princesses of Ombratos pulled out her kerchief and began scrubbing her tongue with it.

The sight tickled Getha in a way nothing else had in a very long time, and though she tried holding back her laughter, a snort escaped.

The princess stopped scrubbing and narrowed her eyes. "You aren't going to eat yours, are you?"

Another snort slipped out. "Not for all the gilding in Seedfall."

Princess Renn's scandalized expression threatened to undo Getha altogether. "It's not humorous," the princess said, though she spoke through a grin. "It's not." She sniggered, then gagged. "Ugh. I think there's a bit stuck in my teeth."

That shattered the last of Getha's composure, and she let loose a howl. The princess lost it too, and together, they floated off on a gale of merriment, soon doubling over and leaning against one another for support as they struggled for breath.

When the strongest gusts passed, Princess Renn, holding her side, said, "You're an ass. As soon as we get back, I'm finding someone else to come out with me."

Insult after insult, yet, the way the princess said them somehow belied their meaning, and Getha found it impossible to take offense. Was that how the other guards were able to jape with one another?

Out of nowhere, a skinny boy with shoulder bones jutting up through his talc-dusted tunic ran up to the princess and tugged at her wrist. Not seeing his approach sobered Getha, and she stood up straight to closer assess their surroundings: scrimple seller with his cart, a knot of young streetlings standing in a nearby alley, and farther down the block, four women sitting along a wall in the shade. No trouble to speak of, but she should have been more certain of that before getting so carried away.

Meanwhile, the princess gazed down at the boy, a smile lingering on her face. "Yes?"

He pointed at her scrimple. "You plannin' to eat the rest of that?"

She seemed surprised to discover she still held it. "I don't believe I am."

"Can I?" While he waited for her answer, he devoured the meat with his eyes.

They didn't let boys as young as him work the mines or the docks, so he had a caretaker, a mother or father or sister or brother, someone who brought home the talc dust on the boy's clothes. Yet neither job paid much to begin with, and Getha had heard rumors of the miners being sent away five days out of ten for lack of work.

Princess Renn crouched in front of the boy and held up the scrimple. "You don't really want this, do you?"

Tears brightened the boy's dark eyes, and Getha wanted to snap at the princess, but then she took a moment to try and see the situation from her perspective. Clearly Princess Renn hadn't gathered much from the boy's bearing and clothing, and since she'd never gone hungry a day in her life, she didn't realize how much the food meant to him.

"Some do like it," Getha said. "Especially when they're hungry enough."

"No, I..." Princess Renn pressed her lips together, then she smiled up at Getha and said, "Thank you." Turning back to the boy, she handed her scrimple to him, and he dug right in, smearing his face with grease.

A girl, also dusted in a fine coating of talc and even skinnier than the boy, darted out of alley. "Me too," she said. She ran up to Getha. "Me too?"

Getha handed her untouched scrimple to the girl, who took it and hurried back to the mouth of her alley, where the other children huddled. The princess rose to walk over there, and the less forward children watched her approach.

"Would you all like some?" she asked. Although slow to understand at times, Getha couldn't fault the princess for her generosity, a reflex that seemed to come as natural to her as breathing.

In response to her question, the children's heads bobbed, giving them the look of a nest filled with hungry baby birds.

"'Ere, now," the scrimple seller said. "You want that many, we'll find us a deal."

"As you say." Princess Renn counted the children, then turned and counted the number of servings on the merchant's spit. "How much for your whole stock?"

The scrimple seller offered the princess a fair deal, but she gave him more than he asked for and refused the change. As he set off with his empty cart, the princess crouched again, held the sticks out to the children like a bouquet, and asked them to form a queue. One by one, the children came forward and she handed them each their own. A few thanked her with words, a couple with shy smiles, and one or two not at all, but every child returned to the alley with a bit of food in hand, and when the princess rose, brushing her hands on her breeches, she did so with a look of well-earned satisfaction.

But it dropped away when she turned away from the feasting children. "Need to do something," she muttered as she resumed walking.

"What's that?"

"Hm?" Princess Renn appeared surprised Getha had heard her. "Oh. It's just that families making their effort for Ombratos shouldn't have children that hungry. It's not right."

Damn me to the pathless hells. The princess from a couple of moons earlier wouldn't have noticed all that. She was learning much, and far faster than Getha had appreciated.

They passed from the narrow streets of the Acorn and onto the wider, tree-lined thoroughfares of the Verdure. "So," Getha said, making her own effort, "what's the coin for?"

Princess Renn took a happy little hop-step. "The last letter you collected was from a family of Fallen living out in Shade's Rest. They moved there because they had a third child, a daughter. But then, several years ago, their first born ran away, and even though they think him dead, my mother refused to approve another bloodmark. So we're going to see a woman about getting one for the girl." She smiled then, looking quite pleased with herself.

Getha stopped, her blood simmering. She couldn't mean...

The princess walked a few steps before realizing Getha was no longer beside her. She turned back. "What is it?"

"When you say we're 'going to see a woman about getting one for the girl,' what do you mean by that?"

Princess Renn furrowed her brow and came back toward Getha. "Do you truly not know?"

Getha was almost certain she understood, but she needed to hear the princess say the word aloud. "Tell me what you mean."

"I mean," the princess said, whispering, "we're going to purchase her a blackmark."

Getha's blood rose to a boil. "A blackmark?" That came out louder than she meant it to, and a group of well-dressed merchant men crossing on the opposite side of the street slowed and gawped at her.

"Let's talk of this somewhere less public, shall we?" Princess Renn took Getha's arm and hastened her along toward the North Gate, toward Shade's Rest.

Angry thoughts roiled through Getha's head as she allowed herself to be pulled a couple of blocks, out of sight of the men, onto an empty road with rows of fine homes lining both sides of the street, and when she couldn't stand it another moment, she planted her feet, jerking the princess to a halt.

Princess Renn stumbled. "Amma's sake, Getha. What—"

"You said we wouldn't do anything illegal."

The princess found her footing. "I know. Believe me, I searched for a patron, but—"

"You said," Getha repeated, "we wouldn't do anything illegal."

"Right. I'm sorry," Princess Renn said, not actually seeming very contrite. "But this is a special circumstance, and I didn't think you'd mind—"

"What?" Getha's temper frothed at the edge of boiling over. "You thought I wouldn't mind committing treason?"

The princess paled. "It's not—"

"Oh, it is," Getha said. "It very much is."

"No, I know it is," Princess Renn snapped. Her color returned, creating bright red splotches on her cheeks. "But I thought you'd understand given"—she looked down at her feet—"your situation." Now she appeared contrite, and even a bit embarrassed, but not for herself. For Getha.

Getha's fingers tingled and her bloodmark throbbed from how tightly she clenched her hands. "You mean because I'm forsaken."

The princess winced.

"I told you that I worked very hard for what I have, so what makes you think I'd enjoy the notion of handing this girl something she didn't even earn?"

Princess Renn's head came up. "Who's to say she hasn't earned it?"

"If she'd earned one, she'd have one, wouldn't she?"

The princess scoffed and waved a dismissive hand, the highborn affectation belying her lowborn guise. "It's more complicated than that."

"Oh, yes?" Getha folded her arms over her chest. "Then explain it to me."

"It's wrong that family can't live within the Gift."

"Mayhaps it is, but that don't make"—Getha caught herself from sliding into her streetling cant—"that doesn't make it complicated."

Princess Renn thrust her shoulders back, her chin out, and in her haughtiest tone, said, "I should have known you would act like this."

The whole afternoon took on a darker cast, and Getha suddenly understood everything. The princess was heedless because she knew someone would always be there to catch her, and she was generous to a fault because she could afford to be. She was also the sort who used the greatest alchemical discovery in hundreds of years for her own gain and who lashed out when pressed to the fences. Born into a different life, or torn from the one in which she already lived, who knew what sort of person might stand in her place?

Staring at the spoiled, sheltered princess, a disappointment almost as bitter as that which she'd tasted when she'd been refused varo coated her tongue. "Complicated or not, I'm not doing it. *We're* not doing it."

"I beg your pardon," she said. "Since when—"

"Since we began. Don't you remember? When I agreed to help you, you said I could put a stop to any venture if I thought it too dangerous." The princess's mouth fell open in disbelief, and Getha continued. "I'm declaring this too dangerous."

Princess Renn stalked away a few steps, and for a moment, Getha thought her charge might attempt to run off without her, but Getha held her ground, as much to see if the princess would let her as anything else.

"Fine," the princess said, through gritted teeth. She stamped her foot. "Fine. Let's go back."

With that, she stomped off again but toward the palace. A rather ungracious concession, yet a concession nonetheless. Getha strode along after the sulking princess, letting her keep her distance. Like the princess' trusting Getha about the rat, this abandonment of her plan demanded consideration, but Getha had tired of trying to piece together the princess's thoughts and motivations, and instead of ruminating further, watched ahead for trouble and counted her steps. Counting was mindless enough so as not to distract her but consuming enough to banish other, unwanted notions from her mind.

Getha and Princess Renn passed through Binding Gate in the Hedgerow, then flashed their chits allowing them easy entry through the palace gates, and after Getha saw the princess back to her brother's work-room on Menders' Row, she turned around and headed right back out into the city.

Out in Shade's Rest, Getha knocked and knocked at the barn door until she heard the latch, then she stood back and prepared to launch herself at Jos the instant he appeared.

The door swung open, and some man, not Jos, poked his head out. "Heyla," the strange man said, a friendly grin splitting his round face. "I own and live over the bakery, and I heard the knocking back here. This barn is mine, too, but I'm letting it out to someone."

"Where's Jos?" Getha said, cutting him off. He looked like the sort who might ramble on if one let him.

The man's smile dimmed. "Not sure. 'Fraid I don't know when he'll be back, either."

"Oh." There it was again—disappointment. When had she started expecting things of people? Why had she?

Without another word, she turned and ran off down the alley in the direction she'd come. When she reached the street, she picked up her pace, and soon she whipped past people and buildings as she tried to outrace her very thoughts. Why had she left the palace and rushed right to Jos's door? If she'd done so to work out her frustrations, she'd passed dozens of taverns filled with men who might serve that purpose. Yet she'd passed them all and headed straight for Jos's because she'd wanted something more than a tumble. She'd wanted—

It doesn't matter. It didn't. She wasn't going back, ever, and that was that.

She kept running. She hadn't sparred with Tumolo in a while, and even if he was on guard, there was always someone at the barracks ready for a fight.

TWENTY-THREE

"A seam can be the strongest part of a garment or the weakest depending on the skill or determination with which it's sewn."
-Master Clothier Elta Derthandera to her apprentice, Lehr Tommel

Are you sure there isn't anything else I can help with, High Alchemist?"

At the top of the tower steps, Kitra Rande touched the handle to her private bedchamber but waited to open the door. "I'm sure."

Alchemist Myka peered up at her from a few steps below. "Have you considered the temperature variant?"

Kitra stifled a sigh. "As I told you last tenday, yes. Now, if you'll excuse me..."

Myka nodded, yet didn't make any move to leave, and Kitra fought the urge to shove the young woman down the steps and out of sight. Alchemist Ithan had been quite happy to pass the task of dealing with Princess Solena's sabotaged working over to the high alchemist. Myka, on the other hand, was struggling with letting go. Whenever Kitra left her chambers, Myka hounded her, taking every chance to corner her and press her about her the investigation.

However, she had kept her oath not to speak of her findings, and Kitra, appreciating that, tried to be gentle with her, but she really did need to return to the young man locked inside her workroom.

"You're dismissed, Alchemist Myka," Kitra said, and when Myka opened her mouth to speak again, Kitra pointed down the steps. "I will tell you when I have news. Please go."

Myka smoothed her already smooth hair back, turned, lifted her robes, and at last, in a manner befitting her highborn upbringing, proceeded down the spiral staircase and out of sight. Kitra would have to give her some more information, and soon, but first...

When the door at the bottom of the tower steps closed, Kitra unlocked the door to her bedchamber, slipped in, and reset the lock from the inside. Despite some of the rumors, she hadn't seen the inside of the chamber—a large, square room with windows looking out onto the surrounding city— until she'd acquired it along with her position, and though she often lingered to marvel at the amazing views, today she crossed the room to the door on the opposite wall without so much as glancing out the windows or at the rest of the rich furnishings.

She pressed her ear to the door of her workroom, and hearing nothing, she undid the second lock and slowly opened the door. *Thank Amma.* There were papers scattered everywhere and the remnants of shattered bottles glittered on the floor, but her newest apprentice, Prince Parneo disguised as Hale Enfoi, sat bent over some pages at the table under one of the room's two windows, calm and quiet. Not wanting to set him off again, she stood in the doorway and waited for him to finish whatever he worked on.

Among the other alchemists of the academy, Kitra referred to Hale as her apprentice, but nothing could have been further from the truth. The young man seated before her had forgotten more about alchemy that she would ever know, and she'd come to anticipate his visits with a mixture of excitement and dread, both stemming from the same place.

Their relationship had begun with him explaining to her his rediscovery of Kastuan's fire, the knowledge that had led to his creation of globes. The working turned out to be rather simple and elegant, but reaching it had required bending his mind around corners not even Marcal had realized were there.

In truth, listening to the explanation had made Kitra feel like the daftest of fools, so she was secretly grateful he'd yet to delve into his work on the Transformation amulet. She had no doubt it would fly over her head, and she still had the sabotaged working that had killed her predecessor, Ithan's wife, and the heir to the throne, to deal with.

After establishing that one of the prince's reasons for coming to the academy was to get to the bottom of the working that had led to his eldest sister's death, Prince Parneo had taken the evidence left over from Ithan and Myka's study and started his own calculations, independent corroboration being the most reliable way to confirm the previous findings.

This morning he'd seemed on the verge of telling Kitra something important when his madness had claimed him, and she'd locked him in her study to rave the gibberish from his system. If Marcal had been the moon, then Prince Parneo was the sun, but, as she'd warned her former mentor, the prince's brilliance came at a cost. He often spoke to beings that weren't there, and this wasn't the first time she'd locked him in her workroom until he'd collected himself. But with him calm again, she hoped he might have some answers for her.

The prince laid down his pen, gathered a stack of pages from the desk, and tapped them against the table to straighten them. Then he turned to face her. "I've been over every aspect of the working's failure and the subjects' deaths"—he always referred to Princess Solena, Marcal, and Claudine as *the subjects*—"were, without a doubt, caused by the unusually high salt content in the sand."

That confirmed one part of Ithan and Myka's findings. "Go on."

"I'm also certain that the salt content doesn't match that of the samples from the Yent Isles."

Another confirmation. But Kitra had been thinking about the salt not being from the Isles and had decided it didn't entirely discount the possibility of Yentish sabotage. "But couldn't someone have added the salt before the subject was—"

"No," the prince said, shaking his head.

He hadn't even heard her out. "Why not?"

"Because the stone composite is wrong too."

Ithan and Myka had never made any mention of the stone, and Kitra's limbs grew heavy with dread. "Wrong in what way?"

The prince glanced down at the page in his hand. "Neither the sand nor the salt came from the Yent Isles."

"Then where?" *Not here. Not here. Not—*

"Tithen."

Kitra stumbled backward until her calves hit the edge of her bed and she dropped down onto it. Tithen? If the prince was right, and she had no doubt he was, then his information not only confirmed the sabotage, it also pointed a finger at Lady Helenia or Prince Dallan.

And a finger pointed in their direction meant war.

She covered her mouth, afraid she might be sick. She'd stepped out of the rain to find herself trapped in a burning building. But she had to contain the depths of her horror. The prince realizing the implications of his findings could very well have been the cause for his earlier fit, and she didn't want to set him off again.

Tucking her emotions away, as she'd been taught, she forced herself to stand, and the moment she regained control, Marcal's voice came to her. *Check your work again, Rande. Don't bring it back until you're certain.* She had to figure out where in Tithen the sample came from, account for any and all possibilities of how it might have ended up in the preparation chamber, and put in place a half dozen other damning details before she took her findings to the throne. She refused to implicate or condemn anyone, or to send her queen to war without specific, irrefutable proof.

She bowed to the prince. "Thank you, Your Highness, for discovering the error." Her voice, Amma bless, came out even. "I will deal with the study from here."

Unless in the midst of a fit, Prince Parneo revealed little in his movements or expressions, but now his shoulders slumped in what appeared to be relief. He, too, stood and came forward to hand her his page. Looking down at his hands, she noticed how smooth they were, how in his Transformed guise he hadn't the ugly, gnarled palms of an alchemist but the silky skin of a highborn or a ductoro. Where had he found his Transformed face and how had he constructed the form's—

"When will you tell my mother?" The prince let the pages go and lowered his hand, hiding it from sight and taking Kitra's curiosity on it along with it.

"Soon," she said, shaking her head and a strange bit of haziness from her mind. *As soon as I am certain.*

AFTER TAKING off her amulet and changing back into her riding leathers, Renn paced back and forth in Parn's work rooms for a while. With her triumph over Guissand Serrimandier and the silliness with the scrimple and feeding the children, it had been such a fine afternoon. Then the argument had come along and ruined things, and the more she thought about her part in it, the more upset she became.

She still believed it was right to try and help that poor girl and her family, regardless of what the law and the queen said. She appreciated Getha's caution, but did she have to be *so* cautious? Then again, Getha had been very clear about what she would and wouldn't do, and that made Renn responsible for her own mistaken assumption.

She also had to claim responsibility for stomping around after she hadn't gotten her way. She'd known it was childish even in the moment, yet she hadn't been able to stop herself. A poor loser. Solena had called Renn that when she was eleven and she'd overturned the terrini board after Solena won six bouts in a row, and it was as true now as it had been then.

When the shutter in the back room opened, Renn worried it might be Getha, because even though she needed to apologize, she hadn't quite worked her way around to it yet. But it wasn't Getha. Instead, a gangly young man balanced on the sill, his upper half inside, his lower half dangling in the alley. Renn hurried over to help her brother inside, then stepped back so he could remove his Transformation amulet and adjust to his own body again.

"How was it today?" she asked once he'd returned to his old self. She wanted to ask if he'd made any progress in his research, but she hated adding to the pressure already on him.

Parneo met her eyes for only an instant before looking away and answered the question she hadn't asked. "A mistake in the calculations, pure and simple."

Renn's breath left her in rush. *A mistake?*

"That stupid alchemist in the Yent Isles with Solena carried a four where she should have carried a six." Then he frowned, perhaps at the carelessness of such a mistake.

"So the alchemists here were working from a flawed formula?" Renn asked just to be certain she understood.

He nodded. "At both ends."

Renn covered her face with her hands. It galled her to think Solena's death the result of such a foolish error. On the other hand, those who had made the error had paid for their mistake with their own lives. That left her with no one to blame. She sorted through her emotions and relief came to the fore. Neither Solena nor Theodora bore any fault, and there was no need for accusations or a trial. No one would be found guilty and strung up on the Table, their body left to rot. No one's life needed to be upset more than it already had been. It was over.

Renn lifted her head from her hands to find Parn staring out the window with an odd expression on his face.

"What?" she asked. He didn't answer. "What is it, Parn?"

At the sound of his name, he blinked and faced her. "I wish I could have done..."

"Done what?"

His helpless expression tugged at her heart. "Done what?" She searched his face for an answer. "Done more?" She reached for him, but he stepped back, avoiding both her eyes and her embrace. "They didn't let you help with the working, remember? And look at everything you've done since. You solved this puzzle, right? Please don't upset yourself by thinking you might have done more. You did what you could."

"That's right." He stared down at his open hands, the palms rough and scarred from his work. "I did what I could."

TWENTY-FOUR

"Lies beget more lies, but every Truth stands alone."
-Nikola Serrimandier to her closest friend, Orane Morovide

Jos lay on his mattress in nothing but his trousers, not quite napping but resting. They'd reached the height of summer, and most Ombratians and Shade's Resters agreed it was the hottest one they'd had in many years. Each day seemed hotter than the last, and Jos had started passing his middays in Ysobello's loft, drawing, dozing, or just letting his thoughts drift where they would. On occasion they wandered to Calyn and Lathan, but more often they found their way to his family or to—

Someone pounded on the barn door, startling the sparrows from the rafters.

Getha! Jos climbed to his feet, slipped on his boots, decided to leave off his tunic, and headed for the loft ladder. Though an odd time for her to come, he hadn't seen her in over half a tenday and he would welcome a visit from her any candlemark of the day. At the bottom of the ladder, he ran a hand through his hair and scratched the night's growth of whiskers on his cheeks and neck, glad he hadn't yet shaved. She'd never said as much, but she seemed to like him with stubble.

The barn door rattled as Getha, sounding as impatient as always, pounded on the door again.

"Coming," he said, hurrying to let her in. Undoing the latch, he took a deep breath, put on his most charming smile, and swung open the door. "To what do I owe..."

A strange woman stood outside, arm raised for another knock, and his spirits fell at the sight of her. She was at least ten or fifteen years older than him, stocky, of middling height. "You Jos?"

"Who are you?" he asked. Her features plucked at a string in his mind, but he couldn't yet catch the tune.

"Believe I asked first." The woman's shoulders and arms bulged with muscle, her tunic and breeches were crusted with white, and she smelled of the sea. A salt farmer, then, and in one hand, she held a rolled-up piece of paper, the sort of paper he preferred to use for his drawings. He returned to her face—same dark brown eyes, same thin lips, though the wrinkles bracketing them weren't quite as deep.

"Are you Calyn's daughter?" he asked.

She nodded. "You Jos, then?" She unrolled the paper and held it out toward him, showing him his drawing of the man with the feather in his hat. "You the one who made this?"

Why hadn't Calyn taken his picture to the guard? "I am. Where's your mother?"

"Ill."

Guilt struck him for thinking poorly of the older woman. "Not too ill, I hope."

"Too soon to tell," the daughter said. She glanced up and down the alley before thrusting the picture at him again. "You do this?"

If the physical resemblance hadn't clued him in to this woman's identity, her disposition would have. Yet Calyn's daughter struck him as being rougher than her mother, a series of overlapping broken lines, heavy but hesitant. "Yes," he said, "I drew that."

"Good." She rolled the drawing back up and tucked it under her arm, flattening and thereby creasing it. It rankled to see his art treated in such a manner, but he reminded himself he'd yielded ownership of it the moment he'd given it away.

"Then I need you to draw someone else," she said.

"Who?"

"Talp." She paused, as if waiting for a reaction, but the name meant nothing to him. Given the way she acted, though, this Talp was important. Or dangerous. Or both. If Calyn had asked him, it would have been one thing, but her daughter had said "I need," and he hadn't agreed to risk himself for her benefit.

"I don't think so," Jos said. "I work for Calyn and—"

"Don't be daft." She reached out and grabbed his arm, her fingers digging into his skin. "This is *for* Calyn."

He yanked his arm away, liking Calyn's daughter less and less. "Then why didn't you say so?"

She stepped back and looked off in the direction of the tenement she and her mother shared. "I said wrong, that's all." She faced him again. "Are you going to help her or not?" He was an instant from refusing when she added, "You're the only one who can."

Her words reminded him of his responsibility, of the vow he'd made to Amma and implicit promise he'd made to Lathan by coming to Shade's Rest. "Fine." He rubbed a hand over his face. "I'll help."

"Good." She let out a sigh. "Right."

"Where can I find this Talp?"

"He's got a tavern down in the Tangles, and on certain days, like this one, he holds court. At his court, he sits there for a candlemark or so and them folk daft enough to work for him or borrow from him, they come and give what's owed. Now, to go there..."

JOS STOOD at the mouth of the alley that led to Talp's Court. Though less than a candlemark past midday, shadows darkened the dirty street around him, as if the sun hurried through the Tangles on its way elsewhere. It was the height of the buildings, their closeness to one another, the narrowness of the streets that made walking through the neighborhood like traversing a canyon. The impression that no one wished to linger in the Tangles, not even those who lived there, not even the sun, was difficult to shake.

Especially when faced with the prospect of entering Talp's Court.

On Jos's way through the city, he'd checked with a few different people to ensure he headed in the right direction, and one by one, each person's friendliness had dried up the instant he'd mentioned the name of the tavern. Then they'd rushed him off quick as quick. With every such incident, his nervousness had grown into the worm that now twisted and writhed in his gut.

The alleyway stretched out before him, a gentle slope downward into an even deeper darkness, and he wished Getha were with him. In all the time they'd spent together, she'd never spoken of what she did, but she'd also never done anything to disabuse him of the notion she served as a guard.

Everything about her, from her brisk manner to the way she moved, each motion imbued with economy and grace, shouted fighter. But because they'd never discussed what she did, he didn't know where she worked or for whom. Given her bloodmark, he assumed she guarded someone inside the Gift, but that still left a whole host of possibilities. She might work for the city guard or as a private guard for a merchant or even one of the highborn, and since he didn't know where she worked or where she lived, that left him alone.

Alone and faced with the prospect of entering Talp's Court.

That's it. Go in or leave. Even as he thought that, his body decided for him, and his feet carried him forward, down into the darkness.

JOS SELDOM VISITED alehouses in the middle of the day, but the number of people in Talp's Court seemed large. As in any busy tavern, bodies crowded the tables and lined the bar, but the atmosphere seemed odd. Quiet. Expectant.

Most sat facing one end of the room, toward a space that looked like it often functioned as a dancing area but which now held a short platform with a chair at its center. It gave the impression of a crude throne, and given that Jos was in Talp's Court, he guessed everyone waited for the man himself to take it.

A strong-armed barmaid carried eight leather jacks brimming over with liquid—four in each hand—away from the bar, leaving a spot right at the corner. Another man saw it when Jos did, but Jos and his longer legs made it there first. The other fellow, a square peg of a person with thick, angular features, bristled at that and looked ready for a clash. Though Jos had little knowledge of how to or any desire to fight, he knew he could appear imposing enough if he wanted to, so he hunched over the bar and flexed his neck and upper arm muscles. The square peg made a disgusted sound as he slunk off.

The mirror behind the bar, though poor in quality, was the longest and largest Jos had ever seen, and it made the large room appear twice as big. It also afforded him a wide view of all the hard, mistrustful souls gathered at the tables. Drawing the whole of the shadowy tavern and those in it would take every piece of charcoal he had and then some. But he sought a single subject—Talp. A shape wavered across the warped mirror, and a bargroom appeared before Jos on the other side of the bar. He ordered a cider and, when it came, sipped from it and hoped Talp might come before he had occasion to order another.

About half a candlemark passed before a rustling at the far end of the room heralded some sort of activity. Almost as one, those at the tables stood, followed by those at the bar. Jos, a moment or two behind, climbed to his feet and craned his neck to see what had prompted the movement.

A group of about ten men and women crossed the far side of the room, headed toward the throne. Every last one of them had the hard look of thieves and cutthroats, but a man near the center of the small parade caught Jos's eye. The man had his deep brown hair tied back in a tail, leaving his ill-composed yet compelling face exposed, and though he was on the shorter end of average for an Ombratian, he seemed to tower above those around him. He stared out at the assembled crowd as he walked, and they stared back, almost every head turning to trace his progress. He called out like a pretty flame or a closed box one had been warned never to open.

Jos couldn't wait to find out how Talp might present on the page. His was the sort of face that made Jos nervous about the truths lying beneath, but he'd expected that from the moment he'd accepted the assignment.

The group reached the platform, and as most of the brigands spread out to surround it, Talp stepped onto the riser, boot heels thudding against the wood. Another man followed him up, and Jos only just noticed him.

If Talp drew the eye, then the other man drove it away, his countenance of such utter plainness that it almost begged for disregard. A secretary or a scribe, then. Someone to take notes as Talp conducted his business. But then Talp walked past the throne while the other man, the plain one, stopped before it, and it wasn't until he sat that Jos realized his mistake. The man who drew one's attention like a lodestone wasn't Talp; he was Talp's distraction. A human mask.

Jos's wariness grew.

The plain man gestured for everyone to sit, and Jos resettled himself at his stool. Without any signal Jos could discern, a man rose from his seat at a table near the platform and walked over to stand before it. Most of the audience remained seated, yet others stood, their heads and shoulders rising above those seated at various spots amongst the crowd, and those men and women fell in behind him, creating a line of about thirty people snaking along the far wall of the room.

Not waiting for any announcement or fanfare, Talp nodded for the first man to come forward, and the business of the day began. The supplicant or lackey or whoever he was wore a white, sleeveless tunic and carried himself with the bearing of a highborn, as if he imagined himself a messero. He walked over and knelt at the platform's edge.

"What have you brought for me, Serrimandier?" asked Talp in a voice that sounded both familiar and strange, in a tone seeming to carry to Jos's ears and no farther.

The other man, Serrimandier, reached into either a pocket or a purse on his belt—his body blocked Jos's view of the movement—pulled something out, bowed his head, and in his cupped hands, offered that something to Talp.

Talp appeared indifferent to the man's actions, but Talp's supposed disinterest was belied in the vigilant way he never took his eyes off Serrimandier. The whole scene reminded Jos of a Xantish cathedral, with all the silver-eyed worshippers sitting in attentive silence while the priest and priestess chanted their intertwining prayers for Those to Come. But here the petitioners listened with a concentration that would put even the most devout Xantish to shame.

After a long moment, Talp said, "Natts," and his distraction, Natts, sauntered over to Serrimandier, his steps slow and heavy in the quiet. He neared and then stopped and stood there, peering down. A couple of people, Jos included, sucked in a sharp breath as Natts, in a single, sudden movement, fell into a crouch before Serrimandier. He spoke, his words too soft to carry, and the man spoke back. Natts rose in another smooth motion, his control signaling a good amount of strength, and plucked the item from Serrimandier's cupped hands. The gold coin caught the light before Natts brought it to his mouth and bit it. Then he inspected the results before flipping the coin into the air with his thumb. He caught it when it came down and spun on his heel to return to his spot near Talp's throne.

A few people, perhaps the same ones who'd gasped before, sighed as Serrimandier stood and returned to his seat, a spot next to a hard-faced Tithen woman who looked more at home in the rough tavern, and though Jos didn't sigh with them, he shared their relief. He had no idea what he'd thought might happen had the man presented a false coin or none at all, but he was glad it hadn't. The next man in line came forward and knelt at the platform's edge, Talp asked him what he'd brought, and Jos turned his attention to the reason he'd come to this awful tavern in the first place.

He did his best work with his subject in sight, but thought better of taking his supplies out in this place. Instead, he watched Talp with a hawkish eye, doing his best to catalogue every detail of the man's body and face, every little tic and movement.

That was harder than it should have been. The man almost never moved, aside from the occasional wave or nod, and he reacted not at all to those who came before him. In addition to that, or perhaps because of it, Jos's attention wandered from him at even the slightest provocation. It didn't help that, after the fifth person, Natts pulled a stone-headed mallet from his belt and started playing with it, twirling it around by its leather thong or dropping the head into his palm over and over—*slap, slap, slap.*

The line moved along at a good pace. A couple of people asked for and received coin, but most gave it, apparently paying some form of tax or debt, and the line shrank until two people remained, a man of about forty and a young woman half his age, and they appeared to be together. From their similar profiles and coloring, and the way he rubbed her upper back as they waited, Jos marked them as related. Father and daughter, perhaps. Or uncle and niece. Jos's thoughts drifted to his father and Anell, what they were doing, whether or not they missed him, and because his mind was on his family, it took him a few moments to realize how much quieter the already silent room had become.

Even Natts held his mallet still.

The young woman shook, and Jos took it for an ailment, but then Natts winked at her and her shivers lessened. Jos wished he'd found that wink as reassuring as she seemed to. Instead, it set his teeth on edge. He waited for things to go along as they had before, and the man and the young woman knelt at the platform's edge as everyone else had, but then things took a turn.

Talp's expression remained the same, yet his question changed and his tone at last took on some color, a shading of menace. "Do you have it?"

Jos had no idea what "it" was, but he held his breath and prayed to Amma that the man or the young woman had it. When the man shook his head, Jos released his breath in a shaky sigh before reclaiming another. Farther down the bar, a woman perched on the edge of her stool, a hungry expression on her ratty face. Others, such as the hale, white-haired man seated at the table nearest to Jos, appeared resigned. But no matter their bearing or expression, no one looked away.

Talp raised his hand, and with a flick of his finger, five of his brigands rushed forward, two to grab the daughter and three for the father. Both cried out, their terrified shouts ringing through the hall, and both fought as the brigands dragged the girl to the nearest table. Those seated there scattered away as a group; one man squeezed onto the edge of a bench at another table, and the rest sought refuge along the side wall. The brigands bent the young woman over the table, and while one pinned her to it from behind, the other came around in front of her to stretch out her arms. Terror seemed to overwhelm her, and she swooned. Her forehead fell against the tabletop and her limbs went slack. The brigand holding her wrists shook out one of the girl's limp hands and slapped it back down against the table, holding it there with the girl's fingers splayed.

"No!" the father screamed, giving form to his wordless shouts. "She didn't do anything!" Sweat soaked his tunic and tears wet his face. "Give me one more day. Please. I swear, one more day, and I'll find you the coin."

The young woman roused and resumed struggling, grunting and whimpering in futile effort.

"Be still, dearest," the father said. "I'm just... Just..." His wild gaze flew back and forth between his daughter and Talp. "Just be still."

The young woman nodded. Talp stared at her. Jos wanted to turn away, to leave, but he felt rooted to the spot. *Please. Please let the threat be enough.* A moment passed, and then another, and the father's ragged breathing slowed as it seemed Talp might let him and his daughter go. Then Natts moved, and Jos's gut clenched as Natts's eyes revealed his cruel smile an instant before it reached his lips.

Father and daughter both screamed and fought with a renewed fervor as Natts strode around the table, raised his stone-headed mallet, and with one sharp, heavy swing, brought it down on the girl's outstretched hand.

TALP'S COURT cleared out soon after, the proceedings ending without signal or fanfare, and Jos joined the throng of those who spilled out onto the street. Without a set destination in mind, he wandered through the city and out into Shade's Rest, where he fetched up at the tavern where he'd met Getha.

There, in an effort to drown out the echo of the wet, meaty crunch of shattering bones, Jos ordered a shot of thorno. He hated the stuff, the acrid stench, the burn of it, but he needed something stronger than ale. He had no idea how much that father might have owed Talp, but could any amount have warranted such brutality? The thing that kept returning to Jos, aside from the sound of a young woman being made a cripple, was

Natts's smile. So Jos drank and drank and drank, until the night snuffed out like a candle.

He awoke to the shaking of the loft as someone ascended the ladder. He didn't know how he'd gotten back to the barn, let alone how he'd made it up into the loft. He wore all of his clothes, including his boots, and he cradled his bag of supplies against his chest like one might hold a child. At least he hadn't left them behind anywhere.

His visitor turned out to be Ysobello with a bucket slung over one forearm. From the bucket, Ysobello pulled out a skin of what Jos hoped was water and a rye trencher, set those on the table, then placed the bucket near the mattress close to Jos's head, and crouched down next to him with a quiet grunt.

"Sounds like you had a mad night last night." Ysobello pitched his voice low, gentle, but Jos still pressed his hands to the side of his head so it wouldn't split in two. "Thought you might like to know that a woman came by while you were out, bangin' on the barn door, lookin' for you."

Of all the Amma-forsaken nights... Jos began to sit up and then decided against it. "She called Getha?" His mouth couldn't have tasted worse if it was filled with dirty stockings.

"Didn't give a name, but she were tall, had a strongish way about her, brown hair." Ysobello shook his head. "Not much of a smiler, that one. Told her you were out, and I weren't certain when to expect you back."

Jos groaned. Ysobello described Getha, all right, and wasn't that just the golden cap to a truly awful day?

"Right," Ysobello said, easing himself back up with a louder grunt and returning to the ladder. "Don't know what prompted this, but I don't suppose it matters. I expect it'll be out of you soon enough."

Jos opened his mouth to thank Ysobello, but what came up wasn't appreciation. He spent the rest of the morning bent over the bucket, and in between bouts of heaving up everything he'd eaten in the last moon, he pieced together a few things.

Calyn's request to draw Talp explained a lot more than it didn't, such as her initial urgency for Jos to come to town or her pointless directive for him to sketch Orli. That had been a test, one he'd passed, and Calyn had moved on to her real reason for requesting Jos's help in the first place: Talp. Granted, Talp lived and worked within the walls of the city, but Jos had no doubt his reach extended out into the Tangles, and since he continued to operate, it seemed the Ombratos city guards were unwilling to, or incapable of, taking him down. Not that a picture could do all that, but one of Jos's drawings might end up being an anchoring knot in a much larger tapestry, and his pride swelled to think Lathan had considered his skill genuine enough to be worthy of such a task.

That afternoon, when he could at last move without his gullet heaving like a ship on a stormy sea, he took out his supplies, sat at his table, and dredged forth a mental image of Talp. He feared what might come, but Calyn's daughter had been right when she'd said she needed him to do this. He had to do it for her, for that poor young woman and her mangled hand, and for anyone else who ever had or ever would cross his or Natts's path.

Hand trembling just the slightest, Jos concentrated on drawing out Talp's truth. He placed his charcoal to the page and...nothing. He concentrated harder, centering all his thoughts on Talp's plain features, his spare mannerisms, his forgettable voice. Jos focused everything he had, every drop of his skill on the man, and soon his head started to pound from the effort, but nothing came.

He dropped his charcoal, covered his eyes with his hands, and sat back, bewildered. He'd never encountered a person who didn't bring forth anything.

But that wasn't right. Something did come when Jos thought of Talp, and that something was nothing. Jos couldn't have explained it aloud, but Talp's nothing bore a presence, rendering it unlike the utter absence of something, and it refused to translate to the page because how did one draw nothing?

Then draw him without his truth. Jos picked up the charcoal to do just that, but Talp's nothingness held him and wouldn't let him go.

JOS RETURNED to Talp's Court three more times. On the first visit, he discovered Talp held court every third day and left. On his second and third visits, he stayed for less than a quarter of a candlemark and then spent the remainder of each day staring at and struggling with the same blank page.

In between his visits to Talp, he ate little, slept less, and drew not at all, and though he prayed for Getha to stop by again, she never did.

Two days after his third visit to the tavern, he decided he needed to get out of his stinking loft, and he passed the morning in Ombratos, sitting on the edge of a canal near a bridge leading to the Meet. Due to the heat and the dryness of the season, the water had lowered far enough that his dangling feet didn't even skim the slow moving surface of the branch.

More out of habit than an actual desire to create, he'd brought his materials with him, and as a young man, his expression set with joyful determination, crossed the bridge toward Jos, he had the sudden urge to draw. He pulled out his paper, set it on his drawing board, and took out a length of charcoal. His hand shook, so he closed his eyes and took a deep breath to steady himself. As he did, the young man's truth rose from the muddiness of his thoughts like a spring crocus. Jos opened his eyes, and with a steady hand, drew the young man on his knees, arms outstretched as he offered a flowering charm to the pretty young woman standing before him, her hands already open to claim it.

The picture released something within Jos, and in a near frenzy, he began sketching almost everyone who came across the bridge, one person right after the next, covering page after page with dozens of drawings. Though rough and rushed, every image came out with enough detail to carry some measure of truth, and every one of them, even the foul ones, reassured him he hadn't lost the precious gift Amma had bestowed upon him.

As the sun neared its zenith, a girl of seven or eight skipped onto the bridge, stopped at its peak, and leaned over the side. She cast two very long plaits of light, almost white-yellow hair over the stone rail and rocked back and forth, seemingly just for the joy of watching her braids swing. He didn't even bother trying to capture her youth, her exuberance. Instead, he watched her playing and laughed with her when one of her plaits swung around and smacked her across the face.

He covered his mouth to muffle his laughter, but she must have heard him because she stopped her silliness and looked over at him, her bright blue eyes wide. With her light hair, eyes, skin, the girl didn't resemble his sister in the slightest, but she reminded him of Mouse just the same. A longing for her, for his caravan, for Gent and Nora, and his aunt Bosk, and even his father, swept through him with such ferocity that, for a moment, he found it hard to breathe.

"What are you doin'?"

Jos started and almost dropped his paper and drawing board into the branch. A few lengths of charcoal slid off and fell into the water, dipping below the surface before rising again to float away on the sluggish current.

"Sorry," the girl said, her voice low and raspy. She wore a sack of a dress

—or an actual sack, with holes cut into it for her head and arms—and her braids, thick as ropes, hung down to her calves. She sat down beside him and dangled her bare, dirty feet over the side. "What are you doin'?" she repeated.

"Drawing," he said, still gripped by his melancholy.

"Drawin' what?"

"People."

She seemed to think about this. Or something else. Her nose wrinkled, and she pinched it. "You smell very bad."

He tried recalling when last he'd bathed and failed. With a renewed awareness of his own body, he held out the neck of his tunic and dipped his chin down for a good whiff. The sour, sweaty reek brought tears to his eyes and made him cough. It also almost made him grateful Getha hadn't come looking for him. "I suppose I should do something about that."

The girl shrugged. "Why for you drawin' people?"

"What's that?"

"You're drawin' people." She peered up at him. "Why for?"

A good question, one he hadn't allowed himself to consider until now. Why was he sitting near this bridge drawing whichever random Fallen who happened to cross it? Suddenly he faced his own truth—Talp's nothingness was a chasm too wide for him to leap across. Though it pained him to consider quitting, he needed to accept that before it drove him mad.

"Can I see?" she asked. Then, heedless of his stench, she leaned in close and peered at the images on his board, at the ten faces and truths captured there.

While she looked, he considered his revelation. *I have to stop.* But if that was the right choice, then why did it also seem like failure? What if his father had been right about his Tempting? What if he'd failed that too?

The girl leaned back. "I seen drawers workin' in the Blossom, but none of they's pictures are like yours. Yours is..." She smiled up at him, and her parted lips revealed two missing front teeth. "Yours is magic."

FEELING LIGHTER and freer than he had in days, Jos returned to Shade's Rest. His first stop: a bathing house. The girl had begged to watch him work, but he'd left her with a promise to return to that spot near the bridge the next day.

With most Shade's Resters out at their jobs or going about their days,

Jos had the common pool to himself. Grabbing a handful of sand and oil, he entered the pool, and while he scrubbed away the past few days, he did his best to accept the fact that he was about to disappoint Calyn and, by extension, his friend Lathan, even though he didn't know how or why. Really, he might never know how or why.

He knocked at Calyn's for over a minute and, remembering her illness, began to worry for her when the door of the next building over flew open, and a man charged out. Dark curls hung over his brow and a scraggy beard did little to hide his sunken cheeks and weak chin. He seemed ready for a fight, but taking a good look at Jos, stopped several feet away.

"Enough of that," the man said. "No point, anyhow. Thems is off."

"Off?" Jos asked. That didn't make any sense. "When? Where?"

The man scowled. "I hain't their keeper."

"Well, do you know when they'll be back?" Another thought occurred to Jos. "Are they even coming back?" The man's scowl deepened, and Jos held his hands up in surrender. "Right," he said. "Not their keeper."

Wondering where Calyn and her daughter might have gone, why they might have gone, Jos went to his loft intending to drop off his supplies before going to the bakery for his supper, but he lay down on his bed for a moment, closed his eyes, and didn't reopen them until dawn.

He went back to the bridge for the next two mornings, and both times, the plait-haired moppet, Dessa, found him and sat beside him, watching him work. Like Mouse, she sensed his gift more than understanding it outright, and like Mouse, she chided him along from any sad or unpleasant subjects and delighted in the happy and humorous ones. It seemed a little pathetic to have a child bolstering his confidence, but pitiable or not, her awe helped him reclaim much of that which he'd lost.

In the afternoons, he wandered around the city plying his trade—he had almost emptied his coffer during his Talp obsession—and in the evenings, he returned to Shade's Rest to knock on Calyn's door, then to sit in his loft. Neither Calyn nor her daughter answered, and he spent both evenings alone.

His third day near the bridge, Dessa came, but refused his offer to sit. "Can you come with me?" she asked.

"Where?"

"I want to show my brother your pictures," she said, tying her braids into a knot on the top of her head.

He packed up his supplies, glad for the excuse to avoid his loft for a little while longer. With Calyn gone or hiding from him and Getha perhaps never to return, more than a few hard decisions awaited him. "Is your brother somewhere far away?"

"No." She shook her head, and the knot came undone. "Not too far."

She skipped ahead of him, hurrying him along with her excitement, leading him away from the Meet and into the Mire. Jos, fearing the Mire to be much like the Tangles, had avoided it, but the neighborhood, at least the small part they traversed, bore little of the Tangles's hopelessness. They passed skinny people wearing clothes worn with age and use, just like the homes and shops that lined the streets, but holes were patched and bright flowers grew in the weatherworn wooden boxes hanging from the sills.

It warmed him to think Dessa might live in such a nice part of the city. But then they passed a crossroads, and the next block seemed less nice, as did the next. He worried that the closer they were to the docks, the harder the neighborhoods would continue to get, and he considered begging off when Dessa stopped at the mouth of an alleyway. She turned to face him, her smile gone, and a sense of foreboding skittered down his spine.

"Where's your brother?" he asked.

"Right here." A strong, calloused hand clamped around the back of Jos's neck, and something sharp jabbed into his ribs.

Idiot. Jos opened his empty hands and held them out in surrender. *Even a blind man could have seen this was a trap.* "All the coin I have is in the purse on my belt, and you're welcome to every last copper."

"Ta," the man said, "but I have all the coin I need. I'm after somethin' a bit rarer."

"What—" Jos glanced over his shoulder, and Natts stared back at him. Jos had never been kicked in the chest by a horse, but he now knew what it must feel like.

Natts, perhaps seeing recognition on Jos's face, smirked, and the cruelty in the expression was even more pronounced up close. Nothing, not even a glimmer of kindness or light shone from his eyes. His was a soul cloaked in utter darkness. He shoved at Jos's neck, and they began walking down the road with Dessa skipping along ahead of them.

They had gone less than a block when Natts spoke. "Care to tell me why a'fore last tenday I never saw you, then, without no word to no one, you're showin' up at court three times in a run?"

Jos scrabbled for a lie. "I—I was looking for an old friend."

"That so?" Natts sucked on his teeth. "You find him?"

"Or her," Dessa said, reminding Jos of her presence. "Might of been a her." She sounded indignant but not worried or scared.

"Too right," Natts said, his smirk returning. "It might of been a *her*." He tightened his grip on Jos's neck and shook him a little. "Mightn't it?"

There was something in the way he'd said "her."

"What did you do to Calyn?" Jos asked before he'd even considered whether or not he should mention her name.

"I don't know any Calyn," Natts said, sounding sincere. "You know a Calyn, Dessa?"

She shrugged. "Had a cousin named Calyn once, but she's been dead for years."

Jos couldn't tell if they lied or not, but given his brief history with Natts, he worried for the old woman and her daughter.

"We don't know Calyn from anyone, tofter," Natts said, "but I do know this. You're goin' to do somethin' for me."

"Am I?" Jos said, surprised by his own bravado.

But his courage left as quick as it had come when Natts chuckled, the sound like thunder on the horizon. "You are. Unless, a'course, you want to join me back at Talp's Court for a more thorough discussion."

Natts flipped Dessa a silver, which she caught and pocketed. She smiled at Jos and shrugged in a "What can you do?" sort of way before skipping off without looking back.

Jos let Natts lead him back toward the Meet. Jos had almost a foot on Natts, but whenever he so much as thought about running, the point of Natts's blade dug into his side. At the very edge of the Mire, they cut off from the main road down a narrower street bordered on one side by a canal, and after a few blocks, fetched up on the edge of a busy fountain square. Buildings—they appeared to be tenements—surrounded the square, and the shouts of merchants echoed off them. People went to and from the fountain with empty or freshly filled buckets, and many stopped to chat along the way. On a different day, under different circumstances, Jos might have enjoyed it.

"Here," Natts said, thrusting Jos down onto a bench in the shadow of a fabric merchant's cart.

"Here what?"

"See them across the way?" He pointed across the square. "Take out your paper and your black, and draw them."

Jos followed the gesture, but there were dozens of people "across the way," and without a detail or two—

A familiar silhouette caught his eye, and his heart near stopped. There, in the exact direction in which Natts pointed, stood Getha, hands on her hips as she spoke to a shorter, yellow-haired woman.

Jos struggled for breath. *Not her. Not her, not her, not her.* "Who?" he asked, his voice cracking. He cleared his throat. "I mean, which ones?"

"Them," Natts said, nodding toward Getha. "The muscled one talkin' to the one with the sunny hair."

"I won't." Jos didn't know why Natts wanted a picture of Getha and her friend, but that he did was enough of a reason to refuse.

Natts leaned in. "How about this, then? If you don't, then I'll stick you, go over there, and run them both through."

Sweat or blood trickled down Jos's side. "The muscled one will fight you."

Natts chuckled. "So?"

"She'll win."

"You know her?"

"No," Jos said, frightened he'd given himself away. "I don't. It's... She looks like a fighter."

Natts eyed her. "Agreed. Still, you hain't never seen me fight."

The sound of the young woman's hand breaking beneath Natts's mallet echoed in Jos's ears. "No one who wasn't already being held down, anyway."

He regretted the words the instant they left his mouth, but Natts chuckled again. "Hain't you a pip? If you're as good as Dessa claims, I'll have to make use of you more often." A smile remained on his face as he dug the blade into Jos's side. "Now draw."

A refusal perched on Jos's lips. Natts couldn't want a picture of Getha and her friend for anything good. But Jos had to remind himself that he didn't actually know how well Getha fought. He assumed her skilled, more than skilled enough to take a brawler like Natts, but he wasn't certain. What if she wasn't? What if Jos refused and Natts outmatched her? His imagination provided an image of Getha lying on the stones, blood pooling around her as it gushed from several gaping knife wounds in her chest. He begged Getha to look up, to look his way and notice him, to run or to help him, but when she scanned the square, her precise, practiced eye skimmed right past the shadow in which he sat.

Self-loathing peppered his fear as he made his choice, resolving to draw Getha and her friend just as they appeared, with none of his skill. Then, as soon as Natts left, he'd chase after them and warn them. He couldn't see any other way through.

His plan worked well enough for Getha. The woman on the page reflected the one before him in every way, without any enhancement or embellishment. But when it came to her friend, his gift cut through his exhaustion and terror and took over, forcing him to the back of his own mind as his hand ranged over the page.

The woman's yellow hair refused to stay light. Or short. Or straight. Riotous dark curls spilled from her head and down around her shoulders, framing a face with features sharper and finer than those of the woman before him. On the page, the pretty, yellow-haired lowborn girl became a regal, raven-haired beauty. He had no way of knowing how passable her disguise might be face-to-face, but from the distance at which he sat, it was flawless.

He meant to stop there, but his hand kept going, sketching out the upper edge of her collarbone—exposed, as if she wore a gown and not a plain cotton tunic—before Natts snatched the edge of the page, yanking it away. Surprised by the action and with the charcoal still pressed down, Jos drew a line across the center of the picture by accident, a heavy smear of darkness that sliced through both women's throats.

Natts grunted. Jos peered up at him, but the sun was right behind his head, casting his expression into an impenetrable shadow.

"Ta, then," Natts said, sounding neither pleased nor disappointed, but he moved and a small leather purse dropped onto the bench beside Jos.

Jos forced himself to stare after Natts until the man moved from sight. Jos didn't want to give the impression that he knew Getha. He didn't want to put her or her friend in any more danger than he already had. Natts disappeared in less than half a minute, swallowed up by the crowd, and the instant he did, Jos jumped to his feet and looked back toward Getha.

But she was gone. Panic fluttered inside him until... *Wait! Is that her at the corner?*

Recognizing the color of her hair and her gait, he sighed with relief and started after her. He was a few steps into the alley, and about to call out to her, when a whirlwind of at least a dozen dirty children accosted him, laughing and pushing and pulling at him. Amid the madness, he recognized Dessa's long braids, and then one of the children kicked him in the groin, and he fell to the ground, gagging and gasping for breath.

The children descended on him like ravens on a fresh carcass. They kicked and hit him, claiming anything and everything worth a copper—his purse, chalk, and sketchbook; his belt, boots, and even his tunic, which one of the children cut and tore from his body. They left him naught but his leggings and smallclothes, and thank Amma for that. The harvest of his person seemingly complete, the children ran off in two different groups, one headed the way he'd come and the other headed the way Getha had gone.

All except Dessa. She knelt down next to his head and kissed his cheek. "Weren't personal." He reached for her, but she was far quicker. She dodged him and stood. "Ta, love." Then she skipped away, his purse jingling in her hand.

Jos didn't know how long it took for him to recover. Eventually, though, his mission to find and warn Getha overwhelmed the pain, and he climbed unsteadily to his feet. Then, with a sense of dread in his belly, he leaned heavily against one of the walls of the alley, he staggered to the end where Getha had exited.

Sure enough. Getha and her yellow-haired friend were no longer in sight. Choosing a direction at random, he ran for a few blocks. When he didn't see Getha, he ran back to the square and chose another direction, then another. Back and forth he went, his mind buzzing with panic, his heart heavy with guilt. Here and there, people asked him if he was well or if he needed help, but he brushed them off. He ran until he couldn't breathe, until his legs wouldn't carry him another step, until it was clear Getha and her friend were gone.

He returned to the edge of the square for the last time just as city bells rang, announcing the sunset, and he fell to his knees. The already busy square became even busier as people headed to their homes. Treating him like a stone in a stream, they divided before him, passing by on either side, ignoring him.

A man didn't move fast enough, and his hip bumped Jos's shoulder. Rage, sudden and huge, filled Jos, and he let out a loud, pained roar to keep from bursting. He shouted because he hated Ombratos and the Fallen and his gift. He hated everything and everyone that had driven him to the city and to this moment—his father, Mutta Kirsch, Lathan, Calyn, Natts. He even hated Getha for choosing him in the first place. But most of all, he hated himself.

Throat raw, he dropped his head into his hands and, then and there, swore to himself and to Amma that he wouldn't leave until he somehow found Getha and warned her.

TWENTY-FIVE

"The arrival of the snows is a portent for the moons ahead. If they arrive on a day of joy and good fortune that bespeaks a fine cold season for the tribe. But a day beset with disagreement, anger, or loss brings long, dark moons in its wake."
-Old Rhyllexie saying

It was dark outside when Dace Morovide rose. He gave his short beard a good scratch, then dressed by the dim light of the hearth fire. His back and shoulders protested as he pulled on a thick sweater, but what else could one expect after harvesting chase? The last tenday had passed in a whirlwind of cutting and hauling in bales of Rhyllex's hardy, fast-flowering grain. The sleeves of his sweater ended just below his elbows, leaving his scarred forearms bare. He tugged on oil-treated doeskin breeches and slid his feet into his indoor boots.

Behind him, Agahara turned over in their bed. He went to his *kärlief* and knelt to pull up the snow bear skin they'd slept under since their wedding night over her naked shoulder. A ribbon of long, white hair hung across her face. How she hated her hair and its singular coloring. Because she still slept, he brushed the strands back and kissed her forehead. She leaned into the kiss and sighed, and her lips fell open just wide enough to reveal the sharp tips of her incisors, filed into points the winter of her menarche.

He ran his hands over the scars on his arms. He longed to climb back into bed with her—through the warm moons they had discussed having a third child—but he needed to leave soon if he wanted to traverse the full perimeter of the Nor'east and return before nightfall.

"Tonight," he whispered, a promise to them both. Rising, he turned his mind to the day ahead.

He considered taking his shortsword, mounted crosswise with Agahara's on their wooden headboard. But he planned to ride hard and didn't want the blade bouncing against his back all day, so he left it and grabbed his dirk from the mantel.

The Young waited for Dace the Prince in the hall. Though it would still be summer in Ombratos, the seasons were shifting in Rhyllex. Even so, the Young's hair still held more black than white. That would change soon enough given how fast Rhyllexie hair grew once the snows came. Dace was glad to see his eldest son dressed for indoors. That meant Dace wasn't in for another argument. Or so he hoped. The Young had turned eleven during the warm moons. Eleven and quarrelsome.

"What has you up this early?" Dace asked. "I haven't changed my mind."

"I know." The Young tucked his hands behind his back. "Next year." Then he tilted his chin up in a stubborn way that reminded Dace of Solena, and something—guilt, perhaps—fluttered in his chest.

He didn't regret not going to Solena's funeral, not for Solena's sake, but Renn hadn't written him since then.

"I came to see you off."

"I'm glad," Dace said, and the Young relaxed. "Where's the Seedling?"

"Isaak sleeps."

In silence, father and son made their way through their family's wing of Vomek Keep. The Rhyllexie didn't employ servants, but a few tribemates lived with them all year round, helping with the daily maintenance of the building and the care of the chieftain's family. At this candlemark, several of these tribemates moved from room to room, building up fires and preparing for the day.

Dace and the Young reached the first set of stairs, a cold corridor chilled by its proximity to the outer wall, and headed down. Tendrils of icy air crept around the sides of the tapestries hung over the arrowslit embrasures. The snows approached, no doubt about that.

On the main floor, they cut through the western end of the great hall. Thought dim and quiet, the tent forest once again stretched to every corner of the massive room. Less than a tenday had passed since the migration back into the keep, but everyone had already settled in. Dace loved this time of year, when his fractured tribe came together and became whole.

Halfway down the South Lane, the Young startled Dace by grabbing his wrist and pulling him into one of the hall's shadowy alcoves. "I'm sorry for fighting you, Papa." Then he wrapped his skinny arms around Dace's waist and squeezed.

Dace wanted to forgive his son, but a lump formed in his throat, and he couldn't get the words out as he embraced the Young back. Closing his eyes, he let the words go and savored the moment, knowing this hug might be their last. The Young was to have his sleeves shortened come next spring.

When the Young's arms fell slack, Dace released him, cleared his throat, and pressed the heels of his hands to his eyes. "You're forgiven." His hands came away wet, and he wiped them on his sweater. "Now," Dace said, "watch out for the Seedling today. Don't let him get underfoot."

The Young grunted that he would, then he ran off, disappearing into the tent forest.

Dace continued on to the kitchens. The roads that surrounded the keep were like a wheel; there was an outer circle and then, at the cardinal points on the compass, four additional roads that all lead toward the hub —Vomek Keep. These roads were their tribe's responsibility, and so, every three moons, the Prince and some others rode out to inspect a quarter. Today, they would ride out to the east, until they reached the village of Yost, then they would turn on to the South Road, and head home.

When the Prince shouldered open the swinging door, a wave of warmth hit him, carrying on it the scents of breads and meats cooking and the crashing and clanging of people bustling about, readying themselves for the rush of almost three hundred tribemates looking to break their fasts.

At a table pressed against the far wall, six men sat, eating from bowls. Sometimes, Dace asked for volunteers to help him with his inspections; other times, he purposefully chose a group of young men and women, just in their short sleeves or with their teeth sharpened, as yet another rite of passage.

On this occasion, however, the Prince had simply picked his closest friends. The twins, Pyry the Plain and Pekka the Corner-Eyed, so named for their handsomeness and their cleverness, respectively, had been supportive of Dace from the start, perhaps because they were all of an age. The Bent Tongue, a slightly older man still far from elder status, told the tallest—and best—tales of anyone in the tribe. Knai the Bear was young, strong, and loved wrestling more than just about anything. Swey the Cloud Face, Dace's fellow outsider, was another natural choice.

Lastly, Dace had chosen Jesper the Tree Shaper. They weren't friends, not exactly, because Jesper was a quiet man and hard to know since he'd rather spend his candlemarks carving than talking, tumbling, or wrestling. Dace liked him, though, and hoped this might be his chance to get to know him further.

The Prince's handpicked crew sat around the table, eating and talking with ease, and his eagerness for the day ahead swelled. He looked around, but even though Hannoh the Cook was nowhere to be seen, Dace kept to the kitchen's edge as he made his way over to them to avoid her wrath.

Having grown up on the coast, he'd met his fair share of captains, but the tightness with which Hannoh ran her particular ship put those salty seafarers to shame. As Dace neared the group, the men laughed and banged their spoons on the table, no doubt in response to something Pekka the Corner-Eyed had said. Pekka's handsome brother, Pyry the Plain, laughed the loudest and slapped the table so hard the bowls jumped, their feud from last winter having dried up during the warm moons.

Next to Pyry, the Bent Tongue chuckled and looked up toward the door. He noticed Dace approaching and spread his hands wide. "The Prince has arrived!"

Like the Young, the Bent Tongue had been named for another, his uncle Oskvar. Though a great honor to share a family member's name with a child, an honor for both the family member and the child, to call the child by that name while the family member still lived was a grave insult. To refer to the Young as Gunnur while his Greatmother Gunna lived would be calling his greatmother unfit to carry her own name.

At the Bent Tongue's announcement, the other men looked up or turned around and shouted out their welcomes, save for Pyry, who hunched over, holding his belly while he still shook with laughter.

Dace pointed at him and spoke to Pekka as he sat in the remaining empty chair. "I think you broke him. He will laugh himself to death."

"Good!" Pekka declared. "Then perhaps some of the women will look at me."

Keli, a quick-witted young woman with more than her fair share of suitors, arrived at Dace's elbow and placed a bowl filled with steaming porridge in front of him. Hands empty, Keli perched them on her round hips and addressed Pekka. "Quite a few more men would have to die before any of us looked your way."

The men, many of the workers in the kitchen, and even Pekka crowed and hooted at that response. Everyone enjoyed seeing Pekka the Corner-Eyed put in his place.

"Keli," Hannoh barked, her voice cutting through the joy like a keen blade through soft bread. "I thought I sent you over there to feed the Prince. I don't remember also telling you to stand about sharpening your tongue. I need those ice berries from the caves now, not a tenday from now!"

Chieftain Gunna liked to brag that the caves below Vomek Keep preserved all the supplies stored within its walls indefinitely. "We've never had an apple turn to mush. Never found a rotted sack of chase or a spoiled side of ness." She claimed the effects of the cave had something to do with gifts bestowed upon them by the bones of their tribe's ancestors. Dace knew very little about the caves below the keep, but he suspected the lack of bad food had less to do with this mysterious gift and more to do with the brisk and efficient way Hannoh ran her kitchen.

Keli flashed her pointed smile at the men and collected the empty bowls. "Back to work." Taking a complicated route through the bustling kitchen, she made her way over to the tub-like sinks in the corner.

Dace dashed his porridge down, as eager as the other men to get to their day of riding. While he ate, the others talked of Knai's prospects in taking the title of "the Bear" for the third winter in a row, a second name he'd earned by his skill in the wrestling ring.

"Torska the Stone is coming for you," Jesper warned him.

"Bah!" Knai said, his bare, unscarred arms flashing as he waved Jesper off. "Her teeth have only been sharp for four summers."

"Eh, eh." Swey the Cloud Face scratched at his nest-like beard. "And you have only been in short sleeves for six. Have you seen her yet? She gained a few inches this summer, and she's quicker than a snake."

"Oh, he saw her all right," Pekka said. "Couldn't take his eyes off her."

Knai scowled, and the other men laughed. He turned to Dace. "Aren't you done yet?"

Dace's spoon scraped the bottom of the bowl, as he scooped the last bit of porridge and stuffed it into his mouth. He swallowed the thick mush and set the bowl in the center of the table. "Done. Let's be off."

The roads around Vomek Keep formed a sort of four-spoked wagon wheel. There were roads that led north, south, east, and west. Connecting their end points were roads to the northeast, southeast, southwest, and northwest. The Denkiefer Forest filled the inner part of the wheel and farmland surrounded the outer edges. Twice a year, at the beginning and the end of the cold season, four different groups rode the four different circuits, checking the quality of the roads, watching for dangerous game, examining the fields, and checking up on the tribe's two villages. Volunteers took these patrols, and Dace had put his name forward for every one since his arrival in Rhyllex.

Pyry and the Bent Tongue led the way into the keep's antechamber, where they all donned their *vervärmen klädij*. Dace shrugged on his favorite coat, one of the few with sleeves long enough to reach his wrists, and strapped his sea cat belt across his chest. To the belt, he tied the scabbard holding his dirk. He needn't check the dagger's sharpness; Rhyllexie treated their weapons with constant, conscious care. Finally, he pulled on over-boots, lacing them tight, put on his red woolen cap, and tucked his gloves into his belt. Overwarm, he hurried outside, the cool, crisp air a welcome relief.

A sparkling frost coated the ground, and his breath left his mouth in white plumes. A half-moon hung heavy in a sky darkened by a leaden predawn. He followed the others down the path toward the stables. They all wore shortswords on their belts or hatchets strapped to their backs, and Swey, his bow slung over his shoulder, lingered behind the rest.

Though Swey the Cloud Face had been with the tribe for almost as long as Dace, his title reflected his outsider status. The summer after Dace arrived in the Avers Valley, Swey came and sought out an audience with Chieftain Gunna. He'd begged to join the tribe, and Gunna had allowed him to do so. Changing tribes was a rarity, unheard of before the Peace and not much practiced even to this day. Swey's second name—the Cloud Face—was a title he'd held since his arrival. Cloud Face meant "one whose intentions aren't wholly clear," so he would continue to be known thusly until he did something to prove his loyalty or another outsider arrived to take his place.

Because of this, Dace had always felt a kinship to Swey, and he sped up to match the man's pace. "Fair morning."

Swey started, as if his thoughts had been elsewhere. "Hm? Oh, yes. Fair morning."

"Copper for your thoughts."

Swey scratched his beard. "What does that mean? Eh, eh."

"Oh." Dace tried to avoid sayings from Ombratos, but even after so many years, they slipped out. "It's a way of asking someone what they're thinking about."

"But why did you offer me coin?" Swey asked. Bartering still prevailed over monetary exchanges in Rhyllex.

Dace shook his head. Sometimes explaining sayings or actions from his home ceased to be worth the effort. "What were you thinking?"

Swey looked off toward the stables, then turned back. "You know? Eh, eh. I don't remember."

Dace laughed. "Then let the snows take it. Ready to ride?"

"I have been waiting for this day all summer long."

"Me too."

Their group headed out on the East Road, and Dace, with his long-legged Windspear, bred for both beauty and speed, left them behind not too far from the keep. Mile after mile of forest passed by in a blur, and he reached the Moeter River far ahead of the others.

He dismounted in the middle of the bridge, near the drinking buckets. One of the buckets had a carving of a person in the side, the other a carving of a horse, both attached by rope to a pole. He dropped the buckets over the edge, into the rushing waters, then drew them up, glad to note that his warmed arms and shoulders no longer protested the effort.

He and Windspear drank from their respective buckets, but he had his fill long before she did, so he sat back on his heels and watched her for a moment, his guilt returning. On the note sent with Windspear six years earlier, Renn had written *To remind you of home.* Now she might never forgive him. Perhaps someday, when she had a husband and children of her own...

Windspear raised her dripping muzzle from the bucket, and Dace stood to lead her off the other side of the bridge to graze at the brittle, yellow grasses along the road's verge. Then he unlaced his breeches, closed his eyes, and enjoyed the simple pleasure of pissing out-of-doors. He finished his business just as he heard the other horses approaching. Tucking himself in and relacing his pants, he stretched his legs, readying himself to return to the saddle.

After the other men watered their horses, Dace hung back with them as they rode. Dark, ponderous clouds laid heavy over the lightening sky, but the bright mood of their group contrasted with the gloom. They talked of everything and nothing, arriving at their first stop before he knew it.

At the Eastern Point, three roads—the East, the Nor'east, and the Sou'east—all met. To the north and south of the point, harvested chase fields stretched off into the distance, and between them lay the small village of Yost, closed up tight for the snow moons, the huts hidden under *kursi*. The staked-down *kursi*, woven from chase stalks, kept the worst of the elements from the empty homes, and without snow covering them, they looked like a collection of huge, overturned reed baskets awaiting the use of some giant.

The men wandered through the *kursi*-dotted village to reach the well sitting at its heart. While Jesper and the Bent Tongue rummaged in their saddle packs for a bite to eat, Pyry, Pekka, and Knai checked on their *kursi* and those of their neighbors, making sure the stakes held and tucking the grasses along the bases tighter. Dace and Swey uncovered the well and set to pulling up buckets of water so that the men and beasts might slake their thirsts. With the various chores seen to, Jesper passed out straps of dried ness, and the men sat around gnawing on them and discussing the impending snows.

"They aren't coming for another tenday." Knai the Bear pounded his fist on his chest to reaffirm his confidence.

"Says who?" the Bent Tongue asked before tearing off a strip of ness with his teeth.

"Says me!"

"And the elders," said Pekka. "I have ears too, Bear."

Pyry stroked the three plaits of his fine beard and squinted at the sky. "The snows are coming in five days, men. I'd bet my whiskers on it."

"What do you think, Dace?" Jesper asked in earnest. The young man spoke no other way, but amusement already colored the other men's expressions.

In all of Dace's life, no more than seven inches of snow had ever fallen in Ombratos in a given winter, and even after a decade spent in the North, he always guessed wrong. Preparing himself for the mocking that would follow his statement, Dace swallowed a bite and breathed deeply. Underneath the thick scent of pine, the loamy rot of the forest floor, and the echo of ripened chase, the air smelled sharp and wet.

"Today," he said. "The snows will come today."

The others laughed and shook their heads.

"Perhaps," Pekka said, the sharp tilt of his smile belying the generosity of his statement.

But for once, Dace didn't feel foolish about his guess. Even so, he held his tongue and let the conversation carry on without him.

Soon enough, the men decided to return to their ride. They covered the well and climbed up on their horses, then they returned to the crossroads, Dace leading the way toward the Nor'east.

Before he'd gone thirty feet, Swey called out, "Wait!"

Dace pulled Windspear to a halt and turned in his saddle. "What goes?"

Swey rode to him, his face sweaty under his beard. "I thought—eh, eh —we were riding the Sou'east."

Dace looked to the other men. "Didn't we ride that in the spring?"

Pekka shook his head. "We rode Sou'west in the spring, remember? We spent all afternoon fixing the Wessow side of the bridge."

How could Dace have forgotten that day? Or the ride home, caked in mud from tip to toe. He guided Windspear around to the south, and Swey wiped the sweat from his brow. Together, they rode back to join the others, then the whole group set off for the Southern Point.

The sun continued to hide its face behind the thick clouds, which grew heavier and grayer with each passing mile, and again, Dace hung back with the others, enjoying their worried glances at the sky as the threat of snow loomed ever closer.

Only Swey kept his eyes to the forest and the road, looking out for beasts. *Good man.* Swey never seemed to take for granted the goodwill of his adopted tribe. Following his fine example, Dace left off watching the sky and joined the Cloud Face in his vigilant scanning of the Denkiefer Forest to their right, the fallow chase fields to the left, and the road, ahead and behind.

The first flakes—large, fluffy clumps of whiteness—fell just as their group reached the cairn marking the road's halfway point, and everyone stopped to look up, even Swey.

Without thinking, Dace shouted in wordless triumph, then held on tight as Windspear skittered beneath him. He couldn't wait to return home, to tell Agahara he had predicted the snows. In her maddening, wonderful way she would say something like, "Of course, *kärlief.*" If he was lucky, she might also gift him with one of her sharp, lovely smiles.

Pekka clapped his hands, the sound muffled by the hide of his leather gloves. "See there, now? It took eleven years, but the Prince has shown us all up." He pointed at Pyry. "Ho, brother! Did you not bet your fine beard the snows would come in five days?"

Pyry's dark eyes widened. *A man without a beard is like a man without balls.* His beard would grow back, but not before he endured more than his fair share of mocking.

"He did," said Knai.

A toothy grin split the Bent Tongue's face. "That's how I remember it."

Jesper waved a hand at the frowning Pyry. "Don't worry. We won't hold you to it."

"By our ancestors," Pekka said, "I will! So will Father once he hears of this." He rode up next to Pyry, who glared at him. "Never wager anything you aren't ready to lose, isn't that right?"

Shoulders tight, Pyry growled at Pekka, anger and frustration both evident in the sound. Then he bent low over his horse's neck, dug his heels into the beast's sides, and took off down the road at a gallop. So much for their peaceful winter. Ever the fine friend, Swey charged off after him, and Pekka watched them both go.

Jesper frowned, but Knai met Dace's gaze, rolled his eyes, and pretended to toss something to the ground, which meant that Knai thought Pyry's anger was unimportant and would be short-lived. Dace, agreeing, echoed the gesture. With any luck, Swey would be able to calm Pyry down, and the men would be waiting at the Southern Point.

Thick flakes brushed against Dace's face, clinging to his eyelashes and beard. Regardless of whether or not Swey and Pyry would wait, the rest of them needed to hurry onward, the first snow seldom a gentle reminder of the coming season. He clucked at Windspear. "Let's go."

Within a mile, the storm dropped over them like a blanket, and whiteness filled the air, lessening Dace's sight of the road ahead in frightening measures. He grew anxious to reunite with Swey and Pyry, and to get back. But as they neared the Southern Point, a frigid gust of wind parted the snows, revealing a dark mound lying in the center of the crossroads.

Pekka kicked his horse into a gallop. The other horses sped up too and so they came upon Pyry as a group. His horse had collapsed, a cluster of black-fletched arrows bristling its bloodied chest. Under the horse, Pyry the Plain's faced the sky with one dark, blank eye open. A black-fletched arrow stuck out from the other.

Dace, his heart pounding, rose in his saddle and scanned the crossroads, but of Swey or an attacker there was no sign. Then Pekka screamed, and Dace whirled around, recognizing as he did so that the cry was one of pain and surprise rather than grief. The sight of Pekka slumped in his saddle, the bloody tip of an arrow poking from his chest, seemed to hold Dace, Knai, Jesper, and the Bent Tongue in a frozen state of shock.

But a second arrowhead sprouted from Pekka's chest and broke the spell. Heralded by the crashing of branches and the pounding of hooves, attackers—too many for Dace to count—burst from the forest.

"Run!" Knai yelled, pulling a hatchet from the sheath on his back.

Dace, who had spent the first eighteen years of his life under the careful watch of the palace guard, did not need to be told twice. He leaned down over Windspear's neck and dug his heels hard into her sides. Windspear charged off at a breakneck speed, and it was all Dace could do to remain in the saddle.

They went at least a mile before he glanced back, expecting to find Knai, Jesper, and the Bent Tongue hard on his heels, but the only rider behind him was a fur-clad stranger on a Rhyllexie stallion. What had happened to the others? Should he turn back? He didn't know. What he did know was that after twenty miles of riding, Windspear was starting to flag.

Run! Knai's order echoed in Dace's mind, imploring him onward. *Run!* He couldn't spare any more thoughts for what was happening or why. He had to get back to the keep. An image of Agahara and their boys flashed though his mind. Though unsure of what was happening, he needed to warn the rest of the tribe.

In what seemed like an eye blink, they covered another half a mile, and Windspear's pace dropped off even further. Dace glanced back and found the man gaining ground on him. Dace had to reach the forest. *The game trail.* If he could make it to the river path and then the game trail, he might have a chance to lose the motherless bastard.

The Denkiefer surrounded him on both sides, and he kept expecting another attacker to exit the forest in front of him. The cold air burned as it rushed in and out of his lungs, and he didn't see the bridge until they were almost on top of it. Windspear's hooves thundered across the wooden planks. He reined her in and guided her to the right. Windspear slid a little in the layer of snow already covering the trail, and for a wild moment, he feared they might fall into the churning waters of the Moeter, but Windspear found her footing, and they bolted down the river path.

Another set of pounding hooves crossed the bridge behind him.

Windspear charged around the curves of the path, each turn bringing with it the terrifying risk of plunging into the river. Dace searched the path ahead. He didn't know when he'd last used the game trail, and he didn't dare miss it. They rounded a blind curve and... There!

Tucked between two massive sentinel pines, a stone cairn marked the head of the path. With the cairn all but buried in the snow, and there was the smallest chance the stranger might not see it for what it was.

While the man rode behind the curve, Dace sent up a prayer to Amma and guided Windspear onto the trail, reaching up and hitting a snow-covered branch as they turned, and a shower of icy flakes burst into the air, rejoining their falling brethren. He hoped it might help to obscure Windspear's tracks. On the trail, snow covered the thick pine branches overhead, forming a canopy that turned midday into twilight. Shadows loomed on either side of the path, and branches tugged at his coat as he rode past. He urged Windspear on, but her breathing had grown labored and a thick lather of sweat covered her flanks.

"Please, girl," he whispered. "Please."

Behind them, branches cracked and another set of hooves thudded across the forest floor. Dace gritted his teeth. His bid to lose the man had failed. He would have to stand and fight.

Dace looked back. The stranger, who gained on him with every passing foot, brandished a long, silver blade in his right hand. Dace couldn't face the man on horseback; a dirk was no match for a true sword, especially when astride a horse unaccustomed to battle. Dismounting gave the stranger yet another advantage, but not if they both dismounted. It was settled, then. Dace's best chance laid in getting them both on the ground.

He pulled back just a little on Windspear's reins, and it was a testament to her fatigue that she didn't fight him in the slightest. Inch by inch, they fell back, while inch by inch, the stranger gained on them. Dace rode Windspear to the far left of the trail, forcing the stranger to approach on the right. If he wanted to swing, he'd have to do so across his body and his horse's neck. Dace cocked his head to the side and unsheathed his dirk. His timing needed to be perfect.

The stallion's head came even with Windspear's rump, and Dace parried the man's first swipe, a hard blow that might have unsaddled Dace had he been caught unawares. Above the muff the stranger wore across his mouth and below the hat pulled far down on his brow, the man's eyes glittered in his wind-burned face like polished onyx.

In that moment Dace vowed he would see his wife and children again, no matter what it took. He yanked hard on Windspear's reins, and the man almost raced right by them, but at the right instant, Dace hurled himself out of the saddle and across the stallion's back, arms wide. He grabbed the stranger, pinning the motherless bastard's arms to his sides and forcing him from his mount. They dropped as one, and together, both men hit the forest floor.

Dace fell on top, but the man's elbow jammed into his stomach as they landed, knocking the wind from him. Dace rolled away from the man and struggled to regain both his breath and his feet. Beside him, the stranger also fought to find his footing.

When Dace managed to stand, he discovered he'd lost his dirk in the fall. He searched the ground, brushing back the undergrowth in wild swaths. His blood rushed through his veins and his pulse pounded at his temples. Where was the blade? Where was the man? Dace spun around. The man still clambered to his feet.

Dace turned again, catching a glint several feet back, along the edge of the trail. He rushed to grab it. His gloved hand closed around the dirk's hilt when the man slammed into his back. The wooden handle slipped between his grasping fingers, and though he was the one moving, a thick pine trunk seemed to barrel toward him, leaving him just enough time to shift so that his left shoulder rammed into the tree instead of his head.

As Dace and the tree made contact, a pain unlike any he had ever known before lanced fire down the whole left side of his body. Still moving, he and the man tumbled to the ground in a heap. For a moment, the pain held Dace in its powerful grip, then his whole body jerked and his thoughts reasserted themselves, warning him to expect the sharp punch of a blade in his neck or back.

But the blade didn't come. Instead, hard fists pounded down on his head, padded almost not at all by the man's gloves. So they had both lost their blades. A small mercy, that.

Lightning bolts of pain sheared down Dace's side as he twisted under the man, who continued to pummel him. Once Dace had turned onto his back, he tried to lift both arms to block the swings, but only the right arm responded. Above him, the man stank of horse and sweat and something else, something darker, and his muff had fallen far enough to reveal his nose.

Dace, furious he might die at the hands of a faceless man, bucked under him and reached out with his working hand to pull away the stranger's muff. The fur came away to reveal a mouth full of rotted teeth and rancid breath foul enough to make Dace gag.

The man's gimlet eyes glittered in the darkness. Taking a couple of direct blows, Dace tore off his glove with his teeth and again sought out the man's face. His thumb found the soft indentation of an eye, and steeling himself, he gouged as hard as he could between the closed lids. With a sudden but gentle release, the surface of the man's eye gave way under Dace's nail, releasing a gush of warm fluid rushed over his hand and down his wrist, into his sleeve.

The man screamed and rolled away.

Dace moved in the opposite direction, spinning over and over until something hard jabbed him. He rolled once more and looked back. The hard thing was a rock, a jagged chunk the size of his fist. He grabbed for it with both hands, and his left arm moved, but the fingers wouldn't close, so he seized the rock with his right hand and tried to lift it from its spot packed tight in the soil.

Not far away, the man, one hand clutched to his ruined eye, crawled in the direction where Dace had last seen the dirk. Dace yanked at the rock, rocking it back and forth, loosening it bit by tiny bit while the man shuffled his hands in wide arcs through the undergrowth. Dace leaned back, gave the rock a sharp kick with his heel, and it burst from the ground in a shower of dirt clods and pine needles. With a dark cry of triumph, the man lifted the blade from the mast and whirled around to find Dace. Dace scrabbled forward and picked up the rock, the weight of it both wrong and right in his hand. He turned, sighted on the man, and hurled the rock with every bit of his remaining strength.

Flying true, the stone crashed into the man's ear and sent him sprawling, and Dace leapt to his feet, closing the distance between them. With one hand, the groaning, half-blinded man clutched the bloody side of his head. Dace grabbed the rock from the ground and fell to his knees beside the stranger. In a flash, the man lashed out with his other hand, which still held the dirk. The sharp blade sliced through Dace's furs and into his side, stuttering against his ribs.

Dace screamed and brought down the stone.

A primal fury forced his arm up and back down, again and again. Each strike punctuated with a wet crunch. On the sixth or seventh blow, the man's head caved in and his legs ceased to twitch, and by the ninth blow, the last of Dace's rage was spent.

He sat back on his heels. He had no idea how long he remained there, staring at the mess, struggling to catch his breath, before a searing rush of vomit rose in his throat. He turned away from the man and was sick.

As he retched, the world beyond the dead man returned, and the vicious throbbing in Dace's shoulder vied for attention with the burning pain in his right side, where a spreading pool of warmth crept down toward his breeches. The man was dead, but Dace was not out of danger yet.

He pried his dirk out of the man's hand and gave his ruined face one last look. There was a mark on his brow. Pushing back the edge of the man's hat, Dace revealed a complicated blue tattoo, the distinctive markings of a Tithen.

His mind reeled. Nothing connected this man to the Vomek tribe. The

Rhyllexie had no use for Tithen or its mercenaries, and Tithens had no reason to venture so far north. The only tie the Vomek tribe had to the Tithen was Dace. The former crown prince, and the family he'd left behind in Ombratos. If a mercenary had been sent to kill Dace, then the long-standing alliance between Ombratos and Tithen was breaking. Or had already broken.

He staggered to a standing position. Twenty or thirty feet down the trail, Windspear's reins were caught in the branches of pine. *To remind you of home.*

He hurried toward the horse in a shambling run. But Ombratos and Tithen were allies, weren't they? He hadn't heard much since Solena's death. He hadn't gone home and something had happened. Windspear's eyes grew wide as he neared and she smelled blood on him. Blood. The Tithen's and his own. In his mind's eye, he once again saw Pekka, an arrow sprouting from his chest like a hellish flower. Something had happened, and perhaps was still happening back at the keep or at Seedfall.

A Morovide's first duty...

He took a few steps, then time stuttered, and he found himself on his knees, clutching Windspear's reins. Get back to the keep, he thought as he climbed to his feet. Though lightheaded and exhausted beyond reasoning, he had to get back.

TWENTY-SIX

"Whether the job be large or small, do it well or not at all."
-Old Tithen saying

Renn lifted a crate of black feathers, sending a cloud of dust up into the hot, musty room. She set the box on a hip-high stack of books and tried to wave the dust away, but only succeeded in stirring up more. It clung to her sweaty skin, and she breathed some of it in, choking.

Putting her hand over her nose and mouth, she coughed as she followed the path between the forgotten towers of crates and books and busts and sculptures and paintings in one of the rooms up on the top floor of the palace where many of her family's antiquities had been stored away and left to languish. As children, she and Parneo had played hide-and-find among them. Now she stumbled through the door out into the hall, where her varo waited.

"Are you well, Your Highness?" Varo Kolson asked. A line of white circled her thin, pursed lips, and her single brow dipped into a point above her upturned nose.

Renn coughed a few more times and sucked in some clean air. "I am." A four-legged wooden stool two hundred years older than either of them stood near the wall. She walked to it and sat, finding it far sturdier than she expected it to be. "Can you think of a single reason why anyone might need a crate full of raven's feathers?"

The point at the center of Kolson's brow deepened. "Is that a riddle?"

"It is to me."

Renn's quip might have earned her a response from Getha, but Kolson just stared at her. Renn shook her head. "I appreciate your concern. It's nothing."

With a sharp bow, Kolson returned to her post beside the door. Renn wished Kolson was Getha, but was also glad she wasn't. Getha's hard demeanor made her difficult to read, and Renn always felt like she needed to be her best self in front of her. Some days Renn welcomed the challenge. Others...

Renn had make a mistake in suggesting they help that family procure a blackmark—an illegal bloodmark—for their daughter, and although Renn and Getha had gone out once more, they'd barely spoken then and hadn't talked at all in the two tendays since.

A warm breeze, as wet and heavy as a lurid breath, blew in through the open window at the end of the short hall, stirring Renn's hair. She pulled the bottom edge of her tunic up to wipe her face, and it came away smudged with sweat and dirt. Leaning against the wall, she gave in to a small measure of her weariness.

Her nightmare about Solena had woken her a half a candlemark before the sunrise. She'd grown used to the nightmares and could often fall asleep again after, but this dream had been different, though it had begun the same.

In the dream, the Binding ceremony had played out as it always did, with the chanting, Solena coming through, her Yentish husband trying to follow, Solena closing the portal, still unable to breathe. But then Solena had, while she knelt in the pool of her own blood, blood that poured from the gaping hole in her chest in an endless rush, somehow managed to bring her palms together to lace her fingers in her and Renn's special signal. She'd looked up at Renn, who always stood where she had on the balcony, and screamed a single word, a word that had chased Renn into wakefulness.

"Run!"

Renn had tried to return to sleep after that, but every time she'd closed her eyes, she'd seen Solena staring up at her and that word—the instruction or warning or whatever it had been—echoed in her ears. She didn't know what to make of the dream or if there was even anything to make of it in the first place. Getha would have an opinion about it because she had opinions about everything, but until they talked again, Renn preferred not to think about it.

So, unable to get back to sleep, she'd decided to go pillaging.

She called her actions "pillaging" because that sounded better than "stealing," but she remained unconvinced it could rightly be called either. The items she took from Seedfall belonged to her family and that meant she had a lawful claim to them. Whether or not the queen might see it that way was a different matter, one Renn wasn't curious to explore, so she chose her items with care, never taking anything of true value, like one of the former queens' Binding blades or something.

Whenever she worried about the queen finding her out, she thought of all the lowborn she'd helped, all the ones still left to help. They were worth the risk. Between her studies and her forays into the Branches, she'd never been so exhausted, but she'd also never felt so useful. She had a purpose, a reason to get up every morning. People counted on her, and that was scary but good. Solena might not have approved of Renn's methods, but she also wouldn't have been able to argue with their outcome.

Footsteps came up the steps and into the hall, so Renn opened her eyes and sat upright. She had a story ready in case anyone came to question her reason for being up there—"I'm just looking for some of Solena's old things"—but she'd yet to need it. It seemed she still didn't. Her maid Editi approached with one of the small silver dishes the servants used to carry letters.

Varo Kolson, hand near her varo blade, watched the servant draw closer, then nodded to her as she passed and relaxed her stance.

Aside from Renn's messages from the Branches and the many letters from Dace, none of which she'd yet to reply to, she seldom received correspondence.

Dallan?

She'd been so consumed by her disagreement with Getha that she hadn't thought about him in a day or two, but now her heart leapt and her excitement banished a measure of her tiredness. Editi knelt at Renn's feet and offered the dish. In its center sat a dirty, water-wrinkled, half-torn fold of paper, but her name and full title, written in Dallan's flowing hand, were just visible under the grime.

She picked up the letter. On the back, a mere sliver of the seal—a shard of dull, blue-green wax—remained, not enough to keep the note closed. "This was open when it arrived?" she asked.

Editi nodded. "Yes, Your Highness. The runner swore over and over in Amma's name that it was already open when it came to him."

Renn held the folded letter flat between her palms, unsure why she was so hesitant to read its contents.

"If I may, Your Highness," Editi said, "shall I fill a cool bath for you?"

"Thank you," Renn said. "That sounds wonderful. Please do so, and I'll be down in a short bit." She stood, as did Editi, who bowed and left.

Renn took the letter into the stifling, windowless storage room and closed the door behind her. Then she sat on the floor against the wall, right under a globe, and unfolded the page. Sand, finer than that found on the shores near Ombratos, fell from the letter into her lap, and she brushed it away.

The salutation read *My dearest Renn*, and at the bottom, in place of a signature, a collection of straight lines had been piled together like a nest made of sticks. An old Tithen rune. She remembered the first time she saw it, drawn in the dirt outside of the stables while she, Dallan, and some others waited for their horses to be saddled, and tears burned her eyes.

My dearest Renn,

It has been long, too long, since our last embrace. Your flowering charm reminds me of your love, but I ache to hold you, to kiss you, to move inside you once more...

The letter continued on like that, bringing gooseflesh and a hot flush to her already warm skin, his intimate words being the sort that would serve her well on her more lonely nights. She devoured the letter and planned to read it over again before she went to her bath, but then she reached the end, and the final paragraph pulled her up short.

I have found my way back. Someone told me recently that love forgives much, and I hope with all my heart she is right. Please hold your love for me close, and never doubt that everything I do, I do for us. For you.

She read those lines five more times, but they remained as obscure the fifth time as they had the first. What could he possibly hope to do that might require her forgiveness? Perhaps he just worried their distance and the moons they'd spent apart had changed things between them.

Had it? Before everything with the amulet and her trips into the city, she would have leapt for joy to read *I have found my way back*, but now thoughts of how her life would change when Dallan returned plagued her. What would happen to her work with the lowborn? Would he approve of her secrets forays out and about, or would they worry him too much? If they did, how much would she, or should she, care?

Intending to write back yet unsure what to say, she climbed to her feet. A drop of sweat rolled down her brow and into her eye, and she decided she could think better in a cool bath. Rubbing the sting of sweat away, she started for the door.

Outside the palace guard barracks, Getha stretched, her muscles tight and her eyes gritty. Four candlemarks of sleep just wasn't enough, especially after the night she'd had. She clasped her hands above her head, reaching toward the cloudless sky. The heat and thickness in the air already promised a hot, heavy afternoon, but she wasn't on duty, so when the warmest part of the day arrived, she planned to find a shady corner and sleep right through it.

She lowered her arms, and a yawn stole over her just as Guards Hoefen and Lorri came trudging around the side of the building. Coming from the last shift, they wore their full uniforms, and when Hoefen noticed Getha, he nudged Lorri in the side with his elbow.

"Dear me. Is the messera looking a bit tired to you?"

Lorri pressed her hands to her round cheeks in mock dismay. "This cannot be! Shall we carry you to your bed, messera?"

At Princess Renn's behest, to keep her and Getha out of the city at night, Palace Guard Leader Selm had put Getha on the afternoon and evening shifts, and that had led to a new nickname—"messera." The title annoyed her, but she preferred it to "forsaken," so she let it stand.

Besides, their words meant nothing to her. They had no clue that in addition to training and executing her guard duties she spent her off-duty candlemarks performing the role of a varo, if not in name, then at least in deed. The likes of Hoefen and Lorri thought Getha stood on the same rung of the ladder as them, unaware she now climbed high above them.

She showed the other guards her back, tied her hair into a tail at her nape with a leather thong, and set off in a slow run toward the palace gates. Her boots tended to slip on the crushed-shell paths, so she kept to the grass. When she reached the gate, sweat already slicked her face and back, but she'd found her rhythm. She ran in place while Guard Milo opened the postern gate, and slipped by him the instant the door cracked wide enough for her to pass.

Out in the Bole, none of the highborn woke so early, but the streets bustled with servants arriving at their posts or merchants making their deliveries. The lowborn could wait until midday for their eggs or their milk, but a highborn expected them to appear before he or she rose for the day.

Most days Getha tried to measure her steps, to keep a steady pace when running down the hill, but a giddy urge, no doubt born from a lack of sleep, took over and she let the incline pull her into a mad dash. The Transformation Gate, open for the day, beckoned her like a line marking the end of a race, and she flew through it.

"You!" a woman's voice called out behind her.

Getha slowed to a stop and turned. A vaguely familiar city guardswoman old enough to be her greatmother rushed toward her. She put her hands on her knees and tried to regain her breath.

"Hain't your mother never taught you any respect?" The woman's flushed face sat atop her sloped shoulders like an overripe tomato. "You about stopped my heart bursting through the gate like that."

Getha held her hands up, palms out, in apology. She hadn't done anything wrong, but she also didn't need to start a fight with the woman.

"Bah!" The woman flapped her hands at Getha as if driving away a flock of sea birds. "Off with you, then." She shuffled back to her post and her partner, a skinny little chit with no more than the sixteen years required to enter the guard in the first place. "Amma-lost palace guards..."

The boy waved to Getha. She nodded and continued on. On the Meet, several merchants stood outside their tents or beside their wagons selling their services or wares, and Ombratians going about their day walked in the large spaces between them. There were rules for who was allowed to sell in the Meet when and where, but Getha had forgotten them the moment she was admitted into the palace guard.

Starting next to the Table, she ran an even-paced lap of the Meet, slowing once for a parade of twenty-odd grey-clad ductoran headed toward the Commons, and again for a fool trying to coax his ancient cow over the steepest bridge in the city. Her lap ended where it began, and she stepped into the long shadow the Table cast across the Meet.

Anyone looking at her might think she'd stopped there to cool down, but they would see only part of the truth. Stretching her arms, she reached up under the edge of the Table, anticipating, hoping for splintered wood but finding the crispness of new paper.

Getha's stomach dropped. Her and the princess's last trip out, the only one since their argument about the blackmark, had been seventeen shades of awkward, and she and Princess Renn hadn't spoken since. She tucked the folded note against her palm, then leaned on the Table's leg, stretched, and slipped the paper into her purse. She wondered about the contents of the note—*Was it another plea for a blackmark? Something worse?*—but it wasn't hers to open, so she left it alone.

Whenever she found a message, on the slight chance someone watched her take it, she ran elsewhere and pretended to drop the note there before returning to the palace. Today she headed into the Acorn, and far ahead, the North Gate called to her. Or less the gate and more what lay beyond it. Since no one expected her anywhere, she could slip out into Shade's Rest and be back in no time.

But a block away from the North Gate, she veered from it and back into the Acorn, ignoring the twinge in her chest. She'd kept her promise to herself and still hadn't returned to Jos's. She wanted to—oh, how she wanted to—but that was exactly why she couldn't.

She stopped at a well, drank several ladles of the icy water, then poured one over her head. The next she held to the giant purple-red bruise on her arm she'd earned in a sparring match the day before. If she fought hard enough and long enough, at some point she was bound to work Jos from her system. She had to.

Forcing thoughts of him from her mind, she resumed her run and turned to the larger, more pressing problem in her life—her arrangement with the princess. Getha passed from the Acorn into the Verdure and from the Verdure into the Chestnut. Part of her wanted to keep helping Princess Renn, but as Waltham had taught her, there was a point at which risk outweighed reward.

She stopped again in an alley beside a draper's shop. Kneeling in the darkest corner, she left a broken feather taken from the ground outside the fletcher's. The feather held no meaning; it just served as a potential distraction for anyone who might be watching.

The princess had listened to Getha about the blackmark, but what if she didn't listen next time? Princess Renn had also promised to take responsibility for anything that happened while they were together, but the queen and Princess Linore thought little of her, so what if she didn't have the sway she assumed?

On the other hand, Princess Renn had done much good for the lowborn, and Getha swelled with pride knowing the small part she had helped play in those deeds. But was that pride blinding her? So many problems and so few answers. Had Getha spoken to Waltham, he might have been able to help her, yet talking to him meant involving him, and she still refused to do that.

Frustrated, she stood, brushed off her hands, and walked out the alley. The heat continued to rise, and she longed for the respite of her shaded nap. Taking to the street and turning toward home, she readied herself to run back up the hill.

HELENIA SAT on the edge of her sagging rope bed and waited. *Two, one, two, two, three. Two, one, two, two, three.* Bright sunlight shone through the cracks in the shutters and around the flimsy door. The heat in the small room had been rising since dawn, but she didn't stand to open the window, nor did she wish to open her door. The room was just large enough for a bed, a bedside table, and the satchel resting at her feet. On the bedside table, a single candle added to the warmth and cast shadows into every corner of the room. The stink of fish, the rot of the ocean, had long since wormed its way into every scrap of wood, every stitch of fabric. In the storehouse below, dock workers shouted to one another.

She smoothed her sweating hands down the legs of her black trousers and ran her fingers under the tight brim of her woolen cap.

Less than a day, Carhal, she promised her dead husband. *Less than a day.* Less than a day left of the dark clothing, the lowborn trousers. Less than a day of hiding her hair and tattoos under a hood or a hat. Less than a day until Dallan...

Let it harden you.

Despite her hatred for Mayve, Helenia kept that bit of advice foremost in her mind. She would bear the burden of Dallan's death for a while, perhaps the rest of her life, but it was the only thing that could set the balance to rights.

She also worried about Orli in the wake of Princess Renn's death, hence the further need for Talp's fighters. Timing was crucial. She wouldn't tell Orli about Renn until after he and his varos had pushed back the Tithen mercenaries. Then, if Orli chose to turn against Helenia, he and his varos might be weary enough that Talp's people could fight them back.

She disliked that she'd never received a drawing of Talp like the one of Orli, the one where he worshipped at her feet and eschewed the attention of his queen, but she'd waited and waited, and had hit the point where she couldn't wait any longer. After all, the first drawing had simply served as confirmation, and she didn't need another one to tell her what she already knew in her heart. She no longer trusted Mayve, but she trusted in Mayve's arrogance, in Orli's subservience, in Talp's greed. She trusted that Carhal, her father, and Burk watched over her, and most of all, she trusted herself.

A thousand things might go wrong and send her plans off in another direction, but all she could do was take each moment as it came. By the next morning, the die would be cast.

Helenia hadn't slept well since sending Mayve word to set the ball rolling. A constant worry that someone might discover her plans in this final stage kept the wheels in her mind turning, and even now, she feared that members of the city watch or the palace guard might be on their way to arrest her for treason. Her heartbeat almost stopped when heavy footfalls landed on the staircase leading up to her room, shaking her floor.

Two, one, two, two, three. That was the secret knock she awaited. Though her knees shook, she leapt to her feet. She would not be taken sitting. The steps stopped on the landing, and the brief silence that followed seemed large enough to fill the sea.

Knock, knock. The pause after those first two brought a small measure of relief, but she held her breath and counted the sequence just in case it was a polite guard who did wait for permission to enter the home of a traitor or a stranger at the wrong door.

Helenia waited for the rest of the pattern. *Knock... knock, knock...knock, knock... knock, knock, knock.*

"Come in," she said, proud that she kept her voice from shaking.

The latch lifted; the door swung inward. A rush of fresh air entered the room, quenching the candle, and she squinted in the sunlight. Just as Mayve had promised, a Xantish sailor—a short, leather-skinned bald man with silvery irises and a hooked nose—stood before her. If he stood before her here, then Mayve's other promises would come to fruition elsewhere. A pity Prince Dace had to die so far from home.

The silver-eyed sailor looked Helenia up and down. This was the first and last day she and this man would spend in each another's company. "Early yet, no?" he asked in his musical accent. "Am thought I be one waking you."

She ignored his broken chatter. "Has the boat arrived?"

"In harbor, no? Less than five hundred feet gone." He frowned. "No, not gone. Away."

Practice your Norrish on someone else. Lifting her satchel from the floor onto her shoulder, she said, "Then let's go."

The sailor clomped down the stairs, and she stepped out onto the landing. Without a single backward glance at the place where she'd lived for the past two moons, she closed the door to the tiny room behind her.

That done, she took a moment to stare out at the calm vastness of the sea. She neared the pinnacle; for her, total success and utter failure were the only possible outcomes. When next she laid her head down, it would be between silk sheets or on the dank stone floor of a prisoner's cell. In which case, she'd kill herself. She'd rather chew through her own wrists and join her Carhal on the other side than be locked up again.

A sense of relief, of setting down a burden, slipped over her. With all the wheels in motion, the events of the day rested in Burk's hands. She traced the sign of the Ever-Watchful Eye on her brow and walked down the steps, glad to be descending the rickety staircase for the last time.

To the north, large ships bobbed against the piers, their masts and riggings rising and dipping with the waves. On shore, people scurried between stacks of crates and ivory hills of talc. Down near her end of the docks, much smaller ships bobbed hull-by-hull along the narrow wooden pathways jutting from the pebbled beach.

The sailor waited for her at the bottom. When she joined him, he took the satchel from her shoulder and led her toward the open gates and then to the end of the docks and across the beach toward the narrower pathways. She walked with her head down so that the brim of her hat hid her face.

An urgent whisper cut through her thoughts. "Helenia!"

The peace brought on by her relief shattered. She whirled around, anxious to discover who called her name. From behind a massive boulder fringed with leafy, red-purple moss, a figure in a dark cloak beckoned to her.

Orli.

An image of him clapping her into irons surfaced in her mind, but his skulking didn't suggest a man about to arrest someone. Ahead of her, the sailor had stopped halfway up the ramp to the docks, and he stood there, again waiting for her. She gestured for him to wait a moment more, then she joined Orli by the rock.

She understood the reason for his mad visit the instant he moved close enough for her to see the sweat pouring down his brow and the way his gaze darted about. He teetered on the edge of losing his nerve. Without hesitation, she reached into his cloak and took his clammy hands in hers. The stink of his fear sweat enveloped her. She smiled, peered up at him from beneath the brim of her cap, and affected the lightest tone possible. "You came to see me off? How bold."

"I don't..." he said, his voice thick, his breaths coming in short gasps. "I don't think I can..." His darting gaze settled on her face. "Forgive me. I don't think..."

She released one of his hands and laid a finger over his lips. "Shh, darling. Shh. Slow down."

He took a couple of deep breaths through his nose and that seemed to relax him a bit. After a few more breaths, he nodded, and she removed her finger.

"Now speak."

"I don't know what to do."

"Return to Seedfall and wait for sundown." She touched his cheek, but he jerked away from her.

"Don't you worry even the slightest bit that what we're doing is wrong?"

Though Orli was a pebble and he hadn't Carhal's skill in hearing truths, he wasn't a fool. His devotion depended on hers, and she needed to say something genuine to him or all would be lost. "I do worry, Luca. But you and I have both seen how this city has started to crumble under Theodora's reign. The complacency of the Morovides mustn't be allowed to destroy this great nation."

He thought for a moment. Then a crease formed between his brows. "Luca?"

"Short for Lucador." The nickname had been a whim. Had she over-played her hand? "Do you mind?"

Tightness in his jaw and the lines of worry around his eyes eased. "Not at all."

She touched his cheek again, and he let her.

"I love you, Helenia. If anything goes wrong tonight, I want you to know that."

An easy enough sentiment to return—they were only words, after all—but that lie wouldn't come, so she grabbed the back of his neck and kissed him as if her life depended on it, not pulling away until they'd both grown breathless. When she at last broke their kiss, every vestige of his anxiety seemed to have fled. He reached up with steady hands and resettled her hat, which had come askew in their embrace. Then he tucked a strand of hair behind her ear and straightened her collar.

Helenia, surprised by the sudden change in him, let him fiddle with her clothing. *Was his nervousness an act all along? Was it a test? If so, did I pass or fail?*

Orli finished and lifted his hood back up, casting his face into shadow. "Safe travels, my darling. I hope to see you again before the dawn." He walked away, and she watched him go.

He had wished her well, called her "my darling," both good signs, right? But what if they weren't? What if this facet of Orli revealed something hidden outside a certain slant of light? *What if he plays a game as long and twisted as my own?*

An intriguing thought, but one with a stronger foundation in her suspicions than in the real world. She swept the clutter of her emotions through a door in her mind and closed it. She had Talp for her protection, and she could puzzle over Orli another day. If he survived, then she'd make the effort to sort it out. For now, he would do as he'd promised.

She rejoined the waiting sailor and waved him on, following him to the very end of the pier, to a single-masted longboat. Less than a dozen other sailors scuttled over the boat's deck, hauling and hoisting as their captain bade them. The Xantish vessel would take her past the breakers, to the point where a Tithen boat waited. That Tithen boat would then take her even farther out, to the fleet of Tithen ships that waited just beyond the horizon.

Wind wives, dozens of them, also waited. Helenia did not doubt that more than one of them would give their lives driving the Tithen fleet to shore, and she took comfort in the knowledge she had done all she could to ensure those lives might not be wasted.

Her sailor jumped from the dock to the boat as it rocked near, with practiced ease. He set down her satchel and offered her a hand to help her step off the steady pier onto the boat. Another risk. What if these Xantish planned to take her prisoner and make her a slave?

Take each moment as it comes.

With resolve and the vague notion she might hurl herself into the water if anyone tried anything, she reached out to take the sailor's hand and stepped onto the deck. No one yanked her arm behind her or held a blade to her throat or looked otherwise intent on harming her. The sailors just ran around, following the foreign orders of their captain while she stood off to the side, and as they moved out to sea, Helenia walked to the aft rail.

Ombratos stood safe and secure behind its wall. People across Althea referred to Ombratos as "The Nut," implying that it couldn't be cracked. She hoped it was as defensible as they said. Because once Mayve learned what had happened to her son, she would come with an army. Helenia wanted to keep her city, but the thing she hungered for even more than that was to see the anguish on Mayve's face.

After that, who cared if the whole world burned?

TWENTY-SEVEN

*"The two faces of Balance, Creation and Destruction, suffer from the same
ruinous flaw. Just as one cannot make something from nothing, once a thing is
made, it can never entirely be unmade."*
-page separated from private journal, author unknown

Getha's wet hair dripped the cool waters of the Sap down her back,
a small relief from the oppressive heat. She drank a few cupped
palmfuls of water and then splashed one over her face.

She had returned to the palace slicked from top to toe in sweat. After
passing the note she'd collected at the Table to a gardening apprentice—
who would in turn pass it to a kitchen girl, who would pass it to a foot
servant, who would pass it to the princess's maid, a chain that had yet to
break—she'd returned to her barracks to grab clean clothing, then on to the
bathing trough. Though the water in the trough was changed daily, it stood
in a sunny clearing, and the temperature had already risen from cool to
tepid, so she had gone instead to dip her head in the Sap.

As she knelt on the bank now, the rush from her run and the icy waters
left her all at once, making her even more tired than she had been before
she left, but the weariness from her run had a well-earned quality to it. She
picked up her vambraces, put them on, and stood. A shaded clearing in the
northern part of the woods called her name. A fallen tree rested in the

clearing, and she couldn't wait to prop her back against it and close her eyes.

She intended to stop by her barracks to grab an old tunic to wad up for a pillow, but not fifteen feet from the Sap, she passed an old elm, and Waltham, who must have been waiting for her, came out from behind it.

Shit.

She didn't stop, but she did slow, and he fell into step beside her. "Why have you been avoiding me?"

"I haven't been..." *No lies.* "I've been busy." She picked up her pace. "We'll talk later."

Waltham fell back, but then a hand closed around her arm. He pulled her up short and whipped her around. "We'll talk now."

Her concern for herself faded as she stared down at him. They'd spoken a few days ago, but he seemed suddenly smaller, frailer, more bowed, and his bones pressed against his ashen skin as if they might jut through. The wrinkles in his face had deepened, dark marks like bruises circled his eyes, and his fine white hair stuck out in all directions. It was as if all of his years, the ones he had been holding back for so long with his stubborn vigor, had piled on him at once.

"Amma's name, Waltham. What in the pathless hells have you been doing? You look like twice-trampled horse shit."

He yanked on her arm. "When were you going to tell me that you've been helping a member of the royal family fence goods stolen from the palace?"

Her mouth fell open.

"No answer? Then I suppose I'll have to go by your expression and assume never."

"How did you—"

"How did I find out?" Though he appeared frail, his anger seemed to lend him strength. "When you came back this morning, I followed you. Then I followed that damned note all the way back to the princess. People have noticed how often she visits the stores these days and how seldom you're on the palace grounds. From there, I just had to fit the pieces together."

So he didn't know everything. He didn't know about the amulet or that Getha and Princess Renn had been sneaking out together. But he'd put together quite a bit.

"And if I know"—he pointed up at the palace—"then it's only a matter of time before someone else figures it out too."

"No one else knows." She and the princess hadn't spoken in days, but the princess would warn her if they were about to get caught.

Waltham sighed. "Damn it, Getha. This is the life I was hoping to keep you from."

The disappointment in his voice pierced her heart like a dagger. "I hain't skimmin'!" Just like that, she was back in the Shade's Rest guard, a girl of fifteen charged with taking bribes from tofters to keep them out of prison. She had thought that version of herself long gone, but it turned out she was just buried, and in that moment, Getha hated Waltham for unearthing her.

She jabbed a finger in his bony chest. "Go twist yourself, you motherless bastard. We're using that coin for a good cause."

"Oh, for Amma's sake." He gritted his teeth and shook her. "*You* are a good cause. What you're doing with the princess? *That* is a childish game that will end badly."

She wanted nothing more than to walk away, but her feet refused to move.

His tone softened. "What's going to happen if you're caught?"

"We won't be."

"But if you are?"

"The princess said she'll protect me." The promise sounded silly when Getha said it aloud, but she would be damned to the pathless hells before she admitted it.

He grabbed her arms tighter than he should have been able to, his fingertips digging into her skin. "How? You and I both know she holds no sway over her mother or anyone else at court. If you're caught, the princess will be locked up in the palace or sent away to marry some foreign noble." He pulled her in until they were almost nose-to-nose. "You will be hanged."

His words bore a dreadful certainty. Even in the blistering heat, a chill ran through her, raising bumps along her bare arms, and a full confession burbled up in her throat.

"Barei!"

The shout came from behind her, sounding very much like Lead Varo Orli. Waltham let her go, and she turned, relieved to find Varo Maurius instead. Dressed in his fighting leathers, he rushed toward her.

"Don't—" That was all Waltham got out before Maurius descended upon them.

Sweat-darkened strands of ginger hair clung to Maurius's neck and face. "Why aren't you at the practice yards, Barei?"

An odd question, especially coming from a man who wasn't her direct superior. "This is my rest day."

He shook his head. "That doesn't matter. Every palace guard who isn't on duty must report to the yards for training."

Waltham stepped up beside her. "By whose order?"

"Lead Varo Orli."

Maurius examined her clothing. "Hasten to your barracks and change. He expected everyone there more than a quarter of a candlemark past."

Waltham turned her to face him. "We aren't done speaking of this. Come to my office the moment you're done." The urgency with which he spoke sent another shiver through her. "The very moment."

"I will," she said. "I swear it."

"Stop dallying, Barei." Maurius gestured for her to precede him back toward the barracks.

Waltham nodded to her, but his attempt at a comforting smile—upturned lips pressed into a hard line beneath worried eyes—was anything but.

Unsure of what else to do, she walked away, and Maurius fell in behind her.

Renn, wearing a thin dressing gown, her wet curls piled high on her head, sat at her desk and reread Dallan's letter for the hundredth time. When she reached the end, she set the page down and traced over his name rune with her finger. Another piece of paper sat next to his letter on the desk. Her response.

My love,

Dallan, I don't

She hadn't made it any further. She had so much to say, so many questions about him and their future, but she didn't have any idea where to start. A knock came at the door, and Renn, glad for the distraction, bade the knocker enter.

Editi came in, once again carrying the silver message platter. It would be foolish to think it another letter from Dallan, but Renn feared and hoped for it anyway. Editi brought the tray forward, knelt, and held it out. "Another one, Your Highness."

A barefaced letter sat on the tray—a letter for Alyse. Her confusion over

Dallan and the rift between her and Getha tempered the usual rush of excitement that came with the letters asking for assistance.

Editi smiled as she waited for Renn to take the message. At least her good humor hadn't been dimmed.

"I bet you were happy to see this," Renn said.

Editi's cheeks darkened. "Mayhaps."

Renn had chosen Editi to take the letters from the foot servant Getha picked out for a couple of reasons. Editi wasn't the sort to ask questions, but even if she had been, Renn might still have chosen her. She'd noticed the maid and the foot servant making eyes at each another on more than one occasion, and she liked the idea of playing some part in bringing them together.

From the dreamy cast of Editi's smile, Renn's meddling was having the desired effect. She envied Editi her simple flirtation, and taking the message, she sent her maid from the room. Once alone, Renn cracked the plain seal and unfolded the stiff paper, expecting the letter to be written in the even, steady hand of a scribe. An alarming number of lowborn couldn't read or write, and scribes penned most of the notes she'd received.

But someone had scrawled the words in a sloppy hand, with careless drops of ink scattered over the page, as if the person writing the note had been rushed or upset when they wrote it.

This is both a plea and a warning. There are people in this city who think you are not who you claim to be. These same people seem to believe that I know who you truly are, even though I do not. I did not want to involve you in this, but they told me that if I do not tell them what they wish to know by tomorrow, then they will hurt him.

Please help me. My messero is everything, and I cannot bear the thought of living without him.

Renn's heart thudded hard. Though no one had signed the letter, the clue in the final line—*My messero is everything*—identified the sender. Not only did someone suspect Renn's secret, that person was willing to hurt Guissand Serrimandier in order to confirm her or his suspicions. Renn had to find Getha. They had to go and help...

Renn realized she'd never learned Guissand's Tithen lover's name. Everyone at court referred to her as "the Tithen" or, among The Spares, as "that ink-faced sellsword."

Well, surely someone knew her name; if not a highborn, then someone out in the Branches. Renn tucked the note into her purse, then reached for the drawer on her desk that held her amulet. She knocked against the open bottle of ink, and it toppled over, spilling across Dallan's message and her attempt at a reply. She attempted to save Dallan's letter by lifting it from the spill, but only succeeded in dripping ink onto her bare feet and the floor. The thick linen paper had soaked up the spill in an instant, anyway, his words already lost.

She hated to see his profession of love obscured, but at the moment she had more pressing matters to worry over than the loss of Dallan's letter or his possible return to Ombratos. Dropping the soggy page back onto the desk, she stood, grabbed her Transformation amulet from its drawer, and hurried to dress.

GETHA EXITED THE BARRACKS, adjusting her leathers as she descended the short staircase outside the door. She looked up to find Princess Renn coming toward her. With Waltham's censures still echoing in Getha's mind, she had hoped for a day or two to think before crossing paths with the princess again.

"Thank Amma," the princess said as she neared. "I was hoping I'd find you here." In one hand she held the bag containing her amulet, in the other the note Getha had taken from the Table.

In the midst of all else, Getha had forgotten about the note. Not looking forward to being trained by Orli but grateful for the excuse, Getha bowed. "If you'll pardon me, Your Highness, I've been instructed to report to the practice yards."

The princess seemed surprised. "This is far more important that anything happening in the practice yards."

What you're doing with the princess, that *is a childish game that can only end badly.*

Studying the intensity in the princess's face, Getha knew she was going to have to be the one to bring an end to their game. "We need to talk before we go back out. I—"

As if to drive home Waltham's warnings, Princess Renn stamped her foot in her spoiled highborn way, and Getha felt even more foolish for getting caught up in her silliness.

"We will, but we can't right now," the princess said. "That's what I'm trying to tell you. The note—"

"Please. I must report to the varo practice yards."

Hurt and confusion marred the princess's fine features. "Is this about the"—she lowered her voice—"blackmark?"

"No." At least, not in the way the princess thought it was. Getha took a deep breath. She might as well end things now. "I don't think I can help you anymore."

Princess Renn stiffened. "Why not?"

"Because what we're doing is pointless." The cruel lie sickened Getha, but things would be easier for both of them in the long run if she broke their alliance and discouraged the princess from forging a new one with anyone else in a single blow. "You should go back to riding and leave helping the lowborn up to someone who can do more than hang healing charms on one tiny problem at a time."

The princess's lower lip quivered, but she raised her chin and her expression grew cold. "I see. Go, then."

Getha stood there. After all they'd been through together, after all they'd done, she wanted to say something more, but if she said anything kind—

"You are dismissed, Guard Barei."

The stubborn tilt of the princess's jaw concerned Getha, but she had been formally dismissed, so she straightened her back, saluted, turned sharply on her heel, and marched off toward the practice yards.

She didn't look back. She couldn't.

RENN HAD ALREADY SHIFTED into Alyse and was lacing up her boots in the back room of Parneo's study when she heard the door to the row open.

"Renn?" Parneo called.

"It's me." She waited until she heard the front door close and then opened the door between the rooms. "I was changing."

Parneo had a large bag slung over one shoulder. He took it off and stowed it under his worktable. "Why are you here so early?"

She knew her twin well enough to know he hid something in that bag, but she hadn't the time to press him. Besides, he would show her eventually. He always did. In response to his question, she pulled the note out of her purse and handed it to him.

He unfolded the page and read it.

334

"Do you know the Tithen's name?" she asked, when he flipped it over to check for more writing on the back.

"It doesn't matter," he said. "This is a trap."

"A trap?"

The thought hadn't occurred to her, though it probably would have to Getha. Her harsh words rang in Renn's ears. *Forget her.* Unable to remain still, Renn paced back and forth across the small room. Besides, the idea of a trap seemed absurd. What possible reason could Serrimandier have to trap her? Then again, what about the Tithen? But Renn couldn't think of any reason why the mercenary might want to hurt her, either, unless the mercenary had become embroiled in some sort of trouble related to Renn and Serrimandier's dealings. That still put Serrimandier in danger.

Renn stopped and turned to Parn. "I can't bear the thought of anyone being hurt for my sake."

He raised an eyebrow. "Where's your guard friend?"

She caught his implication and snatched the note from his hand. "No one forced Getha to join the guard, and no one forced her to help me." Thinking of the way Getha had treated her, how callously Getha had dismissed her, she refolded the page and stuffed it back into her purse. "It doesn't matter. I'm going." She walked into the back room, grabbed a stool, and propped it up under the window.

"Wait."

"What?" she barked, impatient to leave.

In the front room, it sounded like Parneo dug through a wooden box filled with stones. "Here." He came through the door holding a thin needle and a stone the pink-orange color of the sky at sunset and no larger than a pea. He set it down on the worktable in front of her.

"What is that for?" she asked.

Instead of answering, he reached out and grabbed her left hand, turning it palm up. Fast as a snake, he stuck the needle into the middle of her blood-mark, and she cried out, though more from surprise than actual pain.

A single drop of blood welled up from the wound. Still holding her hand, he put down the needle and picked up the stone. He smeared it through the small pool of blood in her palm, and then he told her a short incantation. She repeated the words, and the crimson soaked into the stone quicker than ink being sucked up by a linen page.

He grabbed the stone and closed his eyes. After a moment, he smiled and opened them. "Good."

"Good what?" She closed her eyes, but all she saw was darkness. "What's supposed to happen?"

"Think of yourself," he said, setting the stone back in her hand.

It was the last thing she wished to think of, but the sooner she followed his orders the sooner she could leave. The darkness persisted for another moment before—as if she had opened her eyes, even though she hadn't—a vivid image of Parneo and the room in front of her replaced the darkness. She turned her head back and forth, and the image swept back and forth. Her wonder cut through her anger and nervousness. She opened her eyes, and for the briefest moment, saw two versions of the same room, one laid right on top of the other—Parneo's perspective and her own.

"There," he said. "Now you can be found." He plucked the stone out of her hand, slipped it into his pocket, then looked away from her to fuss over his already well-ordered desk. "If you don't return by sundown, I'm sending someone after you." He meant Getha, and Renn knew, despite what Getha had said, that if she got into real trouble, Getha would come.

The stone and the threat were the closest Parneo had come to an open display of affection in years. Renn crossed the room and, even though he tried to duck away, she planted a kiss on his cheek. "I love you too, dear brother."

He wiped at the spot where she'd kissed and hurried back into the front room, and she let him go. Climbing up on the stool in front of the window, she threw open the shutters.

Twenty-Eight

"If one ne'er learns to fly, then one must learn to fall."
-Favored saying of Phineas Talp

The Xantish sailors didn't take Helenia prisoner. As promised, they sailed over the horizon, beyond the view of those who patrolled the wall along the docks, and delivered her to *The Searcher*, one of three Tithen ships anchored in an area called the Shallows, a place most sailors dared not sail due to the rumors of the ships that had gone missing there.

Once Helenia was aboard, a man about her age, with a sun-bleached cap of hair and a close-trimmed beard, approached her. "I'm Captain Fintan, and I welcome you aboard."

The sour expression only partly hidden by his beard belied that statement. He didn't care to have her or a full company of mercenaries on his ship, but as long as he did as she asked, he could pout all he liked.

"Well met, Captain Fintan," Helenia said, then she excused herself. She needed to review the day's plan with him, but she had something more pressing to attend to first.

She went down in the ship's hold with her bag and changed into her whites. The power and control she felt while donning them seemed akin to how a soldier might feel when putting on her armor. Stepping back out onto the deck, the sun kissed her face and a brisk wind snapped her skirts out like a sail. This was a day meant for battle, a day meant for victory.

A day meant for justice.

Movement on the deck of the *Bountiful Morn* caught her eye, and she turned to find Dallan waving at her. She waved back to her nephew, grateful for the distance between them, then walked to the other side of the ship, putting him out of her sight and out of her mind.

And so began the long wait for sundown.

GETHA DIDN'T THINK she'd ever been so tired in her entire life. Maurius prowled between the rows of exhausted palace guards in the practice yard. Lead Varo Orli had spent the morning forcing them through an endless repetition of fighting positions, but he had disappeared after their too-short midday break and left his second-in-command in charge of their continued torture.

Getha had hoped Marius might go a bit easier on them, but he seemed to have turned into Orli in his absence.

"Again!" Maurius barked. Had she her eyes closed when he'd said it, she wouldn't have known if it was him or the lead varo.

In the back row, Getha crouched, put her palms on the hot dirt, kicked her feet back, lowered her chest and stomach to the ground, pushed her body up, pulled her feet forward, and stood. Her head swam, and her mouth felt lined with wool.

Maurius moved into the row in front of her. "Again!"

She crouched and jumped through the same sequence of movements. Every muscle in her body burned. Next to her, Tumolo grunted with every change in position. He barely regained his feet before Maurius said, "Again!"

He ran them through the sequence over and over. Just as he started down her row, someone up near the front collapsed.

Maurius sighed. "Take a few moments and drink some water, but *do not* leave."

Getha followed Tumolo over to one of the water buckets set around the edges of the yard. He shuffled along, kicking up dirt, and she might have complained, except she couldn't do much better.

When Tumolo reached the bucket, Zeppen handed him the ladle. "It's warm."

Tumolo took it. "Wonderful." He sagged against the fence. "Do you think we're dead?"

Zeppen raised an eyebrow at him. "Your brain sun-cooked?"

"Probably." Tumolo scooped up some water and drank. "But maybe we're dead and we all went to the pathless hells. Mayhaps this is it." Turning, he handed the ladle to Getha. "What do you think, Barei?"

Those were the most civil words he had said to her in moons. What was it about shared suffering that brought out the good fellowship in people? She dipped the ladle into the bucket for herself. "That mean we're trapped here for eternity?"

Zeppen, who had never before even spoken to Getha, stretched her arms up over her head and winced. "For the love of Amma, I hope not."

Maurius clapped his hands. "Back to it!"

Getha groaned along with the others.

Renn walked through the Mire down the shaded side of the street, though the shade did little to combat the pressing heat of the afternoon. As an added bonus, the warmth brought out the many putrid fragrances of the neighborhood, so she did her best not to breathe through her nose. She passed few people—a couple of dock laborers, some merchants who sat outside their shop doors or stood next to their carts—and none of them looked any happier than she did to be out and about.

Not knowing who she could trust and who she couldn't, she'd spent the morning trying to track down Guissand Serrimandier's Tithen directly. First she'd asked around at the palace, and though all of the servants she spoke to had heard about the messero's defection, none knew the Tithen's name. Next she'd gone to the Serrimandier's hearth—one of the largest and stateliest of the homes in the Bole, as Guissand's ancestor had been one of the first queen's closest advisors—but the servants there were very tight-lipped about their former messero.

Renn considered shifting back to her true face in order to speak to someone from Guissand's family, but it would take a while to ease around to the subject of their wayward child without arousing suspicion, and bringing him up at all might reopen wounds that had taken years to heal. Uncertain her efforts would yield the information she sought, she hadn't bothered them.

Nearing midday and having failed with the direct approach, Renn went to The Lost Waif, to the bearded barkeep who had put her in contact with Guissand the Buyer in the first place. To her irritation, the pretty-eyed bargroom was working, which meant she'd had to shout at him in order to have a few moments alone with the barkeep. Even after all that, he hadn't known the Tithen's name or where she and Serrimandier lived. But he said he knew someone who might, and he'd sent her across the city to a cheese-monger's shop in the Blossom.

As it turned out, the Tithen's name and the place where she lived were two of the most closely guarded secrets in the whole of Ombratos. The ignorant cheesemonger had pointed Renn toward a milliner in the Chest-nut, who had pointed her at an ostler who worked at a merchant's home in the Verdure, who had sent her to another ostler back in the Chestnut, who had at last given her a possible address for the couple down in the Mire.

Renn trudged through the neighborhood, worried she might reach the tenement only to reach the end of the road. If the people who lived there didn't know where to find Guissand's home, or if, Amma forbid, no one lived there at all, if the place was empty or turned out to be a shop or some-thing, then Renn had no clue where to go next.

Go home?

She supposed she would have to.

"Wet your gullet?" a woman with a cart of fruits called out to Renn as she passed.

She had to keep moving, but her mouth was as dry as the hot stones on which she walked, and her head swam from hunger and thirst. Looking over the fruit seller's wares, she chose a plum, and when she bit into the sweet, overripe fruit, juice dribbled down her chin. Wiping it off with her collar, she leaned against the shaded wall behind the seller for a moment and pulled out her eating knife.

She had Getha to thank for the ease with which the sharp edge sliced through the skin and the soft flesh beneath. On their second or third trip out into the city, Getha had brought up the idea of Renn carrying a weapon, but not knowing how to use one and with no real desire to learn, she had refused.

After going around and around about it, Getha had given up, saying "Fine. Let me see your eating knife." Renn had pulled it from her belt and handed it to her, and Getha had told her to at least keep the blade sharper than it needed to be.

"What good will that do me?"

Getha had held the blade and offered the knife back to Renn handle-first. "You never know, do you?"

So Renn had gone by the bladesmith's the next time she was on the row to have her eating knife sharpened, and she'd kept it well-honed ever since.

Renn carved off another slice of plum and popped it into her mouth. Over the course of the day, her anger had disappeared. It had dried up in the endless heat, and she missed her friend. *Friend.* Was that what Getha had become to her? Was that even possible, a friendship between a princess and her guard? After all, things could never be equal, and wasn't that part of what a true friendship was based on?

She finished her plum, cast the pit into the gutter, then covered the last few blocks to Serrimandier and the Tithen's tenement, where they supposedly lived on the third floor. Her hopes fell when she laid eyes on it. The front door to the rickety building stood open, as did the shutters on all of the windows, and through one window came the sound of a crying babe. It wasn't the sort of place Renn could imagine any messero, even a messero who'd given up everything as Serrimandier had, living. But she'd come too far to walk away without at least checking.

Renn stood in the entryway for a moment to let her eyes adjust to the dimness, the inside of the building as dark and hot as the inside of an oven. When she could see well enough, she climbed the creaky stairs.

The doors to most of the tenements stood open, revealing the state of the rooms within, and the sight of so much poverty tugged at her; she wanted to help them all. To ease her guilt, she stopped at the second floor, by the rooms with the crying child. A haggard father walked his screaming, skinny, red-faced babe around the messy room. On a different day, she would have offered to clean the place or to hold the child while the father took a moment for himself. As she didn't have the time for either, she entered and gave the man a handful of silvers.

"Ta," he said, dropping the coins down on his beaten table without counting them. He kissed the babe's head and jostled her on his hip. "Her ma works in the mines, as many shifts as they'll give her, but it never seems enough, you ken?"

Renn nodded. A few moons ago she hadn't, but she did now. Wishing his family the best and making a mental to note to return and help him further, she continued on. She had come to learn how much struggling happened out in the Branches. The actual distance between her home and the Mire was less than three miles, and yet this man might as well live on the opposite side of the world. No matter what Getha had said, their work hadn't been pointless, but Renn did need to do more. She had to muster up her courage and return to the convocation. She had to...

She reached the third floor and found the door to Serrimandier's supposed living quarters closed, so she went to knock, but the moment she touched the door, it eased open a crack.

"Heyla?" she called. "Anyone home?"

No one answered, so she pushed the door open farther. With the shutters on the windows closed, and the room beyond was dark. Parneo's warning about letter being a trap returned to her as she took a tentative step over the threshold. "Heyla?"

Sweat ran down the back of her neck, and she'd never missed Getha more. Had the room been empty, she would have run away then and there, but her foot landed on a rug, and in the slivers of sunlight coming through the closed shutters, she spied the shadowy shapes of furniture. Certain the nice man living on the floor below would come if she screamed, she sucked in a breath, opened the door all the way, propped it open with a chair, and hurried over to the nearest window.

The sunlight illuminated very little—an eating table set for a meal, a high bench lined with earthenware bowls, a small hearth, the threadbare rug on which Renn stood, a trunk with a lock, and a colorful quilt spread over the bed. Next to the bed, on a stand with a drawer in it, rested a shuttered globe and a five-inch-tall bust of Queen Elissianne.

Renn smiled. She had done it; she'd found Serrimandier's place. But with neither he nor the Tithen present, what did she do now?

She sat on the edge of the bed. She'd thought finding Guissand's tenement would lead to something, but without anyone there, she'd reached the end of the road. She looked around, helpless, and that was when she noticed something on the wall behind the open door. She stood, crossed the room, moved the chair, and swung the door away from the wall. Someone had left a message on the wall in ash.

Meet Market Way and Bimley's Close one candlemark past sundown.

She touched a letter and her finger came away stained with black. Whoever had written the message had done so recently. But who for? The corner of Market Way and Bimley's Close was on the edge of the Tangles, the darkest and dankest neighborhood in Ombratos, the part of the city she hadn't dare step foot into since her and Getha's flight from Talp's Court.

Renn made sure to close the door of the tenement behind her, then she made haste for the stairs, anxious to leave the small room, anxious for some space, some room to think. She had to return to the palace. She couldn't do this without Getha.

Out in the street, the sun had already fallen below the edge of the Gift, and that meant less than half a candlemark remained until sundown. It was too late for her to get back up to the palace, not if she wanted to be in the Tangles on time. Was that what she wanted? Who knew what might face her there? Then again, what could happen on a street corner? A street corner in the Tangles, sure, but a wide open street corner nonetheless. The chance going there might put her in a position to help Guissand was too great. She had to go.

A candlemark past sundown. Parneo had promised to send Getha after Renn if she didn't make it home before sundown, and as long as he remained present and aware, he would. Of course, given her and Getha's fight, Getha might not come even if he did ask her. Renn touched her eating knife and her worry subsided. If Parneo told Getha she was missing, then the guard would come.

She'll come. Renn said the words over and over to herself, both in an effort to calm her pounding heart and to make them come true.

She'll come. She'll come. She'll come...

A KNOCK CAME at the door to the boat's hold shortly after the nauseating leaping of the ship ceased. Helenia sat up on the bunk, swallowing hard. When it seemed as if everything in her stomach would remain there, she spoke. "Enter."

Captain Fintan opened the door, a silhouette against the twilit sky. "We've arrived, my lady." Then he disappeared from sight.

She stood, her legs shaky, and clambered up onto the deck. Twenty-five mercenaries sat or stood about, windswept and wet with spray. One heaved over the rail, and a couple of others released the spent body of a wind wife over the other side, returning her to the sea as was only right for those of her order.

The nearest mercenary, a man little taller than Helenia, kissed his fingers and touched them to the deck. "Ever-Watchful Eye of Burk watch over you, *brídgaoh*."

Helenia echoed his blessing, then asked, "How many did we lose?"

"One to each ship," the mercenary said, his face somber.

If all went to plan, so many more lives, perhaps even that of the man standing beside her, would be soon lost. She smoothed her white skirts and thought of Carhal. "The sacrifices will not be in vain."

"I hope not, my lady." The mercenary bowed and left to attend to some other business.

She strode to the rail and looked out. The ship bobbed in the waves just off Crown Bay. In the distance, in the city, lamps had been lit and globes unshuttered against the coming night. Seedfall already glittered like a beacon, calling to her.

Not too far off, Dallan stood at the prow of the *Bountiful Morn*. He was so still, his profile so strong and handsome, one could almost imagine him as a statue, a figure carved from wood and placed at the ship's fore as some sort of talisman.

She closed her eyes and imagined Mayve's reaction when she learned of what Helenia had done. Would her son's death harden her or bring her to her knees?

Helenia opened her eyes and stared out at the docks. When Orli and his varos completed their work at the palace, he would set off the signal.

Again, that left Helenia with naught to do but wait.

Is this what it feels like to be run through a wringer?

Getha's muscles felt like wet paper, her joints like they were held together by worn twine that might snap at any moment. She wanted to dive headlong into the Sap, current be damned. She wanted to fall onto her bed, close her eyes, and sleep for days. She barely had the strength to walk over to the varo wing of the palace, let alone have a serious conversation with Waltham, but she had made him a promise.

When he sees the state I'm in, perhaps he'll agree to defer this talk for a day or two. Besides, she hadn't yet decided if she should tell him the whole story or not. She groaned as she trudged up the steps leading into the palace. *Will this Amma-forsaken day never end?*

It wasn't until she stepped into the deathly quiet hall that she realized how few people she'd passed out on the grounds. As with the palace guards, the varo changed shifts at suppertime, and since that was when all of the guards were awake, it tended to be the most social part of the day. Maybe Orli had the varo out doing their own nightmarish training.

She reached Waltham's office door, leaned against the frame, and knocked. Then she closed her eyes and might have, for a moment or two, fallen asleep on her feet. When he didn't call out for her to enter or open the door, she knocked again. He had told her to come to his office, hadn't he? Golden sunlight spilled through the crack at the bottom of the door. She tried the latch. It gave, and so she swung the door inward. He'd left his globes shuttered, but both windows stood wide open and the glare of the setting sun blinded her.

She squinted and stepped into the room. "Waltham? You here?"

"I am," he said, an edge to his tone. Was he still so angry with her?

She waited by the door for her eyes to adjust to the brightness. As they did, she could make out the details of the office—the filled bookshelves along the north wall, the shape of the Althian map next to the window, his sword hanging above the fireplace, the ugly carpet on the floor, the matching chairs in front of his orderly desk—and the shadow of Waltham himself sitting in the high-backed chair behind it.

"Come in and close the door." Though he sounded angry, his blank, expressionless face told another tale.

Her instincts, dulled by weariness, immediately sharpened. Something was wrong and it seemed to have nothing to do with their earlier disagreement. While she tried to figure it out, she did as he'd asked.

Waltham stood, taller and straighter than he had been able to for years, and walked around the desk, every step ragged, as if he wanted to take it and yet fought against it. He stopped in front of the desk and gestured toward one of the two chairs. "Sit."

Everything in her cried out for her to run, or at the very least remain by the door, but she forced herself to step forward. This was Waltham. Whatever was happening, she had to help him. He watched her cross the room and sit on the edge of the seat. Perhaps she could get him talking and—

In the distance, a woman screamed. She turned her head and, with that, he attacked.

He wrapped his hands around her neck and dug his thumbs into her throat, cutting off her air as the cold expanse of his face loomed above hers. She clawed at his hands, but he had gained an impossible strength and his fingers tightened around her neck like a vise. She scrabbled at him, and the world turned grey at the edges. Waltham was going to kill her. Waltham. The last thing she wanted to do was to hurt him, but her desire to live exceeded even that.

She lowered her arm, flexing her wrist. A dagger dropped into her hand, and she drove it into his thigh.

He cried out and released her. Sucking in a wheezing breath, she shoved him away, back into the desk. She tried to stand, to run, but her legs gave out and she toppled to the floor. Drawing in gusty, gasping breaths, she crawled across the floor to get away from him. He hobbled by her, hot blood raining from his wound as he passed. Closing the door, he threw his body against it and slumped to the floor, blocking her escape.

"No!" The word rubbed like gravel against the raw skin of her throat. He was going to force her to kill him. "Why are you doing this?"

Waltham grabbed his hurt leg with one hand and held the other up toward her, palm out. "Stop." Blood spread onto the floor around him, and the blank expression slid away, replaced by a face contorted with pain. "Wait."

She sat there, but released her other dagger. "Why are you doing this?"

"It's the blood oa—" He gagged on the word. Gritting his teeth, he dug his fingers into the skin around the blade and screamed. Then, between shallow breaths, he spoke. "It's him... It's the blood oath...I took when I... I made varo... We're all Bound...to Orli."

"Orli forced you to attack me?" This was Waltham, her Waltham, speaking, and she believed him, but why would Orli do such a thing?

"Yes." The ever-widening pool of blood around Waltham crept toward her. "He ordered me to wait here, for you." He coughed, his eyes watering. "To kill you."

Right outside the window, a man shouted wordlessly, the sound followed by the *crack* of breaking wood. She worried who might be out there, but she needed to see to Waltham first. The shoulder of one of his sleeves gaped, the seam having torn in their fight. Getha ripped off the sleeve and tucked it around the blade. He cursed, but she pressed his hands over the makeshift bandage, and he held it there. Then she stood, stumbled over to grab his sword, and ran to the window. She didn't know what she expected out there, but on the ground, less than six feet below her, a spindly young man crouched over an insensible varo with what appeared to be a broken balustrade clutched in both hands.

Seeming to sense her presence, the young man looked up and relief filled his face. "There you are, guard. I've been searching for you."

A charm hung around his lank neck. Not a charm, a amulet, identical to the one the princess wore, and Princess Renn had sworn the only other person who had one was her twin. "Prince Parneo?"

The young man nodded. Four riderless, untacked horses came around the side of the palace in a panicked gallop, headed out toward the woods.

Getha set down the sword, tucked away her dagger, and offered the prince her hand. He took it, propped his leg up on an outcropping on the palace wall, and with her help, climbed in through the window.

Once he made it inside, she took the sword from the desk and dropped to the floor. The prince followed her lead, and together they crawled back to Waltham, whose skin had turned the color of talc.

She set the sword down just out of his reach. "If Orli ordered you to kill me, then why did you leave your blade on the wall?"

He smiled grimly. "He didn't say how I had to do it. Knew you'd fight back. Knew you'd stop me from hurting anyone else."

"Like who?"

Waltham's smile receded. "After you, he ordered me to search the palace and kill everyone."

The prince knelt on the floor just beyond the pool of blood, staring at it with an unsettling intentness. "My family?"

"Who is your family?" Waltham looked to Getha. "Who is this? An alchemist?"

Did they have time for an explanation of the amulets? Before Getha might decide one way or another, the prince said, "I'm Parneo."

Getha readied herself to answer any number of questions, but Waltham turned to the prince and asked, "May I?"

She didn't understand the question, but the prince seemed to. He nodded. "Go ahead. But hurry."

Waltham closed his eyes, and had they not shifted beneath his eyelids, flicking back and forth, she might have thought he'd passed out. Then he started, and his eyes flew open. "How?"

"How what?" she asked.

Ignoring her, the prince pulled the amulet from under his tunic and let it fall against his chest. "I recovered one of the Lost Pillars."

Waltham huffed, but didn't show any sign of being as shaken by the revelation as she had. "I see."

"What is happening?" Getha demanded.

"I'm sorry," Waltham said, touching her arm. "There isn't time."

As if to echo this sentiment, the prince repeated his question. "My family?"

Waltham coughed, and moved to cover his mouth, leaving behind a bloody handprint on her sleeve. "Orli instructed us to kill everyone outside our order. Every Morovide, every highborn, every guard and servant. He told us to slaughter everyone at Seedfall." He shook his head. "But his words... I can't hear them anymore."

Getha's stomach roiled with Waltham's news, but the prince reacted not at all.

Instead, he dipped a finger in the blood and held it up in front of his face. "*Exsanguor ruvene*. Spill enough blood and the Binding weakens."

A glimmer of hope sparked among the falling darkness, and Waltham voiced the question on her lips. "Can a blood oath be fully broken?"

"Perhaps," the prince said, rubbing the blood between his finger and thumb, "in more controlled circumstances. But not here. Not like this."

Without thinking, Getha reached out and grabbed the front of his tunic. "Why not? If you can do it, then do it."

"I can't," the prince said, his eyes wide as he at last showed some emotion. "I can't make him empty and then fill him up. I don't have enough."

"Speak sense!" she cried, her voice breaking.

"You would almost have to bleed me dry," Waltham said, and the resignation in his voice cut her down to her very soul. "Isn't that right?"

Parneo nodded, and prince or no, Getha wanted to shake him. She wanted to shake him and strike him until he agreed to try. They couldn't just leave Waltham as Orli's poppet.

Waltham coughed. "Getha, please. Let him go."

She unclenched her hands, and the prince jerked away from her. Keeping his gaze on her, he rooted around in a purse on his belt and pulled out a healing charm that he handed it to Waltham. "Use this or you will bleed to death soon."

Waltham reached out and took the charm, and she pictured his empty eyes as he had choked the life from her.

"Wait." Getha wrapped her hand around his. "Mayhaps it's better if you... " She couldn't say the word. "If you let go while you're you. While you're free."

Somehow, Waltham chuckled, the sound dried leaves scraping over stone. "That's no way for an old soldier to die."

He'd said the same thing to her on the roof of the stables. Then, even given his age, the idea of Waltham dying had seemed as impossible as Amma disappearing from the sky. She shouldn't have laughed then, because looking his death in the face now, she was lost.

Waltham muttered the healing incantation and, with the last word, his whole body tensed like a rope yanked taut. His eyes rolled up until only the whites showed, and his heels drummed against the floor as his body shook.

Getha grabbed his arms to keep him from toppling over. "What did you give him?" she asked the prince. "Healing charms don't act this way."

The prince shook his head. He was a Morovide, and she respected him for that and for his alchemical skills, but he and Princess Renn were like night and day, and she didn't much care for his more nocturnal disposition.

"The weak ones don't," he said. "But he's emptier now. He has a few minutes." While Getha tried to figure that out, Prince Parneo turned his head to one side, and as if drawing a spear from a barrel, he plucked the blade from Waltham's leg. "There."

Waltham stopped shaking, and his limbs relaxed. He blinked a few times. "What happened?" He removed the sleeve from his leg. The wound had disappeared, not even leaving a scar in its wake. "How am I still me?"

The prince's words suddenly made sense. "Your blood loss," she said. "It's giving you a few moments before..."

Waltham nodded. "Before my oath traps me again."

Stealing some of their precious remaining moments, the prince turned to Getha. "You have to go after Renn. She's out in the city."

This day was like being crushed under the weight of a thousand boulders, each heavier than the last. "She's out in the city? Where?"

"I don't know." The prince dug through his purse again and took out a stone the color of a sunset. He handed it to her. "But you can find her."

Waltham touched her arm. "Help me up."

She stood and helped him to his feet. He took a few steps, his leg working as well as it ever had, and picked his sword up from the floor where she'd left it. "Orli wants the throne. It's the only explanation." He looked at her. "Go to the princess. Get her out of Ombratos."

Another boulder of responsibility set on her back. "What good will that do?"

He went to the door, opened it, and peered outside. "As long as a Morovide woman lives, the throne will never be his, not truly. But you only have a year and a day."

A year and a day? "Why?"

"A year and a day, and not one moment more. After that, all is lost." He stepped out into the hall; she and the prince followed. "Go," he said, pointing toward the door leading outside. "While you still can."

"You're not coming with us?"

Waltham broke her heart by giving her the look he always did when she asked him a question to which she already knew the answer.

A lump formed in her throat. "No," she said around it. "I can't leave you."

His expression softened. "You can."

"I don't want to."

"I know." He stepped closer to her. "Listen, squirrel. The demands of war are seldom fair and never easy. But you must make the best choices you can with the information you have."

A final lesson. Tears clouded her sight as she grabbed his hand and pressed her bloodmark to his. "I'm sorry." She apologized for leaving him, and for everything else that she felt but didn't have the words to say.

"There is nothing to be sorry for." He pulled his hand gently from hers and lifted it to her cheek. "Remember. Be fast, be bold... "

"Be—" She swallowed hard, and a tear slipped down her cheek. "Be brave and wise."

He wiped the tear away and smiled. "That's my girl." Then the old soldier turned and hobbled off, sword in hand, and too soon, he moved around the corner, out of sight.

Waltham didn't make it much farther before Orli's orders returned, and they blazed in his mind, threatening to destroy all else. *Kill the Morovides. Kill the guards and the servants. Kill until every last man, woman, and child in Seedfall is dead, then return to me.*

It was already too late stop Orli's treachery, too late to save most of the family he had been Bound to protect. Just as Waltham had felt Solena die on that awful morning, this day, through his Binding to them, he had felt the queen's violent death, followed in almost immediate succession by the brutal deaths of Heshiette and Linore.

Only the youngest lived now—no longer outshone by her mother and sisters, Princess Renn glowed bright in his mind—and he trusted Getha to keep her safe.

Unable to stop himself, he stalked through the halls, through the bloody chaos the varos' slaughter had wrought. Everywhere he looked, the hollow, accusatory eyes of the dead stared at him, blaming him for not doing more to stop Orli while he had the chance.

"Waltham!" Neesi, a maid who'd worked in the palace for almost thirty years, cried out to him as he passed an open door. Crouched over, she ran toward him.

He tried to warn her off, but the effects of the *exsanguor ruvene* had faded, and the words refused to come.

As Neesi neared, she opened her arms as if to embrace him. "Help me, Waltham! They're murdering everyone. They murdered—"

With hands that moved of their own accord, with a sword forged to honor and protect, Waltham brought his blade up and cleaved it down through Neesi's unarmored shoulder, far into her chest. Her mouth froze in a rictus of surprise and terror. Stricken, he wrenched his blade from her torso, and her body slumped to the ground to join the rest.

He licked his lips, and a salty, coppery mix of her blood and his tears coated his tongue. No more, he swore to himself. Not one more. He struggled to bring Getha's face to mind. He thought of her, thought of the sharp-edged, mistrustful girl he'd found out in Shade's Rest, a young woman wasting the remarkable skills she wasn't even aware she possessed. Coaxing her to trust him had been like taming a wild animal, but he remembered the pride on her face the day she received her bloodmark, and his own pride in her. A mentor's pride. A father's.

Waltham stumbled on. At least he had saved her. At least he had done that.

He tripped over a severed arm, and Orli's orders wormed through his mind. *Kill until every last man, woman, and child in Seedfall is dead.* The ordered varo would follow these instructions no matter what. They had started outside with the guards, and most would be inside now, hunting down the last of the servants. They would fight tirelessly, heedless of their own wellbeing until they fulfilled their mission.

It was too late to stop Orli's treachery, but it wasn't too late to strip him of his title. After all, what use was a lead varo without any varo left to lead? Waltham had to take care of them all. Somehow.

He climbed to his feet. A footman, barely more than a boy, burst out of a nearby room, and he looked to Waltham, his eyes wide with fear.

Waltham brought to mind the image of Getha buckling on her vambraces for the first time. "Run," he bellowed, raising his sword even as he did. "Run, you fool!"

Praise Amma, the boy ran. With every last bit of will left to him, Waltham brought his blade down wide, meaning to lodge it in the wall. Instead, he slammed the sword into a globe, shattering the glass and releasing a torrent of liquid flame. Laughter bubbled up inside Waltham as the fire splashed onto the honeywood panels and thick rugs. He clutched his sword close and slid down the opposite wall. Let flame and smoke take him. Let it take him, the palace, and every other varo left inside.

Tipping his head back, Waltham yelled to be heard above the rising roar. "We're going to burn, you Amma-forsaken, motherless bastard! How do you like that?"

Orli had poisoned his varo, but now they would all die together.

TWENTY-NINE

"One cannot know the number of seeds in an orange by the color of its peel."
-Yentish Proverb

Renn spat in the gutter and gripped the bottom edge of her tunic to keep her hands from shaking. She'd been waiting at the corner of Market Way and Bimley's Close for a quarter of a candlemark, and had started to worry that she'd missed the meeting or that no one would show. False sunset, when the sun dipped below the Gift, had given way to true sunset—torch lighters were even now running up and down the streets—and Getha had also yet to arrive, leaving Renn alone and exposed.

People walked by, and she tried to watch them without seeming to stare. Any moment the Tithen or Serrimandier or someone else might arrive, and she didn't want to be taken unawares.

"Heyla."

Renn spun around, then looked down to meet the light eyes of a skinny girl of eight or nine. "You Alyse?" the girl asked, tugging on the thick, yellow braids that reached down to her calves.

Hearing her lowborn name come from the girl's mouth startled Renn. "Who are you?"

The girl crossed the braids in front of her neck and tossed one over her shoulder like a scarf. "No matter. Serrimandier sent me."

Renn glanced around. "Where is he?" Thick shadows blanketed the streets beyond the flickering light of the street torches.

The girl used her other braid to point in the direction of Bimley's Close, the road leading farther into the Tangles. "In the paper mill." She whipped the braid up. "In the loft."

A tower on a building in the center of the street rose above all the others, the shutters on the tower closed, with no light escaping between them. Renn heard Parneo's dismissive *It's a trap.* But, another part of her insisted, *what if it isn't?*

Renn took a deep breath. *Getha will come.* She nodded. "Lead the way."

But the girl waved her off. "I'm just the messenger." She turned on her heel and skipped off in the opposite direction, her bare feet rasping against the stones, her braids dancing.

Renn watched the girl until she disappeared in the shadows, then she touched the eating knife on her belt. Serrimandier needed her, and she wouldn't let him down. She set off for the mill and had made it a quarter of the way down the block when, from far off in the distance, came the deep, unmistakable ringing of the Tower Bell. As neither dusk nor dawn encroached upon the darkness, the sound of the bells meant one thing.

Fire.

One by one, the bells in the smaller towers scattered throughout Ombratos also rang, until a clangorous din filled the night.

Up and down the block, doors opened and half-dressed men, women, and children rushed out into the street. Several left their homes with buckets in hand and ran off to lend their strong arms and backs, built up from years of hard labor, to the effort of putting the fire out, wherever it might be. In the valley of the street, Renn couldn't tell if the fire raged across town or on the next block over.

Other lowborn knocked on the doors of their neighbors to rouse them. With a fire about no one wanted to be caught in their beds. Renn had to get to the loft as soon as possible, but she couldn't bear to walk by those closed doors knowing that families might soon be trapped behind them, so she took a moment to join the knockers.

She banged on doors with the flat of her hand, crying "Fire! Fire!" One door flew open as she came to it, and a man and a woman, both in night-shifts and each with a sleep-rumpled child half-awake in their arms, emerged.

"Where's the fire?" the woman asked, an edge of panic in her voice. The child in her arms clung to her like a limpet, and her partner sniffed the air, no doubt for smoke.

"I don't know," Renn said, careful to sound calm. Taking the rise and fall of the land on which the city had been built into account, the loft in Talp's mill was the highest point in the Branches, higher even than the bell towers. Her destination, the responsibilities she had given herself, would not be denied. She pointed up to the loft. "I'm going to go up there and see."

The woman nodded and held back a sob. With a gentle hand, Renn took her arm and turned her toward the nearest permanent bridge. "Go," Renn said. "Head for the bay." She cupped her hands around her mouth and addressed the rest of the Fallen standing in the street. "Head for the bay! Head for the bay!"

One or two others took up the cry and then a few more, and then, almost as one, the crowd turned in the direction of the docks.

Renn wished them well and struggled against the tide of humanity to the mill. Sighting a side door on the massive building, she ran over, yanked it open, and rushed through. With the sluices closed and the wheel still, the quietness in the large space pressed in on her. She ran past bins of linen rags, between hulking pulpers and pressers, straight for the staircase leading to the loft. She charged up the stairs, taking them two at a time, her hand on her eating knife, readying herself for anything.

But soon she reached the top and an empty room with a single, naked globe hanging from the ceiling. Confused, she struggled to catch her breath and stumbled over to the window facing east, where she threw back the shutters.

After Waltham disappeared from sight, Getha turned to the prince. "How are we going to leave the palace grounds?" Her heart ached, but she couldn't think about Waltham. She wouldn't, not until the princess was safe.

Prince Parneo stared at her. "What do you mean?"

Exasperated but determined not to lose her temper, she said, "If Orli wants everyone dead, then his varo are watching the walls and waiting at the gate."

The prince seemed to think about this, tipping his head one way, then the other, as if weighing his options.

"Help me," she said. "I have to get to Renn."

He closed his eyes and kept leaning his head back and forth. Getha wanted to reach out and shake him and was just about to when, in a hall not too far off, someone screamed, and the prince's eyes snapped open.

"Come," he said. He grabbed a globe from a sconce on the wall, then started off toward the outside, gesturing for her to follow.

Not seeing any other choice, she did. He led her outside, heedless of anyone who might be waiting for them. Trying to look in every direction at once, she kept close to him as they skirted the edge of the building. The sunset washed the grounds in golden light with orange, pink, and purple clouds streaked across the sky. It would have been stunning sunset but for the strange emptiness of the grounds and the shouts ringing out in the distance.

The prince rounded the corner to the north wing, and they passed into the shadow of some tall hedges. Stiff branches clawed at Getha, raking their fingers over her bare arms and face, but at least they hid her and the prince from sight. Halfway along the wall, he stopped.

"Why are we here?" Getha whispered.

Prince Parneo slapped the wall, except it wasn't the wall but a door she had somehow never noticed before. Placing his hand on it, he said a few words, and it swung open, releasing a pungent, musty odor and revealing a set of wooden stairs leading down into the earth. He started down them, leaving her to do as she would. Again not seeing any other choice, she joined him on the stairs, closing the door behind her.

The ragged dirt wall gave way to stone, and the stairs ended at the opening to a narrow pathway. The prince rushed ahead of her, his globe a bobbing light sliding along the slick stone walls in the otherwise absolute darkness. Anxious not to be left behind in the dark, she made haste to catch up with him. "Why didn't you ever tell the princess about this?"

Prince Parneo whirled on her, eyes wild, the globe he carried casting sinister shadows across his strange face. "Quiet! The walls have ears. They hear you down here and—" He snapped his head to the side and looked at the stone wall, and she jumped when he shouted a string of gibberish at it.

Princess Renn had told Getha that alchemy helped the prince keep his madness at bay. But with a amulet hanging around his neck and a purse filled with charms at his belt, it seemed alchemy no longer worked quite so well. Still shouting, he started forward again, and she chased after him, releasing one of her blades.

With each step, the pungent odor grew, and the familiarity of the scent tickled at the edges of her senses. Less than fifty feet from where they'd stopped, the prince broke into a run, and though her sore legs protested, she did the same.

Ahead of her, the prince suddenly leaped, his long legs carrying him over something laying across the pathway. She slowed to get a better look at the something and reeled back at the sight of two corpses, their rotting bodies the source of the odor. In the receding light of the prince's globe she could only make out their shapes—one tall and lanky, the other shorter and capped with a shock of white, or perhaps once yellow, hair.

She shivered. "Who...?"

She wanted to ask who these people had been and where they'd come from, but her thoughts turned slimy and slippery, sliding away from the bodies and their possible origins. Up ahead, the prince still ran, leaving her far behind. Hugging the wall opposite the corpses, she edged around them, then dashed away toward the glow of the globe, the greasiness in her mind diminishing with every step. The prince grew winded and slowed to a walk, and she jogged into his small pool of light. The stench of *something* filled her nostrils, but her recognition of the smell lingered just out of reach.

They traveled in silence for what seemed like an age, but eventually they approached the end of the pathway and another set of stairs, this one carved into the rock leading up and, with Amma's merciful grace, out. The prince ascended with a measured step, and Getha had to fight the urge to shove past and run up the stairs. She clutched the charm the prince had given her. For some reason, she held one of her daggers in her other hand.

Though it was tricky on the steps, she slipped the dagger back into its vambrace and reset the trigger. "What does this charm do?"

He explained it to her, stopping halfway up the steps to demonstrate. "Close your eyes and think of Renn."

Getha clenched her fist around the charm and thought of the princess. *Amma save me. I'm never going to make it to her in time.* Then she closed her eyes, and it was as if she closed them and then opened them somewhere else. The princess, if that's whose view she saw, hurried down a darkened street. The rundown buildings marked it as a street in the Tangles, but Getha couldn't place anything else. *Look around!* But it appeared the magic only flowed into one direction because the princess didn't look around; she kept her gaze pinned ahead of her. *She knows where she's going.* A clue. Yet, after the past few moons, after all of the places the princess and Getha had been together, it meant little.

The prince screamed, and the noise invaded Getha's mind. Her view, the princess', blinked out.

Prince Parneo held the sides of his head, with the globe pressed to one side of his face before it slipped away. It hit a step and bounced off, back down into the tunnel. The prince screamed and screamed, the sound coloring the blackness and echoing around her until she thought she might go mad.

The princess needed her. Getha gripped the prince's arms and slid past him, then, holding his wrist, she dragged him upward. After a few steps, her head slammed into a door, but she barely felt the pain. For a terrifying moment, the massive slab of wood wouldn't budge. She wedged her back against the door and her feet under her, and bit by bit, the door rose, letting a crack of light in around the edge, and the prince's screams stopped as if someone had cut them in two. He crept up beside her, touched the door with a finger, and it flew up and over on its hinges, slamming against the floor.

Or the ground. The prince rushed out past her, and she climbed up behind him. They appeared to be at the end of an alley, the sky above them dark with stars. While they had been down in the tunnel, full night had fallen. "Where are we?"

Without a word, the prince ran off toward the street.

She chased after him. "Wait!"

He turned right out of the alley, and the academy loomed ahead. She slowed, but he ran on. The alchemist guarding the gates seemed to know him because she opened them a crack to allow him inside. Never once looking back, he slid through, and the guard slammed the gates closed behind him.

Getha stopped. She had to leave the prince's life in Amma's hands. The princess mattered more. Waltham's instructions returned to her. *Get her out of Ombratos. As long as a Morovide woman lives, the throne will never be his.* Followed by that ominous threat, *A year and a day, and not one moment more. After that, all is lost.* She buried the image of her mentor, her patron, the closest thing she'd ever had to a father walking away from her. If she didn't do as he had asked, then his death, all the deaths this night, would mean nothing.

She clutched the charm the prince had given her and closed her eyes. More darkness, but walls pressed in around the princess and then the view shifted downward. Steps. She climbed steps. From the number of them, Getha could guess the princess's location, but she waited to be certain. *Faster!*

Princess Renn reached the top step and looked around a room with shuttered windows against every wall. She hurried to the first and pulled back the shutters.

Getha opened her eyes. The princess was alone in the loft of Talp's paper mill, but Amma only knew how long that would last. Getha tucked the stone into her pocket and ran.

At first, smoke rose in tendrils from the palace, like smoke from cooking fires spiraling out of chimneys. It took Helenia a moment to realize her mistake. With *The Searcher* still out beyond the breakers, she was too far away, especially in the fading light, to see a detail like the thin thread of smoke from a chimney, which meant the fire was larger than it looked. Much larger.

"Fire!"

The cry came out from the deck of the *Bountiful Morn*, then spread to the decks of *The Searcher* and the *Shadowed Moon*. All of the sailors and mercenaries on *The Searcher* crowded around Helenia to stare out at Seed-fall, where the fire grew and spread.

This wasn't right. She hadn't instructed anyone to burn the palace. Something had gone wrong, very wrong, and yet Helenia still felt in control.

Captain Fintan reached the rail next to Helenia. "What do we do, my lady?"

Logic dictated they run away and cut their losses. But they had come too far to turn back. Helenia had come too far to turn back. She had bet every single coin down to her last on Ombratos, and she would win everything or lose it all.

She smoothed her hands down her skirt. "Sail into the bay." The captain hesitated, and she turned on him. "Sail into the bay!"

THIRTY

"The Unknown can only be Known when the time is right."
-From Galathar Morovide's *Treatise of a Bloody Wanderer*

The bell inside High Alchemist Kitra Rande's office door rang. Without looking up from the formula she studied, she grabbed for the pull and signaled for whoever it was to come in. After a lot of discreet work, she had sourced the sabotaging sand to the beaches around the Tithen capital of Galleford, and with that, had gone her last excuse to keep the information from the queen.

The inside bell rang again. Irritated that the ringer hadn't entered the first time, Kitra glared at the door, tugged on her pull, and waited. All of a sudden, the bell above her door rang wildly, as if someone hoped to yank it off its cord.

"What in Amma's name...?" She wanted to call out and demand for the mad ringer to enter, but thanks to the Binding on the office, she'd just be shouting at herself. Rising to her feet, she charged across the room and threw open the door.

The prince, in his Transformed guise, rushed in. He never came to the academy so late. Something was wrong. Fost chased after him, but Kitra stopped her secretary just inside the door.

"I'm sorry," he said, looking up at her from beneath his fringe. "I tried to—"

"That's fine," Kitra said, herding him out. "I'll deal with him." She got him into the hall, then she shut the door on him and turned to face the prince.

"My family," he said, slumping down in one of her chairs. "They're dead. All dead. Dead, dead, dead, dead..."

An icy hand wrapped around her, numbing her face and snatching her breath away. She knelt in front of the prince and took his hot, sweaty hands in hers. "What? Who is dead?"

"Solena, Mother Queen, Father, Linore, Heshi..."

With every name, it became harder and harder to breathe. Gasping, she waited for his twin's name, the final death that would damn them all.

"Dead, dead, dead, dead, dead."

"And Princess Renn?"

The prince looked out her window, the one overlooking the courtyard and the Gift. "The guardswoman spilled a lot of the varo's blood, almost too much, but he told her to find Renn and keep her safe. So I..." He cocked his head to the side and took his hands back, grabbing at his ears. "No!" he shouted, as if speaking to someone outside her window. "No, no, no!"

If he spoke the truth, they couldn't wait for one of his fits to pass. A burst of inspiration came to her. Climbing to her feet, she rounded her desk and opened the center drawer, finding her old ceremonial dagger and a minor healing charm. She returned to the shouting prince and took a firm hold of his left hand. Then, as quick and lightly as she could, she pricked his palm in the middle of his bloodmark.

A drop of blood welled up. She slipped the dagger into her belt, dropped the charm into his palm, and closed his hand around it. As if by instinct, he shouted the words to activate it. A glow emanated from between his fingers, and his ragged breathing eased. When the charm stopped glowing, having spent its minor effects, he'd returned to himself.

He rolled the charm around in his hand. "I wasn't supposed to, but I gave the guard something to help her find Renn. The guard promised to keep her safe."

He wasn't supposed to? According to whom? Who had told him not to protect his twin? "Tell me everything you know."

The prince, in a rambling, disjointed fashion, explained about Lead Varo Orli's treachery and the varos' slaughter. "And the Gift," he said. "The Gift is broken."

She glanced out at the pristine, implacable wall that looked no different than it ever had. "What does that mean?"

"It's broken," he insisted. He stood, pulled her to her feet, and dragged her to the window, where he pointed out at the Gift. "Can't you see the cracks?"

She couldn't, but she didn't want to send him into another spiral. "Yes, of course."

He sighed with obvious relief. "At last."

She eased him down into her chair, then she left his side to pace the room.

Amma's breath, what was Orli thinking? He knew as well as any of them the law about keeping a Morovide on the throne. Was that why Princess Renn still lived? But what could he want with her? Did he still long for the role of prince-consort? Surely his missing toe was enough to remind him of that impossibility. Unless he saved the princess for someone else. Someone from Tithen, from Galleford, had sabotaged the working, mayhaps even a member of their royal family. Prince Dallan? Could he the one behind the Morovides' deaths?

She shook her head. She'd waited too long, and none of that really mattered, not anymore. All that mattered now were those under her watch —Prince Parneo and the alchemists.

She and the prince had to run, but what about her alchemists? If she left them behind, what might befall them? With the Gift being product of alchemy, so if it truly was broken, then it only made sense the alchemists could be blamed for breaking it.

Her thoughts came together with such remarkable celerity it made her head spin. The time for planning was over; it was time to run.

Part of her wanted to stop, to think further, to check her work, but she'd already waited too long. Guilt that she might be a little responsible for everything that had happened tried to rise up within her, but she crushed it beneath her heel.

Rushing to the door, she opened it and poked her head out.

Fost stood just outside, wringing his hands. "Yes, High Alchemist?"

She sent him for Alchemist Myka Berren. "Be very quick about it," she said. "Speak to no one except for her, and don't stop for any reason."

He bobbed his head, his hair flopping in his eyes, and scurried off.

Ducking back into her office and closing her door behind her, she returned to her desk, eased behind the chair, opened the window, and poked her head outside. She breached the office's Binding and was greeted by people in the courtyard yelling and the strong scent of burning. Up on the Gift, someone screamed, a sound unlike any she'd ever heard before.

The screaming person was dying, of that she was sure, and in some awful way.

Those wailing atop the Gift might be city guards dying at the hands of invaders, but it seemed equally likely that their demises were connected to the wall. The face of it had changed. It shone with an oily gleam and...it beckoned to her, until all she wanted to do was touch it. Prince Parneo was right. Somehow, the Gift was broken.

A few alchemists approached the changed wall, their hands outstretched. Alarm flashed through Kitra like lightning.

"No!" she shouted at the ensorcelled alchemists. "Stay away from the Gift! Stay away!"

Her warning seemed to cut through the wall's siren song, and they stopped, looking around as if they'd just awoken.

"Stuff waxed cotton in your ears and then keep everyone away from it!"

The dazed alchemists nodded, and Kitra reentered the office's silent bubble. *Amma, please help them.*

A sheaf of blank papers sat in one corner of her desk. She set a sheet in front of the prince and took one for herself.

The prince stared down at his. "What is this for?"

She handed him a pen and grabbed her own, then she opened a bottle of ink between them. "Write nonsense, but make it look like a formula," she told him. "Quick as you can."

Less than five minutes later, the bell rang. She tugged her pull, and with a shot of final inspiration, added the parting line to her letter and her signature. The door behind her opened and someone stepped inside.

"...is the meaning of this, High Alchemist?"

Kitra bade the prince to finish up—he made an abstracted grunt as he kept writing—and turned. With her cheek red and marked with pillow creases, Myka looked so young. Only twenty-six. Misgivings tugged at Kitra, but she'd made her choices and around her laid the rubble of what happened when she doubted herself at every turn.

"I'm leaving," Kitra said, with certainty, and before Myka even thought to ask, Kitra held up a hand. "I can't tell you where or anything else, so please, no questions."

What was left? She needed to pack. Grabbing her alchemical supply bag, she tossed her worn copy of Galathar Morovide's *Treatise of a Bloody Wanderer* into it, then fell to the floor and tore away several of the boards.

Myka gasped as Kitra revealed the opening and the safe bearing the queen's true crown, an old and rusted iron case about one-foot square with a sole alchemical formula etched into its door. Using her dagger, Kitra sliced along the edge of her palm and spoke the incantation as her blood splashed onto the formula. When she finished speaking, the formula flashed and the door sprang open.

"What is that?" Myka asked, as Kitra reached in and pulled out the thin wooden case holding the circlet.

With care, Kitra placed the box in her supply bag, right next to the copy of Galathar's book. "It's better if you don't know."

She closed the safe, replaced the boards, and climbed to her feet. *Anything else?* She returned to her desk to collect her extra pair of spectacles and a handful of flowering and healing charms, using one of those to heal the cut on her hand. Ignoring her, the prince continued to write. She'd asked him to pen a nonsense formula in the hopes someone might mistake it for a working to break the wall.

"Almost done?"

"No!" the prince shouted. "It must never be done! Never-ever, ever-never!" He tossed the pen to the floor and pressed his hands to his ears.

She rubbed his forearms. "That's fine."

"That's fine," he repeated. "Fine, fine, fine, fine..." Bit by bit, he dropped his hands to the desktop.

As he calmed, she eased him out of the chair and toward the window. Orli or one of his varo could arrive any moment. "Go," she told the prince. "Wait in the bushes right below the window."

To her surprise and extreme relief, he climbed outside.

"He seems upset. Do you think he'll stay put?" Myka asked, reminding Kitra of her presence.

"He has to." Kitra glanced at the formula he'd written. "I'm the only person he has left to watch out for him."

"What does that mean?"

As briefly as she could, and without explaining about the prince's identity or revealing his rediscovery of Transformation, Kitra told Myka everything he had said about the Morovides, Orli, and the Gift. With each word, the horror on Myka's face deepened, and when Kitra reached the end, Myka looked as if she might be sick. Too late, Kitra remembered Myka had grown up in the Bole and remained friends with Princess Linore.

"You're an alchemist," Kitra reminded her. "Tuck it away."

It obviously took some effort, but Myka's face cleared, until only the ashen cast to her skin remained. "Why me?" she asked. "There are at least ten more alchemists with more skill and more experience."

"I wanted someone who knows the truth of what happened to Princess Solena."

"Why me?" Myka repeated. "Why not Ithan?"

"I sent his wife to the Yent Isles. Marcal asked me for a recommendation; I told him to send her. I think Ithan knows that, and I think he blames me for her death."

"So you don't trust him?"

"No," Kitra said. "I don't trust him, and neither should you. Don't trust anyone. Tuck your emotions away, tuck your friendships away, and watch out for yourself." She picked up the confession she'd written and handed it to Myka. "If anyone comes asking about the Gift, show them that. Blame me for anything. Blame me for *everything*."

"But—"

"Go along with the new ruler, whoever it might be. Do as she or he asks, and you'll be safe."

Someone clambered at the windowsill. "Come now," the prince whispered. "Hurry."

Kitra grabbed her bag, then circled the desk to pull Myka into a crushing hug. One day she might regret leaving the young alchemist to face the danger alone, but there was nothing for it. The prince had to survive, and as Kitra had told Myka, she was all he had left.

"Here." Kitra guided Myka around the desk and sat her in the chair. "You're the high alchemist now. You must believe it so others will too."

Myka touched her hand. "Good luck."

Kitra tried to offer her a brave smile. "And to you."

She handed her bag out to the prince, and with his help, she climbed into the courtyard. Removing her crimson robe, she turned it so the black silken lining faced out—a betrayal that somehow also felt right.

Taking up her bag, she and the prince set out. Together, they rounded the side of the academy, while up on the hill, Seedfall burned.

THROUGH THE WINDOW to the east, a menacing orange glow haloed Seedfall, and its dozens of windows blazed with light. A pillar of smoke rose into the darkness, the dark, billowing cloud blocking out Bright Amma and all other stars from view. With a thunderous burst Renn felt more than she heard, gouts of fire flooded from some of the windows on the ground floor, and thick fingers of flame reached out and up, like a massive burning god, clawing its way up from the pathless hells to crush her home in its infernal grip.

Stunned, she couldn't look away, couldn't move, couldn't breathe.

Strong hands grabbed her from behind, spun her around, and slammed her back against the wall. Echoes of the flames crowded her vision, and she struggled blindly until the cold bite of steel touched her throat.

A shadow leaned in, pressed its cheek to hers, and a familiar voice said, "They're all dead. You're the last of your line." Then he—Talp's man, Natts—laughed, and said, "Fancy that. I thought I was going to be killin' a princess tonight, but if you think about it, I got myself a queen."

He pulled the knife back and turned it this way and that. The carved-bone handle and long, curved blade marked it for it was—a killing blade. Pressing it to her cheek, he smiled and took a folded piece of paper from his pocket. He shook it open, and on it someone had sketched a picture of her standing beside Getha, with a dark, heavy line drawn through both their throats. Where had he found such a thing?

"Heyla, Your Majesty. Been following you for a while."

The drawing, his words, the blade, Seedfall ablaze. It was all too much, so her mind clung to her last sane thought. "Did you hurt Serrimandier?"

He tipped his head to the side. "I tell you your family's dead, and the first person you ask me about is some Amma-forsaken messero who didn't know well enough to keep hold of what good fortune he had?"

Her hand shook as she brought it up between them.

"Serrimandier's dead, my queen. Dead and gone."

A tear slipped down her cheek as she found the handle of her eating knife.

"Don't cry now." He caught the tear with his knife and let it roll across the blade. "You'll be with the rest of your family soon enough."

The meaning of his earlier words at last sunk in. "You killed them?" She slid the knife from its sheath and drew it back.

He shook his head. "That was Orli's job. Him and the varos."

Shock stilled her hand. "The varos?"

Natts looked past her, out the window, and his face hardened. "Enough talk."

"Wait! Why did the varos betray us?"

"Don't know," he said. "When you're gone, I'll go ask the Tithens."

GETHA WAS HALFWAY up the stairs to the loft, with four or five of Talp's men hard on her heels, when she heard the scream. Her heart in her throat, she did the only thing she could, and ran even faster.

NATTS SCREAMED AGAIN and stumbled away from Renn, his face twisted in pain, her eating knife protruding from the middle of his chest. Blood soaked into his light-colored tunic and blossomed out around the knife. He looked down at it and back at her. Then he dropped the drawing and his knife, took a few drunken steps toward the stairs, and collapsed.

Was he dead? Reaching past him, she grabbed the drawing, crumpled it up, and stuck it in her purse. Was her family dead? Was Serrimandier?

"That was Orli's job... I'll go ask the Tithens," he had said.

Why the Tithens? In front of her, the only person who could answer that laid as still as the grave. Had she killed him? Her blade had slid too easily into his chest, slicing through skin and scraping against bone. Bile rose in her throat.

A figure bounded up the stairs and tripped over Natts' body. Getha barely caught herself before she hit the floor. "Renn!"

"Getha!" Renn wanted to go to her, but her legs wouldn't move. "I knew you'd come."

"Stay there!" Getha went to the center of the room, turned to face the stairs, and cast her arms out to both sides. Blades appeared in both hands just as two more figures came up the steps.

The first man also tripped over Natts, but the second leapt over him and closed on Getha. Renn's fear for her released her enough to take a single step, but Getha flew into motion, and any idea she might be of help fled Renn's mind.

Stepping back against the wall, she slid along it until she reached the corner, then she slumped to the floor and curled into a ball, too scared to watch, and yet, as two more people came up the stairs and entered the fight, unable to look away.

When they'd first started working together, Renn had attended a few of Getha's practices, and though she'd recognized the woman's skill, she understood now she'd never witnessed it exercised to its true extent. Getha parried and thrust with a savage speed, meeting the others' blades wherever they fell or dodging between them with an inhuman grace. She fought as if born to it, slicing through her opponents one by one, cutting them down as if she were death itself.

It wasn't until the last body fell, eyes open and mouth gaping as blood poured from a wound in her throat, that Renn recognized the woman as Serrimandier's Tithen. Somewhere along the line, Serrimandier or his woman—or both—had betrayed Renn, and she doubted the Tithen would be here unless Serrimandier was already dead.

And if he was dead, then all the rest...

Breathing hard, Getha wiped her blades on her tunic and slid them back into her vambraces. She'd wanted to try her hand against the Tithen, but she hated to think why she might have just gotten the chance.

"We have to go."

The princess huddled in the corner, shivering and staring wide-eyed at the bodies littering the floor. Getha crossed the room in a few short steps and touched her arm. "We have to go."

Princess Renn looked up at her. "Is it true? Is my family dead?" She pointed at the body near the stairs, the one with her eating knife in his chest. "Natts said that Orli killed them."

Waltham and the prince had seemed certain enough, and given the state of the palace, she had to assume they were. "Yes."

"All of them?" The princess sounded as lost as Getha had felt watching Waltham walk away from her. "Even Parn?"

Getha wanted to tell the princess that her twin lived, to give her that small bit of comfort, but the words stuck in her throat. Getha had come to know her too well. If Getha told the princess Prince Parneo still lived, she would insist they go after him.

"Please, Getha." The desperation the princess' voice tore at her. "Even him?"

The demands of war are seldom fair and never easy. Getha knew what she had to do, but she couldn't quite bring herself to speak the lie. Instead, like a coward, she looked down at the floor and let her silence speak for her.

"No!" The princess's anguished cry ripped through Getha, the gut-wrenching sobs that followed were almost more than she could bear.

"Come," Getha said, pulling the weeping princess to her feet. "We have to go."

Princess Renn stood and let Getha lead her toward the stairs. They needed somewhere to go now, somewhere to hide. Getha's mind whirled, and in her desperation, she could think of only one person left in the world who might possibly be able to help her.

RENN LET Getha steer her along the streets of Ombratos, out of the Tangles and into the Mire. She tried to marshal her thoughts, bring them into some sort of shape, but they refused, and in an impossibly short time, they reached the wall road. Screams, dozens of them, joined in a hellish chorus, rained down. Up on the Gift, men and women died at the hands of someone. Talp's men? Orli? The Tithens?

"Where are we going?"

Renn wasn't aware she'd spoken aloud until Getha said, "North Gate. Shade's Rest."

That was where they were, skirting the Acorn, approaching North Gate. Not too far, a couple of blocks left. The screams continued, sharp, high, almost inhuman screams. Were the guards being tortured?

Forty or fifty feet ahead, a door opened and a man wearing only his smallclothes stumbled out. Getha stopped and held an arm up to stop Renn too. The man didn't even look at them. As if drawn by some unseen force, he dashed across the road and pressed his hand to the Gift.

Nothing happened. Then his hand...sank into the wall? His hand and forearm disappeared, like something pulled him into—*into?*—the wall up to his elbow. He let out a surprised grunt, yet nothing more. It didn't make sense, but nothing of this night made sense. All Renn understood was that she'd failed at everything, but she could help this man.

Shoving Getha aside, she broke into a run.

"Renn!"

Getha's hand brushed the back of her tunic, so she ran faster. Getha wanted to protect her, but she had to save one person, just one. She reached the man's side, and a powerful urge to touch the wall swept over her. *No! Save the man.*

She gripped his arm, the one not in—*in?*—the wall, and the strength of a raging multitude flooded into her.

GETHA COULDN'T MAKE sense of what was happening to the man, and she didn't care. She simply had to keep Renn safe. So she grabbed for Renn, prepared to drag her from the city if she had to, but the instant Getha touched Renn's arm, something like an invisible giant's hand smacked her back. She flew half a dozen feet and hit the road hard, knocking the back of her head against the stones.

Stars swam in Getha's vision, as she clambered to her feet. She tried to blink them away, afraid of reaching for Renn and accidentally touching the wall. Getha prodded the throbbing spot at the back of her skull and winced. When her sight cleared, she saw Renn and the man just standing there with identical slack expressions on their faces.

"Renn?"

As one, Renn and the man turned to Getha and opened their mouths. Then a piercing shriek stabbed into Getha's head with all the force of a sharp blade. She screamed and clapped her hands over her ears, though that did nothing to block out the sound. She fell to her knees and begged Amma to stop the screaming, praying aloud, feeling the words tearing from her throat and the rush of air leaving her mouth, but unable to hear herself.

It seemed Amma couldn't hear her either, because the unbroken cry went on and on and the pain in her head spread through her body like a poison. She clawed at her ears and sobbed, but the Amma-forsaken wailing continued, as uncaring and unrelenting as waves crashing against the beach.

All at once, the noise stopped, and Getha looked up through blurred eyes, blinking as the shapes of Renn and the man sharpened. As one, they leaned forward and again opened their mouths. She scrambled to get her feet under her. She had to get Renn away before they cried out.

But instead of the scream, voices, thousands of them, poured from their open mouths in a gabbling, clicking language Getha had never heard before. Even so, terror turned her blood to ice. She didn't know the words, but she understood the tone—wrathful. They repeated the same phrase over and over as some sort of declaration or threat.

Or promise.

The voices cut off abruptly, and for a heartbeat, their faces cleared. Then the man screamed, a human scream of pain, and his arm was yanked even farther into the Gift as the wall consumed him. If Getha didn't get Renn away from him, it would eat her too.

She grabbed Renn's arm as tightly as she could and pulled. Renn let loose a final, inhuman scream. Then there came a tearing sound, loud enough that it could be Amma rending the sky in two, and Renn's hand detached from the man's.

RENN RETURNED to herself as she and Getha tumbled to the ground. They fell hard, but she landed on top of Getha, and Getha protected her from hitting the ground.

Fragments of memories, all of them drenched in blood, flashed through her mind. Her throat was raw, and the voices echoed in her ears. They were so angry. They were starving. The thoughts hollowed her out and filled her with writhing, rotting snakes.

Just when she feared they might never leave her, Getha touched her arm, and the howling diminished to a whisper. Getha dragged her away from the wall and pulled her to her feet. When she looked, the only thing left of the man was his hand, clawing and grasping at nothing as the hungry wall ate him.

"Come on," Getha said. All color had left her face, and she looked near to collapse, but the bruising grip she had on Renn's arm suggested she might never let go again.

Renn nodded and walked a few steps. Then another shriek came down from the wall, and it resonated in her very bones. Those were her people, her responsibility, and she was fleeing, abandoning them to this nightmare. She glanced over her shoulder. The last of the man had disappeared. How could she go and leave them to this wall, this gift turned curse?

"We can't go," Renn said, tears rolling down her cheeks. "Not like this."

Getha kept moving. "There's no other choice right now, but we will return."

"Do you promise?"

Getha stopped, looked back, and met her gaze. "I swear it."

WITH CLUMSY HANDS, Jos finished harnessing Thunder and Lightning to his fully packed wagon. Beyond the Gift, the palace fire raged and smoke covered the sky, blocking Blessed Amma from sight, and people stood around him in the street, entranced by the destruction. Not Ysobello, though. After a heartfelt farewell, he had locked himself and his family in their bakery.

From inside the city came the shattering of glass, the tearing cracks of breaking wood, and the screams. So many screams. Jos couldn't even begin to imagine what all this might mean for the Morovides or the Fallen.

Or Getha.

Since the last time he'd seen her, he had spent countless candlemarks searching the city for her, his only fact about her life that she bore a blood-mark. He'd knocked on doors in the Chestnut and the Verdure, asking the family's personal guards if they knew anyone who answered to her name or matched her description.

He'd also tried drawing her again and again to discover something new, but all he'd revealed was Getha as he'd seen her, entering the tavern, lying in his bed, talking with that strange woman wearing the disguise. Thinking the other woman's image might lead him somewhere, he'd sketched her again and shown the picture to Ysobello, but Ysobello had said she looked a little like one of the royal princesses, an utter absurdity and no help at all.

Even so, Jos had agreed that she looked highborn, and so he'd entered the Bole one day determined to knock on every door there, too, only to be turned away at the first house and snatched up by the city guard before he might reach the second.

He'd passed that night in an Ombratian cell, worried every moment Getha might return to his loft and again find him missing. He paid forsaken children to watch his loft during the day when he was out looking, but he wasn't sure they'd stick around once night fell.

In the morning, a magistrate deemed his transgression unworthy of attention, casting him back out on the street with a warning, and Jos went back to his loft to find the boy dozing in the alley outside his door. As it turned out, Getha hadn't come by during the long night.

Three days had passed since then, three long days of knocking on doors in the Branches at which he'd already knocked, but that was only because it took him three days to accept that he, heartsick and defeated, had given up on her ever returning.

Jos checked Lightning's traces yet again, then he climbed up on the driver's bench and waited. He had to leave before things turned even worse, but something held him, and he sat there until the enthralled people standing around him roused and began eyeing him and his wagon.

Shadows etched ugly lines in their faces, and he could almost see them thinking how unprepared they were and how prepared he was, and his mother's story about her caravan returned to him, sparking in him a fear that ran even deeper than whatever force held him in place.

I'm so sorry, Getha.

He clicked his tongue and drove his beasts through the slowly parting crowd. It took him long, tense minutes to reach the crossroads. When he did, he glanced down the road toward the city one last time, and hardly believing his eyes, he caught a glimpse of a tall, bloodied woman dragging along a smaller, yellow-haired woman.

Yanking Thunder and Lightning to a stop, he stood. "Getha!"

The woman didn't answer, and he feared he might have conjured her from his imagination, but then he called her name again—"Getha!"—and she looked up.

He jumped from his wagon and ran to her. As he reached her side, she eased the yellow-haired woman's arm off her shoulder and handed her over to him. The small woman seemed insensate, so Jos swept a hand under her legs and cradled her to his chest.

"Thank you," she whispered, then closed her eyes.

"Leaving town?" Getha asked. From the weariness in her voice, the look on her face, she'd been to the pathless hells and back, but he'd never seen a more beautiful sight in all his life.

"Yes," he said, guilt and relief warring within him. "Need a ride?"

She nodded and started off for his wagon. Jos glanced back at the city. Up on the hill, the fires of Seedfall roared like a vengeful beast.

Getha had found him, but the possibility of what could have been haunted him like a specter. He resettled his grip on the yellow-haired woman in his arms and spared a thought of mercy for the Morovides, wherever they might be.

THIRTY-ONE

"Bent is not always broken."
-Old Tithen saying

Helenia's head pounded as the sailors guided *The Searcher* into a slip. She stood at the rail while the ropes were tied, and the moment the board bridging the ship to the dock had been set, she crossed it, anxious to return to solid land.

Her feet hit the pier, and as the mercenaries paid from Mayve's coffers scrambled off the ship after her, she tried to take stock. The signal had never been lit, Orli and his varo were nowhere to be seen, and above the city, the fires at Seedfall burned. For all she knew, Orli and his soldiers were dead in the blaze and the Morovides had escaped unscathed. The city guard might even, at the very moment, being making their way through the city to arrest her and Dallan.

Let them try, she thought, as Dallan's ship slid alongside the dock. The Tithens would fight to the very last, and she would die in the tumult, by her own hand if need be, anything to not be captured, and Dallan would die or be arrested. Either way, she would still have her revenge.

She checked the gate to see if the city guard approached. They didn't, but a man, short and remarkable only for his un-remarkableness, strolled out from the city with a phalanx of brigands trailing him, and the pain in her head gave a nasty jolt.

"Stay back," she shouted at the mercenaries as she charged down the dock. She met Talp at the point where the pier joined the docks. "What are you doing here?" she whispered, glancing over her shoulder to make sure no one had followed her.

"Fair night to you too, my lady."

The mercenaries hadn't followed her and neither had the sailors, but they all stared at her. As did Dallan, who now stood on the pier with a perplexed expression on his face.

She turned back to Talp. "What do you want? Is it done? Are the varos..." The thought of Orli's death disturbed her so much she couldn't finish the sentence. Another wretched surprise in a night already filled with them.

Talp cocked his head to the side in the way that bespoke taking her measure. "Orli is alive, but his varos are dead. Lost"—he pointed up at the palace—"in that."

She quashed the relief that came with hearing of Orli's survival. Without the varo, she had no way to fight back the Tithens, no way to deal with Dallan, no way to face down Talp and his people. "What about the Morovides? The princess?"

Talp frowned but continued as if she hadn't said anything. "The lead varo stopped by the academy, but he's on his way. Should be here any moment."

Then why had Talp come? Did he think to fight Orli and the Tithens? If so, to what end? Talp had less than a dozen people at his back, no match for three shiploads of mercenaries. The pounding in her head increased as she tried to think.

Talp sighed. "The Morovides are dead. The varo are dead. The princess is gone." He leaned in. "Don't you see? I've come to collect."

Collect? She'd promised him the city's mines because she'd never thought he'd be alive to take them. But here he was, standing before her, demanding his payment, which meant he thought she had the authority to give it. Which meant the Morovides truly were gone, and Talp had come to confront her outmatched.

A triumph drove back the ache in her head. "You're a fool. Leave now and I won't have you cut down where you stand."

Talp laughed. "Did you not hear me when I told you Orli rides this way as we speak?" He looked past her and bowed. "Heyla, Your Highness."

Helenia whirled around. She hadn't heard Dallan approach, and he stood less than ten feet away. "Dallan! I was just—"

"Who is this?" he asked. "What's happening? Are the Morovides alive? Is Renn safe?"

Before she could think of a plausible lie, Talp jumped in. "This lady and I were just discussing the arrangements we made for this night, Your Highness. Or should I say, Your Majesty?"

Helenia felt like a rat trapped in a cage. If Talp spoke now of their plan, the sole death would be her own, and where was the justice in that? "We owe this man."

Talp crooked a finger over his shoulder and one of his brigands, a woman who resembled a boulder, separated from the group and came forward carrying a sheaf of folded papers. She set the pages in Talp's waiting hand, and he offered them to Helenia.

She took them and glanced toward the gate. Dallan didn't know who this man was, but there was a risk Orli might recognize him. Still. "We will look these over and—"

Talp tsked at her and shook his head. "You will sign them this instant." He crooked his finger again, and the boulder took a quill and a bottle of ink from an inside pocket of her coat. Then another brigand broke from the group, a man of Talp's same height and coloring, but with black, fathomless, unforgettable eyes that drilled into her, making her glad when he turned away from her to offer his back.

Talp snatched the papers from Helenia and laid them upon it. He flipped to the last page and pointed to a line at the bottom. "Sign."

Helenia's mind spun, but the pain had returned tenfold, and she couldn't think of any better option. She had made a deal with an Ombratian, and little surprise, he was bleeding her dry.

She reached for the quill, but Talp plucked it up before she could take it. "No." He pointed over her shoulder. "Him. Our new king."

Dallan stared at her. "Sign what? What is this?"

Talp rocked back and forth on his heels. "It is your first act as king."

A man ran out through the gate, and for a moment, Helenia mistook it for Orli. She realized her mistake in an instant, but her heart still raced. She took the quill from Talp and shoved it into Dallan's hand. "Just sign."

He hesitated as he read the bottom page. "What does this say about the products of the mines?"

"For Burk's sake!" Helenia shouted, her temper straining at the furthest reaches of its tether. "It's part of the cost of your throne. Sign it!"

Dallan shook his head, but he dipped the quill into the proffered bottle of ink and put the tip to the page. As he signed his name, the boulder put away the ink and pulled out a stick of sealing wax. Dallan finished signing and stepped back. From the group of brigands, an older woman in a skirt came forth with an already lit candle, and the boulder melted a glob of bloodred wax onto the page.

Dallan glanced at Helenia with trepidation, but he licked the face of his signet ring and pressed it into the center of the wax. She had no idea how she was going to explain this to him since she'd hadn't planned on explaining anything. He was supposed to be dead, and she was supposed to be behind the walls of her city on her freshly usurped throne.

Talp took the contract and handed it to the man whose back he'd used as a desk. The black-eyed man inspected Dallan's signature, then looked up, his gaze once again boring into her. "Thank you."

He turned and walked off, waving the pages in the air as if drying them. The human boulder rolled along behind him, and the rest of the brigands fell into step at his heel, all but the unremarkable man.

"Talp thanks you." The man—*Talp?*—kissed his fingers at her. "Do watch out for the wall, love." He grinned at Dallan and fell into another bow. "Good luck, Your Majesty." Then he straightened and hastened off to join the others.

Helenia wanted to chase after him to find out what had just happened, but no sooner had the group passed through the gate when out strode Orli.

With his slight limp and his shoulders bowed, he looked every inch as tired as her, and she had to stop herself from going right to him. Perhaps later, after they had spoken, and after he had shed his anger over the princess's death, perhaps then they could sit together as he liked to, and she could find a few candlemarks of sleep with her head on his shoulder.

But, here and now, she measured her steps as she walked to meet him, and Dallan hung back. She didn't worry about him or the others telling Orli about her meeting with Talp. The Tithens thought her on their side, and Dallan...

She expected Orli to spread his arms to her as she neared and had to hide her disappointment when he didn't.

He threw her even further off-balance when he stopped several feet from her and bowed. "Lady Helenia," he said, his rugged voice even raspier than usual.

Unable to read anything other than weariness in his face, she matched his formality. "Please report, Lead Varo Orli."

An emotion surfaced beneath his exhaustion, but she couldn't make it out. "It is done."

"The Morovides are dead?"

"As you wished." He spoke as if every word cost him something. "I also went to the academy."

"Why? What happened to the varo?"

He shook his head. "High Alchemist Rande is gone." He pulled a folded page from the pouch at his belt and handed it to her. "She left this."

Helenia took the page from him. Was this how Ombratos thought to fight back against her, by drowning her in paper? She read the letter. The confession. The high alchemist spoke of Orli's treason, and her part in executing the alchemist's long-standing plan to "poison the well" should anyone ever take the city over from the inside.

"What does she mean?" Helenia asked. "What did they do?"

Orli glanced over his shoulder. "The wall is... Something is wrong with the wall. People are dying on it. Against it."

A spike of pain drove through Helenia's head, right behind her eyes. "What does that mean?"

He shrugged, and the desire to slap him overtook the last of her urge to fall into his arms. Frustrated beyond speech, Helenia turned her attention back to the letter. It explained nothing more, and the final lines were, *Long live the Morovides! Long live the Fallen! Long live Ombratos!*

The spike of pain turned into a steady, sickening throb. "Why did you bring this to me? Are you here to take us into the city?"

"There is a coach inside the gates," he said sharply.

"Fine." She turned away from him to collect Dallan and their retinue.

"I lost every last one of my varo," Orli said as she walked away from him, the fury in his tone making his words loud. "In that clever little fire of yours, I lost all of them."

She stopped and faced him. "I didn't—"

Dallan rushed over. "The Morovides? You lost them? How?"

Will this night never relent? "Dallan, stop. We will discuss this later."

"Where?" he demanded. "Where are they? Where is Renn?"

The throbbing threatened to swallow her whole head, and her temper snapped. "They're all dead. The queen? Dead. The princesses? Dead. *Your* princess? She's dead!"

Dallan was stricken. "Dead?"

"Yes!" she shouted at the same instant Orli said, "No."

What? "How do you—"

"It doesn't matter, does it?" Orli said. "I know." His certainty left no room for doubt. "I also know we have a year and a day to see her Bound to the throne."

"Or...?" she prompted.

He held his hands out, palms up. "Or may Amma have mercy on us all."

The urge to slap him returned in force. "Are you being purposefully obtuse or do you really not know?"

His glare might have been enough to cow a lesser person, but Helenia returned it inch for inch. "I truly do not know," he said at last, looking away.

Her skirt and hair danced in a wild gust. The wind that had been driving the smoke and ash toward the mountains shifted seaward, and within minutes, grey clouds carrying the stench of burned buildings and bodies filled the city and poured out through the gate.

Clumps of ash caught in Helenia's hair and brushed against her white gown. So much of her plan lay around her in shambles. This was supposed to be her victory, her triumph. She was supposed to be at the top of the city, in the golden throne room at Seedfall. Instead, she stood at the bottom, having all of her failures heaped upon her.

The pounding in her head became so strong, and her disappointment so overwhelming, she needed a moment of comfort. She went to Orli and took his hands, then she turned her face up to his and waited for him to kiss her. He brought their clasped hands up and kissed her knuckles, and she readied herself to be pulled into one of his sloppy embraces.

But rather than bring her closer, he spoke. "You're back in your whites." He lowered her hands, stepped back, and let her go.

His repudiation hurt far worse than it should have. "What is this? You are done with me because I am back in my whites? What would you have me do, disrespect the memory of my husband?"

"No," he said. "Not if you truly loved him."

For that, she had no answer.

"I am your loyal servant, Lady Helenia. I suppose that will have to be enough for both of us." He bowed to her. "If you will excuse me, I shall wait by your carriage." He turned away and walked back toward the city.

She could do nothing but watch him go.

Dallan grabbed her arm. "Why did you do this?"

Looking at him, she saw only Mayve in his features. Damned Mayve. Somehow she still had control. Somehow Helenia remained tied to the ends of Mayve's strings, backed against her own wall.

Facing into the smoke, Helenia held her eyes open until they teared up.

Then she pulled out the last card she could think to play. "It was Mayve," she said. "All of this was Mayve."

Dallan stared at her. "She said the Morovides should die? She wanted to kill Renn?"

"She thought it best," Helenia said. She bowed her head. "Yes."

Perhaps it was the moons they'd spent together in Ombratos or their days on the road. Perhaps Dallan bore some measure of his dead uncle's gift, and he heard the honesty in her words. Whatever it was, he dropped her arm, and when she peeked up though her lashes, his handsome face had been marred with a mixture of sadness and anger that could only have been brought on by the beginnings of belief. She'd planted just a seed, but if she tended it well enough...

Her headache slipped away, and she held back a laugh. This wasn't the revenge she'd planned for. It was better.

Helenia shook the ash from her hair and skirts. She set her shoulders, tipped her chin up, and charged into the smoke. For all its troubles, Ombratos was her city now, and nothing else would keep her from it.

EPILOGUE

"The voices call to me as they did the others. I know they want something, but part of me recognizes they ask for more than I could give, and my solace is that I do not understand their pleas.
But this I beg of you, Amma. Please watch over the wretched soul who can."
-Julian Morovide, twin of Queen Theodora, final private journal entry

In the deepest darkness of the moonless night, Parneo sat in the shadow of a shadow, the absence of light hiding him from Kitra's prying eyes. She looked for him, called his name. They always came to look for him. All except Renn. She used to, but not anymore.

He missed her presence, her kindnesses, but at least she was still out there, still alive. The voices told him she lived; the voices entered his dreams, hissing her name and howling for her blood. He hated those dreams and how they reminded him that one day he would be forced to choose.

He'd thought the day had come, yet they hadn't stopped him from helping the guard. They had let him help. They made him hurt, but they let him help, and Renn escaped. Gone. Safe.

For now, but not forever.

Parneo sat with his legs tucked under him, his knees scant inches from the Gift. Because it was the safest and most reliable means back to the palace grounds, he and Kitra had traveled the secret path, hurrying past the bodies—*don't look, don't look, don't looooook*—and rising from it like worms from the earth. Then they'd hidden from the sun, the burning ball of the false sun—*farewell, Seedfall*—in the royal forest. Kitra had wanted to leave while he wanted to stay, but now she tramped through the undergrowth, not seeing, never seeing except what he wanted.

Even in the shadows, the starlight made the Gift shine like the whites of a person's eyes. The other Fallen hadn't always been afraid of it. They had believed it just a wall, made to shield them, to protect them. Did they now know it was alive, that it hated them, that it wanted to hurt them?

Perhaps. But the Gift had always hated them. It had always wanted to hurt them. Too bad they couldn't hear the voices. Not like Parneo. No screams for them. No cries, no desperate pleas for vengeance, for release.

They hadn't heard the promises, either. The whispers in the night. *We beg of you, Special One. Do this for us. Set us free.*

Only the men of Parneo's family heard the voices, only those boys born with a twin. A set of twins for every queen, always a girl and a boy, a leader for the throne and a mad alchemist to sacrifice on the altar of their name. He had read about it in the hidden books, the warped pages of journals stinking sweet of rot, words they hid from prying eyes within Seedfall, meant for the others and others and others. But there wouldn't be more others because Galathar had written the secret words just for him.

The others. They had heard the voices too. They had spilled enough ink to fill the sea with their doubts, their fears. *Am I going mad? Why can no one else hear them?* The others had heard the voices, but they had never understood the forgotten language, never understood what was being asked of them.

Not like Parneo.

That is because you are our chosen, the voices explained. They always explained. *You are our Special One.*

A cool breeze slid along the Gift, and Parneo remembered standing in the preparation chamber the morning of Solena's return. The voices had been so loud, a clamoring tumult all begging him for the same thing, the thing they wanted above all else—freedom.

One miscalculation, one tiny slip, one pinch of the wrong sand, dropped from his hand into the right phial, tiny grains hitting the surface of the blood and sinking below before anyone saw. Doubt and pain and fear and so much doubt had filled his heart. Solena, like the rest of his siblings, had never spared him much attention, but Renn loved her, worshipped her, and hurting Renn hurt like hurting himself.

A necessary sacrifice, Special One. We were enslaved, but you shall set us free.

The results had been bloody and ruinous, but they had stolen the details of Solena's death from his mind.

A gift from the Gift. The only one we have ever willingly given.

Parneo had found the words, found the calculations and laid them bare, but he kept a sliver of regret in his head and his hand and his heart. One day the voices would force him to choose between them and Renn. They always made him choose. The day of Solena's death, he had chosen them. He had chosen them because they had promised freedom.

But freedom hadn't come, not yet. They were still trapped, and he was alone.

"Parneo!" Kitra called, her voice poking into his thoughts like a needle piercing a palm. She would find him in a few moments. She would find him and insist they leave before he had a chance to ask his question.

He leaned forward until his forehead almost touched the wall. He knew what happened when people touched it now; they had shown him. The Gift had awoken enough to pull them in, to devour them whole.

Parneo placed his lips next to the shining surface. "When?" he whispered. "When?" Then he reached out his hand and laid his palm against the warm, smooth face of the Gift. The bright outline of a postern door flashed and then a plain wooden door simply appeared.

The other Fallen had reason to fear the Gift, but he didn't. The wall would never hurt him. Not their Special One. "When?"

The wind blew stronger, lifting Parneo's hair from his brow, carrying Kitra's calls away into the night. He closed his eyes and listened as the wall pulsed beneath his hand.

Soon, the voices promised, soothing him with their familiar clicks and shrieks. *We will all be free soon.*

END OF BOOK ONE

ACKNOWLEDGMENTS

As I'm sure you've heard/read a million times, it takes a village to write and publish a book. This is true, but some villages are bigger than others, and mine is kind of huge, so put your mittens around your kittens and away we go!

First and foremost, I'd like to give a major shout-out to my OG agent, Margaret Bail. (No relation...that we know of!) Without her myriad insights and relentless tenacity, this book would never have found a home. "Never give up; never surrender," amirite? Also, thank you to fantastic Emily Keyes, who adopted me when Margaret retired. I'm so glad I got to remain a part of the Fuse Literary family.

And thank you to whichever agent adopts me next. Just so you know, I'm house-trained and good with children!

Much love to Mr. John G. Hartness for bringing me aboard at Falstaff Books. I've always been a misfit toy, and I'm filled with joy to have found my tribe. Additional smooches to John for being one of my biggest cheer-leaders. *Your* belief in me restored *my* belief in me, and your skirt and pom-poms are in the mail.

Sending love and hugs to my editrix supreme, Venessa Giunta. I'll stop writing those annoying, Proustian sentences someday. Until then, I know you'll keep cracking the whip. Big ups to Sarah Joy Adams for her thoughtful and incisive copy edits. If there are any remaining plot holes or confusing sections, the fault is all mine. And thank you to my eagle-eyed proofer Joe Crowe. I really do know the difference between "it's" and "its," I promise!

I was lucky to first meet Venessa Giunta at Seton Hill University (no, *not* Seton Hall University), where I completed my MFA in Writing Popular Fiction. My life changed significantly the day I was accepted into that program, and only for the better.

Thank you to my first mentor at SHU, David Bischoff, for encouraging me when I really needed it, and thank you to my second mentor, Timons Esaias, for telling it like it was/is. Renn really was TSTL (too stupid to live) in my earlier drafts, but I think she's come a long way, baby! David passed away a few years back, but, Tim, I'm glad to still have you in my life. You're a friend, an inspiration, and an endless font of incredible stories and obscure information.

All of the professors/mentors/guest lecturers I encountered at SHU were impactful in at least one way or another, but I have to give one last, special hooty-hoo to Anne Harris, who has also become a good friend. You are invincible, hilarious, and the undisputed Prankster Queen. *Viva la Conciergerie!*

P.S. The opossum is in the toolbox.

I met too many amazing friends at SHU to name them all individually, so here's the short-list of my personal VIPs. Lee Stokes went above and beyond; he welcomed me into the program, listened to me talk for hours about a book which will most likely never be written, helped me get an awesome editing gig, fought off countless nerds to get me a *Mass Effect: Andromeda* backpack, and a million other things. Also, Genevieve Iseult Eldredge, who, undeterred by my rampant shyness, took me under her wing and advised me to select the project for my thesis that would get my butt in the chair, even on the days when I really didn't want to write. Even now, she keeps me going when things get rough. *heart fingers*

No tea, no shade to the other classes at Seton Hill, but the June 2011 Ones will always be the best. I was randomly thrown together with a diverse, crazy-talented group of people, and even though we went through an avalanche of hardships, we still managed to graduate together. To you, I say, "Look at this stuff. Isn't it neat? Wouldn't you think my collection's complete?" Also, Ursula, Journey, fireflies, and WESTEROS!

To my dearest fishes among the Ones—Stephanie Call Dunn, Danielle Modafferi, and Ariel Raia—you are my people. If/when we get together in Japan, things are gonna get clown shoes! (I'm comin' for ya, Fuji-Q Highland.)

Family roll call! Thank you to my most steadfast fans, starting with my mom/marmu/mamacita/marmoset, Karen Bales. I very literally could not have done this without you. Much love and appreciation to Georgia Nelson, another early adopter, my siblings and their partners, and to my aunts, uncle, and cousins. Kelly and Huhnars, you have contributed greatly to my success; I appreciate you both beyond measure. Hugs and a hundred kisses to each of my nephlets as well: John, Mary, Gavin, Mayala, Milo, Owen,

Pele, and Zoey. I'm sorry that most of you won't be able to read this for a while, but I hope you like it when you do get old enough for it. I love you all bigger than the Universe. Finally, thanks to my uncle Kirk Bales, my Gma Connie, and my dad Steve Bales, all of whom recently passed away. I love you all, and if the Good Place has a bookstore, help a girl out up there!

To my friends outside of SHU, thank you to Steph and Tom Nielsen and the rest of my game-night posse. It has been waaaaaaay too long, and I miss you all. Thank you to my peeps at the Barrington Area Library and the Palatine Public Library District. Libraries are happy places for me, and these two feel like homes away from home.

Thank you to the Women, especially Stacia McClure. We've shared high highs, low lows, and everything in between. You are my BFF, my partner-in-crime, and my number-one person. You're also one of the strongest, kindest, and most compassionate people I've ever met, and you love with an enviable ferocity. Don't ever let anyone take that away from you.

One day, we shall once again gaze upon the glory of the Disco Yeti and cheer its magnificence!

I would also like to thank two more supportive people who were never able to see this book in print: Rhonda Nicol and Jason Blatt.

Rho, I miss you. I miss our deep (and sometimes deeply silly) chats. I miss our shenanigans, and if there is an afterlife, I hope you'll have forgiven me for my part in the Iced-Tea Fiasco by the time I get there.

Jason, thank you for being a great friend and the best critique partner a gal could ask for. I could always count on you for your helpful comments, your encouragement, a great political discussion, and a ride to and/or from the airport. (PIT Crew 4-life!) You meant more to me than you'll ever know, and you'll forever own a piece of my heart.

Last but never least, thank *you*, dear reader. Double exploding fist-bumps to everyone who made it this far. Your dedication is truly unparalleled. I hope you enjoyed this book, and I hope you're excited for the future adventures of Renn, Getha, and co. TTFN, my lovelies!

About the Author

Spawned in another dimension, Erin S. Bales spends her days writing, sourcing comestibles, and negotiating the pitfalls of a gravity-based environment. She has also developed a penchant for video games, horror movies, tattoos, and competition-based reality shows. Erin has published many other titles, but they are written in a scent only marsupials can detect. This is her first human-form novel.

FRIENDS OF FALSTAFF

Thank You to All our Falstaff Books Patrons, who get extra digital content each month! To be featured here and see what other great rewards we offer, go to www.patreon.com/falstaffbooks.

PATRONS

Dino Hicks
John Hooks
John Kilgallon
Larissa Lichty
Travis & Casey Schilling
Staci-Leigh Santore
Sheryl R. Hayes
Scott Norris
Samuel Montgomery-Blinn
Junkle

CPSIA information can be obtained
at www.ICGtesting.com
Printed in the USA
LVHW010043290322
714682LV00016B/707/J

9 781645 541486